O. Henry, the pen name of William Sydney Porter (1862–1910), was born in Greensboro, North Carolina. Young Porter went to work in a drugstore at age fifteen. Later he traveled to Texas to work on a ranch and spent ten years in Austin, where he married, worked as a bank teller, and purchased a weekly newspaper, *The Rolling Stone*. But the paper failed, and in 1894, Porter was accused of embezzling bank funds. Eventually, he fled to Honduras and returned only in 1897 to be with his dying wife. Committed to a federal penitentiary in Ohio, he began writing under the name O. Henry. Following his release in 1901, he lived in New York City. A prolific writer, often turning out a story a week, he kept his real identity a   rst book, *Cabbages and   as followed by thirteen o   ich have been translated   are so popular that they

Burton Raffel has taught English, classics, and comparative literature at universities in the United States, Israel, and Canada. He is the author of such acclaimed translations as *Beowulf*; *The Essential Horace: Odes, Epodes, Epistles and Satires*; *The Complete Poetry and Prose of Chairil Anwar*; *Poems from the Old English*; and *The Annotated Milton*; as well as several critical studies, including *Introduction to Poetry* and *The Forked Tongue: A Study of the Translation Process*.

Laura Furman, professor of English at the University of Texas at Austin and a Guggenheim Fellow, is the author of two novels, three collections of short stories, and a memoir. Her fiction, essays, and journalism have appeared in *The New Yorker*, *Southwest Review*, *Yale Review*, *The American Scholar*, *Ploughshares*, and elsewhere. Since 2002, she has been series editor of the O. Henry Prize Stories.

41
STORIES
BY
O. HENRY

Selected and with an Introduction by
Burton Raffel
and with an Afterword by
Laura Furman

SIGNET CLASSICS

SIGNET CLASSICS
Published by New American Library, a division of
Penguin Group (USA) Inc., 375 Hudson Street,
New York, New York 10014, USA
Penguin Group (Canada), 90 Eglinton Avenue East, Suite 700, Toronto,
Ontario M4P 2Y3, Canada (a division of Pearson Penguin Canada Inc.)
Penguin Books Ltd., 80 Strand, London WC2R 0RL, England
Penguin Ireland, 25 St. Stephen's Green, Dublin 2,
Ireland (a division of Penguin Books Ltd.)
Penguin Group (Australia), 250 Camberwell Road, Camberwell, Victoria 3124,
Australia (a division of Pearson Australia Group Pty. Ltd.)
Penguin Books India Pvt. Ltd., 11 Community Centre, Panchsheel Park,
New Delhi - 110 017, India
Penguin Group (NZ), 67 Apollo Drive, Rosedale, Auckland 0632,
New Zealand (a division of Pearson New Zealand Ltd.)
Penguin Books (South Africa) (Pty.) Ltd., 24 Sturdee Avenue,
Rosebank, Johannesburg 2196, South Africa

Penguin Books Ltd., Registered Offices:
80 Strand, London WC2R 0RL, England

Published by Signet Classics, an imprint of New American Library,
a division of Penguin Group (USA) Inc.

First Signet Classics Printing, December 1984
First Signet Classics Printing (Furman Afterword), July 2007
30   29   28   27   26   25   24

Introduction copyright © New American Library, an imprint of Penguin Group
(USA) Inc., 1984
Afterword copyright © Laura Furman, 2007

 REGISTERED TRADEMARK—MARCA REGISTRADA

Printed in the United States of America

ALWAYS LEARNING   PEARSON

Contents

~

Introduction

~

Born in Greensboro, North Carolina, in 1862, William Sydney Porter was the son of a neurotic, largely self-trained doctor and a tubercular mother of good family. His maternal grandfather had been a successful newspaper editor; his mother had a degree from a women's college. His mother died of tuberculosis when he was three, and his paternal grandmother—and especially his father's sister—raised the boy. His father drifted into drinking, worked at a perpetual-motion machine, and died in 1886, as much out of contact with the world at large as with his son.

His grandmother was a firm, outspoken woman who, after her husband's death, ran a boardinghouse. His aunt ran a small private school where Porter got what education he received; she also pushed him to read and to read well. "I did more reading between my thirteenth and nineteenth years than I have done in all the years since," he noted, "and my taste at that time was much better than it is now, for I used to read nothing but the classics. . . . I never have time to read now. I did all my reading before I was twenty."

At age 15, he was apprenticed as a pharmacist in a drugstore owned and operated by a paternal uncle, and his formal schooling was over. At age 19, he was a licensed pharmacist; within a year, showing signs of the tuberculosis that had killed his mother, he was sent to a sheep and cattle ranch in southwest Texas where outdoor life might arrest the disease. After working on the ranch for two years, he moved to Austin, Texas, worked at assorted jobs, and in 1887 married the daughter of a successful Austin businessman. He had always been interested in drawing and sketching; now he secured a reasonably well-paying post as a draftsman in the Texas Land Office and began to raise a family. His first child, a son, died a few hours after birth; his second child, a daughter, survived her father. His wife became ill with tuberculosis, Porter lost his drafting post, took a job as a bank teller, and tried to establish himself as a humorist, writing both for the Houston *Post* and also buying a printing press and the rights to a small scandal sheet, promptly renamed *The Rolling Stone*. It was an eight-page affair, for which he wrote most of the material and did the typesetting and printing, simultaneously keeping his bank post. The magazine did not flourish: Porter slid into a life of dissolution and illicit borrowing from various bank accounts. His father-in-law repaid his embezzlement, and a jury acquitted him on criminal charges, but the Federal bank examiners moved for a new trial. *The Rolling Stone* died in 1895, Porter was rearrested in 1896, and promptly fled, first to New Orleans and then to Honduras. He stayed two years. Roughly a year later, learning that his wife was near death, he returned. She died a few months afterward; the next year, 1898, he was tried, convicted, and sentenced to five years in the penitentiary in Columbus, Ohio, where he, in fact, served over three years.

Jail was deeply traumatic for him, though he received favorable treatment as a pharmacist and was given reasonable freedom to continue writing. No one knows exactly how or why he transformed himself, in those years, into what became his internationally celebrated pen name, O.Henry, nor does anyone know precisely what (if anything) the pseudonym is supposed to mean. Clearly, the important thing is that it *is* a pseudonym. The use of the name O.Henry was a way of separating himself from much of the reality he had no inclination to deal with. His letters to his small daughter never revealed why he was away from home or, indeed, where he was, but the letters he wrote to his in-laws indicate keen awareness of prison conditions. Though fellow prisoners urged him to write on such topics, he neither did nor would. "I will forget that I ever breathed behind these walls," he affirmed even before his discharge. His personal disguise, equally clearly, melted into the many disguises and transformations of his fiction, in which from the start nothing was ever exactly what it seemed to be and the laws of causation scarcely seem to hold. Secrets are magical charms in the world of his fiction, as after his release from prison the secret of his criminal conviction became a potentially destructive spell that had to be forever contained.

O.Henry drew on his own life and the lives of his fellow prisoners in the stories he wrote in those prison years and afterward. But he also taught himself how to transform mundane materials into magical fiction—an art he practiced, thereafter, with immense and quite conscious aplomb. In a restaurant one day, Irvin Cobb, himself a humorist, asked O.Henry how he developed his plots, where on earth he found them all. "Oh, everywhere," O.Henry is reported to have answered. "There are stories in everything." He then picked up the menu and, glancing at it, declared, "There's a story in this." And he improvised the plot of "Springtime à la Carte," perfectly typical of the best of his tales.

And "perfectly typical" is an unusually appropriate term for the hundreds of stories that poured from his pen. No writer of equivalent stature, with the possible exception of Anton Chekhov, has ever written so distinctly to formula, and Chekhov did not write that way for his entire creative life but only at the start. O.Henry's beginning was his end: It is almost impossible to tell from internal evidence when a particular story was written, nor is there any significant difference in quality. There are good stories and bad ones, and there are superb stories, throughout his work. His many published collections, similarly, are a chronological jumble, for it simply does not matter in what book a story occurs, any more than it matters when it was written. At one point, under contract with a New York newspaper, the *World*, he turned out a story a week for the paper's Sunday edition and kept it up for thirty months and over one hundred stories. The results were neither better nor worse than during any other period of the roughly nine years after he left jail. O.Henry made his own conditions: the pressure to write, to publish, to succeed did not come from signing a contract.

He rapidly became famous, and he began to earn large sums of money. The *World* paid him $100 a week, a sum probably equal to ten times that amount today. He lived well but almost as anonymously as the way he hid himself behind his literary name. He was deathly afraid of meeting someone from the penitentiary, of being found out, of being exposed as William Sydney Porter, bank embezzler and convict. *Cabbages and Kings,* his first collection, came out in 1904, and was well received. *The Four Million* (i.e., the four million residents of New York City at that time), published in 1906, made him famous. From that day to this, his works have never been out of print. Book after book rolled into print; even after his death in 1910, there were stories enough for four more volumes, plus, in 1920 and then in 1936, still further gleanings, largely of very early material.

It was a literally killing pace, and O.Henry had begun to feel the effects and to slow down by about 1907. He had also managed to marry for a second time, to a childhood sweetheart and spinster who was close to forty and temperamentally about as unsuited to him as he was unsuited to marriage itself. His daughter lived with them briefly, but the marriage fell apart: by 1909 the second Mrs. Porter had gone home to mother, the young Miss Porter had been sent off to school, and O.Henry, weary, as always in debt, was desperately trying to recoup. As always he wrote, and he schemed; fortune beckoned, and he looked the other way while plunging still further into debt and imminent physical collapse, drinking too much, living too high, and yet perpetually hopeful, perpetually dreaming, planning, scrambling. He took money for a novel that was never written and wrote a failed musical comedy instead. He took $500 for the dramatic rights to "A Retrieved Reformation," instead of writing the play himself, as the producer had wanted. *Alias Jimmy Valentine* was a tremendous hit, earning more than $100,000 in royalties by the time its first run ended. He drank more and more, wrote less and less, unwilling to admit that the tuberculosis that had killed his mother and his first wife, and which three decades earlier had threatened him, had now caught up to him and was eating his life away. He died sordidly, suffering simultaneously from tuberculosis, diabetes, and an advanced stage of cirrhosis of the liver.

It would be hard to put it better than Jesse F. Knight has done in a little-known journal, *The Romantist:*

O.Henry realized that Romance is not in a specific locale. Romance is not inherent anywhere. Rather, it is within ourselves. . . . It is how we view life which determines Romance; not life itself. . . . One of O. Henry's most remarkable achievements was his successful blending of Romanticism and the modern, industrial, urban city. O.Henry brought Romanticism squarely into the 20th century.

The realists of his time, Stephen Crane and Frank Norris and Theodore Dreiser, tried in their differing ways to confront their world. O.Henry had no great interest in confrontation: what he primarily wanted, and what he created in his fiction, was escape. And yet as Mr. Knight suggests, it is not so simple and straightforward, for one could write a good part of a social history of New York City in the first decade of the twentieth century from his stories alone. Poverty is everywhere, and misery, and death, too. The heroine of "The Furnished Room" has killed herself in poverty and desperation. The hero kills himself, too, once he learns what has happened to her. The hero of "Brickdust Row" discovers, to his horror, what the city can do to young women and then discovers that without having known it, he is what we would today call a slumlord. "It's too late, I tell you," he exclaims at the end, realizing that the girl he would like to love has been too badly affected. "It's too late. It's too late. It's too late." At the end of "An Unfinished Story" not here reprinted, the narrator dreams himself in heaven, being interrogated by an angelic policeman. Is he one of the prosperous lot standing nearby?

"Who are they?" I asked.

"Why," said he, "they are the men who hired working-girls, and paid 'em five or six dollars a week to live on. Are you one of the bunch?"

"Not on your immortality," said I. "I'm only a fellow that set fire to an orphan asylum, and murdered a blind man for his pennies."

That deft, wry combination of pain and humor is a special and rare accomplishment. To quote Mr. Knight again, the "pain he undoubtedly felt became one of his greatest assets as he projected it through his fiction. He often poked good-natured fun at human follies, but it is a gentle irony born out of affection, out of love for the human race. His humor . . .

is not corrosive. . . . [Overall] there is about his fiction a sense of gaiety and lightness, comparable to a Viennese waltz.'' He cannot keep himself from seeing, somehow, that evil exists, and often triumphs—and not only in cities. ''The Caballaro's Way'' is powerful evidence that O.Henry did not unduly romanticize human nature wherever he found it. But one of the major tools he wielded, in fashioning the many forms of escape that he wove so artfully, was humor. He poked fun; he made puns, some of them as outrageous as any execrable pun ever concocted. In ''Masters of Arts,'' not here reprinted, a con man reproaches an unwilling artist partner. '' 'Now, sonny,' he said with gentle grimness, 'you and me will have an Art to Art talk.' '' In ''Springtime à la Carte,'' the story mentioned earlier as having been spun out of a glance at a restaurant menu, a novel by Charles Reade that O.Henry liked is referred to as ''the best non-selling book of the month.'' In ''Seats of the Haughty,'' not here reprinted, a con man ''hustles away with a kind of Swiss movement toward a jewelry store.'' He can get almost as verbally playful as James Joyce, though in a very different cause. '' 'It's part of my business,' '' says a character in ''The Man Higher Up,'' not here reprinted, '' 'to play up to the ruffles when I want to make a riffle as Raffles. 'Tis loves that makes the bit go 'round' ''—referring, in this last atrocious pun, to the bit with which the burglar bores his way into his chosen victim's premises.

This kind of wordplay, to be sure, is the farthest thing from the hack work of which O.Henry is so freely accused. It is true that he wrote a great deal and that he never, so far as is known, revised. He also wrote with great art and with immense zest, which are not qualities associated with hack work. There is sentimentality in much of O.Henry (as there is, it must be noted, in much of Frank Norris, Theodore Dreiser, and even Stephen Crane), but there is far more artistic discipline and vivid love of craft than some of his critics are prepared to admit. ''The club of realism,'' a marvelously apt phrase from ''The Caliph, Cupid and the Clock,'' ought not to be wielded against O.Henry: He was trying to do something very different, and doing it, much of the time, superlatively well.

Nor is O.Henry the flighty, fundamentally unserious writer

he is sometimes made out to be. (No more are Strauss waltzes flighty. They are neither Bach-like nor Brahms-like, but they do not purport to be. Do we reproach a beautiful dog for not being a beautiful horse, or a handsome boy for not being a dashing man?) There is intense seriousness in his stories, even intense seriousness about the craft he practiced so secretively. "The art of narrative," declares the narrator in "The Phonograph and the Graft," not here reprinted, "consists in concealing from your audience everything it wants to know until after you expose your favorite opinions on topics foreign to the subject. A good story is like a bitter pill with the sugar coating inside of it." In "Springtime à la Carte," again, he begins with a short, one-sentence paragraph, "It was a day in March," and then goes on, brilliantly:

> Never, never begin a story this way when you write one. No opening could possibly be worse. It is un-imaginative, flat dry, and likely to consist of mere wind. But in this instance it is allowable. For the following paragraph, which should have inaugurated the narrative, is too wildly extravagant and preposterous to be flaunted in the face of the reader without preparation.

This is the art which, proclaiming artlessness, neatly conceals art. We are all no more than common men together, O. Henry keeps insisting, but what common man could have written phrases like "Women are the natural enemies of clocks," "We are grown stiff with the ramrod of convention down our backs," or "Women do not read the love stories in the magazines. . . . The love stories are read by fat cigar drummers and little ten-year-old girls"? What common man could say of a commemorative statue standing in New York City traffic that "the great General must feel, unless his nerves are iron, that rapid transit gloria mundi"? Or could gloriously destroy one of the most famous schoolboy phrases in all of Latin literature and then redeem the farce with as deft a bit of social comment as could possibly be written?

> I'm mindful of Mr. Julius Caesar's account of 'em where he says: *"Omnia Gallia in tres partes divisa est"*; which is the same as to say, "We will need all of our gall in devising means to tree them parties." I

hated to make a show of education; but I was disinclined to be overdone in syntax by a mere Indian, a member of a race to which we owe nothing except the land on which the United States is situated.

What common man could dispose of female do-gooders one minute, saying of a cabman's horse "that he was stuffed with oats until one of those old ladies who leave their dishes unwashed at home and go about having expressmen arrested, would have smiled—yes, smiled—to have seen him," and then, the next minute, declare that a character "found in altruism more pleasure than his riches, his station and all the grosser sweets of life had given him?"

O. Henry, at his best, is both brilliant and wise, both serious and funny. He mixes and he pours, and his concoctions, though brewed according to formula, are nevertheless dazzlingly potent at their best, for the formula is unique, it is his alone, and it is framed out of materials as true as much of what goes into the heaviest, most ponderous tomes. Art does not have to be dull, to be effective; the artist does not have to be a bore, to be real. O. Henry is many things, and like all good artists, he is sometimes a contradictory, complex mixture of many different things, but he is almost never boring—and certainly not in any of the stories here spread out for your enlightenment, instruction, and entertainment.

—BURTON RAFFEL

41
STORIES
BY
O. HENRY

The Social Triangle

At the stroke of six Ikey Snigglefritz laid down his goose. Ikey was a tailor's apprentice. Are there tailors' apprentices nowadays?

At any rate, Ikey toiled and snipped and basted and pressed and patched and sponged all day in the steamy fetor of a tailor-shop. But when work was done Ikey hitched his wagon to such stars as his firmament let shine.

It was Saturday night, and the boss laid twelve begrimed and begrudged dollars in his hand. Ikey dabbled discreetly in water, donned coat, hat and collar with its frazzled tie, and chalcedony pin, and set forth in pursuit of his ideals.

For each of us, when our day's work is done, must seek our ideal, whether it be love or pinochle or lobster à la Newburg, or the sweet silence of the musty bookshelves.

Behold Ikey as he ambles up the street beneath the roaring "El" between the rows of reeking sweatshops. Pallid, stooping, insignificant, squalid, doomed to exist forever in penury of body and mind, yet, as he swings his cheap cane and projects the noisome inhalations from his cigarette you perceive that he nurtures in his narrow bosom the bacillus of society.

Ikey's legs carried him to and into that famous place of entertainment known as the Café Maginnis—famous because it was the rendezvous of Billy McMahan, the greatest man, the most wonderful man, Ikey thought, that the world had ever produced.

Billy McMahan was the district leader. Upon him the Tiger purred, and his hand held manna to scatter. Now, as Ikey entered, McMahan stood, flushed and triumphant and mighty, the centre of a huzzaing concourse of his lieutenants and constituents. It seems there had been an election; a signal victory had been won; the city had been swept back into line by a resistless besom of ballots.

Ikey slunk along the bar and gazed, breath-quickened, at his idol.

How magnificent was Billy McMahan, with his great, smooth, laughing face; his gray eye, shrewd as a chicken hawk's; his diamond ring, his voice like a bugle call, his prince's air, his plump and active roll of money, his clarion call to friend and comrade—oh, what a king of men he was! How he obscured his lieutenants, though they themselves loomed large and serious, blue of chin and important of mien, with hands buried deep in the pockets of their short overcoats! But Billy—oh, what small avail are words to paint for you his glory as seen by Ikey Snigglefritz!

The Café Maginnis rang to the note of victory. The white-coated bartenders threw themselves featfully upon bottle, cork and glass. From a score of clear Havanas the air received its paradox of clouds. The leal and the hopeful shook Billy McMahan's hand. And there was born suddenly in the worshipful soul of Ikey Snigglefritz an audacious, thrilling impulse.

He stepped forward into the little cleared space in which majesty moved, and held out his hand.

Billy McMahan grasped it unhesitatingly, shook it and smiled.

Made mad now by the gods who were about to destroy him, Ikey threw away his scabbard and charged upon Olympus.

"Have a drink with me, Billy," he said familiarly, "you and your friends?"

"Don't mind if I do, old man," said the great leader, "just to keep the ball rolling."

The last spark of Ikey's reason fled.

"Wine," he called to the bartender, waving a trembling hand.

The corks of three bottles were drawn; the champagne bubbled in the long row of glasses set upon the bar. Billy McMahan took his and nodded, with his beaming smile at Ikey. The lieutenants and satellites took theirs and growled "Here's to you." Ikey took his nectar in delirium. All drank.

Ikey threw his week's wages in a crumpled roll upon the bar.

"C'rect," said the bartender, smoothing the twelve one-dollar notes. The crowd surged around Billy McMahan again. Some one was telling how Brannigan fixed 'em over in the Eleventh. Ikey leaned against the bar a while, and then went out.

He went down Hester Street and up Chrystie, and down Delancey to where he lived. And there his women folk, a bibulous mother and three dingy sisters, pounced upon him for his wages. And at his confession they shrieked and objurgated him in the pithy rhetoric of the locality.

But even as they plucked at him and struck him Ikey remained in his ecstatic trance of joy. His head was in the clouds; the star was drawing his wagon. Compared with what he had achieved the loss of wages and the bray of women's tongues were slight affairs.

He had shaken the hand of Billy McMahan.

Billy McMahan had a wife, and upon her visiting cards was engraved the name "Mrs. William Darragh McMahan." And there was a certain vexation attendant upon these cards; for, small as they were, there were houses in which they could not be inserted. Billy McMahan was a dictator in politics, a four-walled tower in business, a mogul, dread, loved and obeyed among his own people. He was growing rich; the daily papers had a dozen men on his trail to chronicle his every word of wisdom; he had been honored in caricature holding the Tiger cringing in leash.

But the heart of Billy was sometimes sore within him. There was a race of men from which he stood apart but that he viewed with the eye of Moses looking over into the promised land. He, too, had ideals, even as had Ikey Snigglefritz; and sometimes, hopeless of attaining them, his own solid success was as dust and ashes in his mouth. And Mrs. William Darragh McMahan wore a look of discontent upon her plump but pretty face, and the very rustle of her silks seemed a sigh.

There was a brave and conspicuous assemblage in the dining saloon of a noted hostelry where Fashion loves to display her charms. At one table sat Billy McMahan and his wife. Mostly silent they were, but the accessories they enjoyed little needed the indorsement of speech. Mrs. McMahan's diamonds were outshone by few in the room. The waiter bore the costliest brands of wine to their table. In evening dress, with an expression of gloom upon his smooth and massive countenance, you would look in vain for a more striking figure than Billy's.

Four tables away sat alone a tall, slender man, about thirty, with thoughtful, melancholy eyes, a Van Dyke beard and peculiarly white, thin hands. He was dining on filet mignon, dry toast and apollinaris. That man was Cortlandt Van Duyckink, a man worth eighty millions, who inherited and held a sacred seat in the exclusive inner circle of society.

Billy McMahan spoke to no one around him, because he knew no one. Van Duyckink kept his eyes on his plate because he knew that every one present was hungry to catch his. He could bestow knighthood and prestige by a nod, and he was chary of creating a too extensive nobility.

And then Billy McMahan conceived and accomplished the most startling and audacious act of his life. He rose deliberately and walked over to Cortlandt Van Duyckink's table and held out his hand.

"Say, Mr. Van Duyckink," he said, "I've heard you was talking about starting some reforms among the poor people down in my district. I'm McMahan, you know. Say, now, if that's straight I'll do all I can to help you. And what I says goes in that neck of the woods, don't it? Oh, say, I rather guess it does."

Van Duyckink's rather somber eyes lighted up. He rose to his lank height and grasped Billy McMahan's hand.

"Thank you, Mr. McMahan," he said, in his deep, serious tones. "I have been thinking of doing some work of that sort. I shall be glad of your assistance. It pleases me to have become acquainted with you."

Billy walked back to his seat. His shoulder was tingling from the accolade bestowed by royalty. A hundred eyes were now turned upon him in envy and new admiration. Mrs. William Darragh McMahan trembled with ecstasy, so that her diamonds smote the eye almost with pain. And now it was apparent that at many tables there were those who suddenly remembered that they enjoyed Mr. McMahan's acquaintance. He saw smiles and bows about him. He became enveloped in the aura of dizzy greatness. His campaign coolness deserted him.

"Wine for that gang!" he commanded the waiter, pointing with his finger. "Wine over there. Wine to those three gents by that green bush. Tell 'em it's on me. D——n it! Wine for everybody!"

The waiter ventured to whisper that it was perhaps inexpedient to carry out the order, in consideration of the dignity of the house and its custom.

"All right," said Billy, "if it's against the rules. I wonder if 'twould do to send my friend Van Duyckink a bottle? No? Well, it'll flow all right at the caffy to-night, just the same. It'll be rubber boots for anybody who comes in there any time up to 2 A.M."

Billy McMahan was happy.

He had shaken the hand of Cortlandt Van Duyckink.

The big pale-gray auto with its shining metal work looked out of place moving slowly among the push carts and trash-heaps on the lower east side. So did Cortlandt Van Duyckink, with his aristocratic face and white, thin hands, as he steered carefully between the groups of ragged, scurrying youngsters in the streets. And so did Miss Constance Schuyler, with her dim, ascetic beauty, seated at his side.

"Oh, Cortlandt," she breathed, "isn't it sad that human beings have to live in such wretchedness and poverty? And you—how noble it is of you to think of them, to give your time and money to improve their condition!"

Van Duyckink turned his solemn eyes upon her.

"It is little," he said, sadly, "that I can do. The question is a large one, and belongs to society. But even individual effort is not thrown away. Look, Constance! On this street I have arranged to build soup kitchens, where no one who is hungry will be turned away. And down this other street are the old buildings that I shall cause to be torn down and there erect others in place of those death-traps of fire and disease."

Down Delancey slowly crept the pale-gray auto. Away from it toddled coveys of wondering, tangle-haired, bare-footed, unwashed children. It stopped before a crazy brick structure, foul and awry.

Van Duyckink alighted to examine at a better perspective

one of the leaning walls. Down the steps of the building came a young man who seemed to epitomize its degradation, squalor and infelicity—a narrow-chested, pale, unsavory young man, puffing at a cigarette.

Obeying a sudden impulse, Van Duyckink stepped out and warmly grasped the hand of what seemed to him a living rebuke.

"I want to know you people," he said, sincerely. "I am going to help you as much as I can. We shall be friends."

As the auto crept carefully away Cortlandt Van Duyckink felt an unaccustomed glow about his heart. He was near to being a happy man.

He had shaken the hand of Ikey Snigglefritz.

Tobin's Palm

Tobin and me, the two of us, went down to Coney one day, for there was four dollars between us, and Tobin had need of distractions. For there was Katie Mahorner, his sweetheart, of County Sligo, lost since she started for America three months before with two hundred dollars, her own savings, and one hundred dollars from the sale of Tobin's inherited estate, a fine cottage and pig on the Bog Shannaugh. And since the letter that Tobin got saying that she had started to come to him not a bit of news had he heard or seen of Katie Mahorner. Tobin advertised in the papers, but nothing could be found of the colleen.

So, to Coney me and Tobin went, thinking that a turn at the chutes and the smell of the popcorn might raise the heart in his bosom. But Tobin was a hard-headed man, and the sadness stuck in his skin. He ground his teeth at the crying balloons; he cursed the moving pictures; and, though he would drink whenever asked, he scorned Punch and Judy, and was for licking the tintype men as they came.

So I gets him down a side way on a board walk where the attractions were some less violent. At a little six by eight stall Tobin halts, with a more human look in his eye.

" 'Tis here," says he, "I will be diverted. I'll have the palm of me hand investigated by the wonderful palmist of the Nile, and see if what is to be will be."

Tobin was a believer in signs and the unnatural in nature. He possessed illegal convictions in his mind along the subjects of black cats, lucky numbers, and the weather predictions in the papers.

We went into the enchanted chicken coop, which was fixed mysterious with red cloth and pictures of hands with lines crossing 'em like a railroad centre. The sign over the door says it is Madame Zozo the Egyptian Palmist. There was a fat woman inside in a red jumper with pothooks and beasties embroidered upon it. Tobin gives her ten cents and extends one of his hands. She lifts Tobin's hand, which is own brother to the hoof of a drayhorse, and examines it to see whether 'tis a stone in the frog or a cast shoe he has come for.

"Man," says this Madame Zozo, "the line of your fate shows—"

" 'Tis not me foot at all," says Tobin, interrupting. "Sure, 'tis no beauty, but ye hold the palm of me hand."

"The line shows," says the Madame, "that ye've not arrived at your time of life without bad luck. And there's more to come. The mount of Venus—or is that a stone bruise?—shows that ye've been in love. There's been trouble in your life on account of your sweetheart."

" 'Tis Katie Mahorner she has references with," whispers Tobin to me in a loud voice to one side.

"I see," says the palmist, "a great deal of sorrow and tribulation with one whom ye cannot forget. I see the lines of designation point to the letter K and the letter M in her name."

"Whist!" says Tobin to me; "do ye hear that?"

"Look out," goes on the palmist, "for a dark man and a light woman; for they'll both bring ye trouble. Ye'll make a voyage upon the water very soon, and have a financial loss. I see one line that brings good luck. There's a man coming into your life who will fetch ye good fortune. Ye'll know him when ye see him by his crooked nose."

"Is his name set down?" asks Tobin. " 'Twill be convenient in the way of greeting when he backs up to dump off the good luck."

"His name," says the palmist, thoughtful looking, "is not spelled out by the lines, but they indicate 'tis a long one, and the letter 'o' should be in it. There's no more to tell. Goodevening. Don't block up the door."

" 'Tis wonderful how she knows," says Tobin as we walk to the pier.

As we squeezed through the gates a nigger man sticks his lighted segar against Tobin's ear, and there is trouble. Tobin hammers his neck, and the women squeal, and by presence of mind I drag the little man out of the way before the police comes. Tobin is always in an ugly mood when enjoying himself.

On the boat going back, when the man calls "Who wants the good-looking waiter?" Tobin tried to plead guilty, feeling the desire to blow the foam off a crock of suds, but when he felt in his pocket he found himself discharged for lack of evidence. Somebody had disturbed his change during the commotion. So we sat, dry, upon the stools, listening to the Dagoes fiddling on deck. If anything, Tobin was lower in spirits and less congenial with his misfortunes than when we started.

On a seat against the railing was a young woman dressed suitable for red automobiles, with hair the colour on an unsmoked meerschaum. In passing by Tobin kicks her foot without intentions, and, being polite to ladies when in drink, he tries to give his hat a twist while apologizing. But he knocks it off, and the wind carries it overboard.

Tobin came back and sat down, and I began to look out for him, for the man's adversities were becoming frequent. He was apt, when pushed so close by hard luck, to kick the best dressed man he could see, and try to take command of the boat.

Presently Tobin grabs my arm and says, excited: "Jawn," says he, "do ye know what we're doing? We're taking a voyage upon the water."

"There now," says I; "subdue yeself. The boat'll land in ten minutes more."

"Look," says he, "at the light lady upon the bench. And have ye forgotten the nigger man that burned me ear? And isn't the money I had gone—a dollar sixty-five it was?"

I thought he was no more than summing up his catastrophes so as to get violent with good excuse, as men will do, and I tried to make him understand such things was trifles.

"Listen," says Tobin. "Ye've no ear for the gift of prophecy or the miracles of the inspired. What did the palmist lady tell ye out of me hand? 'Tis coming true before your eyes. 'Look out,' says she, 'for a dark man and a light woman; they'll bring ye trouble.' Have ye forgot the nigger man, though he got some of it back from me fist? Can ye show me a lighter woman than the blonde lady that was the cause of me hat falling in the water? And where's the dollar sixty-five I had in me vest when we left the shooting gallery?"

The way Tobin put it, it did seem to corroborate the art of prediction, though it looked to me that these accidents could happen to any one at Coney without the implication of palmistry.

Tobin got up and walked around on deck, looking close at the passengers out of his little red eyes. I asked him the interpretation of his movements. Ye never know what Tobin has in his mind until he begins to carry it out.

"Ye should know," says he, "I'm working out the salvation promised by the lines in me palm. I'm looking for the crooked-nose man that's to bring the good luck. 'Tis all that will save us. Jawn, did ye ever see a straighter-nosed gang of hellions in the days of your life?"

'Twas the nine-thirty boat, and we landed and walked up-town through Twenty-second Street, Tobin being without his hat.

On a street corner, standing under a gas-light and looking over the elevated road at the moon, was a man. A long man he was, dressed decent, with a segar between his teeth, and I saw that his nose made two twists from bridge to end, like the wriggle of a snake. Tobin saw it at the same time, and I heard him breathe hard like a horse when you take the saddle off. He went straight up to the man, and I went with him.

"Good-night to ye," Tobin says to the man. The man takes out a segar and passes the compliments, sociable.

"Would ye hand us your name," asks Tobin, "and let us look at the size of it? It may be our duty to become acquainted with ye."

"My name," says the man, polite, "is Friedenhausman— Maximus G. Friedenhausman."

" 'Tis the right length," says Tobin. "Do you spell it with an 'o' anywhere down the stretch of it?"

"I do not," says the man.

"*Can* ye spell it with an 'o'?" inquires Tobin, turning anxious.

"If your conscience," says the man with the nose, "is indisposed toward foreign idioms ye might, to please yourself, smuggle the letter into the penultimate syllable."

" 'Tis well," says Tobin. "Ye're in the presence of Jawn Malone and Daniel Tobin."

" 'Tis highly appreciated," says the man, with a bow. "And now since I cannot conceive that ye would hold a spelling bee upon the street corner, will ye name some reasonable excuse for being at large?"

"By the two signs," answers Tobin, trying to explain, "which ye display according to the reading of the Egyptian palmist from the sole of me hand, ye've been nominated to offset with good luck the lines of trouble leading to the nigger man and the blonde lady with her feet crossed in the boat, besides the financial loss of a dollar sixty-five, all so far fulfilled according to Hoyle."

The man stopped smoking and looked at me.

"Have ye any amendments," he asks, "to offer to that statement, or are ye one too? I thought by the looks of ye ye might have him in charge."

"None," says I to him, "except that as one horseshoe resembles another so are ye the picture of good luck as predicted by the hand of me friend. If not, then the lines of Danny's hand may have been crossed, I don't know."

"There's two of ye," says the man with the nose, looking up and down for the sight of a policeman. "I've enjoyed your company immense. Good-night."

With that he shoves his segar in his mouth and moves

across the street, stepping fast. But Tobin sticks close to one side of him and me at the other.

"What!" says he, stopping on the opposite sidewalk and pushing back his hat; "do ye follow me? I tell ye," he says, very loud, "I'm proud to have met ye. But it is my desire to be rid of ye. I am off to me home."

"Do," says Tobin, leaning against his sleeve. "Do be off to your home. And I will sit at the door of it till ye come out in the morning. For the dependence is upon ye to obviate the curse of the nigger man and the blonde lady and the financial loss of the one-sixty-five."

" 'Tis a strange hallucination," says the man, turning to me as a more reasonable lunatic. "Hadn't ye better get him home?"

"Listen, man," says I to him. "Daniel Tobin is as sensible as he ever was. Maybe he is a bit deranged on account of having drink enough to disturb but not enough to settle his wits, but he is no more than following out the legitimate path of his superstitions and predicaments, which I will explain to you." With that I relates the facts about the palmist lady and how the finger of suspicion points to him as an instrument of good fortune. "Now, understand," I concludes, "my position in this riot. I am the friend of me friend Tobin, according to me interpretations. 'Tis easy to be a friend to the prosperous, for it pays; 'tis not hard to be a friend to the poor, for ye get puffed up by gratitude and have your picture printed standing in front of a tenement with a scuttle of coal and an orphan in each hand. But it strains the art of friendship to be true friend to a born fool. And that's what I'm doing," says I, "for, in my opinion, there's no fortune to be read from the palm of me hand that wasn't printed there with the handle of a pick. And, though ye've got the crookedest nose in New York City, I misdoubt that all the fortune-tellers doing business could milk good luck from ye. But the lines of Danny's hand pointed to ye fair, and I'll assist him to experiment with ye until he's convinced ye're dry."

After that the man turns, sudden, to laughing. He leans against a corner and laughs considerable. Then he claps me and Tobin on the backs of us and takes us by an arm apiece.

" 'Tis my mistake," says he. "How could I be expecting anything so fine and wonderful to be turning the corner upon me? I came near being found unworthy. Hard by," says he, "is a café, snug and suitable for the entertainment of idiosyncrasies. Let us go there and have a drink while we discuss the unavailability of the categorical."

So saying, he marched me and Tobin to the back room of a saloon, and ordered the drinks, and laid the money on the table. He looks at me and Tobin like brothers of his, and we have the segars.

"Ye must know," says the man of destiny, "that me walk in life is one that is called the literary. I wander abroad be night seeking idiosyncrasies in the masses and truth in the heavens above. When ye came upon me I was in contemplation of the elevated road in conjunction with the chief luminary of night. The rapid transit is poetry and art: the moon but a tedious, dry body, moving by rote. But these are private opinions, for, in the business of literature, the conditions are reversed. 'Tis me hope to be writing a book to explain the strange things I have discovered in life."

"Ye will put me in a book," says Tobin, disgusted; "will ye put me in a book?"

"I will not," says the man, "for the covers will not hold ye. Not yet. The best I can do is to enjoy ye meself, for the time is not ripe for destroying the limitations of print. Ye would look fantastic in type. All alone by meself must I drink this cup of joy. But, I thank ye, boys; I am truly grateful."

"The talk of ye," says Tobin, blowing through his moustache and pounding the table with his fist, "is an eyesore to me patience. There was good luck promised out of the crook of your nose, but ye bear fruit like the bang of a drum. Ye resemble, with your noise of books, the wind blowing through a crack. Sure, now, I would be thinking the palm of me hand lied but for the coming true of the nigger man and the blonde lady and—"

"Whist!" says the long man; "would ye be led astray by physiognomy? Me nose will do what it can within bounds. Let us have these glasses filled again, for 'tis good to keep idiosyncrasies well moistened, they being subject to deterioration in a dry moral atmosphere."

So, the man of literature makes good, to my notion, for he pays, cheerful, for everything, the capital of me and Tobin being exhausted by prediction. But Tobin is sore, and drinks quiet, with the red showing in his eye.

By and by we moved out, for 'twas eleven o'clock, and stands a bit upon the sidewalk. And then the man says he must be going home, and invites me and Tobin to walk that way. We arrives on a side street two blocks away where there is a stretch of brick houses with high stoops and iron fences. The man stops at one of them and looks up at the top windows which he finds dark.

" 'Tis me humble dwelling," says he, "and I begin to perceive by the signs that me wife has retired to slumber. Therefore I will venture a bit in the way of hospitality. 'Tis me wish that ye enter the basement room, where we dine, and partake of a reasonable refreshment. There will be some fine cold fowl and cheese and a bottle or two of ale. Ye will be welcome to enter and eat, for I am indebted to ye for diversions."

The appetite and conscience of me and Tobin was congenial to the proposition, though 'twas sticking hard in Danny's superstitions to think that a few drinks and a cold lunch should represent the good fortune promised by the palm of his hand.

"Step down the steps," says the man with the crooked nose, "and I will enter by the door above and let ye in. I will ask the new girl we have in the kitchen," says he, "to make ye a pot of coffee to drink before ye go. 'Tis fine coffee Katie Mahorner makes for a green girl just landed three months. Step in," says the man, "and I'll send her down to ye."

The Last Leaf

In a little district west of Washington Square the streets have run crazy and broken themselves into small strips called "places." These "places" make strange angles and curves. One street crosses itself a time or two. An artist once discovered a valuable possibility in this street. Suppose a collector with a bill for paints, paper and canvas should, in traversing this route, suddenly meet himself coming back, without a cent having been paid on account!

So, to quaint old Greenwich Village the art people soon came prowling, hunting for north windows and eighteenth-century gables and Dutch attics and low rents. Then they imported some pewter mugs and a chafing dish or two from Sixth Avenue, and became a "colony."

At the top of a squatty, three-story brick Sue and Johnsy had their studio. "Johnsy" was familiar for Joanna. One was from Maine; the other from California. They had met at the *table d'hôte* of an Eighth Street "Delmonico's," and found their tastes in art, chicory salad and bishop sleeves so congenial that the joint studio resulted.

That was in May. In November a cold, unseen stranger, whom the doctors called Pneumonia, stalked about the colony, touching one here and there with his icy fingers. Over on the east side this ravager strode boldly, smiting his victims by scores, but his feet trod slowly through the maze of the narrow and moss-grown "places."

Mr. Pneumonia was not what you would call a chivalric old gentleman. A mite of a little woman with blood thinned by California zephyrs was hardly fair game for the red-fisted, short-breathed old duffer. But Johnsy he smote; and she lay, scarcely moving, on her painted iron bedstead, looking through the small Dutch window-panes at the blank side of the next brick house.

One morning the busy doctor invited Sue into the hallway with a shaggy, gray eyebrow.

"She has one chance in—let us say, ten," he said, as he shook down the mercury in his clinical thermometer. "And that chance is for her to want to live. This way people have of lining-up on the side of the undertaker makes the entire pharmacœia look silly. Your little lady has made up her mind that she's not going to get well. Has she anything on her mind?"

"She—she wanted to paint the Bay of Naples some day," said Sue.

"Paint?—bosh! Has she anything on her mind worth thinking about twice—a man, for instance?"

"A man?" said Sue, with a jew's-harp twang in her voice.

"Is a man worth—but, no, doctor; there is nothing of the kind."

"Well, it is the weakness, then," said the doctor. "I will do all that science, so far as it may filter through my efforts, can accomplish. But whenever my patient begins to count the carriages in her funeral procession I subtract 50 per cent. from the curative power of medicines. If you will get her to ask one question about the new winter styles in cloak sleeves I will promise you a one-in-five chance for her, instead of one in ten."

After the doctor had gone Sue went into the workroom and cried a Japanese napkin to a pulp. Then she swaggered into Johnsy's room with her drawing board, whistling ragtime.

Johnsy lay, scarcely making a ripple under the bedclothes, with her face toward the window. Sue stopped whistling, thinking she was asleep.

She arranged her board and began a pen-and-ink drawing to illustrate a magazine story. Young artists must pave their way to Art by drawing pictures for magazine stories that young authors write to pave their way to Literature.

As Sue was sketching a pair of elegant horseshow riding trousers and a monocle on the figure of the hero, an Idaho cowboy, she heard a low sound, several times repeated. She went quickly to the bedside.

Johnsy's eyes were open wide. She was looking out the window and counting—counting backward.

"Twelve," she said, and a little later "eleven"; and then "ten," and "nine"; and then "eight" and "seven," almost together.

Sue looked solicitously out of the window. What was there to count? There was only a bare, dreary yard to be seen, and the blank side of the brick house twenty feet away. An old, old ivy vine, gnarled and decayed at the roots, climbed half way up the brick wall. The cold breath of autumn had stricken its leaves from the vine until its skeleton branches clung, almost bare, to the crumbling bricks.

"What is it, dear?" asked Sue.

"Six," said Johnsy, in almost a whisper. "They're falling faster now. Three days ago there were almost a hundred. It made my head ache to count them. But now it's easy. There goes another one. There are only five left now."

"Five what, dear? Tell your Sudie."

"Leaves. On the ivy vine. When the last one falls I must go, too. I've known that for three days. Didn't the doctor tell you?"

"Oh, I never heard of such nonsense," complained Sue, with magnificent scorn. "What have old ivy leaves to do with your getting well? And you used to love that vine, so, you naughty girl. Don't be a goosey. Why, the doctor told me this morning that your chances for getting well real soon were— let's see exactly what he said—he said the chances were ten to one! Why, that's almost as good a chance as we have in New York when we ride on the street cars or walk past a new building. Try to take some broth now, and let Sudie go back to her drawing, so she can sell the editor man with it, and buy port wine for her sick child, and pork chops for her greedy self."

"You needn't get any more wine," said Johnsy, keeping her eyes fixed out the window. "There goes another. No, I don't want any broth. That leaves just four. I want to see the last one fall before it gets dark. Then I'll go, too."

"Johnsy, dear," said Sue, bending over her, "will you promise me to keep your eyes closed, and not look out the window until I am done working? I must hand those drawings in by to-morrow. I need the light, or I would draw the shade down."

"Couldn't you draw in the other room?" asked Johnsy, coldly.

"I'd rather be here by you," said Sue. "Besides, I don't want you to keep looking at those silly ivy leaves."

"Tell me as soon as you have finished," said Johnsy, closing her eyes, and lying white and still as a fallen statue, "because I want to see the last one fall. I'm tired of waiting. I'm tired of thinking. I want to turn loose my hold on everything, and go sailing down, down, just like one of those poor, tired leaves."

"Try to sleep," said Sue. "I must call Behrman up to be my model for the old hermit miner. I'll not be gone a minute. Don't try to move 'til I come back."

Old Behrman was a painter who lived on the ground floor beneath them. He was past sixty and had a Michael Angelo's Moses beard curling down from the head of a satyr along the body of an imp. Behrman was a failure in art. Forty years he had wielded the brush without getting near enough to touch the hem of his Mistress's robe. He had been always about to paint a masterpiece, but had never yet begun it. For several years he had painted nothing except now and then a daub in the line of commerce or advertising. He earned a little by serving as a model to those young artists in the colony who could not pay the price of a professional. He drank gin to excess, and still talked of his coming masterpiece. For the rest he was a fierce little old man, who scoffed terribly at softness in any one, and who regarded himself as especial mastiff-in-waiting to protect the two young artists in the studio above.

Sue found Behrman smelling strongly of juniper berries in his dimly lighted den below. In one corner was a blank canvas on an easel that had been waiting there for twenty-five years to receive the first line of the masterpiece. She told him of Johnsy's fancy, and how she feared she would, indeed, light and fragile as a leaf herself, float away, when her slight hold upon the world grew weaker.

Old Behrman, with his red eyes plainly streaming, shouted his contempt and derision for such idiotic imaginings.

"Vass!" he cried. "Is dere people in de world mit der foolishness to die because leafs dey drop off from a confounded vine? I haf not heard of such a thing. No, I will not bose as a model for your fool hermit-dunderhead. Vy do you allow dot silly pusiness to come in der brain of her? Ach, dot poor leetle Miss Yohnsy."

"She is very ill and weak," said Sue, "and the fever has left her mind morbid and full of strange fancies. Very well, Mr. Behrman, if you do not care to pose for me, you needn't. But I think you are a horrid old—old flibbertigibbet."

"You are just like a woman!" yelled Behrman. "Who said I will not bose? Go on. I come mit you. For half an hour I haf peen trying to say dot I am ready to bose. Gott! dis is not any blace in which one so goot as Miss Yohnsy shall lie sick. Some day I vill baint a masterpiece, and ve shall all go away. Gott! yes."

Johnsy was sleeping when they went upstairs. Sue pulled the shade down to the window-sill, and motioned Behrman into the other room. In there they peered out the window fearfully at the ivy vine. Then they looked at each other for a moment without speaking. A persistent, cold rain was falling, mingled with snow. Behrman, in his old blue shirt, took his seat as the hermit miner on an upturned kettle for a rock.

When Sue awoke from an hour's sleep the next morning she found Johnsy with dull, wide-open eyes staring at the drawn green shade.

"Put it up; I want to see," she ordered, in a whisper.

Wearily Sue obeyed.

But, lo! after the beating rain and fierce gusts of wind that had endured through the livelong night, there yet stood out against the brick wall one ivy leaf. It was the last on the vine. Still dark green near its stem, but with its serrated edges tinted with the yellow of dissolution and decay, it hung bravely from a branch some twenty feet above the ground.

"It is the last one," said Johnsy. "I thought it would surely fall during the night. I heard the wind. It will fall to-day, and I shall die at the same time."

"Dear, dear!" said Sue, leaning her worn face down to the pillow, "think of me, if you won't think of yourself. What would I do?"

But Johnsy did not answer. The lonesomest thing in all the world is a soul when it is making ready to go on its mysterious, far journey. The fancy seemed to possess her more strongly as one by one the ties that bound her to friendship and to earth were loosed.

The day wore away, and even through the twilight they could see the lone ivy leaf clinging to its stem against the wall. And then, with the coming of the night the north wind was again loosed, while the rain still beat against the windows and pattered down from the low Dutch eaves.

When it was light enough Johnsy, the merciless, commanded that the shade be raised.

The ivy leaf was still there.

Johnsy lay for a long time looking at it. And then she called to Sue, who was stirring her chicken broth over the gas stove.

"I've been a bad girl, Sudie," said Johnsy. "Something has made that last leaf stay there to show me how wicked I was. It is a sin to want to die. You may bring me a little broth now, and some milk with a little port in it, and—no; bring me a hand-mirror first, and then pack some pillows about me, and I will sit up and watch you cook."

An hour later she said:

"Sudie, some day I hope to paint the Bay of Naples."

The doctor came in the afternoon, and Sue had an excuse to go into the hallway as he left.

"Even chances," said the doctor, taking Sue's thin, shaking hand in his. "With good nursing you'll win. And now I must see another case I have downstairs. Behrman, his name is—some kind of an artist, I believe. Pneumonia, too. He is an old, weak man, and the attack is acute. There is no hope for him; but he goes to the hospital to-day to be made more comfortable."

The next day the doctor said to Sue: "She's out of danger. You've won. Nutrition and care now—that's all."

And that afternoon Sue came to the bed where Johnsy lay, contentedly knitting a very blue and very useless woolen shoulder scarf, and put one arm around her, pillows and all.

"I have something to tell you, white mouse," she said. "Mr. Behrman died of pneumonia to-day in the hospital. He was ill only two days. The janitor found him on the morning of the first day in his room downstairs helpless with pain. His shoes and clothing were wet through and icy cold. They couldn't imagine where he had been on such a dreadful night. And then they found a lantern, still lighted, and a ladder that had been dragged from its place, and some scattered brushes, and a palette with green and yellow colors mixed on it, and—look out the window, dear, at the last ivy leaf on the wall. Didn't you wonder why it never fluttered or moved when the wind blew? Ah, darling, it's Behrman's masterpiece—he painted it there the night that the last leaf fell."

Schools and Schools

Old Jerome Warren lived in a hundred-thousand-dollar house at 35 East Fifty-Soforth Street. He was a downtown broker, so rich that he could afford to walk—for his health—a few blocks in the direction of his office every morning and then call a cab.

He had an adopted son, the son of an old friend named Gilbert—Cyril Scott could play him nicely—who was becoming a successful painter as fast as he could squeeze the paint out of his tubes. Another member of the household was Barbara Ross, a step-niece. Man is born to trouble; so, as old Jerome had no family of his own, he took up the burdens of others.

Gilbert and Barbara got along swimmingly. There was a tacit and tactical understanding all round that the two would stand up under a floral bell some high noon, and promise the minister to keep old Jerome's money in a state of high commotion. But at this point complications must be introduced.

Thirty years before, when old Jerome was young Jerome, there was a brother of his named Dick. Dick went West to seek his or somebody else's fortune. Nothing was heard of him until one day old Jerome had a letter from his brother. It was badly written on ruled paper that smelled of salt bacon and coffee-grounds. The writing was asthmatic and the spelling St. Vitusy.

It appeared that instead of Dick having forced Fortune to stand and deliver, he had been held up himself, and made to give hostages to the enemy. That is, as his letter disclosed, he was on the point of pegging out with a complication of disorders that even whiskey had failed to check. All that his thirty years of prospecting had netted him was one daughter, nineteen years old, as per invoice, whom he was shipping East, charges prepaid, for Jerome to clothe, feed, educate, comfort, and cherish for the rest of her natural life or until matrimony should them part.

Old Jerome was a board-walk. Everybody knows that the world is supported by the shoulders of Atlas; and that Atlas stands on a rail-fence; and that the rail-fence is built on a turtle's back. Now, the turtle has to stand on something; and that is a board-walk made of men like old Jerome.

I do not know whether immortality shall accrue to man; but if not so, I would like to know when men like old Jerome get what is due them?

They met Nevada Warren at the station. She was a little girl, deeply sunburned and wholesomely good-looking, with a manner that was frankly unsophisticated, yet one that not even a cigar-drummer would intrude upon without thinking twice. Looking at her, somehow you would expect to see her in a short skirt and leather leggings, shooting glass balls or taming mustangs. But in her plain white waist and black skirt she sent you guessing again. With an easy exhibition of strength she swung along a heavy valise, which the uniformed porters tried in vain to wrest from her.

"I am sure we shall be the best of friends," said Barbara, pecking at the firm, sunburned cheek.

"I hope so," said Nevada.

"Dear little niece," said old Jerome, "you are as welcome to my house as if it were your father's own."

"Thanks," said Nevada.

"And I am going to call you 'cousin,' " said Gilbert, with his charming smile.

"Take the valise, please," said Nevada. "It weighs a million pounds. It's got samples from six of dad's old mines in it," she explained to Barbara. "I calculate they'd assay about nine cents to the thousand tons, but I promised him to bring them along."

II It is a common custom to refer to the usual complications between one man and two ladies, or one lady and two men, or a lady and a man and a nobleman, or—well, any of these problems—as the triangle. But they are never unqualified triangles. They are always isosceles—never equilateral. So, upon the coming of Nevada Warren, she and Gilbert and Barbara Ross lined up into such a figurative triangle; and of that triangle Barbara formed the hypotenuse.

One morning old Jerome was lingering long after breakfast over the dullest morning paper in the city before setting forth to his downtown fly-trap. He had become quite fond of Nevada, finding in her much of his dead brother's quiet independence and unsuspicious frankness.

A maid brought in a note for Miss Nevada Warren.

"A messenger-boy delivered it at the door, please," she said. "He's waiting for an answer."

Nevada, who was whistling a Spanish waltz between her teeth, and watching the carriages and autos roll by in the street, took the envelope. She knew it was from Gilbert, before she opened it, by the little gold palette in the upper left-hand corner.

After tearing it open she pored over the contents for a while, absorbedly. Then, with a serious face, she went and stood at her uncle's elbow.

"Uncle Jerome, Gilbert is a nice boy, isn't he?"

"Why, bless the child!" said old Jerome, crackling his paper loudly; "of course he is. I raised him myself."

"He wouldn't write anything to anybody that wasn't exactly—I mean that everybody couldn't know and read, would he?"

"I'd just like to see him try it," said uncle, tearing a handful from his newspaper. "Why, what—"

"Read this note he just sent me, uncle, and see if you think it's all right and proper. You see, I don't know much about city people and their ways."

Old Jerome threw his paper down and set both his feet upon it. He took Gilbert's note and fiercely perused it twice, and then a third time.

"Why, child," said he, "you had me almost excited, although I was sure of that boy. He's a duplicate of his father, and he was a gilt-edged diamond. He only asks if you and Barbara will be ready at four o'clock this afternoon for an automobile drive over to Long Island. I don't see anything to criticize in it except the stationery. I always did hate that shade of blue."

"Would it be all right to go?" asked Nevada, eagerly.

"Yes, yes, yes, child, of course. Why not? Still, it pleases me to see you so careful and candid. Go, by all means."

"I don't know," said Nevada, demurely. "I thought I'd ask you. Couldn't you go with us, uncle?"

"I? No, no, no, no! I've ridden once in a car that boy was driving. Never again! But it's entirely proper for you and Barbara to go. Yes, yes. But I will not. No, no, no, no!"

Nevada flew to the door, and said to the maid:

"You bet we'll go. I'll answer for Miss Barbara. Tell the boy to say to Mr. Warren, 'You bet we'll go.' "

"Nevada," called old Jerome, "pardon me, my dear, but wouldn't it be as well to send him a note in reply? Just a line would do."

"No, I won't bother about that," said Nevada, gayly. "Gilbert will understand—he always does. I never rode in an automobile in my life; but I've paddled a canoe down Little Devil River through the Lost Horse Cañon, and if it's any livelier than that I'd like to know!"

III   Two months are supposed to have elapsed.

Barbara sat in the study of the hundred-thousand-dollar house. It was a good place for her. Many places are provided in the world where men and women may repair for the purpose of extricating themselves from divers difficulties. There are cloisters, wailing-places, watering-places, confessionals, hermitages, lawyers' offices, beauty-parlors, air-ships, and studies; and the greatest of these are studies.

It usually takes a hypotenuse a long time to discover that it is the longest side of a triangle. But it's a long line that has no turning.

Barbara was alone. Uncle Jerome and Nevada had gone to the theatre. Barbara had not cared to go. She wanted to stay at home and study in the study. If you, miss, were a stunning New York girl, and saw every day that a brown, ingenuous Western witch was getting hobbles and a lasso on the young man you wanted for yourself, you, too, would lose taste for the oxidized silver setting of a musical comedy.

Barbara sat by the quartered-oak library table. Her right arm rested upon the table, and her dextral fingers nervously manipulated a sealed letter. The letter was addressed to Nevada Warren; and in the upper left-hand corner of the envelope was Gilbert's little gold palette. It had been delivered at nine o'clock, after Nevada had left.

Barbara would have given her pearl necklace to know what that letter contained; but she could not open and read it by the aid of steam, or a pen-handle, or a hair-pin, or any of the generally approved methods, because her position in society forbade such an act. She had tried to read some of the lines of the letter by holding the envelope up to a strong light and pressing it hard against the paper, but Gilbert had too good a taste in stationery to make that possible.

At eleven-thirty the theatre-goers returned. It was a delicious winter night. Even so far as from the cab to the door they were powdered thickly with the big flakes downpouring diagonally from the east. Old Jerome growled good-naturedly about villainous cab service and blockaded streets. Nevada, colored like a rose, with sapphire eyes, babbled of the stormy nights in the mountains around dad's cabin. During all these wintry apostrophes, Barbara, cold at heart, sawed wood—the only appropriate thing she could think of to do.

Old Jerome went immediately upstairs to hot-water-bottles and quinine. Nevada fluttered into the study, the only cheerfully lighted room, subsided into an armchair, and, while at the interminable task of unbuttoning her elbow gloves, gave oral testimony as to the demerits of the "show."

"Yes, I think Mr. Fields is really amusing—sometimes," said Barbara. "Here is a letter for you, dear, that came by special delivery just after you had gone."

"Who is it from?" asked Nevada, tugging at a button.

"Well, really," said Barbara, with a smile, "I can only guess. The envelope has that queer little thing in one corner that Gilbert calls a palette, but which looks to me rather like a gilt heart on a school-girl's valentine."

"I wonder what he's writing to me about," remarked Nevada, listlessly.

"We're all alike," said Barbara; "all women. We try to find out what is in a letter by studying the postmark. As a last resort we use scissors, and read it from the bottom upward. Here it is."

She made a motion as if to toss the letter across the table to Nevada.

"Great catamounts!" exclaimed Nevada. "These centre-fire buttons are a nuisance. I'd rather wear buckskins. Oh, Barbara, please shuck the hide off that letter and read it. It'll be midnight before I get these gloves off!"

"Why, dear, you don't want me to open Gilbert's letter to you? It's for you, and you wouldn't wish any one else to read it, of course!"

Nevada raised her steady, calm, sapphire eyes from her gloves.

"Nobody writes me anything that everybody mightn't read," she said. "Go on, Barbara. Maybe Gilbert wants us to go out in his car again tomorrow."

Curiosity can do more things than kill a cat; and if emotions, well recognized as feminine, are inimical to feline life, then jealousy would soon leave the whole world catless. Barbara opened the letter, with an indulgent, slightly bored air.

"Well, dear," she said, "I'll read it if you want me to."

She slit the envelope, and read the missive with swift-travelling eyes; read it again, and cast a quick, shrewd glance at Nevada, who, for the time, seemed to consider gloves as the world of her interest, and letters from rising artists as no more than messages from Mars.

For a quarter of a minute Barbara looked at Nevada with a strange steadfastness; and then a smile so small that it widened her mouth only the sixteenth part of an inch, and narrowed her eyes no more than a twentieth flashed like an inspired thought across her face.

Since the beginning no woman has been a mystery to another woman. Swift as light travels, each penetrates the heart and mind of another, sifts her sister's words of their cunningest disguises, reads her most hidden desires, and plucks the sophistry from her wiliest talk like hairs from a comb, twiddling them sardonically between her thumb and fingers before letting them float away on the breezes of fundamental doubt. Long ago Eve's son rang the door-bell of the family residence in Paradise Park, bearing a strange lady on his arm, whom he introduced. Eve took her daughter-in-law aside and lifted a classic eyebrow.

"The Land of Nod," said the bride, languidly flirting the leaf of a palm. "I suppose you've been there, of course?"

"Not lately," said Eve, absolutely unstaggered. "Don't

you think the applesauce they serve over there is execrable? I rather like that mulberry-leaf tunic effect, dear; but, of course, the real fig goods are not to be had over there. Come over behind this lilac-bush while the gentlemen split a celery tonic. I think the caterpillar-holes have made your dress open a little in the back.''

So, then and there—according to the records—was the alliance formed by the only two who's-who ladies in the world. Then it was agreed that women should forever remain as clear as a pane of glass—though glass was yet to be discovered—to other women, and that she should palm herself off on a man as a mystery.

Barbara seemed to hesitate.

"Really, Nevada," she said, with a little show of embarrassment, "you shouldn't have insisted on my opening this. I—I'm sure it wasn't meant for any one else to know."

Nevada forgot her gloves for a moment.

"Then read it aloud," she said. "Since you've already read it, what's the difference? If Mr. Warren has written to me something that any one else oughtn't to know, that is all the more reason why everybody should know it."

"Well," said Barbara, "this is what it says: 'Dearest Nevada—Come to my studio at twelve o'clock to-night. Do not fail.' " Barbara rose and dropped the note in Nevada's lap. "I'm awfully sorry," she said, "that I knew. It isn't like Gilbert. There must be some mistake. Just consider that I am ignorant of it, will you, dear? I must go upstairs now, I have such a headache. I'm sure I don't understand the note. Perhaps Gilbert has been dining too well, and will explain. Good night!"

IV Nevada tiptoed to the hall, and heard Barbara's door close upstairs. The bronze clock in the study told the hour of twelve was fifteen minutes away. She ran swiftly to the front door, and let herself out into the snowstorm. Gilbert Warren's studio was six squares away.

By aërial ferry the white, silent forces of the storm attacked the city from beyond the sullen East River. Already the snow lay a foot deep on the pavements, the drifts heaping themselves like scaling-ladders against the walls of the besieged town. The Avenue was as quiet as a street in Pompeii. Cabs now and then skimmed past like white-winged gulls over a moonlit ocean; and less frequent motor-cars—sustaining the comparison—hissed through the foaming waves like submarine boats on their jocund, perilous journeys.

Nevada plunged like a wind-driven storm-petrel on her way. She looked up at the ragged sierras of cloud-capped buildings that rose above the streets, shaded by the night lights and the congealed vapors to gray, drab, ashen, lavender, dun, and cerulean tints. They were so like the wintry mountains of her Western home that she felt a satisfaction such as the hundred-thousand-dollar house had seldom brought her.

A policeman caused her to waver on a corner, just by his eye and weight.

"Hello, Mabel!" said he. "Kind of late for you to be out, ain't it?"

"I—I am just going to the drug store," said Nevada, hurrying past him.

The excuse serves as a passport for the most sophisticated. Does it prove that woman never progresses, or that she sprang from Adam's rib, full-fledged in intellect and wiles?

Turning eastward, the direct blast cut down Nevada's speed one half. She made zigzag tracks in the snow; but she was as tough as a piñon sapling, and bowed to it as gracefully. Suddenly the studio-building loomed before her, a familiar landmark, like a cliff above some well-remembered cañon. The haunt of business and its hostile neighbor, art, was darkened and silent. The elevator stopped at ten.

Up eight flights of Stygian stairs Nevada climbed, and rapped firmly at the door numbered "89." She had been there many times before, with Barbara and Uncle Jerome.

Gilbert opened the door. He had a crayon pencil in one hand, a green shade over his eyes, and a pipe in his mouth. The pipe dropped to the floor.

"Am I late?" asked Nevada. "I came as quick as I could. Uncle and me were at the theatre this evening. Here I am, Gilbert!"

Gilbert did a Pygmalion-and-Galatea act. He changed from a statue of stupefaction to a young man with a problem to tackle. He admitted Nevada, got a whiskbroom, and began to brush the snow from her clothes. A great lamp, with a green shade, hung over an easel, where the artist had been sketching in crayon.

"You wanted me," said Nevada, simply, "and I came. You said so in your letter. What did you send for me for?"

"You read my letter?" inquired Gilbert, sparring for wind.

"Barbara read it to me. I saw it afterward. It said: 'Come to my studio at twelve to-night, and do not fail.' I thought you were sick, of course, but you don't seem to be."

"Aha!" said Gilbert, irrelevantly. "I'll tell you why I asked you to come, Nevada. I want you to marry me immediately—to-night. What's a little snowstorm? Will you do it?"

"You might have noticed that I would, long ago," said Nevada. "And I'm rather stuck on the snowstorm idea, myself. I surely would hate one of those flowery church noon-weddings. Gilbert, I didn't know you had grit enough to propose in this way. Let's shock 'em—it's our funeral, ain't it?"

"You bet!" said Gilbert. "Where did I hear that expression?" he added to himself. "Wait a minute, Nevada; I want to do a little 'phoning."

He shut himself up in a little dressing-room, and called upon the lightnings of the heavens—condensed into unromantic numbers and districts.

"That you, Jack? You confounded sleepy-head! Yes, wake up; this is me—or I—oh, bother the difference in grammar! I'm going to be married right away. Yes! Wake up your sister—don't answer me back; bring her along, too—you *must*. Remind Agnes of the time I saved her from drowning in Lake Ronkonkoma—I know it's caddish to refer to it, but she *must* come with you. Yes! Nevada is here, waiting. We've been engaged quite a while. Some opposition among the relatives, you know, and we have to pull it off this way. We're waiting here for you. Don't let Agnes out-talk you— bring her! You will? Good old boy! I'll order a carriage to call for you, double-quick time. Confound you, Jack, you're all right!"

Gilbert returned to the room where Nevada waited.

"My old friend, Jack Peyton, and his sister were to have been here at a quarter to twelve," he explained; "but Jack is so confoundedly slow. I've just 'phoned them to hurry. They'll be here in a few minutes. I'm the happiest man in the world, Nevada! What did you do with the letter I sent you to-day?''

"I've got it cinched here," said Nevada, pulling it out from beneath her opera-cloak.

Gilbert drew the letter from the envelope and looked it over carefully. Then he looked at Nevada thoughtfully.

"Didn't you think it rather queer that I should ask you to come to my studio at midnight?" he asked.

"Why, no," said Nevada, rounding her eyes. "Not if you needed me. Out West, when a pal sends you a hurry call—ain't that what you say here?—we get there first and talk about it after the row is over. And it's usually snowing there, too, when things happen. So I didn't mind.''

Gilbert rushed into another room, and came back burdened with overcoats warranted to turn wind, rain, or snow.

"Put this raincoat on," he said, holding it for her. "We have a quarter of a mile to go. Old Jack and his sister will be here in a few minutes." He began to struggle into a heavy coat. "Oh, Nevada," he said, "just look at the headlines on the front page of that evening paper on the table, will you? It's about your section of the West, and I know it will interest you."

He waited a full minute, pretending to find trouble in the getting on of his overcoat, and then turned. Nevada had not moved. She was looking at him with strange and pensive directness. Her cheeks had a flush on them beyond the color that had been contributed by the wind and snow; but her eyes were steady.

"I was going to tell you," she said, "anyhow, before you—before we—before—well, before anything. Dad never gave me a day of schooling. I never learned to read or write a darned word. Now if—"

Pounding their uncertain way upstairs, the feet of Jack, the somnolent, and Agnes, the grateful, were heard.

V   When Mr. and Mrs. Gilbert Warren were spinning softly homeward in a closed carriage, after the ceremony, Gilbert said:

"Nevada, would you really like to know what I wrote you in the letter that you received to-night?"

"Fire away!" said his bride.

"Word for word," said Gilbert, "it was this: 'My dear Miss Warren—You were right about the flower. It was a hydrangea, and not a lilac.' "

"All right," said Nevada. "But let's forget it. The joke's on Barbara, anyway!"

Springtime à la Carte

It was a day in March.

Never, never begin a story this way when you write one. No opening could possibly be worse. It is unimaginative, flat, dry, and likely to consist of mere wind. But in this instance it is allowable. For the following paragraph, which should have inaugurated the narrative, is too wildly extravagant and preposterous to be flaunted in the face of the reader without preparation.

Sarah was crying over her bill of fare.

Think of a New York girl shedding tears on the menu card!

To account for this you will be allowed to guess that the lobsters were all out, or that she had sworn ice-cream off during Lent, or that she had ordered onions, or that she had just come from a Hackett matinée. And then, all these theories being wrong, you will please let the story proceed.

The gentleman who announced that the world was an oyster which he with his sword would open made a larger hit than he deserved. It is not difficult to open an oyster with a sword. But did you ever notice any one try to open the terrestrial bivalve with a typewriter? Like to wait for a dozen raw opened that way?

Sarah had managed to pry apart the shells with her unhandy weapon far enough to nibble a wee bit at the cold and clammy world within. She knew no more shorthand than if she had been a graduate in stenography just let slip upon the world by a business college. So, not being able to stenog, she could not enter that bright galaxy of office talent. She was a free-lance typist and canvassed for odd jobs of copying.

The most brilliant and crowning feat of Sarah's battle with the world was the deal she made with Schulenberg's Home Restaurant. The restaurant was next door to the old red brick in which she hall-roomed. One evening after dining at Schulenberg's 40-cent, five-course *table d'hôte* (served as fast as you throw the five baseballs at the colored gentleman's head) Sarah took away with her the bill of fare. It was written in an almost unreadable script neither English nor German, and so arranged that if you were not careful you began with a toothpick and rice pudding and ended with soup and the day of the week.

The next day Sarah showed Schulenberg a neat card on which the menu was beautifully typewritten with the viands temptingly marshalled under their right and proper heads from "hors d'œuvre" to "not responsible for over-coats and umbrellas."

Schulenberg became a naturalized citizen on the spot. Before Sarah left him she had him willingly committed to an agreement. She was to furnish typewritten bills of fare for the twenty-one tables in the restaurant—a new bill for each day's dinner, and new ones for breakfast and lunch as often as changes occurred in the food or as neatness required.

In return for this Schulenberg was to send three meals per diem to Sarah's hall room by a waiter—an obsequious one if possible—and furnish her each afternoon with a pencil draft of what Fate had in store for Schulenberg's customers on the morrow.

Mutual satisfaction resulted from the agreement. Schulenberg's patrons now knew what the food they ate was called even if its nature sometimes puzzled them. And Sarah had food during a cold, dull winter, which was the main thing with her.

And then the almanac lied, and said that spring had come. Spring comes when it comes. The frozen snows of January still lay like adamant in the cross-town streets. The hand-organs still played "In the Good Old Summertime," with their December vivacity and expression. Men began to make thirty-day notes to buy Easter dresses. Janitors shut off steam. And when these things happen one may know that the city is still in the clutches of winter.

One afternoon Sarah shivered in her elegant hall bedroom; "house heated; scrupulously clean; conveniences; seen to be appreciated." She had no work to do except Schulenberg's menu cards. Sarah sat in her squeaky willow rocker, and looked out the window. The calendar on the wall kept crying to her: "Springtime is here, Sarah—springtime is here, I tell you. Look at me, Sarah, my figures show it. You've got a neat figure yourself, Sarah—a—nice springtime figure—why do you look out the window so sadly?"

Sarah's room was at the back of the house. Looking out the window she could see the windowless rear brick wall of the box factory on the next street. But the wall was clearest crystal; and Sarah was looking down a grassy lane shaded with cherry trees and elms and bordered with raspberry bushes and Cherokee roses.

Spring's real harbingers are too subtle for the eye and ear. Some must have the flowering crocus, the wood-starring dogwood, the voice of bluebird—even so gross a reminder as the farewell handshake of the retiring buckwheat and oyster before they can welcome the Lady in Green to their dull bosoms. But to old earth's choicest kind there come straight, sweet messages from his newest bride, telling them they shall be no stepchildren unless they choose to be.

On the previous summer Sarah had gone into the country and loved a farmer.

(In writing your story never hark back thus. It is bad art, and cripples interest. Let it march, march.)

Sarah stayed two weeks at Sunnybrook Farm. There she learned to love old Farmer Franklin's son Walter. Farmers have been loved and wedded and turned out to grass in less time. But young Walter Franklin was a modern agriculturist. He had a telephone in his cow house, and he could figure up exactly what effect next year's Canada wheat crop would have on potatoes planted in the dark of the moon.

It was in this shaded and raspberried lane that Walter had wooed and won her. And together they had sat and woven a crown of dandelions for her hair. He had immoderately praised the effect of the yellow blossoms against her brown tresses;

and she had left the chaplet there, and walked back to the
house swinging her straw sailor in her hands.

They were to marry in the spring—at the very first signs of
spring, Walter said. And Sarah came back to the city to
pound her typewriter.

A knock at the door dispelled Sarah's visions of that happy
day. A waiter had brought the rough pencil draft of the Home
Restaurant's next day fare in old Schulenberg's angular hand.

Sarah sat down to her typewriter and slipped a card between the rollers. She was a nimble worker. Generally in an
hour and a half the twenty-one menu cards were written and
ready.

To-day there were more changes on the bill of fare than
usual. The soups were lighter; pork was eliminated from the
entrées, figuring only with Russian turnips among the roasts.
The gracious spirit of spring pervaded the entire menu. Lamb,
that lately capered on the greening hillsides, was becoming
exploited with the sauce that commemorated its gambols. The
song of the oyster, though not silenced, was *diminuendo con
amore*. The frying-pan seemed to be held, inactive, behind
the beneficent bars of the broiler. The pie list swelled; the
richer puddings had vanished; the sausage, with his drapery
wrapped about him, barely lingered in a pleasant thanatopsis
with the buckwheats and the sweet but doomed maple.

Sarah's fingers danced like midgets above a summer stream.
Down through the courses she worked, giving each item its
position according to its length with an accurate eye.

Just above the desserts came the list of vegetables. Carrots
and peas, asparagus on toast, the perennial tomatoes and corn
and succotash, lima beans, cabbage—and then——

Sarah was crying over her bill of fare. Tears from the
depths of some divine despair rose in her heart and gathered
to her eyes. Down went her head on the little typewriter
stand; and the keyboard rattled a dry accompaniment to her
moist sobs.

For she had received no letter from Walter in two weeks,
and the next item on the bill of fare was dandelions—dandelions
with some kind of egg—but bother the egg!—dandelions, with
whose golden blooms Walter had crowned her his queen of
love and future bride—dandelions, the harbingers of spring,

her sorrow's crown of sorrow—reminder of her happiest days.

Madam, I dare you to smile until you suffer this test: Let the Marechal Niel roses that Percy brought you on the night you gave him your heart be served as a salad with French dressing before your eyes at a Schulenberg *table d'hôte*. Had Juliet so seen her love tokens dishonored the sooner would she have sought the lethean herbs of the good apothecary.

But what witch is Spring! Into the great cold city of stone and iron a message had to be sent. There was none to convey it but the little hardy courier of the fields with his rough green coat and modest air. He is a true soldier of fortune, this *dent-de-lion*—this lion's tooth, as the French chefs call him. Flowered, he will assist at love-making, wreathed in my lady's nut-brown hair; young and callow and unblossomed, he goes into the boiling pot and delivers the word of his sovereign mistress.

By and by Sarah forced back her tears. The cards must be written. But, still in a faint, golden glow from her dandelion dream, she fingered the typewriter keys absently for a little while, with her mind and heart in the meadow lane with her young farmer. But soon she came swiftly back to the rock-bound lanes of Manhattan, and the typewriter began to rattle and jump like a strike-breaker's motor car.

At 6 o'clock the waiter brought her dinner and carried away the typewriten bill of fare. When Sarah ate she set aside, with a sigh, the dish of dandelions with its crowning ovarious accompaniment. As this dark mass had been transformed from a bright and love-indorsed flower to be an ignominious vegetable, so had her summer hopes wilted and perished. Love may, as Shakespeare said, feed on itself: but Sarah could not bring herself to eat the dandelions that had graced, as ornaments, the first spiritual banquet of her heart's true affection.

At 7:30 the couple in the next room began to quarrel; the man in the room above sought for A on his flute; the gas went a little lower; three coal wagons started to unload—the only sound of which the phonograph is jealous; cats on the back fences slowly retreated toward Mukden. By these signs Sarah knew that it was time for her to read. She got out "The Cloister and the Hearth," the best non-selling book of the

month, settled her feet on her trunk, and began to wander
with Gerard.

The front door bell rang. The landlady answered it. Sarah
left Gerard and Denys treed by a bear and listened. Oh, yes;
you would, just as she did!

And then a strong voice was heard in the hall below, and
Sarah jumped for her door, leaving the book on the floor and
the first round easily the bear's.

You have guessed it. She reached the top of the stairs just
as her farmer came up, three at a jump, and reaped and
garnered her, with nothing left for the gleaners.

"Why haven't you written—oh, why?" cried Sarah.

"New York is a pretty large town," said Walter Franklin.
"I came in a week ago to your old address. I found that you
went away on a Thursday. That consoled some; it eliminated
the possible Friday bad luck. But it didn't prevent my hunting
for you with police and otherwise ever since!"

"I wrote!" said Sarah, vehemently.

"Never got it!"

"Then how did you find me?"

The young farmer smiled a springtime smile.

"I dropped into that Home Restaurant next door this
evening," said he. "I don't care who knows it; I like a dish
of some kind of greens at this time of the year. I ran my eye
down that nice typewritten bill of fare looking for something
in that line. When I got below cabbage I turned my chair
over and hollered for the proprietor. He told me where you
lived."

"I remember," sighed Sarah, happily. "That was dandelions below cabbage."

"I'd know that cranky capital W 'way above the line
that your typewriter makes anywhere in the world," said
Franklin.

"Why, there's no W in dandelions," said Sarah in surprise.

The young man drew the bill of fare from his pocket and
pointed to a line.

Sarah recognised the first card she had typewritten that
afternoon. There was still the rayed splotch in the upper
right-hand corner where a tear had fallen. But over the spot
where one should have read the name of the meadow plant,

the clinging memory of their golden blossoms had allowed her fingers to strike strange keys.

Between the red cabbage and the stuffed green peppers was the item:

"DEAREST WALTER, WITH HARD-BOILED EGG."

Best-Seller

One day last summer I went to Pittsburgh—well, I had to go there on business.

My chair-car was profitably well filled with people of the kind one usually sees on chair-cars. Most of them were ladies in brown-silk dresses cut with square yokes, with lace insertion and dotted veils, who refused to have the windows raised. Then there was the usual number of men who looked as if they might be in almost any business and going almost anywhere. Some students of human nature can look at a man in a Pullman and tell you where he is from, his occupation and his stations in life, both flag and social; but I never could. The only way I can correctly judge a fellow-traveller is when the train is held up by robbers, or when he reaches at the same time I do for the last towel in the dressing-room of the sleeper.

The porter came and brushed the collection of soot on the windowsill off to the left knee of my trousers. I removed it with an air of apology. The temperature was eighty-eight. One of the dotted-veiled ladies demanded the closing of two more ventilators, and spoke loudly of Interlaken. I leaned back idly in chair No. 7, and looked with the tepidest curiosity at the small, black, bald-spotted head just visible above the back of No. 9.

Suddenly No. 9 hurled a book to the floor between his

chair and the window, and, looking, I saw that it was "The Rose Lady and Trevelyan," one of the best-selling novels of the present day. And then the critic or Philistine, whichever he was, veered his chair toward the window, and I knew him at once for John A. Pescud of Pittsburgh, travelling salesman for a plate-glass company—an old acquaintance whom I had not seen in two years.

In two minutes we were faced, had shaken hands, and had finished with such topics as rain, prosperity, health, residence, and destination. Politics might have followed next; but I was not so ill-fated.

I wish you might know John A. Pescud. He is of the stuff that heroes are not often lucky enough to be made of. He is a small man with a wide smile, and an eye that seems to be fixed upon that little red spot on the end of your nose. I never saw him wear but one kind of necktie, and he believes in cuff-holders and button-shoes. He is as hard and true as anything ever turned out by the Cambria Steel Works; and he believes that as soon as Pittsburgh makes smoke-consumers compulsory, St. Peter will come down and sit at the foot of Smithfield Street, and let somebody else attend to the gate up in the branch heaven. He believes that "our" plate-glass is the most important commodity in the world, and that when a man is in his home town he ought to be decent and law-abiding.

During my acquaintance with him in the City of Diurnal Night I had never known his views on life, romance, literature, and ethics. We had browsed, during our meetings, on local topics and then parted, after Château Margaux, Irish stew, flannel-cakes, cottage-pudding, and coffee (hey, there!—with milk separate). Now I was to get more of his ideas. By way of facts, he told me that business had picked up since the party conventions, and that he was going to get off at Coketown.

II "Say," said Pescud, stirring his discarded book with the toe of his right shoe; "did you ever read one of these best-sellers? I mean the kind where the hero is an American swell—sometimes even from Chicago—who falls in love with a royal princess from Europe who is travelling under an alias, and follows her to her father's kingdom or principality? I guess you have. They're all alike. Sometimes this going-

away masher is a Washington newspaper correspondent, and
sometimes he is a Van Something from New York, or a
Chicago wheat-broker worth fifty millions. But he's always
ready to break into the king row of any foreign country that
sends over their queens and princesses to try the new plush
seats on the Big Four or the B. and O. There doesn't seem to
be any other reason in the book for their being here.

"Well, this fellow chases the royal chair-warmer home as I
said, and finds out who she is. He meets her on the *corso* or
the *strasse* one evening and gives us ten pages of conversation.
She reminds him of the difference in their stations, and that
gives him a chance to ring in three solid pages about America's
uncrowned sovereigns. If you'd take his remarks and set 'em
to music, and then take the music away from 'em, they'd
sound exactly like one of George Cohan's songs.

"Well, you know how it runs on, if you've read any of
'em—he slaps the king's Swiss bodyguards around like everything whenever they get in his way. He's a great fencer, too.
Now, I've known of some Chicago men who were pretty
notorious fences, but I never heard of any fencers coming
from there. He stands on the first landing of the royal stair-
case in Castle Schutzenfestenstein with a gleaming rapier in
his hand, and makes a Baltimore broil of six platoons of
traitors who come to massacre the said king. And then he has
to fight duels with a couple of chancellors, and foil a plot by
four Austrian arch-dukes to seize the kingdom for a gas-
oline-station.

"But the great scene is when his rival for the princess'
hand, Count Feodor, attacks him between the portcullis and
the ruined chapel, armed with a mitrailleuse, a yataghan, and
a couple of Siberian bloodhounds. This scene is what runs the
best-seller into the twenty-ninth edition before the publisher
has had time to draw a check for the advance royalties.

"The American hero shucks his coat and throws it over the
heads of the bloodhounds, gives the mitrailleuse a slap with
his mitt, says 'Yah!' to the yataghan, and lands in Kid
McCoy's best style on the count's left eye. Of course, we
have a neat little prize-fight right then and there. The count—in
order to make the go possible—seems to be an expert at the
art of self-defence, himself; and here we have the Corbett-
Sullivan fight done over into literature. The book ends with

the broker and the princess doing a John Cecil Clay cover under the linden-trees on the Gorgonzola Walk. That winds up the love-story plenty good enough. But I notice that the book dodges the final issue. Even a best-seller has sense enough to shy at either leaving a Chicago grain-broker on the throne of Lobsterpotsdam or bringing over a real princess to eat fish and potato salad in an Italian chalet on Michigan Avenue. What do you think about 'em?"

"Why," said I, "I hardly know, John. There's a saying: 'Love levels all ranks,' you know."

"Yes," said Pescud, "but these kind of love-stories are rank—on the level. I know something about literature, even if I am in plate-glass. These kind of books are wrong, and yet I never go into a train but what they pile 'em up on me. No good can come out of an international clinch between the Old World aristocracy and one of us fresh Americans. When people in real life marry, they generally hunt up somebody in their own station. A fellow usually picks out a girl that went to the same high-school and belonged to the same singing-society that he did. When young millionaires fall in love, they always select the chorus-girl that likes the same kind of sauce on the lobster that he does. Washington newspaper correspondents always marry widow ladies ten years older than themselves who keep boarding-houses. No, sir, you can't make a novel sound right to me when it makes one of C. D. Gibson's bright young men go abroad and turn king-doms upside down just because he's a Taft American and took a course at a gymnasium. And listen how they talk, too!"

Pescud picked up the best-seller and hunted his page.

"Listen at this," said he. "Trevelyan is chinning with the Princess Alwyna at the back end of the tulip-garden. This is how it goes:

"Say not so, dearest and sweetest of earth's fairest flowers. Would I aspire? You are a star set high above me in a royal heaven; I am only—myself. Yet I am a man, and I have a heart to do and dare. I have no title save that of an uncrowned sovereign; but I have an arm and a sword that yet might free Schutzenfestenstein from the plots of traitors.

* * *

"Think of a Chicago man packing a sword, and talking about freeing anything that sounded as much like canned pork as that! He'd be much more likely to fight to have an import duty put on it."

"I think I understand you, John," said I. "You want fiction-writers to be consistent with their scenes and characters. They shouldn't mix Turkish pashas with Vermont farmers, or English dukes with Long Island clamdiggers, or Italian countesses with Montana cowboys, or Cincinnati brewery agents with the rajahs of India."

"Or plain business men with aristocracy high above 'em," added Pescud. "It don't jibe. People are divided into classes, whether we admit it or not, and it's everybody's impulse to stick to their own class. They do it, too. I don't see why people go to work and buy hundreds of thousands of books like that. You don't see or hear of any such didoes and capers in real life."

III "Well, John," said I, "I haven't read a best-seller in a long time. Maybe I've had notions about them somewhat like yours. But tell me more about yourself. Getting along all right with the company?"

"Bully," said Pescud, brightening at once. "I've had my salary raised twice since I saw you, and I get a commission, too. I've bought a neat slice of real estate out in the East End, and have run up a house on it. Next year the firm is going to sell me some shares of stock. Oh, I'm in on the line of General Prosperity, no matter who's elected!"

"Met your affinity yet, John?" I asked.

"Oh, I didn't tell you about that, did I?" said Pescud with a broader grin.

"O-ho!" I said. "So you've taken time enough off from your plate-glass to have a romance?"

"No, no," said John. "No romance—nothing like that! But I'll tell you about it.

"I was on the south-bound, going to Cincinnati, about eighteen months ago, when I saw, across the aisle, the finest looking girl I'd ever laid eyes on. Nothing spectacular, you know, but just the sort you want for keeps. Well, I never was up to the flirtation business, either handkerchief, automobile, postage-stamp, or door-step, and she wasn't the kind to start anything. She read a book and minded her business, which was to make the world prettier and better just by residing in it. I kept on looking out of the side doors of my eyes, and finally the proposition got out of the Pullman class into a case of cottage with a lawn and vines running over the porch. I never thought of speaking to her, but I let the plate-glass business go to smash for a while.

"She changed cars at Cincinnati and took a sleeper to Louisville over the L. and N. There she bought another ticket, and went on through Shelbyville, Frankford, and Lexington. Along there I began to have a hard time keeping up with her. The trains came along when they pleased, and didn't seem to be going anywhere in particular, except to keep on the track and the right of way as much as possible. Then they began to stop at junctions instead of towns, and at last they stopped altogether. I'll bet Pinkerton would outbid the plate-glass people for my services any time if they knew how I managed to shadow that young lady. I contrived to keep out of her sight as much as I could, but I never lost track of her.

"The last station she got off at was away down in Virginia, about six in the afternoon. There were about fifty houses and four hundred niggers in sight. The rest was red mud, mules, and speckled hounds.

"A tall old man, with a smooth face and white hair, looking as proud as Julius Caesar and Roscoe Conkling on the same post-card, was there to meet her. His clothes were frazzled, but I didn't notice that till later. He took her little satchel, and they started over the plank walks and went up a road along the hill. I kept along a piece behind 'em, trying to look like I was hunting a garnet ring in the sand that my sister had lost at a picnic the previous Saturday.

"They went in a gate on top of the hill. It nearly took my breath away when I looked up. Up there in the biggest grove I ever saw was a tremendous house with round white pillars about a thousand feet high, and the yard was so full of rose-bushes and box-bushes and lilacs that you couldn't have seen the house if it hadn't been as big as the Capitol at Washington.

" 'Here's where I have to trail,' says I to myself. I thought before that she seemed to be in moderate circumstances, at least. This must be the Governor's mansion, or the Agricultural Building of a new World's Fair, anyhow. I'd better go back to the village and get posted by the postmaster, or drug the druggist for some information.

"In the village I found a pine hotel called the Bay View House. The only excuse for the name was a bay horse grazing in the front yard. I set my sample-case down, and tried to be ostensible. I told the landlord I was taking orders for plate-glass.

" 'I don't want no plates,' says he, 'but I need another glass molasses-pitcher.'

"By-and-by I got him down to local gossip and answering questions.

" 'Why,' says he, 'I thought everybody knowed who lived in the big white house on the hill. It's Colonel Allyn, the biggest man and finest quality in Virginia, or anywhere else. They're the oldest family in the State. That was his daughter that got off the train. She's been up to Illinois to see her aunt, who is sick.'

"I registered at the hotel, and on the third day I caught the young lady walking in the front yard, down next to the paling fence. I stopped and raised my hat—there wasn't any other way.

" 'Excuse me,' says I, 'can you tell me where Mr. Hinkle lives?'

"She looks at me as cool as if I was the man come to see about the weeding of the garden, but I thought I saw just a slight twinkle of fun in her eyes.

" 'No one of that name lives in Birchton,' says she. 'That is,' she goes on, 'as far as I know. Is the gentleman you are seeking white?'

"Well, that tickled me. 'No kidding,' says I. 'I'm not looking for smoke, even if I do come from Pittsburgh.'

" 'You are quite a distance from home,' says she.

" 'I'd have gone a thousand miles farther,' says I.

" 'Not if you hadn't waked up when the train started in Shelbyville,' says she; and then she turned almost as red as one of the roses on the bushes in the yard. I remembered I had dropped off to sleep on a bench in the Shelbyville station, waiting to see which train she took, and only just managed to wake up in time.

"And then I told her why I had come, as respectful and

earnest as I could. And I told her everything about myself, and what I was making, and how that all I asked was just to get acquainted with her and try to get her to like me.

"She smiles a little, and blushes some, but her eyes never get mixed up. They look straight at whatever she's talking to.

" 'I never had any one talk like this to me before, Mr. Pescud,' says she. 'What did you say your name is—John?'

" 'John A.,' says I.

" 'And you came mighty near missing the train at Powhatan Junction, too,' says she, with a laugh that sounded as good as a mileage-book to me.

" 'How did you know?' I asked.

" 'Men are very clumsy,' said she. 'I knew you were on every train. I thought you were going to speak to me, and I'm glad you didn't.'

"Then we had more talk; and at last a kind of proud, serious look came on her face, and she turned and pointed a finger at the big house.

" 'The Allyns,' says she, 'have lived in Elmcroft for a hundred years. We are a proud family. Look at that mansion. It has fifty rooms. See the pillars and porches and balconies. The ceilings in the reception-rooms and the ball-room are twenty-eight feet high. My father is a lineal descendant of belted earls.'

" 'I belted one of 'em once in the Duquesne Hotel, in Pittsburgh,' says I, 'and he didn't offer to resent it. He was there dividing his attentions between Monongahela whiskey and heiresses, and he got fresh.'

" 'Of course,' she goes on, 'my father wouldn't allow a drummer to set his foot in Elmcroft. If he knew that I was talking to one over the fence he would lock me in my room.'

" 'Would you let me come there?' says I. 'Would you talk to me if I was to call? For,' I goes on, 'if you said I might come and see you, the earls might be belted or suspendered, or pinned up with safety-pins, as far as I am concerned.'

" 'I must not talk to you,' she says, 'because we have not been introduced. It is not exactly proper. So I will say good-bye, Mr.——'

" 'Say the name,' says I. 'You haven't forgotten it.'

" ' "Pescud," ' says she, a little mad.

" 'The rest of the name!' I demands, cool as could be.

" 'John,' says she.

" 'John—what?' I says.

" 'John A.,' says she, with her head high. 'Are you through, now?'

" 'I'm coming to see the belted earl to-morrow,' I says.

" 'He'll feed you to his fox-hounds,' says she, laughing.

" 'If he does, it'll improve their running,' says I. 'I'm something of a hunter myself.'

" 'I must be going in now,' says she. 'I oughtn't to have spoken to you at all. I hope you'll have a pleasant trip back to Minneapolis—or Pittsburgh, was it? Good-bye!'

" 'Good-night,' says I, 'and it wasn't Minneapolis. What's your name, first, please?'

"She hesitated. Then she pulled a leaf off a bush, and said:

" 'My name is Jessie,' says she.

" 'Good-night, Miss Allyn,' says I.

"The next morning at eleven, sharp, I rang the doorbell of that World's Fair main building. After about three quarters of an hour an old nigger man about eighty showed up and asked what I wanted. I gave him my business card, and said I wanted to see the colonel. He showed me in.

"Say, did you ever crack open a wormy English walnut? That's what that house was like. There wasn't enough furniture in it to fill an eight-dollar flat. Some old horsehair lounges and three-legged chairs and some framed ancestors on the walls were all that met the eye. But when Colonel Allyn comes in, the place seemed to light up. You could almost hear a band playing, and see a bunch of old-timers in wigs and white stockings dancing a quadrille. It was the style of him, although he had on the same shabby clothes I saw him wear at the station.

"For about nine seconds he had me rattled, and I came mighty near getting cold feet and trying to sell him some plate-glass. But I got my nerve back pretty quick. He asked me to sit down, and I told him everything. I told him how I followed his daughter from Cincinnati, and what I did it for, and all about my salary and prospects, and explained to him my little code of living—to be always decent and right in your home town; and when you're on the road never take more than four glasses of beer a day or play higher than a twenty-five-cent limit. At first I thought he was going to throw me out of the window, but I kept on talking. Pretty soon I got a chance to tell him that story about the Western Congressman who had lost his pocketbook and the grass widow—you remember that story. Well, that got him to laughing, and I'll bet that was the first laugh those ancestors and horsehair sofas had heard in many a day.

"We talked two hours. I told him everything I knew; and then he began to ask questions and I told him the rest. All I asked of him was to give me a chance. If I couldn't make a hit with the little lady, I'd clear out, and not bother any more. At last he says:

" 'There was a Sir Courtenay Pescud in the time of Charles I, if I remember rightly.'

" 'If there was,' says I, 'he can't claim kin with our bunch. We've always lived in and around Pittsburgh. I've got an uncle in the real-estate business, and one in trouble somewhere out in Kansas. You can inquire about any of the rest of us from anybody in old Smoky Town, and get satisfactory replies. Did you ever run across that story about the captain of the whaler who tried to make a sailor say his prayers?' says I.

" 'It occurs to me that I have never been so fortunate,' says the colonel.

"So I told it to him. Laugh! I was wishing to myself that he was a customer. What a bill of glass I'd sell him! And then he says:

" 'The relating of anecdotes and humorous occurrences has always seemed to me, Mr. Pescud, to be a particularly agreeable way of promoting and perpetuating amenities between friends. With your permission, I will relate to you a fox-hunting story with which I was personally connected, and which may furnish you some amusement.'

"So he tells it. It takes forty minutes by the watch. Did I laugh? Well, say! When I got my face straight he calls in old Pete, the super-annuated darky, and sends him down to the hotel to bring up my valise. It was Elmcroft for me while I was in the town.

"Two evenings later I got a chance to speak a word with Miss Jessie alone on the porch while the colonel was thinking up another story.

" 'It's going to be a fine evening,' says I.

" 'He's coming,' says she. 'He's going to tell you, this time, the story about the old negro and the green watermelons. It always comes after the one about the Yankees and the game rooster. There was another time,' she goes on, 'that you nearly got left—it was at Pulaski City.'

" 'Yes,' says I, 'I remember. My foot slipped as I was jumping on the step, and I nearly tumbled off.'

" 'I know,' says she. 'And—and I—*I was afraid you had, John A. I was afraid you had.*'

"And then she skips into the house through one of the big windows."

IV "Coketown!" droned the porter, making his way through the slowing car.

Pescud gathered his hat and baggage with the leisurely promptness of an old traveller.

"I married her a year ago," said John. "I told you I built a house in the East End. The belted—I mean the colonel—is there, too. I find him waiting at the gate whenever I get back from a trip to hear any new story I might have picked up on the road."

I glanced out of the window. Coketown was nothing more than a ragged hillside dotted with a score of black dismal huts propped up against dreary mounts of slag and clinkers. It rained in slanting torrents, too, and the rills foamed and splashed down through the black mud to the railroad-tracks.

"You won't sell much plate-glass here, John," said I. "Why do you get off at this end-o'-the-world?"

"Why," said Pescud, "the other day I took Jessie for a little trip to Philadelphia, and coming back she thought she saw some petunias in a pot in one of those windows over there just like some she used to raise down in the old Virginia home. So I thought I'd drop off here for the night, and see if I could dig up some of the cuttings or blossoms for her. Here we are. Good-night, old man. I gave you the address. Come out and see us when you have time."

The train moved forward. One of the dotted brown ladies insisted on having windows raised, now that the rain beat against them. The porter came along with his mysterious wand and began to light the car.

I glanced downward and saw the best-seller. I picked it up

and set it carefully farther along on the floor of the car, where the raindrops would not fall upon it. And then, suddenly, I smiled, and seemed to see that life has no geographical metes and bounds.

"Good-luck to you, Trevelyan," I said. "And may you get the petunias for your princess!"

The Gift of the Magi

One dollar and eighty-seven cents. That was all. And sixty cents of it was in pennies. Pennies saved one and two at a time by bulldozing the grocer and the vegetable man and the butcher until one's cheeks burned with the silent imputation of parsimony that such close dealing implied. Three times Della counted it. One dollar and eighty-seven cents. And the next day would be Christmas.

There was clearly nothing to do but flop down on the shabby little couch and howl. So Della did it. Which instigates the moral reflection that life is made up of sobs, sniffles, and smiles, with sniffles predominating.

While the mistress of the home is gradually subsiding from the first stage to the second, take a look at the home. A furnished flat at $8 per week. It did not exactly beggar description, but it certainly had that word on the lookout for the mendicancy squad.

In the vestibule below was a letter-box into which no letter would go, and an electric button from which no mortal finger could coax a ring. Also appertaining thereunto was a card bearing the name "Mr. James Dillingham Young."

The "Dillingham" had been flung to the breeze during a former period of prosperity when its possessor was being paid $30 per week. Now, when the income was shrunk to $20, the letters of "Dillingham" looked blurred, as though they were thinking seriously of contracting to a modest and unassuming D. But whenever Mr. James Dillingham Young came home and reached his flat above he was called "Jim" and greatly hugged by Mrs. James Dillingham Young, already introduced to you as Della. Which is all very good.

Della finished her cry and attended to her cheeks with the powder rag. She stood by the window and looked out dully at a gray cat walking a gray fence in a gray backyard. Tomorrow would be Christmas Day, and she had only $1.87 with which to buy Jim a present. She had been saving every penny she could for months, with this result. Twenty dollars a week doesn't go far. Expenses had been greater than she had calculated. They always are. Only $1.87 to buy a present for Jim. Her Jim. Many a happy hour she had spent planning for something nice for him. Something fine and rare and sterling—something just a little bit near to being worthy of the honor of being owned by Jim.

There was a pier-glass between the windows of the room. Perhaps you have seen a pier-glass in an $8 flat. A very thin and very agile person may, by observing his reflection in a rapid sequence of longitudinal strips, obtain a fairly accurate conception of his looks. Della, being slender, had mastered the art.

Suddenly she whirled from the window and stood before the glass. Her eyes were shining brilliantly, but her face had lost its color within twenty seconds. Rapidly she pulled down her hair and let it fall to its full length.

Now, there were two possessions of the James Dillingham Youngs in which they both took a mighty pride. One was Jim's gold watch that had been his father's and his grandfather's. The other was Della's hair. Had the Queen of Sheba lived in the flat across the airshaft, Della would have let her hair hang out the window some day to dry just to depreciate Her Majesty's jewels and gifts. Had King Solomon been the janitor, with all his treasures piled up in the basement, Jim would have pulled out his watch every time he passed, just to see him pluck at his beard from envy.

So now Della's beautiful hair fell about her rippling and shining like a cascade of brown waters. It reached below her knee and made itself almost a garment for her. And then she did it up again nervously and quickly. Once she faltered for a minute and stood still while a tear or two splashed on the worn red carpet.

On went her old brown jacket; on went her old brown hat. With a whirl of skirts and with the brilliant sparkle still in her eyes, she fluttered out the door and down the stairs to the street.

Where she stopped the sign read: "Mme. Sofronie. Hair Goods of All Kinds." One flight up Della ran, and collected herself, panting. Madame, large, too white, chilly, hardly looked the "Sofronie."

"Will you buy my hair?" asked Della.

"I buy hair," said Madame. "Take yer hat off and let's have a sight at the looks of it."

Down rippled the brown cascade.

"Twenty dollars," said Madame, lifting the mass with a practised hand.

"Give it to me quick," said Della.

Oh, and the next two hours tripped by on rosy wings. Forget the hashed metaphor. She was ransacking the stores for Jim's present.

She found it at last. It surely had been made for Jim and no one else. There was no other like it in any of the stores, and she had turned all of them inside out. It was a platinum fob chain simple and chaste in design, properly proclaiming its value by substance alone and not by meretricious ornamentation—as all good things should do. It was even worthy of The Watch. As soon as she saw it she knew that it must be Jim's. It was like him. Quietness and value—the description applied to both. Twenty-one dollars they took from her for it, and she hurried home with the 87 cents. With that chain on his watch Jim might be properly anxious about the time in any company. Grand as the watch was, he sometimes looked at it on the sly on account of the old leather strap that he used in place of a chain.

When Della reached home her intoxication gave way a little to prudence and reason. She got out her curling irons and lighted the gas and went to work repairing the ravages made by generosity added to love. Which is always a tremendous task, dear friends—a mammoth task.

Within forty minutes her head was covered with tiny,

close-lying curls that made her look wonderfully like a truant schoolboy. She looked at her reflection in the mirror long, carefully, and critically.

"If Jim doesn't kill me," she said to herself, "before he takes a second look at me, he'll say I look like a Coney Island chorus girl. But what could I do—oh! what could I do with a dollar and eighty-seven cents?"

At 7 o'clock the coffee was made and the frying-pan was on the back of the stove hot and ready to cook the chops.

Jim was never late. Della doubled the fob chain in her hand and sat on the corner of the table near the door that he always entered. Then she heard his step on the stair away down on the first flight, and she turned white for just a moment. She had a habit of saying little silent prayers about the simplest everyday things, and now she whispered: "Please God, make him think I am still pretty."

The door opened and Jim stepped in and closed it. He looked thin and very serious. Poor fellow, he was only twenty-two—and to be burdened with a family! He needed a new overcoat and he was without gloves.

Jim stopped inside the door, as immovable as a setter at the scent of quail. His eyes were fixed upon Della, and there was an expression in them that she could not read, and it terrified her. It was not anger, nor surprise, nor disapproval, nor horror, nor any of the sentiments that she had been prepared for. He simply stared at her fixedly with that peculiar expression on his face.

Della wriggled off the table and went for him.

"Jim, darling," she cried, "don't look at me that way. I had my hair cut off and sold it because I couldn't have lived through Christmas without giving you a present. It'll grow out again—you won't mind, will you? I just had to do it. My hair grows awfully fast. Say 'Merry Christmas!' Jim, and let's be happy. You don't know what a nice—what a beautiful, nice gift I've got for you."

"You've cut off your hair?" asked Jim, laboriously, as if he had not arrived at that patent fact yet even after the hardest mental labor.

"Cut it off and sold it," said Della. "Don't you like me just as well, anyhow? I'm me without my hair, ain't I?"

Jim looked about the room curiously.

"You say your hair is gone?" he said, with an air almost of idiocy.

"You needn't look for it," said Della. "It's sold, I tell you—sold and gone, too. It's Christmas Eve, boy. Be good to me, for it went for you. Maybe the hairs of my head were numbered," she went on with a sudden serious sweetness, "but nobody could ever count my love for you. Shall I put the chops on, Jim?"

Out of his trance Jim seemed quickly to wake. He enfolded his Della. For ten seconds let us regard with discreet scrutiny some inconsequential object in the other direction. Eight dollars a week or a million a year—what is the difference? A mathematician or a wit would give you the wrong answer. The magi brought valuable gifts, but that was not among them. This dark assertion will be illuminated later on.

Jim drew a package from his overcoat pocket and threw it upon the table.

"Don't make any mistake, Dell," he said, "about me. I don't think there's anything in the way of a haircut or a shave or a shampoo that could make me like my girl any less. But if you'll unwrap that package you may see why you had me going a while at first."

White fingers and nimble tore at the string and paper. And then an ecstatic scream of joy; and then, alas! a quick feminine change to hysterical tears and wails, necessitating the immediate employment of all the comforting powers of the lord of the flat.

For there lay The Combs—the set of combs, side and back, that Della had worshipped for long in a Broadway window. Beautiful combs, pure tortoise shell, with jewelled rims—just the shade to wear in the beautiful vanished hair. They were expensive combs, she knew, and her heart had simply craved and yearned over them without the least hope of possession. And now, they were hers, but the tresses that should have adorned the coveted adornments were gone.

But she hugged them to her bosom, and at length she was able to look up with dim eyes and a smile and say: "My hair grows so fast, Jim!"

And then Della leaped up like a little singed cat and cried, "Oh, oh!"

Jim had not yet seen his beautiful present. She held it out

to him eagerly upon her open palm. The dull precious metal seemed to flash with a reflection of her bright and ardent spirit.

"Isn't it a dandy, Jim? I hunted all over town to find it. You'll have to look at the time a hundred times a day now. Give me your watch. I want to see how it looks on it."

Instead of obeying, Jim tumbled down on the couch and put his hands under the back of his head and smiled.

"Dell," said he, "let's put our Christmas presents away and keep 'em a while. They're too nice to use just at present. I sold the watch to get the money to buy your combs. And now suppose you put the chops on."

The magi, as you know, were wise men—wonderfully wise men—who brought gifts to the Babe in the manger. They invented the art of giving Christmas presents. Being wise, their gifts were no doubt wise ones, possibly bearing the privilege of exchange in case of duplication. And here I have lamely related to you the uneventful chronicle of two foolish children in a flat who most unwisely sacrificed for each other the greatest treasures of their house. But in a last word to the wise of these days let it be said that of all who give gifts these two were the wisest. Of all who give and receive gifts, such as they are wisest. Everywhere they are wisest. They are the magi.

The Green Door

Suppose you should be walking down Broadway after dinner, with ten minutes allotted to the consummation of your cigar while you are choosing between a diverting tragedy and something serious in the way of vaudeville. Suddenly a hand is laid upon your arm. You turn to look into the thrilling eyes of a beautiful woman, wonderful in diamonds and Russian sables. She thrusts hurriedly into your hand an extremely hot buttered roll, flashes out a tiny pair of scissors, snips off the second button of your overcoat, meaningly ejaculates the one word, "parallelogram!" and swiftly flies down a cross street, looking back fearfully over her shoulder.

That would be pure adventure. Would you accept it? Not you. You would flush with embarrassment; you would sheepishly drop the roll and continue down Broadway, fumbling feebly for the missing button. This you would do unless you are one of the blessed few in whom the pure spirit of adventure is not dead.

True adventurers have never been plentiful. They who are set down in print as such have been mostly business men with newly invented methods. They have been out after the things they wanted—golden fleeces, holy grails, lady loves, treasure, crowns and fame. The true adventurer goes forth aimless and uncalculating to meet and greet unknown fate. A fine example was the Prodigal Son—when he started back home.

Half-adventurers—brave and splendid figures—have been numerous. From the Crusades to the Palisades they have enriched the arts of history and fiction and the trade of historical fiction. But each of them had a prize to win, a goal to kick, an axe to grind, a race to run, a new thrust in tierce to deliver, a name to carve, a crow to pick—so they were not followers of true adventure.

In the big city the twin spirits Romance and Adventure are always abroad seeking worthy wooers. As we roam the streets they slyly peep at us and challenge us in twenty different guises. Without knowing why, we look up suddenly to see in a window a face that seems to belong to our gallery of intimate portraits; in a sleeping thoroughfare we hear a cry of agony and fear coming from an empty and shuttered house; instead of at our familiar curb a cab-driver deposits us before a strange door, which one, with a smile, opens for us and bids us enter; a slip of paper, written upon, flutters down to our feet from the high lattices of Chance; we exchange glances of instantaneous hate, affection, and fear with hurrying strangers in the passing crowds; a sudden souse of rain—and our umbrella may be sheltering the daughter of the Full Moon and first cousin of the Sidereal System; at every corner handkerchiefs drop, fingers beckon, eyes besiege, and the lost, lonely, the rapturous, the mysterious, the perilous changing clues of adventure are slipped into our fingers. But few of us are willing to hold and follow them. We are grown stiff with the ramrod of convention down our backs. We pass on; and some day we come, at the end of a very dull life, to reflect that our romance has been a pallid thing of a marriage or two, a satin rosette kept in a safe-deposit drawer, and a lifelong feud with a steam radiator.

Rudolf Steiner was a true adventurer. Few were the evenings on which he did not go forth from his hall bedchamber in search of the unexpected and the egregious. The most interesting thing in life seemed to him to be what might lie just around the next corner. Sometimes his willingness to tempt fate led him into strange paths. Twice he had spent the night in a station-house; again and again he had found himself the dupe of ingenious and mercenary tricksters; his watch and money had been the price of one flattering allurement. But with undiminished ardor he picked up every glove cast before him into the merry lists of adventure.

One evening Rudolf was strolling along a cross-town street in the older central part of the city. Two streams of people filled the sidewalks—the home-hurrying, and that restless contingent that abandons home for the specious welcome of the thousand-candle-power *table d'hôte*.

The young adventurer was of pleasing presence, and moved serenely and watchfully. By daylight he was a salesman in a piano store. He wore his tie drawn through a topaz ring instead of fastened with a stick pin; and once he had written to the editor of a magazine that "Junie's Love Test," by Miss Libbey, had been the book that had most influenced his life.

During his walk a violent chattering of teeth in a glass case on the sidewalk seemed at first to draw his attention (with a qualm) to a restaurant before which it was set; but a second glance revealed the electric letters of a dentist's sign high above the next door. A giant negro, fantastically dressed in a red embroidered coat, yellow trousers and a military cap, discreetly distributed cards to those of the passing crowd who consented to take them.

This mode of dentistic advertising was a common sight to

Rudolf. Usually he passed the dispenser of the dentist's cards without reducing his store; but to-night the African slipped one into his hand so deftly that he retained it there smiling a little at the successful feat.

When he had travelled a few yards further he glanced at the card indifferently. Surprised, he turned it over and looked again with interest. One side of the card was blank; on the other was written in ink three words, "The Green Door." And then Rudolf saw, three steps in front of him, a man throw down the card the negro had given him as he passed. Rudolf picked it up. It was printed with the dentist's name and address and the usual schedule of "plate work" and "bridge work" and "crowns," and specious promises of "painless" operations.

The adventurous piano salesman halted at the corner and considered. Then he crossed the street, walked down a block, recrossed and joined the upward current of people again. Without seeming to notice the negro as he passed the second time, he carelessly took the card that was handed him. Ten steps away he inspected it. In the same handwriting that appeared on the first card "The Green Door" was inscribed upon it. Three or four cards were tossed to the pavement by pedestrians both following and leading him. These fell blank side up. Rudolf turned them over. Everyone bore the printed legend of the dental "parlors."

Rarely did the arch sprite Adventure need to beckon twice to Rudolf Steiner, his true follower. But twice it had been done, and the quest was on.

Rudolf walked slowly back to where the giant negro stood by the case of rattling teeth. This time as he passed he received no card. In spite of his gaudy and ridiculous garb, the Ethiopian displayed a natural barbaric dignity as he stood, offering the cards suavely to some, allowing others to pass unmolested. Every half minute he chanted a harsh, unintelligible phrase akin to the jabber of car conductors and grand opera. And not only did he withhold a card this time but it seemed to Rudolf that he received from the shining and massive black countenance a look of cold, almost contemptuous disdain.

The look stung the adventurer. He read in it a silent accusation that he had been found wanting. Whatever the mysterious written words on the cards might mean, the black had selected him twice from the throng for their recipient; and now seemed to have condemned him as deficient in the wit and spirit to engage the enigma.

Standing aside from the rush, the young man made a rapid estimate of the building in which he conceived that his adventure must lie. Five stories high it rose. A small restaurant occupied the basement.

The first floor, now closed, seemed to house millinery or furs. The second floor, by the winking electric letters, was the dentist's. Above this a polyglot babel of signs struggled to indicate the abodes of palmists, dressmakers, musicians, and doctors. Still higher up draped curtains and milk bottles white on the window sills proclaimed the regions of domesticity.

After concluding his survey Rudolf walked briskly up the high flight of stone steps into the house. Up two flights of the carpeted stairway he continued; and at its top paused. The hallway there was dimly lighted by two pale jets of gas—one far to his right, the other nearer, to his left. He looked toward the nearer light and saw, within its wan halo, a green door. For one moment he hesitated; then he seemed to see the contumelious sneer of the African juggler of cards; and then he walked straight to the green door and knocked against it.

Moments like those that passed before his knock was answered measure the quick breath of true adventure. What might not be behind those green panels! Gamesters at play; cunning rogues baiting their traps with subtle skill; beauty in love with courage, and thus planning to be sought by it; danger, death, love, disappointment, ridicule—any of these might respond to that temerarious rap.

A faint rustle was heard inside, and the door slowly opened. A girl not yet twenty stood there white-faced and tottering. She loosed the knob and swayed weakly, groping with one hand. Rudolf caught her and laid her on a faded couch that stood against the wall. He closed the door and took a swift glance around the room by the light of a flickering gas jet. Neat, but extreme poverty was the story that he read.

The girl lay still, as if in a faint. Rudolf looked around the room excitedly for a barrel. People must be rolled upon a barrel who—no, no; that was for drowned persons. He began to fan her with his hat. That was successful, for he struck her nose with the brim of his derby and she opened her eyes. And then the young man saw that hers, indeed, was the one missing face from his heart's gallery of intimate portraits. The frank, gray eyes, the little nose, turning pertly outward; the chestnut hair, curling like the tendrils of a pea vine, seemed the right end and reward of all his wonderful adventures. But the face was woefully thin and pale.

The girl looked at him calmly, and then smiled.

"Fainted, didn't I?" she asked, weakly. "Well, who wouldn't? You try going without anything to eat for three days and see!"

"Himmel!" exclaimed Rudolf, jumping up. "Wait till I come back."

He dashed out the green door and down the stairs. In twenty minutes he was back again kicking at the door with his toe for her to open it. With both arms he hugged an array of wares from the grocery and the restaurant. On the table he laid them—bread and butter, cold meats, cakes, pies, pickles, oysters, a roasted chicken, a bottle of milk and one of red-hot tea.

"This is ridiculous," said Rudolf, blusteringly, "to go without eating. You must quit making election bets of this kind. Supper is ready." He helped her to a chair at the table and asked: "Is there a cup for the tea?" "On the shelf by the window," she answered. When he turned again with the cup he saw her, with eyes shining rapturously, beginning upon a huge dill pickle that she had rooted out from the paper bags with a woman's unerring instinct. He took it from her, laughingly, and poured the cup full of milk. "Drink that first," he ordered, "and then you shall have some tea, and then a chicken wing. If you are very good you shall have a pickle to-morrow. And now, if you'll allow me to be your guest we'll have supper."

He drew up the other chair. The tea brightened the girl's eyes and brought back some of her color. She began to eat with a sort of dainty ferocity like some starved wild animal. She seemed to regard the young man's presence and the aid he had rendered her as a natural thing—not as though she undervalued the conventions; but as one whose great stress gave her the right to put aside the artificial for the human. But gradually, with the return of strength and comfort, came also a sense of the little conventions that belong; and she began to tell him her little story. It was one of a thousand such as the city yawns at every day—the shop girl's story of insufficient wages, further reduced by "fines" that go to swell the store's profits; of time lost through illness; and then of lost positions, lost hope, and—the knock of the adventurer upon the green door.

But to Rudolf the history sounded as big as the Iliad or the crisis in "Junie's Love Test."

"To think of you going through all that," he exclaimed.

"It was something fierce," said the girl, solemnly.

"And you have no relatives or friends in the city?"

"None whatever."

"I am all alone in the world, too," said Rudolf, after a pause.

"I am glad of that," said the girl, promptly; and somehow it pleased the young man to hear that she approved of his bereft condition.

Very suddenly her eyelids dropped and she sighed deeply.

"I'm awfully sleepy," she said, "and I feel so good."

Rudolf rose and took his hat.

"Then I'll say good-night. A long night's sleep will be fine for you."

He held out his hand, and she took it and said "good-night." But her eyes asked a question so eloquently, so frankly and pathetically that he answered it with words.

"Oh, I'm coming back to-morrow to see how you are getting along. You can't get rid of me so easily."

Then, at the door, as though the way of his coming had been so much less important than the fact that he had come, she asked: "How did you come to knock at my door?"

He looked at her for a moment, remembering the cards, and felt a sudden jealous pain. What if they had fallen into other hands as adventurous as his? Quickly he decided that she must never know the truth. He would never let her know that he was aware of the strange expedient to which she had been driven by her great distress.

"One of our piano tuners lives in this house," he said. "I knocked at your door by mistake."

The last thing he saw in the room before the green door closed was her smile.

At the head of the stairway he paused and looked curiously about him. And then he went along the hallway to its other end; and, coming back, ascended to the floor above and continued his puzzled explorations. Every door that he found in the house was painted green.

Wondering, he descended to the sidewalk. The fantastic African was still there. Rudolf confronted him with his two cards in his hand.

"Will you tell me why you gave me these cards and what they mean?" he asked.

In a broad, good-natured grin the negro exhibited a splendid advertisement of his master's profession.

"Dar it is, boss," he said, pointing down the street. "But I 'spect you is a little late for de fust act."

Looking the way he pointed Rudolf saw above the entrance to a theatre the blazing electric sign of its new play, "The Green Door."

"I'm informed dat it's a fust-rate show, sah," said the negro. "De agent what represents it pussented me with a dollar, sah, to distribute a few of his cards along with de doctah's. May I offer you one of de doctah's cards, suh?"

At the corner of the block in which he lived Rudolf stopped for a glass of beer and a cigar. When he had come out with his lighted weed he buttoned his coat, pushed back his hat and said, stoutly, to the lamp post on the corner:

"All the same, I believe it was the hand of Fate that doped out the way for me to find her."

Which conclusion, under the circumstances, certainly admits Rudolf Steiner to the ranks of the true followers of Romance and Adventure.

Transients in Arcadia

There is a hotel on Broadway that has escaped discovery by the summer-resort promoters. It is deep and wide and cool. Its rooms are finished in dark oak of a low temperature. Home-made breezes and deep-green shrubbery give it the delights without the inconveniences of the Adirondacks. One can mount its broad staircases or glide dreamily upward in its aërial elevators, attended by guides in brass buttons, with a serene joy that Alpine climbers have never attained. There is a chef in its kitchen who will prepare for you brook trout better than the White Mountains ever served, sea food that would turn Old Point Comfort—"by Gad, sah!"—green with envy, and Maine venison that would melt the official heart of the game warden.

A few have found out this oasis in the July desert of Manhattan. During that month you will see the hotel's reduced array of guests scattered luxuriously about in the cool twilight of its lofty dining-room, gazing at one another across the snowy waste of unoccupied tables, silently congratulatory.

Superfluous, watchful, pneumatically moving waiters hover near, supplying every want before it is expressed. The temperature is perpetual April. The ceiling is painted in water colors to counterfeit a summer sky across which delicate clouds drift and do not vanish as those of nature do to our regret.

The pleasing, distant roar of Broadway is transformed in the imagination of the happy guests to the noise of a waterfall filling the woods with its restful sound. At every strange footstep the guests turn an anxious ear, fearful lest their retreat be discovered and invaded by the restless pleasure-seekers who are forever hounding Nature to her deepest lairs.

Thus in the depopulated caravansary the little band of connoisseurs jealously hide themselves during the heated season, enjoying to the uttermost the delights of mountain and sea-shore that art and skill have gathered and served to them.

In this July came to the hotel one whose card that she sent to the clerk for her name to be registered read "Mme. Héloise D'Arcy Beaumont."

Madame Beaumont was a guest such as the Hotel Lotus loved. She possessed the fine air of the élite, tempered and sweetened by a cordial graciousness that made the hotel employés her slaves. Bell-boys fought for the honor of answering her ring; the clerks, but for the question of ownership, would have deeded to her the hotel and its contents; the other guests regarded her as the final touch of feminine exclusiveness and beauty that rendered the entourage perfect.

This super-excellent guest rarely left the hotel. Her habits were consonant with the customs of the discriminating patrons of the Hotel Lotus. To enjoy that delectable hostelry one must forego the city as though it were leagues away. By night a brief excursion to the nearby roofs is in order; but during the torrid day one remains in the umbrageous fastnesses of the Lotus as a trout hangs poised in the pellucid sanctuaries of his favorite pool.

Though alone in the Hotel Lotus, Madame Beaumont preserved the state of a queen whose loneliness was of position only. She breakfasted at ten, a cool, sweet, leisurely, delicate being who glowed softly in the dimness like a jasmine flower in the dusk.

But at dinner was Madame's glory at its height. She wore a gown as beautiful and immaterial as the mist from an unseen cataract in a mountain gorge. The nomenclature of this gown is beyond the guess of the scribe. Always pale-red roses reposed against its lace-garnished front. It was a gown that the head-waiter viewed with respect and met at the door. You thought of Paris when you saw it, and maybe of mysterious countesses, and certainly of Versailles and rapiers and Mrs. Fiske and rouge-et-noir. There was an untraceable rumor in the Hotel Lotus that Madame was a cosmopolite, and that she was pulling with her slender white hands certain strings between the nations in the favor of Russia. Being a citizeness of the world's smoothest roads it was small wonder that she was quick to recognize in the refined purlieus of the Hotel Lotus the most desirable spot in America for a restful sojourn during the heat of midsummer.

On the third day of Madame Beaumont's residence in the hotel a young man entered and registered himself as a guest. His clothing—to speak of his points in approved order—was quietly in the mode; his features good and regular; his expression that of a poised and sophisticated man of the world. He informed the clerk that he would remain three or four days, inquired concerning the sailing of European steamships, and sank into the blissful inanition of the nonpareil hotel with the contented air of a traveller in his favorite inn.

The young man—not to question the veracity of the register—was Harold Farrington. He drifted into the exclusive and calm current of life in the Lotus so tactfully and silently that not a ripple alarmed his fellow-seekers after rest. He ate in the Lotus and of its patronym, and was lulled into blissful peace with the other fortunate mariners. In one day he acquired his table and his waiter and the fear lest the panting chasers after repose that kept Broadway warm should pounce upon and destroy this contiguous but covert haven.

After dinner on the next day after the arrival of Harold Farrington Madame Beaumont dropped her handkerchief in passing out. Mr. Farrington recovered and returned it without the effusiveness of a seeker after acquaintance.

Perhaps there was a mystic freemasonry between the discriminating guests of the Lotus. Perhaps they were drawn one to another by the fact of their common good fortune in discovering the acme of summer resorts in a Broadway hotel. Words delicate in courtesy and tentative in departure from formality passed between the two. And, as if in the expedient atmosphere of a real summer resort, an acquaintance grew, flowered and fructified on the spot as does the mystic plant of the conjuror. For a few moments they stood on a balcony upon which the corridor ended, and tossed the feathery ball of conversation.

"One tires of the old resorts," said Madame Beaumont, with a faint but sweet smile. "What is the use to fly to the mountains or the seashore to escape noise and dust when the very people that make both follow us there?"

"Even on the ocean," remarked Farrington sadly, "the

Philistines be upon you. The most exclusive steamers are getting to be scarcely more than ferry boats. Heaven help us when the summer resorter discovers that the Lotus is further away from Broadway than Thousand Islands or Mackinac.''

"I hope our secret will be safe for a week, anyhow," said Madame, with a sigh and a smile. "I do not know where I would go if they should descend upon the dear Lotus. I know of but one place so delightful in summer, and that is the castle of Count Polinski, in the Ural Mountains.''

"I hear that Baden-Baden and Cannes are almost deserted this season," said Farrington. "Year by year the old resorts fall in disrepute. Perhaps many others, like ourselves, are seeking out the quiet nooks that are overlooked by the majority.''

"I promise myself three days more of this delicious rest," said Madame Beaumont. "On Monday the *Cedric* sails.''

Harold Farrington's eyes proclaimed his regret. "I too must leave on Monday," he said, "but I do not go abroad.''

Madame Beaumont shrugged one round shoulder in a foreign gesture.

"One cannot hide here forever, charming through it may be. The château has been in preparation for me longer than a month. Those house parties that one must give—what a nuisance! But I shall never forget my week in the Hotel Lotus.''

"Nor shall I," said Farrington in a low voice, "and I shall never *forgive* the *Cedric*.''

On Sunday evening, three days afterward, the two sat at a little table on the same balcony. A discreet waiter brought ices and small glasses of claret cup.

Madame Beaumont wore the same beautiful evening gown that she had worn each day at dinner. She seemed thoughtful. Near her hand on the table lay a small chatelaine purse. After she had eaten her ice she opened the purse and took out a one-dollar bill.

"Mr. Farrington," she said, with the smile that had won the Hotel Lotus, "I want to tell you something. I'm going to leave before breakfast in the morning, because I've got to go back to my work. I'm behind the hosiery counter at Casey's Mammoth Store, and my vacation's up at eight o'clock tomorrow. That paper dollar is the last cent I'll see till I draw my eight dollars salary next Saturday night. You're a real gentleman, and you've been good to me, and I wanted to tell you before I went.

"I've been saving up out of my wages for a year just for this vacation. I wanted to spend one week like a lady if I never do another one. I wanted to get up when I please instead of having to crawl out at seven every morning; and I wanted to live on the best and be waited on and ring bells for things just like rich folks do. Now I've done it, and I've had the happiest time I ever expect to have in my life. I'm going back to my work and my little hall bedroom satisfied for another year. I wanted to tell you about it, Mr. Farrington, because I—I thought you kind of liked me, and I—I liked you. But, oh, I couldn't help deceiving you up till now, for it was all just like a fairy tale to me. So I talked about Europe and the things I've read about in other countries, and made you think I was a great lady.

"This dress I've got on—it's the only one I have that's fit to wear—I bought from O'Dowd & Levinsky on the instalment plan.

"Seventy-five dollars is the price, and it was made to measure. I paid $10 down, and they're to collect $1 a week till it's paid for. That'll be about all I have to say, Mr. Farrington, except that my name is Mamie Siviter instead of Madame Beaumont, and I thank you for your attentions. This dollar will pay the instalment due on the dress to-morrow. I guess I'll go up to my room now."

Harold Farrington listened to the recital of the Lotus's loveliest guest with an impassive countenance. When she had concluded he drew a small book like a checkbook from his coat pocket. He wrote upon a blank form in this with a stub of pencil, tore out the leaf, tossed it over to his companion and took up the paper dollar.

"I've got to go to work, too, in the morning," he said, "and I might as well begin now. There's a receipt for the dollar instalment. I've been a collector for O'Dowd & Levinsky for three years. Funny, ain't it, that you and me both had the same idea about spending our vacation? I've always wanted to put up at a swell hotel, and I saved up out of my twenty per, and did it. Say, Mame, how about a trip to Coney Saturday night on the boat—what?"

The face of the pseudo Madame Héloise D'Arcy Beaumont beamed.

"Oh, you bet I'll go, Mr. Farrington. The store closes at twelve on Saturdays. I guess Coney'll be all right even if we did spend a week with the swells."

Below the balcony the sweltering city growled and buzzed in the July night. Inside the Hotel Lotus the tempered, cool shadows reigned, and the solicitious waiter single-footed near the low windows, ready at a nod to serve Madame and her escort.

At the door of the elevator Farrington took his leave, and Madame Beaumont made her last ascent. But before they reached the noiseless cage he said: "Just forget that 'Harold Farrington,' will you?—McManus is the name—James McManus. Some call me Jimmy."

"Good-night, Jimmy," said Madame.

Brickdust Row

Blinker was displeased. A man of less culture and poise and wealth would have sworn. But Blinker always remembered that he was a gentleman—a thing that no gentleman should do. So he merely looked bored and sardonic while he rode in a hansom to the centre of disturbance, which was the Broadway office of Lawyer Oldport, who was agent for the Blinker estate.

"I don't see," said Blinker, "why I should be always signing confounded papers. I am packed, and was to have left for the North Woods this morning. Now I must wait until to-morrow morning. I hate night trains. My best razors are, of course, at the bottom of some unidentifiable trunk. It is a plot to drive me to bay rum and a monologuing, thumb-handed barber. Give me a pen that doesn't scratch. I hate pens that scratch."

"Sit down," said double-chinned, gray Lawyer Oldport. "The worst has not been told you. Oh, the hardships of the rich! The papers are not yet ready to sign. They will be laid before you to-morrow at eleven. You will miss another day. Twice shall the barber tweak the helpless nose of a Blinker. Be thankful that your sorrows do not embrace a haircut."

"If," said Blinker, rising, "the act did not involve more signing of papers I would take my business out of your hands at once. Give me a cigar, please."

"If," said Lawyer Oldport, "I had cared to see an old friend's son gulped down at one mouthful by sharks I would have ordered you to take it away long ago. Now, let's quit fooling, Alexander. Besides the grinding task of signing your name some thirty times to-morrow, I must impose upon you the consideration of a matter of business—of business, and I may say humanity or right. I spoke to you about this five years ago, but you would not listen—you were in a hurry for a coaching trip, I think. The subject has come up again. The property——"

"Oh, property!" interrupted Blinker. "Dear Mr. Oldport, I think you mentioned to-morrow. Let's have it all at one dose to-morrow—signatures and property and snappy rubber bands and that smelly sealing-wax and all. Have luncheon with me? Well, I'll try to remember to drop in at eleven to-morrow. Morning."

The Blinker wealth was in lands, tenements, and hereditaments, as the legal phrase goes. Lawyer Oldport had once taken Alexander in his little pulmonary gasoline runabout to see the many buildings and rows of buildings that he owned in the city. For Alexander was sole heir. They had amused Blinker very much. The houses looked so incapable of producing the big sums of money that Lawyer Oldport kept piling up in banks for him to spend.

In the evening Blinker went to one of his clubs, intending to dine. Nobody was there except some old fogies playing whist who spoke to him with grave politeness and glared at him with savage contempt. Everybody was out of town. But here he was kept in like a schoolboy to write his name over and over on pieces of paper. His wounds were deep.

Blinker turned his back on the fogies, and said to the club steward who had come forward with some nonsense about cold fresh salmon roe:

"Symons, I'm going to Coney Island." He said it as one might say: "All's off, I'm going to jump into the river."

The joke pleased Symons. He laughed with a sixteenth of a note of the audibility permitted by the laws governing employees.

"Certainly, sir," he tittered. "Of course, sir, I think I can see you at Coney, Mr. Blinker."

Blinker got a paper and looked up the movements of Sunday steamboats. Then he found a cab at the first corner and drove to a North River pier. He stood in line, as democratic as you or I, and bought a ticket, and was trampled upon and shoved forward until, at last, he found himself on the upper deck of the boat staring brazenly at a girl who sat alone upon a camp stool. But Blinker did not intend to be brazen; the girl was so wonderfully good looking that he forgot for one minute that he was the prince incog, and behaved just as he did in society.

She was looking at him, too, and not severely. A puff of wind threatened Blinker's straw hat. He caught it warily and settled it again. The movement gave the effect of a bow. The girl nodded and smiled, and in another instant he was seated at her side. She was dressed all in white, she was paler than Blinker imagined milkmaids and girls of humble stations to be, but she was as tidy as a cherry blossom, and her steady, supremely frank gray eyes looked out from the intrepid depths of an unshadowed and untroubled soul.

"How dare you raise your hat to me?" she asked, with a smile-redeemed severity.

"I didn't," Blinker said, but he quickly covered the mistake by extending it to "I didn't know how to keep from it after I saw you."

"I do not allow gentlemen to sit by me to whom I have not been introduced," she said with a sudden haughtiness that deceived him. He rose reluctantly, but her clear, teasing laugh brought him down to his chair again.

"I guess you weren't going far," she declared, with beauty's magnificent self-confidence.

"Are you going to Coney Island?" asked Blinker.

"Me?" She turned upon him wide-open eyes full of banter-ing surprise. "Why, what a question! Can't you see that I'm riding a bicycle in the park?" Her drollery took the form of impertinence.

"And I'm laying bricks on a tall factory chimney," said Blinker. "Mayn't we see Coney together? I'm all alone and I've never been there before."

"It depends," said the girl, "on how nicely you behave. I'll consider your application until we get there."

Blinker took pains to provide against the rejection of his application. He strove to please. To adopt the metaphor of his nonsensical phrase, he laid brick upon brick on the tall chim-ney of his devoirs until, at length, the structure was stable and complete. The manners of the best society come around finally to simplicity; and as the girl's way was that naturally, they were on a mutual plane of communication from the beginning.

He learned that she was twenty, and her name was Florence; that she trimmed hats in a millinery shop; that she lived in a furnished room with her best chum Ella, who was cashier in a shoe store; and that a glass of milk from the bottle on the window-sill and an egg that boils itself while you twist up your hair makes a breakfast good enough for any one. Flor-ence laughed when she heard "Blinker."

"Well," she said. "It certainly shows that you have imagination. It gives the 'Smiths' a chance for a little rest, anyhow."

They landed at Coney, and were dashed on the crest of a great human wave of mad pleasure-seekers into the walks and avenues of Fairyland gone into vaudeville.

With a curious eye, a critical mind, and a fairly withheld judgment Blinker considered the temples, pagodas and kiosks of popularized delights. Hoi polloi trampled, hustled, and crowded him. Basket parties bumped him; sticky children tumbled, howling, under his feet, candying his clothes. Inso-lent youths strolling among the booths with hard-won canes under one arm and easily won girls on the other, blew defiant smoke from cheap cigars into his face. The publicity gentle-men with megaphones, each before his own stupendous attraction, roared like Niagara in his ears. Music of all kinds that could be tortured from brass, reed, hide, or string, fought in the air to gain space for its vibrations against its competitors. But what held Blinker in awful fascination was the mob, the multitude, the proletariat shrieking, struggling, hurrying, panting, hurling itself in incontinent frenzy, with unabashed abandon, into the ridiculous sham palaces of trumpery and tinsel pleasures. The vulgarity of it, its brutal overriding of all the tenets of repression and taste that were held by his caste, repelled him strongly.

In the midst of his disgust he turned and looked down at Florence by his side. She was ready with her quick smile and upturned, happy eyes, as bright and clear as the water in trout pools. The eyes were saying that they had the right to be shining and happy, for was their owner not with her (for the present) Man, her Gentleman Friend and holder of the keys to the enchanted city of fun.

Blinker did not read her look accurately, but by some miracle he suddenly saw Coney aright.

He no longer saw a mass of vulgarians seeking gross joys. He now looked clearly upon a hundred thousand true idealists. Their offenses were wiped out. Counterfeit and false though the garish joys of these spangled temples were, he perceived that deep under the gilt surface they offered saving and apposite balm and satisfaction to the restless human heart. Here, at least, was the husk of Romance, the empty but shining casque of Chivalry, the breath-catching though safe-guarded dip and flight of Adventure, the magic carpet that transports you to the realms of fairyland, though its journey be through but a few poor yards of space. He no longer saw a rabble, but his brothers seeking the ideal. There was no magic of poesy here or of art; but the glamour of their imagination turned yellow calico into cloth of gold and the megaphone into the silver trumpets of joy's heralds.

Almost humbled, Blinker rolled up the shirt sleeves of his mind and joined the idealists.

"You are the lady doctor," he said to Florence. "How shall we go about doing this jolly conglomeration of fairy tales, incorporated?"

"We will begin there," said the Princess, pointing to a fun pagoda on the edge of the sea, "and we will take them all in, one by one."

They caught the eight o'clock returning boat and sat, filled with pleasant fatigue, against the rail in the bow, listening to the Italians' fiddle and harp. Blinker had thrown off all care. The North Woods seemed to him an uninhabitable wilderness. What a fuss he had made over signing his name—pooh! he could sign it a hundred times. And her name was as pretty as she was—"Florence," he said it to himself a great many times.

As the boat was nearing its pier in the North River a two-funnelled, drab, foreign-looking sea-going steamer was dropping down toward the bay. The boat turned its nose in towards its slip. The steamer veered as if to seek mid-stream, and then yawned, seemed to increase its speed and struck the Coney boat on the side near the stern, cutting into it with a terrifying shock and crash.

While the six hundred passengers on the boat were mostly tumbling about the decks in a shrieking panic the captain was shouting at the steamer that it should not back off and leave the rent exposed for the water to enter. But the steamer tore its way out like a savage sawfish and cleaved its heartless way, full speed ahead.

The boat began to sink at its stern, but moved slowly toward the slip. The passengers were a frantic mob, unpleasant to behold.

Blinker held Florence tightly until the boat had righted itself. She made no sound or sign of fear. He stood on a camp stool, ripped off the slats above his head and pulled down a number of the life preservers. He began to buckle one around Florence. The rotten canvas split and the fraudulent granulated cork came pouring out in a stream. Florence caught a handful of it and laughed gleefully.

"It looks like breakfast food," she said. "Take it off. They're no good."

She unbuckled it and threw it on the deck. She made Blinker sit down and sat by his side and put her hand in his. "What'll you bet we don't reach the pier all right?" she said, and began to hum a song.

And now the captain moved among the passengers and compelled order. The boat would undoubtedly make her slip, he said, and ordered the women and children to the bow, where they could land first. The boat, very low in the water at the stern, tried gallantly to make his promise good.

"Florence," said Blinker, as she held him close by an arm and hand, "I love you."

"That's what they all say," she replied, lightly.

"I am not one of 'they all,'" he persisted. "I never knew any one I could love before. I could pass my life with you and be happy every day. I am rich. I can make things all right for you."

"That's what they all say," said the girl again, weaving the words into her little, reckless song.

"Don't say that again," said Blinker in a tone that made her look at him in frank surprise.

"Why shouldn't I say it?" she asked, calmly. "They all do."

"Who are 'they'?" he asked, jealous for the first time in his existence.

"Why, the fellows I know."

"Do you know so many?"

"Oh, well, I'm not a wall flower," she answered with modest complacency.

"Where do you see these—these men? At your home?"

"Of course not. I meet them just as I did you. Sometimes on the boat, sometimes in the park, sometimes on the street. I'm a pretty good judge of a man. I can tell in a minute if a fellow is one who is likely to get fresh."

"What do you mean by 'fresh'?"

"Who try to kiss you—me, I mean."

"Do any of them try that?" asked Blinker, clenching his teeth.

"Sure. All men do. You know that."

"Do you allow them?"

"Some. Not many. They won't take you out anywhere unless you do."

She turned her head and looked searchingly at Blinker. Her eyes were as innocent as a child's. There was a puzzled look in them, as though she did not understand him.

"What's wrong about my meeting fellows?" she asked, wonderingly.

"Everything," he answered, almost savagely. "Why don't you entertain your company in the house where you live? Is it necessary to pick up Tom, Dick, and Harry on the streets?"

She kept her absolutely ingenuous eyes upon his.

"If you could see the place where I live you wouldn't ask that. I live in Brickdust Row. They call it that because there's red dust from the bricks crumbling over everything. I've lived there for more than four years. There's no place to receive company. You can't have anybody come to your room. What else is there to do? A girl has got to meet the men, hasn't she?"

"Yes," he said hoarsely. "A girl has got to meet a—has got to meet the men."

"The first time one spoke to me on the street," she continued, "I ran home and cried all night. But you get used to it. I meet a good many nice fellows at church. I go on rainy days and stand in the vestibule until one comes up with an umbrella. I wish there was a parlor, so I could ask you to call, Mr. Blinker—are you really sure it isn't 'Smith,' now?"

The boat landed safely. Blinker had a confused impression of walking with the girl through quiet crosstown streets until she stopped at a corner and held out her hand.

"I live just one more block over," she said. "Thank you for a very pleasant afternoon."

Blinker muttered something and plunged northward till he found a cab. A big, gray church loomed slowly at his right. Blinker shook his fist at it through the window.

"I gave you a thousand dollars last week," he cried under his breath, "and she meets them in your very doors. There is something wrong; there is something wrong."

At eleven the next day Blinker signed his name thirty times with a new pen provided by Lawyer Oldport.

"Now let me get to the woods," he said, surlily.

"You are not looking well," said Lawyer Oldport. "The trip will do you good. But listen, if you will, to that little matter of business of which I spoke to you yesterday, and also five years ago. There are some buildings, fifteen in number, of which there are new five-year leases to be signed. Your father contemplated a change in the lease provisions, but never made it. He intended that the parlors of these houses should not be sublet, but that the tenants should be allowed to use them for reception rooms. These houses are in the shopping districts, and are mainly tenanted by young working girls. As it is they are forced to seek companionship outside. This row of red brick—"

Blinker interrupted him with a loud, discordant laugh.

"Brickdust Row for an even hundred," he cried. "And I own it. Have I guessed right?"

"The tenants have some such name for it," said Lawyer Oldport.

Blinker arose and jammed his hat down to his eyes.

"Do what you please with it," he said, harshly. "Remodel it, burn it, raze it to the ground. But, man, it's too late, I tell you. It's too late. It's too late. It's too late. It's too late."

The Enchanted Profile

There are few Caliphesses. Women are Scheherazades by birth, predilection, instinct, and arrangement of the vocal cords. The thousand and one stories are being told every day by hundreds of thousands of viziers' daughters to their respective sultans. But the bow-string will get some of 'em yet if they don't watch out.

I heard a story, though, of one Lady Caliph. It isn't precisely an Arabian Nights story, because it brings in Cinderella, who flourished her dishrag in another epoch and country. So, if you don't mind the mixed dates (which seem to give it an Eastern flavor, after all), we'll get along.

In New York there is an old, old hotel. You have seen woodcuts of it in the magazines. It was built—let's see—at a time when there was nothing above Fourteenth Street except the old Indian trail to Boston and Hammerstein's office. Soon the old hostelry will be torn down. And, as the stout walls are riven apart and the bricks go roaring down the chutes, crowds of citizens will gather at the nearest corners and weep over the destruction of a dear old landmark. Civic pride is strong in New Bagdad; and the wettest weeper and the loudest

howler against the iconoclasts will be the man (originally
from Terre Haute) whose fond memories of the old hotel are
limited to his having been kicked out from its free-lunch
counter in 1873.

At the hotel always stopped Mrs. Maggie Brown. Mrs.
Brown was a bony woman of sixty, dressed in the rustiest
black, and carrying a handbag made, apparently, from the hide
of the original animal that Adam decided to call an alligator.
She always occupied a small parlor and bedroom at the top of
the hotel at a rental of two dollars per day. And always, while
she was there, each day came hurrying to see her many men,
sharp-faced, anxious-looking, with only seconds to spare. For
Maggie Brown was said to be the third richest woman in the
world; and these solicitous gentlemen were only the city's
wealthiest brokers and business men seeking trifling loans of
half a dozen millions or so from the dingy old lady with the
prehistoric handbag.

The stenographer and typewriter of the Acropolis Hotel
(there! I've let the name of it out!) was Miss Ida Bates. She
was a holdover from the Greek classics. There wasn't a flaw
in her looks. Some old-timer in paying his regards to a lady
said: "To have loved her was a liberal education." Well,
even to have looked over the black hair and neat white
shirtwaist of Miss Bates was equal to a full course in any
correspondence school in the country. She sometimes did a
little typewriting for me and, as she refused to take the money
in advance, she came to look upon me as something of a
friend and protégé. She had unfailing kindliness and good
nature; and not even a whitelead drummer or a fur importer
had ever dared to cross the dead line of good behavior in her
presence. The entire force of the Acropolis, from the owner,
who lived in Vienna, down to the head porter, who had been
bedridden for sixteen years, would have sprung to her defence in a moment.

One day I walked past Miss Bates's little sanctum Reming-
torium, and saw in her place a black-haired unit—unmistakably
a person—pounding with each of her forefingers upon the
keys. Musing on the mutability of temporal affairs, I passed
on. The next day I went on a two weeks' vacation. Returning,
I strolled through the lobby of the Acropolis, and saw, with a
little warm glow of auld lang syne, Miss Bates, as Grecian

and kind and flawless as ever, just putting the cover on her machine. The hour for closing had come; but she asked me in to sit for a few minutes in the dictation chair. Miss Bates explained her absence and returned to the Acropolis Hotel in words identical with or similar to these following:

"Well, Man, how are the stories coming?"

"Pretty regularly," said I. "About equal to their going."

"I'm sorry," said she. "Good typewriting is the main thing in a story. You've missed me, haven't you?"

"No one," said I, "whom I have ever known knows as well as you do how to space properly belt buckles, semicolons, hotel guests, and hairpins. But you've been away too. I saw a package of peppermint-pepsin in your place the other day."

"I was going to tell you about it," said Miss Bates, "if you hadn't interrupted me.

"Of course, you know about Maggie Brown, who stops here. Well, she's worth $40,000,000. She lives in Jersey in a ten-dollar flat. She's always got more cash on hand than half a dozen business candidates for vice-president. I don't know whether she carries it in her stocking or not, but I know she's mighty popular down in the part of the town where they worship the golden calf.

"Well, about two weeks ago, Mrs. Brown stops at the door and rubbers at me for ten minutes. I'm sitting with my side to her, striking off some manifold copies of a copper-mine proposition for a nice old man from Tonopah. But I always see everything all around me. When I'm hard at work I can see things through my side-combs; and I can leave one button unbuttoned in the back of my shirtwaist and see who's behind me. I didn't look around, because I make from eighteen to twenty dollars a week, and I didn't have to.

"That evening at knocking-off time she sends for me to come up to her apartment. I expected to have to typewrite about two thousand words of notes-of-hand, liens, and contracts, with a ten-cent tip in sight; but I went. Well, Man, I was certainly surprised. Old Maggie Brown had turned human.

" 'Child,' says she, 'you're the most beautiful creature I ever saw in my life. I want you to quit your work and come and live with me. I've no kith or kin,' says she, 'except a husband and a son or two, and I hold no communication with any of 'em. They're extravagant burdens on a hardworking woman. I want you to be a daughter to me. They say I'm stingy and mean, and the papers print lies about my doing my own cooking and washing. It's a lie,' she goes on. 'I put my washing out, except the handkerchiefs and stockings and petticoats and collars, and light stuff like that. I've got forty million dollars in cash and stocks and bonds that are as negotiable as Standard Oil, preferred, at a church fair. I'm a lonely old woman and I need companionship. You're the most beautiful human being I ever saw,' says she. 'Will you come and live with me? I'll show 'em whether I can spend money or not,' she says.

"Well, Man, what would you have done? Of course, I fell to it. And, to tell you the truth. I began to like old Maggie. It wasn't all on account of the forty millions and what she could do for me. I was kind of lonesome in the world, too. Everybody's got to have somebody they can explain to about the pain in their left shoulder and how fast patent-leather shoes wear out when they begin to crack. And you can't talk about such things to men you meet in hotels—they're looking for just such openings.

"So I gave up my job in the hotel and went with Mrs. Brown. I certainly seemed to have a mash on her. She'd look at me for half an hour at a time when I was sitting, reading, or looking at the magazines.

"One time I says to her: 'Do I remind you of some deceased relative or friend of your childhood, Mrs. Brown? I've noticed you give me a pretty good optical inspection from time to time.'

" 'You have a face,' she says, 'exactly like a dear friend of mine—the best friend I ever had. But I like you for yourself, child, too,' she says.

"And say, Man, what do you suppose she did? Loosened up like a Marcel wave in the surf at Coney. She took me to a swell dressmaker and gave her *à la carte* to fit me out—money no object. They were rush orders, and madame locked the front door and put the whole force to work.

"Then we moved to—where do you think?—no; guess again—that's right—the Hotel Bonton. We had a six-room apartment; and it cost $100 a day. I saw the bill. I began to love that old lady.

"And then, Man, when my dresses began to come in—oh,

I won't tell you about 'em! you couldn't understand. And I began to call her Aunt Maggie. You've read about Cinderella, of course. Well, what Cinderella said when the prince fitted that 3½ A on her foot was a hard-luck story compared to the things I told myself.

"Then Aunt Maggie says she is going to give me a coming-out banquet in the Bonton that'll make moving Vans of all the old Dutch families on Fifth Avenue.

" 'I've been out before, Aunt Maggie,' says I. 'But I'll come out again. But you know,' says I, 'that this is one of the swellest hotels in the city. And you know—pardon me— that it's hard to get a bunch of notables together unless you've trained for it.'

" 'Don't fret about that, child,' says Aunt Maggie. 'I don't send out invitations—I issue orders. I'll have fifty guests here that couldn't be brought together again at any reception unless it were given by King Edward or William Travers Jerome. They are men, of course, and all of 'em either owe me money or intend to. Some of their wives won't come, but a good many will.'

"Well, I wish you could have been at that banquet. The dinner service was all gold and cut glass. There were about forty men and eight ladies present besides Aunt Maggie and I. You'd never have known the third richest woman in the world. She had on a new black silk dress with so much passementerie on it that it sounded exactly like a hailstorm I heard once when I was staying all night with a girl that lived on a top-floor studio

"And my dress!—say, Man, I can't waste the words on you. It was all hand-made lace—where they was any of it at all—and it cost $300. I saw the bill. The men were all baldheaded or white-sidewhiskered, and they kept up a running fire of light repartee about 3-per cent, and Bryan and the cotton crop.

"On the left of me was something that talked like a banker, and on my right was a young fellow who said he was a newspaper artist. He was the only—well, I was going to tell you.

"After the dinner was over Mrs. Brown and I went up to the apartment. We had to squeeze our way through a mob of reporters all the way through the halls. That's one of the things money does for you. Say, do you happen to know a newspaper artist named Lathrop—a tall man with nice eyes and an easy way of talking? No, I don't remember what paper he works on. Well, all right.

"When we got upstairs Mrs. Brown telephones for the bill right away. It came, and it was $600. I saw the bill. Aunt Maggie fainted. I got her on a lounge and opened the bead-work.

" 'Child,' says she, when she got back to the world, 'what was it? A raise of rent or an income-tax?'

" 'Just a little dinner,' says I. 'Nothing to worry about—hardly a drop in the bucket-shop. Sit up and take notice—a dispossess notice, if there's no other kind.'

"But, say, Man, do you know what Aunt Maggie did? She got cold feet! She hustled me out of that Hotel Bonton at nine the next morning. We went to a rooming-house on the lower West Side. She rented one room that had water on the floor below and light on the floor above. After we got moved all you could see in the room was about $1,500 worth of new swell dresses and a one-burner gas-stove.

"Aunt Maggie had had a sudden attack of the hedges. I guess everybody has got to go on a spree once in their life. A man spends his on highballs, and a woman gets woozy on clothes. But with forty million dollars—say! I'd like to have a picture of—but, speaking of pictures, did you ever run across a newspaper artist named Lathrop—a tall—oh, I asked you that before, didn't I? He was mighty nice to me at the dinner. His voice just suited me. I guess he must have thought I was to inherit some of Aunt Maggie's money.

"Well, Mr. Man, three days of that light-housekeeping was plenty for me. Aunt Maggie was affectionate as ever. She'd hardly let me get out of her sight. But let me tell you. She was a hedger from Hedgersville, Hedger County. Seventy-five cents a day was the limit she set. We cooked our own meals in the room. There I was, with a thousand dollars' worth of the latest things in clothes, doing stunts over a one-burner gas-stove.

"As I say, on the third day I flew the coop. I couldn't stand for throwing together a fifteen-cent kidney stew while wearing, at the same time, a $150 house-dress, with Valenciennes lace insertion. So I goes into the closet and puts on the cheapest dress Mrs. Brown had bought for me—it's the one I've got on now—not so bad for $75, is it? I'd left all my own clothes in my sister's flat in Brooklyn.

" 'Mrs. Brown, formerly "Aunt Maggie," ' says I to her, 'I am going to extend my feet alternately, one after the other, in such a manner and direction that this tenement will recede from me in the quickest possible time. I am no worshipper of money,' says I, 'but there are some things I can't stand. I can stand the fabulous monster that I've read about that blows hot birds and cold bottles with the same breath. But I can't stand a quitter,' says I. 'They say you've got forty million dollars— well, you'll never have any less. And I was beginning to like you, too,' says I.

"Well, the late Aunt Maggie kicks till the tears flow. She offers to move into a swell room with a two-burner stove and running water.

" 'I've spent an awful lot of money, child,' says she. 'We'll have to economize for a while. You're the most beautiful creature I ever laid eyes on,' she says, 'and I don't want you to leave me.'

"Well, you see me, don't you? I walked straight to the Acropolis and asked for my job back, and I got it. How did you say your writings were getting along? I know you've lost out some by not having me to typewrite 'em. Do you ever have 'em illustrated? And, by the way, did you ever happen to know a newspaper artist—oh, shut up! I know I asked you before. I wonder what paper he works on? It's funny, but I couldn't help thinking that he wasn't thinking about the money he might have been thinking I was thinking I'd get from old Maggie Brown. If I only knew some of the newspaper editors I'd——"

The sound of an easy footstep came from the doorway. Ida Bates saw who it was with her back-hair comb. I saw her turn pink, perfect statue that she was—a miracle that I share with Pygmalion only.

"Am I excusable?" she said to me—adorable petitioner that she became. "It's—it's Mr. Lathrop. I wonder if it really wasn't the money—I wonder, if after all, he——"

Of course, I was invited to the wedding. After the ceremony I dragged Lathrop aside.

"You an artist," said I, "and haven't figured out why

Maggie Brown conceived such a strong liking for Miss Bates—that was? Let me show you.''

The bride wore a simple white dress as beautifully draped as the costumes of the ancient Greeks. I took some leaves from one of the decorative wreaths in the little parlor, and made a chaplet of them, and placed them on née Bates' shining chestnut hair, and made her turn her profile to her husband.

"By jingo!" said he. "Isn't Ida's head a dead ringer for the lady's head on the silver dollar?''

The Furnished Room

Restless, shifting, fugacious as time is a certain vast bulk of the population of the red brick district of the lower West Side. Homeless, they have a hundred homes. They flit from furnished room to furnished room, transients forever—transients in abode, transients in heart and mind. They sing "Home, Sweet Home" in ragtime; they carry their *lares et penates* in a bandbox; their vine is entwined about a picture hat; a rubber plant is their fig tree.

Hence the houses of this district, having had a thousand dwellers, should have a thousand tales to tell, mostly dull ones, no doubt; but it would be strange if there could not be found a ghost or two in the wake of all these vagrant guests.

One evening after dark a young man prowled among these crumbling red mansions, ringing their bells. At the twelfth he rested his lean hand-baggage upon the step and wiped the dust from his hatband and forehead. The bell sounded faint and far away in some remote, hollow depths.

To the door of this, the twelfth house whose bell he had rung, came a housekeeper who made him think of an unwholesome, surfeited worm that had eaten its nut to a hollow shell and now sought to fill the vacancy with edible lodgers.

He asked if there was a room to let.

"Come in," said the housekeeper. Her voice came from her throat; her throat seemed lined with fur. "I have the third-floor back, vacant since a week back. Should you wish to look at it?"

The young man followed her up the stairs. A faint light from no particular source mitigated the shadows of the halls. They trod noiselessly upon a stair carpet that its own loom would have forsworn. It seemed to have become vegetable; to have degenerated in that rank, sunless air to lush lichen or spreading moss that grew in patches to the stair-case and was viscid under the foot like organic matter. At each turn of the stairs were vacant niches in the wall. Perhaps plants had once been set within them. If so they had died in that foul and tainted air. It may be that statues of the saints had stood there, but it was not difficult to conceive that imps and devils had dragged them forth in the darkness and down to the unholy depths of some furnished pit below.

"This is the room," said the housekeeper, from her furry throat. "It's a nice room. It ain't often vacant. I had some most elegant people in it last summer—no trouble at all, and paid in advance to the minute. The water's at the end of the hall. Sprowls and Mooney kept it three months. They done a vaudeville sketch. Miss B'retta Sprowls—you may have heard of her—Oh, that was just the stage names—right there over the dresser is where the marriage certificate hung, framed. The gas is here, and you see there is plenty of closet room. It's a room everybody likes. It never stays idle long."

"Do you have many theatrical people rooming here?" asked the young man.

"They comes and goes. A good proportion of my lodgers is connected with the theatres. Yes, sir, this is the theatrical district. Actor people never stays long anywhere. I get my share. Yes, they comes and they goes."

He engaged the room, paying for a week in advance. He was tired, he said, and would take possession at once. He counted out the money. The room had been made ready, she said, even to towels and water. As the housekeeper moved away he put, for the thousandth time, the question that he carried at the end of his tongue.

"A young girl—Miss Vashner—Miss Eloise Vashner—do you remember such a one among your lodgers? She would be singing on the stage, most likely. A fair girl, of medium height and slender, with reddish, gold hair and a dark mole near her left eyebrow."

"No, I don't remember the name. Them stage people has names they change as often as their rooms. They comes and they goes. No, I don't call that one to mind."

No. Always no. Five months of ceaseless interrogation and the inevitable negative. So much time spent by day in questioning managers, agents, schools and choruses; by night among the audiences of theatres from all-star casts down to music halls so low that he dreaded to find what he most hoped for. He who had loved her best had tried to find her. He was sure that since her disappearance from home this great, water-girt city held her somewhere, but it was like a monstrous quicksand, shifting its particles constantly, with no foundation, its upper granules of to-day buried to-morrow in ooze and slime.

The furnished room received its latest guest with a first glow of pseudo-hospitality, a hectic, haggard, perfunctory welcome like the specious smile of a demirep. The sophistical comfort came in reflected gleams from the decayed furniture, the ragged brocade upholstery of a couch and two chairs, a foot-wide cheap pier glass between the two windows, from one or two gilt picture frames and a brass bedstead in a corner.

The guest reclined, inert, upon a chair, while the room, confused in speech as though it were an apartment in Babel, tried to discourse to him of its divers tenantry.

A polychromatic rug like some brilliant-flowered, rectangular, tropical islet lay surrounded by a billowy sea of soiled matting. Upon the gay-papered wall were those pictures that pursue the homeless one from house to house—The Huguenot Lovers, The First Quarrel, The Wedding Breakfast, Psyche at the Fountain. The mantel's chastely severe outline was ingloriously veiled behind some pert drapery drawn rakishly askew like the sashes of the Amazonian ballet. Upon it was some desolate flotsam cast aside by the room's marooned when lucky sail had borne them to a fresh port—a trifling vase or two, pictures of actresses, a medicine bottle, some stray cards out of a deck.

One by one, as the characters of a cryptograph become explicit, the little signs left by the furnished room's procession of guests developed a significance. The threadbare space in the rug in front of the dresser told that lovely women had marched in the throng. The tiny fingerprints on the wall spoke of little prisoners trying to feel their way to sun and air. A splattered stain, raying like the shadow of a bursting bomb, witnessed where a hurled glass or bottle had splintered with its contents against the wall. Across the pier glass had been scrawled with a diamond in staggering letters the name "Marie." It seemed that the succession of dwellers in the furnished room had turned in fury—perhaps tempted beyond forbearance by its garish coldness—and wreaked upon it their passions. The furniture was chipped and bruised; the couch, distorted by bursting springs, seemed a horrible monster that had been slain during the stress of some grotesque convulsion. Some more potent upheaval had cloven a great slice from the marble mantel. Each plank in the floor owned its particular cant and shriek as from a separate and individual agony. It seemed incredible that all this malice and injury had been wrought upon the room by those who had called it for a time their home; and yet it may have been the cheated home instinct surviving blindly, the resentful rage at false household gods that had kindled their wrath. A hut that is our own we can sweep and adorn and cherish.

The young tenant in the chair allowed these thoughts to file, soft-shod, through his mind, while there drifted into the room furnished sounds and furnished scents. He heard in one room a tittering and incontinent, slack laughter; in others the monologue of a scold, the rattling of dice, a lullaby, and one crying dully; above him a banjo tinkled with spirit. Doors banged somewhere; the elevated trains roared intermittently; a cat yowled miserably upon a back fence. And he breathed the breath of the house—a dark savor rather than a smell—a cold, musty effluvium as from underground vaults mingled with the reeking exhalations of linoleum and mildewed and rotten woodwork.

Then suddenly, as he rested there, the room was filled with

the strong, sweet odor of mignonette. It came as upon a single buffet of wind with such sureness and fragrance and emphasis that it almost seemed a living visitant. And the man cried aloud: "What, dear?" as if he had been called, and sprang up and faced about. The rich odor clung to him and wrapped him around. He reached out his arms for it, all his senses for the time confused and commingled. How could one be peremptorily called by an odor? Surely it must have been a sound. But, was it not the sound that had touched, that had caressed him?

"She has been in this room," he cried, and he sprang to wrest from it a token, for he knew he would recognize the smallest thing that had belonged to her or that she had touched. This enveloping scent of mignonette, the odor that she had loved and made her own—whence came it?

The room had been but carelessly set in order. Scattered upon the flimsy dresser scarf were half a dozen hairpins—those discreet, indistinguishable friends of womankind, feminine of gender, infinite mood and uncommunicative of tense. These he ignored, conscious of their triumphant lack of identity. Ransacking the drawers of the dresser he came upon a discarded, tiny, ragged handkerchief. He pressed it to his face. It was racy and insolent with heliotrope; he hurled it to the floor. In another drawer he found odd buttons, a theatre programme, a pawnbroker's card, two lost marshmallows, a book on the divination of dreams. In the last was a woman's black satin hair bow, which halted him, poised between ice and fire. But the black satin hair bow also is femininity's demure, impersonal common ornament and tells no tales.

And then he traversed the room like a hound on the scent, skimming the walls, considering the corners of the bulging matting on his hands and knees, rummaging mantel and tables, the curtains and hangings, the drunken cabinet in the corner, for a visible sign, unable to perceive that she was there beside, around, against, within, above him, clinging to him, wooing him, calling him so poignantly through the finer senses that even his grosser ones became cognizant of the call. Once again he answered loudly: "Yes, dear!" and turned, wild-eyed, to gaze on vacancy, for he could not yet discern form and color and love and outstretched arms in the odor of mignonette. Oh, God! whence that odor, and since when have odors had a voice to call? Thus he groped.

He burrowed in crevices and corners, and found corks and cigarettes. These he passed in passive contempt. But once he found in a fold of the matting a half-smoked cigar, and this he ground beneath his heel with a green and trenchant oath. He sifted the room from end to end. He found dreary and ignoble small records of many a peripatetic tenant; but of her whom he sought, and who may have lodged there, and whose spirit seemed to hover there, he found no trace.

And then he thought of the housekeeper.

He ran from the haunted room downstairs and to a door that showed a crack of light. She came out to his knock. He smothered his excitement as best he could.

"Will you tell me, madam," he besought her, "who occupied the room I have before I came?"

"Yes, sir. I can tell you again. 'Twas Sprowls and Mooney, as I said. Miss B'retta Sprowls it was in the theatres, but Missis Mooney she was. My house is well known for respectability. The marriage certificate hung, framed, on a nail over——"

"What kind of a lady was Miss Sprowls—in looks, I mean?"

"Why, black-haired, sir, short, and stout, with a comical face. They left a week ago Tuesday."

"And before they occupied it?"

"Why, there was a single gentleman connected with the draying business. He left owing me a week. Before him was Missis Crowder and her two children, that stayed four months; and back of them was old Mr. Doyle, whose sons paid for him. He kept the room six months. That goes back a year, sir, and further I do not remember."

He thanked her and crept back to his room. The room was dead. The essence that had vivified it was gone. The perfume of mignonette had departed. In its place was the old, stale odor of mouldy house furniture, of atmosphere in storage.

The ebbing of his hope drained his faith. He sat staring at the yellow, swinging gaslight. Soon he walked to the bed and began to tear the sheets into strips. With the blade of his knife he drove them tightly into every crevice around windows and door. When all was snug and taut he turned out the light, turned the gas full on again and laid himself gratefully upon the bed.

It was Mrs. McCool's night to go with the can for beer. So she fetched it and sat with Mrs. Purdy in one of those subterranean retreats where housekeepers foregather and the worm dieth seldom.

"I rented out my third-floor-back this evening," said Mrs. Purdy, across a fine circle of foam. "A young man took it. He went up to bed two hours ago."

"Now, did ye, Mrs. Purdy, ma'am?" said Mrs. McCool, with intense admiration. "You do be a wonder for rentin' rooms of that kind. And did ye tell him, then?" she concluded in a husky whisper laden with mystery.

"Rooms," said Mrs. Purdy, in her furriest tones, "are furnished for to rent. I did not tell him, Mrs. McCool."

" 'Tis right ye are, ma'am; 'tis by renting rooms we kape alive. Ye have the rale sense for business, ma'am. There be many people will rayjict the rentin' of a room if they be tould a suicide has been after dyin' in the bed of it."

"As you say, we has our living to be making," remarked Mrs. Purdy.

"Yis, ma'am; 'tis true. 'Tis just one wake ago this day I helped ye lay out the third-floor-back. A pretty slip of a colleen she was to be killin' herself wid the gas—a swate little face she had, Mrs. Purdy, ma'am."

"She'd a-been called handsome, as you say," said Mrs. Purdy, assenting but critical, "but for that mole she had a'growin' by her left eyebrow. Do fill up your glass again, Mrs. McCool."

Con Men and Hoboes

~

Shearing the Wolf

Jeff Peters was always eloquent when the ethics of his profession were under discussion.

"The only times," said he, "that me and Andy Tucker ever had any hiatuses in our cordial intents was when we differed on the moral aspects of grafting. Andy has his standards and I had mine. I didn't approve of all of Andy's schemes for levying contributions from the public, and he thought I allowed my conscience to interfere too often for the financial good of the firm. We had high arguments sometimes. Once one word led on to another till he said I reminded him of Rockefeller.

" 'I know how you mean that, Andy,' says I, 'but we have been friends too long for me to take offense, at a taunt that you will regret when you cool off. I have yet,' says I, 'to shake hands with a subpœna server.'

"One summer me and Andy decided to rest up a spell in a fine little town in the mountains of Kentucky called Grassdale. We was supposed to be horse drovers, and good decent citizens besides, taking a summer vacation. The Grassdale people liked us, and me and Andy declared a secession of hostilities, never so much as floating the fly leaf of a rubber concession prospectus or flashing a Brazilian diamond while we was there.

"One day the leading hardware merchant of Grassdale drops around to the hotel where me and Andy stopped, and smokes with us, sociable, on the side porch. We knew him pretty well from pitching quoits in the afternoons in the court house yard. He was a loud, red man, breathing hard, but fat and respectable beyond all reason.

107

"After we talk on all the notorious themes of the day, this Murkison—for such was his entitlements—takes a letter out of his coat pocket in a careful, careless way and hands it to us to read.

" 'Now, what do you think of that?' he says laughing—'a letter like that to ME!'

"Me and Andy sees at a glance what it is; but we pretend to read it through. It was one of them old-time typewritten green goods letters explaining how for $1,000 you could get $5,000 in bills that an expert couldn't tell from the genuine; and going on to tell how they were made from plates stolen by an employee of the Treasury at Washington.

" 'Think of 'em sending a letter like that to ME!' says Murkison again.

" 'Lots of good men get 'em,' says Andy. 'If you don't answer the first letter they let you drop. If you answer it they write again asking you to come on with your money and do business.'

" 'But think of 'em writing to ME!' says Murkison.

"A few days later he drops around again.

" 'Boys,' says he, 'I know you are all right or I wouldn't confide in you. I wrote to them rascals again just for fun. They answered and told me to come on to Chicago. They said telegraph to J. Smith when I would start. When I get there I'm to wait on a certain street corner till a man in a gray suit comes along and drops a newspaper in front of me. Then I am to ask how the water is, and he knows it's me and I know it's him.'

" 'Ah, yes,' says Andy, gaping, 'it's the same old game. I've often read about it in the papers. Then he conducts you to the private abattoir in the hotel, where Mr. Jones is already waiting. They show you brand-new real money and sell you all you want at five to one. You see 'em put it in a satchel for you and know it's there. Of course it's brown paper when you come to look at it afterward.'

" 'Oh, they couldn't switch it on me,' says Murkison. 'I haven't built up the best paying business in Grassdale without having witticisms about me. You say it's real money they show you, Mr. Tucker?'

" 'I've always—I see by the papers that it always is,' says Andy.

" 'Boys,' says Murkison, 'I've got it in my mind that them fellows can't fool me. I think I'll put a couple of thousand in my jeans and go up there and put it all over 'em. If Bill Murkison gets his eyes once on them bills they show him he'll never take 'em off of 'em. They offer $5 for $1, and they'll have to stick to the bargain if I tackle 'em. That's the kind of trader Bill Murkison is. Yes, I jist believe I'll drop up Chicago way and take a 5 to 1 shot on J. Smith. I guess the water'll be fine enough.'

"Me and Andy tries to get this financial misquotation out of Murkison's head, but we might as well have tried to keep the man who rolls peanuts with a toothpick from betting on Bryan's election. No, sir; he was going to perform a public duty by catching these green goods swindlers at their own game. Maybe it would teach 'em a lesson.

"After Murkison left us me and Andy sat a while prepondering over our silent meditations and heresies of reason. In our idle hours we always improved our higher selves by ratiocination and mental thought.

" 'Jeff,' says Andy after a long time, 'quite unseldom I have seen fit to impugn your molars when you have been chewing the rag with me about your conscientious way of doing business. I may have been often wrong. But here is a case where I think we can agree. I feel that it would be wrong for us to allow Mr. Murkison to go alone to meet those Chicago green goods men. There is but one way it can end. Don't you think we would both feel better if we was to intervene in some way and prevent the doing of this deed?'

"I got up and shook Andy Tucker's hand hard and long.

" 'Andy,' says I, 'I may have had one or two hard thoughts about the heartlessness of your corporation but I retract 'em now. You have a kind nucleus at the interior of your exterior after all. It does you credit. I was just thinking the same thing that you have expressed. It would not be honorable or praiseworthy,' says I, 'for us to let Murkison go on with this project he has taken up. If he is determined to go let us go with him and prevent this swindle from coming off.'

"Andy agreed with me; and I was glad to see that he was in earnest about breaking up this green goods scheme.

" 'I don't call myself a religious man,' says I, 'or a fanatic in moral bigotry, but I can't stand still and see a man who has built up a business by his own efforts and brains and risk be robbed by an unscrupulous trickster who is a menace to the public good.'

" 'Right, Jeff,' says Andy. 'We'll stick right along with Murkison if he insist on going and block this funny business. I'd hate to see any money dropped in it as bad as you would.'

"Well, we went to see Murkison.

" 'No, boys,' says he. 'I can't consent to let the song of this Chicago siren waft by me on the summer breeze. I'll fry some fat out of this ignis fatuus or burn a hole in the skillet. But I'd be plumb diverted to death to have you all go along with me. Maybe you could help some when it comes to cashing in the ticket to that 5 to 1 shot. Yes, I'd really take it as a pastime and regalement if you boys would go along too.'

"Murkison gives it out in Grassdale that he is going for a few days with Mr. Peters and Mr. Tucker to look over some iron ore property in West Virginia. He wires J. Smith that he will set foot in the spider web on a given date; and the three of us lights out for Chicago.

"On the way Murkison amuses himself with premonitions and advance pleasant recollections.

" 'In a gray suit,' says he, 'on the southwest corner of Wabash Avenue and Lake Street. He drops the paper, and I ask how the water is. Oh, my, my, my!' And then he laughs all over for five minutes.

"Sometimes Murkison was serious and tried to talk himself out of his cogitations, whatever they was.

" 'Boys,' says he, 'I wouldn't have this to get out in Grassdale for ten times a thousand dollars. It would ruin me there. But I know you all are all right. I think it's the duty of every citizen,' says he, 'to try to do up these robbers that prey upon the public. I'll show 'em whether the water's fine. Five dollars for one—that's what J. Smith offers, and he'll have to keep his contract if he does business with Bill Murkison.'

"We got into Chicago about 7 P.M. Murkison was to meet the gray man at half-past 9. We had dinner at a hotel and then went up to Murkison's room to wait for the time to come.

" 'Now boys,' says Murkison, 'let's get our gumption together and inoculate a plan for defeating the enemy. Suppose while I'm exchanging airy bandage with the gray capper you gents come along, by accident, you know, and holler: "Hello, Murk!!" and shake hands with symptoms of surprise and familiarity. Then I take the capper aside and tell him you all are Jenkins and Brown of Grassdale, groceries and feed, good men and maybe willing to take a chance while away from home.'

" ' "Bring 'em along," he'll say, of course, "if they care to invest." Now, how does that scheme strike you?'

" 'What do you say, Jeff?' says Andy, looking at me.

" 'Why, I'll tell you what I say,' says I. 'I say let's settle this thing right here now. I don't see any use of wasting any more time.' I took a nickel-plated .38 out of my pocket and clicked the cylinder around a few times.

" 'You undevout, sinful, insidious hog,' says I to Murkison, 'get out that two thousand and lay it on the table. Obey with velocity,' says I, 'for otherwise alternatives are impending. I am preferably a man of mildness, but now and then I find myself in the middle of extremities. Such men as you,' I went on after he had laid the money out, 'is what keeps the jails and court houses going. You come up here to rob these men of their money. Does it excuse you?' I asks, 'that they were trying to skin you? No, sir; you was going to rob Peter to stand off Paul. You are ten times worse,' says I, 'than that green goods man. You go to church at home and pretend to be a decent citizen, but you'll come to Chicago and commit larceny from men that have built up a sound and profitable business by dealing with such contemptible scoundrels as you have tried to be to-day. How do you know,' says I, 'that that green goods man hasn't a large family dependent upon his extortions? It's you supposedly respectable citizens who are always on the lookout to get something for nothing,' says I, 'that support the lotteries and wild-cat mines and stock exchanges and wire tappers of this country. If it wasn't for you they'd go out of business. The green goods man you was going to rob,' says I, 'studied maybe for years to learn his trade. Every turn he makes he risks his money and liberty and maybe his life. You come up here all sanctified and vanoplied with respectability and a pleasing post office address to swindle him. If he gets the money you can squeal to the police. If you get it he hocks the gray suit to buy supper and says nothing. Mr. Tucker and me sized you up,' says I, 'and came along to see that you got what you deserved. Hand over the money,' says I, 'you grass-fed hypocrite.'

"I put the two thousand, which was all in $20 bills, in my inside pocket.

" 'Now get out your watch,' says I to Murkison. 'No, I don't want it,' says I. 'Lay it on the table and you sit in that chair till it ticks off an hour. Then you can go. If you make any noise or leave any sooner we'll hand-bill you all over Grassdale. I guess your high position there is worth more than $2,000 to you.'

"Then me and Andy left.

"On the train Andy was a long time silent. Then he says: 'Jeff, do you mind my asking you a question?'

" 'Two,' says I, 'or forty.'

" 'Was that the idea you had,' says he, 'when we started out with Murkison?'

" 'Why certainly,' says I. 'What else could it have been? Wasn't it yours, too?'

"In about half an hour Andy spoke again. I think there are times when Andy don't exactly understand my system of ethics and moral hygiene.

" 'Jeff,' says he, 'some time when you have the leisure I wish you'd draw off a diagram and footnotes of that conscience of yours. I'd like to have it to refer to occasionally.' "

Hostages to Momus

I never got inside of the legitimate line of graft but once. But, one time, as I say, I reversed the decision of the revised statutes and undertook a thing that I'd have to apologize for even under the New Jersey trust laws.

Me and Caligula Polk, of Muskogee in the Creek Nation,

was down in the Mexican State of Tamaulipas running a peripatetic lottery and monte game. Now, selling lottery tickets is a government graft in Mexico, just like selling forty-eight cents' worth of postage-stamps for forty-nine cents is over here. So Uncle Porfirio he instructs the *rurales* to attend our case.

Rurales? They're a sort of country police; but don't draw any mental crayon portraits of the worthy constable with a tin star and a gray goatee. The *rurales*—well, if we'd mount our Supreme Court on broncos, arm 'em with Winchesters, and start 'em out after John Doe *et al.* we'd have about the same thing.

When the *rurales* started for us we started for the States. They chased us as far as Matamoras. We hid in a brickyard; and that night we swum the Rio Grande, Caligula with a brick in each hand, absent-minded, which he drops upon the soil of Texas, forgetting he had 'em.

From there we migrated to San Antone, and then over to New Orleans, where we took a rest. And in that town of cotton bales and other adjuncts to female beauty we made the acquaintance of drinks invented by the Creoles during the period of Louey Cans, in which they are still served at the side doors. The most I can remember of this town is that me and Caligula and a Frenchman name McCarty—wait a minute; Adolph McCarty—was trying to make the French Quarter pay up the back trading-stamps due on the Louisiana Purchase, when somebody hollers that the johndarms are coming. I have an insufficient recollection of buying two yellow tickets through a window; and I seemed to see a man swing a lantern and say "All aboard!" I remembered no more, except that the train butcher was covering me and Caligula up with Augusta J. Evans's works and figs.

When we become revised, we find that we have collided up against the State of Georgia at a spot hitherto unaccounted for in time tables except by an asterisk, which means that trains stop every other Thursday on signal by tearing up a rail. We was waked up in a yellow pine hotel by the noise of flowers and the smell of birds. Yes, sir, for the wind was banging sunflowers as big as buggy wheels against the weatherboarding and the chicken coop was right under the window. Me and Caligula dressed and went downstairs. The landlord was shelling peas on the front porch. He was six feet of chills and fever, and Hongkong in complexion though in other respects he seemed amenable in the exercise of his sentiments and features.

Caligula, who is a spokesman by birth, and a small man, though red-haired and impatient of painfulness of any kind, speaks up.

"Pardner," says he, "good-morning, and be darned to you. Would you mind telling us why we are at? We know the reason we are where, but can't exactly figure out on account of at what place."

"Well, gentlemen," says the landlord, "I reckoned you-all would be inquiring this morning. You all dropped off of the nine-thirty train here last night; and you was right tight. Yes, you was right smart in liquor. I can inform you that you are now in the town of Mountain Valley, in the State of Georgia."

"On top of that," says Caligula, "don't say that we can't have anything to eat."

"Sit down, gentlemen," says the landlord, "and in twenty minutes I'll call you to the best breakfast you can get anywhere in town."

That breakfast turned out to be composed of fried bacon and a yellowish edifice that proved up something between pound cake and flexible sandstone. The landlord calls it corn pone; and then he sets out a dish of the exaggerated breakfast food known as hominy; and so me and Caligula makes the acquaintance of the celebrated food that enabled every Johnny Reb to lick one and two-thirds Yankees for nearly four years at a stretch.

"The wonder to me is," says Caligula, "that Uncle Robert Lee's boys didn't chase the Grant and Sherman outfit clear up into Hudson's Bay. It would have made me that mad to eat this truck they call mahogany!"

"Hog and hominy," I explains, "is the staple food of this section."

"Then," says Caligula, "they ought to keep it where it belongs. I thought this was a hotel and not a stable. Now, if we was in Muskogee at the St. Lucifer House, I'd show you some breakfast grub. Antelope steaks and fried liver to begin on, and vension cutlets with *chili con carne* and pine-apple fritters, and then some sardines and mixed pickles; and top it off with a can of yellow clings and a bottle of beer. You won't find a layout like that on the bill of affairs of any of your Eastern restauraws.''

"Too lavish," said I. "I've travelled, and I'm unprejudiced. There'll never be a perfect breakfast eaten until some man grows arms long enough to stretch down to New Orleans for his coffee and over to Norfolk for his rolls, and reaches up to Vermont and digs a slice of butter out of a spring-house, and then turns over a beehive close to a white clover patch out in Indiana for the rest. Then he'd come pretty close to making a meal on the amber that the gods eat on Mount Olympia.''

"Too ephemeral," says Caligula. "I'd want ham and eggs, or rabbit stew, anyhow, for a chaser. What do you consider the most edifying and casual in the way of a dinner?''

"I've been infatuated from time to time," I answers, "with fancy ramifications of grub such as terrapins, lobsters, reed birds, jambolaya, and canvas-covered ducks; but after all there's nothing less displeasing to me than a beefsteak smothered in mushrooms on a balcony in sound of the Broadway street cars, with a hand-organ playing down below, and the boys hollering extras about the latest suicide. For the wine, give me a reasonable Ponty Cany. And that's all, except a *demi-tasse*.''

"Well," says Caligula, "I reckon in New York you get to be a conniseer; and when you go around with a *demi-tasse* you are naturally bound to buy 'em stylish grub.''

"It's a great town for epicures," says I. "You'd soon fall into their ways if you was there.''

"I've heard it was," says Caligula. "But I reckon I wouldn't. I can polish my fingernails all they need myself.''

II After breakfast we went out on the front porch, lighted up two of the landlord's *flor de upas* perfectos, and took a look at Georgia.

The installment of scenery visible to the eye looked mighty poor. As far as we could see was red hills all washed down with gullies and scattered over with patches of piny woods. Blackberry bushes was all that kept the rail fences from falling down. About fifteen miles over to the north was a little range of well-timbered mountains.

That town of Mountain Valley wasn't going. About a

dozen people permeated along the sidewalks; but what you saw mostly was rain-barrels and roosters, and boys poking around with sticks in piles of ashes made by burning the scenery of Uncle Tom shows.

And just then there passes down on the other side of the street a high man in a long black coat and a beaver hat. All the people in sight bowed, and some crossed the street to shake hands with him; folks came out of stores and houses to holler at him; women leaned out of windows and smiled; and all the kids stopped playing to look at him. Our landlord stepped out on the porch and bent himself double like a carpenter's rule, and sung out, "Good-morning, Colonel," when he was a dozen yards gone by.

"And is that Alexander, pa?" says Caligula to the landlord; "and why is he called great?"

"That, gentlemen," says the landlord, "is no less than Colonel Jackson T. Rockingham, the president of the Sunrise & Edenville Tap Railroad, mayor of Mountain Valley, and chairman of the Perry County board of immigration and public improvements."

"Been away a good many years, hasn't he?" I asked.

"No, sir; Colonel Rockingham is going down to the post-office for his mail. His fellow-citizens take pleasure in greeting him thus every morning. The colonel is our most prominent citizen. Besides the height of the stock of the Sunrise & Edenville Tap Railroad, he owns a thousand acres of that land across the creek. Mountain Valley delights, sir, to honor a citizen of such wealth and public spirit."

For an hour that afternoon Caligula sat on the back of his neck on the porch and studied a newspaper, which was unusual in a man who despised print. When he was through he took me to the end of the porch among the sunlight and drying dishtowels. I knew that Caligula had invented a new graft. For he chewed the ends of his mustache and ran the left catch of his suspenders up and down, which was his way.

"What is it now?" I asks. "Just so it ain't floating mining stocks or raising Pennsylvania pinks, we'll talk it over."

"Pennsylvania pinks? Oh, that refers to a coin-raising scheme of the Keystoners. They burn the soles of old women's feet to make them tell where their money's hid."

Caligula's words in business was always few and bitter.

"You see them mountains," said he, pointing. "And you seen that colonel man that owns railroads and cuts more ice when he goes to the post-office than Roosevelt does when he cleans 'em out. What we're going to do is to kidnap the latter into the former, and inflict a ransom of ten thousand dollars."

"Illegality," says I, shaking my head.

"I knew you'd say that," says Caligula. "At first sight it does seem to jar peace and dignity. But it don't. I got the idea out of that newspaper. Would you commit aspersions on a equitable graft that the United States itself has condoned and indorsed and ratified?"

"Kidnapping," says I, "is an immoral function in the derogatory list of the statutes. If the United States upholds it, it must be a recent enactment of ethics, along with race suicide and rural delivery."

"Listen," says Caligula, "and I'll explain the case set down in the papers. Here was a Greek citizen named Burdick Harris," says he, "captured for a graft by Africans; and the United States sends two gunboats to the State of Tangiers and makes the King of Morocco give up seventy thousand dollars to Raisuli."

"Go slow," says I. "That sounds too international to take in all at once. It's like 'thimble, thimble, who's got the naturalization papers?' "

" 'Twas press despatches from Constantinople," says Caligula. "You'll see, six months from now. They'll be confirmed by the monthly magazines; and then it won't be long till you'll notice 'em alongside of photos of the Mount Pelee eruption photos in the while-you-get-your-hair-cut weeklies. It's all right, Pick. This African man Raisuli hides Burdick Harris up in the mountains, and advertises his price to the governments of different nations. Now, you wouldn't think for a minute," goes on Caligula, "that John Hay would have chipped in and helped this graft along if it wasn't a square game, would you?"

"Why, no," says I. "I've always stood right in with Bryan's policies, and I couldn't consciently say a word against the Republican administration just now. But if Harris was a Greek, on what system of international protocols did Hay interfere?"

"It ain't exactly set forth in the papers," says Caligula. "I suppose it's a matter of sentiment. You know he wrote this poem, 'Little Breeches'; and them Greeks wear little or none. But anyhow, John Hay sends the *Brooklyn* and the *Olympia* over, and they cover Africa with thirty-inch guns. And then Hay cables after the health of the *persona grata.* 'And how are they this morning?' he wires. 'Is Burdick Harris alive yet, or Mr. Raisuli dead?' And the King of Morocco sends up the seventy thousand dollars, and they turn Burdick Harris loose. And there's not half the hard feelings among the nations about this little kidnapping matter as there was about the peace congress. And Burdick Harris says to the reporters, in the Greek language, that he's often heard about the United States, and he admires Roosevelt next to Raisuli, who is one of the whitest and most gentlemanly kidnappers that he ever worked alongside of. So you see, Pick,'' winds up Caligula, ''we've got the law of nations on our side. We'll cut this colonel man out of the herd, and corral him in them little mountains, and stick up his heirs and assigns for ten thousand dollars.''

''Well, you seldom little red-headed territorial terror,'' I answers, ''you can't bluff your uncle Tecumseh Pickens! I'll be your company in this graft. But I misdoubt if you've absorbed the inwardness of this Burdick Harris case, Calig; and if on any morning we get a telegram from the Secretary of State asking about the health of the scheme, I propose to acquire the most propinquitous and celeritous mule in this section and gallop diplomatically over into the neighboring and peaceful nation of Alabama.''

III Me and Caligula spent the next three days investigating the bunch of mountains into which we proposed to kidnap Colonel Jackson T. Rockingham. We finally selected an upright slice of topography covered with bushes and trees that you could only reach by a secret path that we cut up the side of it. And the only way to reach the mountain was to follow up the bend of a branch that wound among the elevations.

Then I took in hand an important subdivision of the proceedings. I went up to Atlanta on the train and laid in a two-hundred-and-fifty-dollar supply of the most gratifying and efficient lines of grub that money could buy. I always was an admirer of viands in their more palliative and revised stages. Hog and hominy are not only inartistic to my stomach, but they give indigestion to my moral sentiments. And I thought of Colonel Jackson T. Rockingham, president of the Sunrise & Edenville Tap Railroad, and how he would miss the luxury of his home fare as is so famous among wealthy Southerners. So I sunk half of mine and Caligula's capital in as elegant a layout of fresh and canned provisions as Burdick Harris or any other professional kidnappee ever saw in a camp.

I put another hundred in a couple of cases of Bordeaux, two quarts of cognac, two hundred Havana regalias with gold bands, and a camp stove and stools and folding cots. I wanted Colonel Rockingham to be comfortable; and I hoped after he gave up the ten thousand dollars he would give me and Caligula as good a name for gentlemen and entertainers as the Greek man did the friend of his that made the United States his bill collector against Africa. When the goods came down from Atlanta, we hired a wagon, moved them up on the little mountain, and established camp. And then we laid for the colonel.

We caught him one morning about two miles out from Mountain Valley, on his way to look after some of his burnt umber farm land. He was an elegant old gentleman, as thin and tall as a trout rod, with frazzled shirt-cuffs and specs on a black string. We explained to him, brief and easy, what we wanted; and Caligula showed him, careless, the handle of his forty-five under his coat.

"What?" says Colonel Rockingham. "Bandits in Perry County, Georgia! I shall see that the board of immigration and public improvements hears of this!"

"Be so unfoolhardy as to climb into that buggy," says Caligula, "by order of the board of perforation and public depravity. This is a business meeting, and we're anxious to adjourn *sine qua non.*"

We drove Colonel Rockingham over the mountain and up the side of it as far as the buggy could go. Then we tied the horse, and took our prisoner on foot up to the camp.

"Now, colonel," I says to him, "we're after the ransom, me and my partner; and no harm will come to you if the King of Mor—if your friends send up the dust. In the meantime, we are gentlemen the same as you. And if you give us your word not to try to escape, the freedom of the camp is yours.''

"I give you my word," says the colonel.

"All right," says I; "and now it's eleven o'clock and me and Mr. Polk will proceed to inoculate the occasion with a few well-timed trivialities in the line of grub."

"Thank you," says the colonel; "I believe I could relish a slice of bacon and a plate of hominy."

"But you won't," says I, emphatic. "Not in this camp. We soar in higher regions than them occupied by your celebrated but repulsive dish."

While the colonel read his paper, me and Caligula took off our coats and went in for a little luncheon *de luxe* just to show him. Caligula was a fine cook of the Western brand. He could toast a buffalo or fricassee a couple of steers as easy as a woman could make a cup of tea. He was gifted in the way of knocking together edibles when haste and muscle and quantity was to be considered. He held the record west of the Arkansas River for frying pancakes with his left hand, broiling venison cutlets with his right and skinning a rabbit with his teeth at the same time. But I could do things *en casserole* and *à la creole,* and handle the oil and tabasco as gently and nicely as a French *chef.*

So at twelve o'clock we had a hot lunch ready that looked like a banquet on a Mississippi River steamboat. We spread it on the tops of two or three big boxes, opened two quarts of the red wine, set the olives and a canned oyster cocktail and a ready-made Martini by the colonel's plate, and called him to grub.

Colonel Rockingham drew up his campstool, wiped off his specs, and looked at the things on the table. Then I thought he was swearing; and I felt mean because I hadn't taken more pains with the victuals. But he wasn't; he was asking a blessing; and me and Caligula hung our heads and I saw a tear drop from the colonel's eye into his cocktail.

I never saw a man eat with so much earnestness and application—not hastily like a grammarian or one of the canal, but slow and appreciative, like a anaconda, or a real *vive bonjour.*

In an hour and a half the colonel leaned back. I brought

him a pony of brandy and his black coffee, and set the box of Havana regalias on the table.

"Gentlemen," says he, blowing out the smoke and trying to breathe it back again, "when we view the eternal hills and the smiling and beneficent landscape, and reflect upon the goodness of the Creator who——"

"Excuse me, colonel," says I, "but there's some business to attention to now"; and I brought out paper and pen and ink and laid 'em before him. "Who do you want to send to for the money?" I asks.

"I reckon," says he, after thinking a bit, "to the vice-president of our railroad, at the general offices of the Company in Edenville."

"How far is it to Edenville from here?" I asked.

"About ten miles," says he.

Then I dictated these lines, and Colonel Rockingham wrote them out:

I am kidnapped and held a prisoner by two desperate outlaws in a place which is useless to attempt to find. They demand ten thousand dollars at once for my release. The amount must be raised immediately, and these directions followed. Come alone with the money to Stony Creek, which runs out of Blacktop Mountains. Follow the bed of the creek till you come to a big flat rock on the left bank, on which is marked a cross in red chalk. Stand on the rock and wave a white flag. A guide will come to you and conduct you to where I am held. Lose no time.

After the colonel had finished this, he asked permission to tack on a postscript about how white he was being treated, so the railroad wouldn't feel uneasy in its bosom about him. We agreed to that. He wrote down that he had just had lunch with the two desperate ruffians; and then he set down the whole bill of fare, from cocktails to coffee. He wound up with the remark that dinner would be ready about six, and would probably be a more licentious and intemperate affair than lunch.

Me and Caligula read it, and decided to let it go; for we, being cooks, were amenable to praise, though it sounded out of place on a sight draft for ten thousand dollars.

I took the letter over to the Mountain Valley road and watched for a messenger. By and by a colored equestrian came along on horseback, riding toward Edenville. I gave him a dollar to take the letter to the railroad offices; and then I went back to camp.

IV

About four o'clock in the afternoon, Caligula, who was acting as lookout, calls to me:

"I have to report a white shirt signaling on the starboard bow, sir."

I went down the mountain and brought back a fat, red man in an alpaca coat and no collar.

"Gentlemen," says Colonel Rockingham, "allow me to introduce my brother, Captain Duval C. Rockingham, vice-president of the Sunrise & Edenville Tap Railroad."

"Otherwise the King of Morocco," says I. "I reckon you don't mind my counting the ransom, just as a business formality."

"Well, no, not exactly," says the fat man, "not when it comes. I turned that matter over to our second vice-president. I was anxious after Brother Jackson's safetiness. I reckon he'll be along right soon. What does that lobster salad you mentioned taste like, Brother Jackson?"

"Mr. Vice-President," says I, "you'll oblige us by remaining here till the second V. P. arrives. This is a private rehearsal, and we don't want any roadside speculators selling tickets."

In half an hour Caligula sings out again:

"Sail ho! Looks like an apron on a broomstick."

I perambulated down the cliff again, and escorted up a man six foot three, with a sandy beard and no other dimensions that you could notice. Thinks I to myself, if he's got ten thousand dollars on his person it's in one bill and folded lengthwise.

"Mr. Patterson G. Coble, our second vice-president," announces the colonel.

"Glad to know you, gentlemen," says this Coble. "I came up to disseminate the tidings that Major Tallahassee Tucker, our general passenger agent, is now negotiating a peach-crate full of our railroad bonds with the Perry County Bank for a loan. My dear Colonel Rockingham, was that chicken gumbo or cracked goobers on the bill of fare in your note? Me and the conductor of fifty-six was having a dispute about it.''

"Another white wings on the rocks!'' hollers Caligula. "If I see any more I'll fire on 'em and swear they was torpedo-boats!''

The guide goes down again, and convoys into the lair a person in blue overalls carrying an amount of inebriety and a lantern. I am so sure that this is Major Tucker that I don't even ask him until we are up above; and then I discover that it is Uncle Timothy, the yard switchman at Edenville, who is sent ahead to flag our understandings with the gossip that Judge Prendergast, the railroad's attorney, is in the process of mortgaging Colonel Rockingham's farming lands to make up the ransom.

While he is talking, two men crawl from under the bushes into camp, and Caligula, with no white flag to disinter him from his plain duty, draws his gun. But again Colonel Rockingham intervenes and introduces Mr. Jones and Mr. Batts, engineer and fireman of train number forty-two.

"Excuse us,'' says Batts, "but me and Jim have hunted squirrels all over this mounting, and we don't need no white flag. Was that straight, colonel, about the plum pudding and pineapples and real store cigars?''

"Towel on a fishing-pole in the offing!'' howls Caligula. "Suppose it's the firing line of the freight conductors and brakeman.''

"My last trip down,'' says I, wiping off my face. "If the S. & E. T. wants to run an excursion up here just because we kidnapped their president, let 'em. We'll put out our sign. 'The Kidnapper's Cafe and Trainmen's Home.' ''

This time I caught Major Tallahassee Tucker by his own confession, and I felt easier. I asked him into the creek, so I could drown him if he happened to be a track-walker or caboose porter. All the way up the mountain he driveled to me about asparagus on toast, a thing that his intelligence in life had skipped.

Up above I got his mind segregated from food and asked if he had raised the ransom.

"My dear sir,'' says he, "I succeeded in negotiating a loan on thirty thousand dollars' worth of the bonds of our railroad, and—''

"Never mind just now, major," says I. "It's all right, then. Wait till after dinner, and we'll settle the business. All of you gentlemen," I continues to the crowd, "are invited to stay to dinner. We have mutually trusted one another, and the white flag is supposed to wave over the proceedings."

"The correct idea," says Caligula, who was standing by me. "Two baggage-masters and a ticket agent dropped out of a tree while you was below the last time. Did the major man bring the money?"

"He says," I answered, "that he succeeded in negotiating the loan."

If any cooks ever earned ten thousand dollars in twelve hours me and Caligula did that day. At six o'clock we spread the top of the mountain with as fine a dinner as the personnel of any railroad ever engulfed. We opened all the wine, and we concocted entrées and *pièces de resistance,* and stirred up little savory *chef de cuisines* and organized a mass of grub such as has seldom instigated out of canned and bottled goods. The railroad gathered around it, and the wassail and diversions was intense.

After the feast me and Caligula, in the line of business, takes Major Tucker to one side and talks ransom. The major pulls out an agglomeration of currency about the size of the price of a town lot in the suburbs of Rabbitville, Arizona, and makes this outcry.

"Gentlemen," says he, "the stock of the Sunrise & Edenville railroad has depreciated some. The best I could do with thirty thousand dollars' worth of the bonds was to secure a loan of eighty-seven dollars and fifty cents. On the farming lands of Colonel Rockingham, Judge Prendergast was able to obtain, on a ninth mortgage, the sum of fifty dollars. You will find the amount, one hundred and thirty-seven fifty, correct."

"A railroad president," said I, looking this Tucker in the eye, "and the owner of a thousand acres of land; and yet——"

"Gentlemen," says Tucker, "the railroad is ten miles long. There don't any train run on it except when the crew goes out in the pines and gathers enough lightwood knots to get up steam. A long time ago, when times was good, the net earnings used to run as high as eighteen dollars a week. Colonel Rockingham's land has been sold for taxes thirteen times. There hasn't been a peach crop in this part of Georgia for two years. The wet spring killed the watermelons. No-body around here has money enough to buy fertilizer; and land is so poor the corn crop failed, and there wasn't enough grass to support the rabbits. All the people have had to eat in this section for over a year is hog and hominy, and——"

"Pick," interrupts Caligula, mussing up his red hair, "what are you going to do with that chicken-feed?"

I hands the money back to Major Tucker; and then I goes over to Colonel Rockingham and slaps him on the back.

"Colonel," says I, "I hope you've enjoyed our little joke. We don't want to carry it too far. Kidnappers! Well, wouldn't it tickle your uncle? My name's Rhinegelder, and I'm a nephew of Chauncey Depew. My friend's a second cousin of the editor of *Puck*. So you can see. We are down South enjoying ourselves in our humorous way. Now, there's two quarts of cognac to open yet, and then the joke's over."

What's the use to go into details? One or two will be enough. I remember Major Tallahassee Tucker playing on a jew's-harp, and Caligula waltzing with his head on the watch pocket of a tall baggage-master. I hesitate to refer to the cake-walk done by me and Mr. Patterson G. Coble with Colonel Jackson T. Rockingham between us.

And even on the next morning, when you wouldn't think it possible, there was a consolation for me and Caligula. We knew that Raisuli himself never made half the hit with Burdick Harris that we did with the Sunrise & Edenville Tap Railroad.

A Retrieved Reformation

A guard came to the prison shoe-shop, where Jimmy Valentine was assiduously stitching uppers, and escorted him to the front office. There the warden handed Jimmy his pardon, which had been signed that morning by the governor. Jimmy took it in a tired kind of way. He had served nearly ten months of a four-year sentence. He had expected to stay only about three months, at the longest. When a man with as many friends on the outside as Jimmy Valentine had is received in the "stir" it is hardly worth while to cut his hair.

"Now, Valentine," said the warden, "you'll go out in the morning. Brace up, and make a man of yourself. You're not a bad fellow at heart. Stop cracking safes, and live straight."

"Me?" said Jimmy, in surprise. "Why, I never cracked a safe in my life."

"Oh, no," laughed the warden. "Of course not. Let's see, now. How was it you happened to get sent up on that Springfield job? Was it because you wouldn't prove an alibi for fear of compromising somebody in extremely high-toned society? Or was it simply a case of a mean old jury that had it in for you? It's always one or the other with you innocent victims."

"Me?" said Jimmy, still blankly virtuous. "Why, warden, I never was in Springfield in my life!"

"Take him back, Cronin," smiled the warden, "and fix him up with outgoing clothes. Unlock him at seven in the morning, and let him come to the bull-pen. Better think over my advice, Valentine."

At a quarter past seven on the next morning Jimmy stood in the warden's outer office. He had on a suit of the

126

villainously fitting, ready-made clothes and a pair of the stiff, squeaky shoes that the state furnishes to its discharged compulsory guests.

The clerk handed him a railroad ticket and the five-dollar bill with which the law expected him to rehabilitate himself into good citizenship and prosperity. The warden gave him a cigar, and shook hands. Valentine, 9762, was chronicled on the books "Pardoned by Governor," and Mr. James Valentine walked out into the sunshine.

Disregarding the song of the birds, the waving green trees, and the smell of the flowers, Jimmy headed straight for a restaurant. There he tasted the first sweet joys of liberty in the shape of a broiled chicken and a bottle of white wine—followed by a cigar a grade better than the one the warden had given him. From there he proceeded leisurely to the depot. He tossed a quarter into the hat of a blind man sitting by the door, and boarded his train. Three hours set him down in a little town near the state line. He went to the café of one Mike Dolan and shook hands with Mike, who was alone behind the bar.

"Sorry we couldn't make it sooner, Jimmy, me boy," said Mike. "But we had that protest from Springfield to buck against, and the governor nearly balked. Feeling all right?"

"Fine," said Jimmy. "Got my key?"

He got his key and went upstairs, unlocking the door of a room at the rear. Everything was just as he had left it. There on the floor was still Ben Price's collar-button that had been torn from that eminent detective's shirt-band when they had overpowered Jimmy to arrest him.

Pulling out from the wall a folding-bed, Jimmy slid back a panel in the wall and dragged out a dust-covered suitcase. He opened this and gazed fondly at the finest set of burglar's tools in the East. It was a complete set, made of specially tempered steel, the latest designs in drills, punches, braces and bits, jimmies, clamps, and augers, with two or three novelties invented by Jimmy himself, in which he took pride. Over nine hundred dollars they had cost him to have made at——, a place where they make such things for the profession.

In half an hour Jimmy went downstairs and through the café. He was now dressed in tasteful and well-fitting clothes, and carried his dusted and cleaned suitcase in his hand.

"Got anything on?" asked Mike Dolan, genially.

"Me?" said Jimmy, in a puzzled tone. "I don't understand. I'm representing the New York Amalgamated Short Snap Biscuit Cracker and Frazzled Wheat Company."

This statement delighted Mike to such an extent that Jimmy had to take a seltzer-and-milk on the spot. He never touched "hard" drinks.

A week after the release of Valentine, 9762, there was a neat job of safeburglary done in Richmond, Indiana, with no clue to the author. A scant eight hundred dollars was all that was secured. Two weeks after that a patented, improved, burglar-proof safe in Logansport was opened like a cheese to the tune of fifteen hundred dollars, currency; securities and silver untouched. That began to interest the rogue-catchers. Then an old-fashioned bank-safe in Jefferson City became active and threw out of its crater an eruption of bank-notes amounting to five thousand dollars. The losses were now high enough to bring the matter up into Ben Price's class of work. By comparing notes, a remarkable similarity in the methods of the burglaries was noticed. Ben Price investigated the scenes of the robberies, and was heard to remark:

"That's Dandy Jim Valentine's autograph. He's resumed business. Look at that combination knob—jerked out as easy as pulling up a radish in wet weather. He's got the only clamps that can do it. And look how clean those tumblers were punched out! Jimmy never has to drill but one hole. Yes, I guess I want Mr. Valentine. He'll do his bit next time without any short-time or clemency foolishness."

Ben Price knew Jimmy's habits. He had learned them while working up the Springfield case. Long jumps, quick get-aways, no confederates, and a taste for good society— these ways had helped Mr. Valentine to become noted as a successful dodger of retribution. It was given out that Ben Price had taken up the trail of the elusive cracksman, and other people with burglar-proof safes felt more at ease.

One afternoon Jimmy Valentine and his suitcase climbed out of the mail-hack in Elmore, a little town five miles off the railroad down in the black-jack country of Arkansas. Jimmy, looking like an athletic young senior just home from college, went down the board sidewalk toward the hotel.

A young lady crossed the street, passed him at the corner

and entered a door over which was the sign "The Elmore Bank." Jimmy Valentine looked into her eyes, forgot what he was, and became another man. She lowered her eyes and colored slightly. Young men of Jimmy's style and looks were scarce in Elmore.

Jimmy collared a boy that was loafing on the steps of the bank as if he were one of the stock-holders, and began to ask him questions about the town, feeding him dimes at intervals. By and by the young lady came out, looking royally unconscious of the young man with the suitcase, and went her way.

"Isn't that young lady Miss Polly Simpson?" asked Jimmy, with specious guile.

"Naw," said the boy. "She's Annabel Adams. Her pa owns this bank. What'd you come to Elmore for? Is that a gold watch-chain? I'm going to get a bulldog. Got any more dimes?"

Jimmy went to the Planters' Hotel, registered as Ralph D. Spencer, and engaged a room. He leaned on the desk and declared his platform to the clerk. He said he had come to Elmore to look for a location to go into business. How was the shoe business, now, in the town? He had thought of the shoe business. Was there an opening?

The clerk was impressed by the clothes and manner of Jimmy. He, himself, was something of a pattern of fashion to the thinly gilded youth of Elmore, but he now perceived his shortcomings. While trying to figure out Jimmy's manner of tying his four-in-hand he cordially gave information.

Yes, there ought to be a good opening in the shoe line. There wasn't an exclusive shoe-store in the place. The dry-goods and general stores handled them. Business in all lines was fairly good. Hoped Mr. Spencer would decide to locate in Elmore. He would find it a pleasant town to live in, and the people very sociable.

Mr. Spencer thought he would stop over in the town a few days and look over the situation. No, the clerk needn't call the boy. He would carry up his suitcase, himself; it was rather heavy.

Mr. Ralph Spencer, the phœnix that arose from Jimmy Valentine's ashes—ashes left by the flame of a sudden and alternative attack of love—remained in Elmore, and prospered. He opened a shoe-store and secured a good run of trade.

Socially he was also a success, and made many friends. And he accomplished the wish of his heart. He met Miss Annabel Adams, and became more and more captivated by her charms.

At the end of a year the situation of Mr. Ralph Spencer was this: he had won the respect of the community, his shoe-store was flourishing, and he and Annabel were engaged to be married in two weeks. Mr. Adams, the typical, plodding, country banker, approved of Spencer. Annabel's pride in him almost equalled her affection. He was as much at home in the family of Mr. Adams and that of Annabel's married sister as if he were already a member.

One day Jimmy sat down in his room and wrote this letter, which he mailed to the safe address of one of his old friends in St. Louis:

Dear Old Pal:

I want you to be at Sullivan's place, in Little Rock, next Wednesday night at nine o'clock. I want you to wind up some little matters for me. And, also, I want to make you a present of my kit of tools. I know you'll be glad to get them—you couldn't duplicate the lot for a thousand dollars. Say, Billy, I've quit the old business—a year ago. I've got a nice store. I'm making an honest living, and I'm going to marry the finest girl on earth two weeks from now. It's the only life, Billy—the straight one. I wouldn't touch a dollar of another man's money now for a million. After I get married I'm going to sell out and go West, where there won't be so much danger of having old scores brought up against me. I tell you, Billy, she's an angel. She believes in me; and I wouldn't do another crooked thing for the whole world. Be sure to be at Sully's, for I must see you. I'll bring along the tools with me.

Your old friend,
Jimmy

On the Monday night after Jimmy wrote this letter, Ben Price jogged unobtrusively into Elmore in a livery buggy. He lounged about town in his quiet way until he found out what he wanted to know. From the drug-store across the street from Spencer's shoe-store he got a good look at Ralph D. Spencer.

"Going to marry the banker's daughter are you, Jimmy?" said Ben to himself, softly. "Well, I don't know!"

The next morning Jimmy took breakfast at the Adamses. He was going to Little Rock that day to order his wedding-suit and buy something nice for Annabel. That would be the first time he had left town since he came to Elmore. It had been more than a year now since those last professional "jobs," and he thought he could safely venture out.

After breakfast quite a family party went down town together—Mr. Adams, Annabel, Jimmy, and Annabel's married sister with her two little girls, aged five and nine. They came by the hotel where Jimmy still boarded, and he ran up to his room and brought along his suitcase. Then they went on to the bank. There stood Jimmy's horse and buggy and Dolph Gibson, who was going to drive him over to the railroad station.

All went inside the high, carved oak railings into the banking-room—Jimmy included, for Mr. Adams's future son-in-law was welcome anywhere. The clerks were pleased to be greeted by the good-looking, agreeable young man who was going to marry Miss Annabel. Jimmy set his suitcase down. Annabel, whose heart was bubbling with happiness and lively youth, put on Jimmy's hat and picked up the suitcase. "Wouldn't I make a nice drummer?" said Annabel. "My! Ralph, how heavy it is. Feels like it was full of gold bricks."

"Lot of nickel-plated shoe-horns in there," said Jimmy, coolly, "that I'm going to return. Thought I'd save express charges by taking them up. I'm getting awfully economical."

The Elmore Bank had just put in a new safe and vault. Mr. Adams was very proud of it, and insisted on an inspection by every one. The vault was a small one, but it had a new patented door. It fastened with three solid steel bolts thrown simultaneously with a single handle, and had a time-lock. Mr. Adams beamingly explained its workings to Mr. Spencer, who showed a courteous but not too intelligent interest. The two children, May and Agatha, were delighted by the shining metal and funny clock and knobs.

While they were thus engaged Ben Price sauntered in and leaned on his elbow, looking casually inside between the railings. He told the teller that he didn't want anything; he was just waiting for a man he knew.

Suddenly there was a scream or two from the women, and a commotion. Unperceived by the elders, May, the nine-year-old girl, in a spirit of play, had shut Agatha in the vault. She had then shot the bolts and turned the knob of the combination as she had seen Mr. Adams do.

The old banker sprang to the handle and tugged at it for a moment. "The door can't be opened," he groaned. "The clock hasn't been wound nor the combination set."

Agatha's mother screamed again, hysterically.

"Hush!" said Mr. Adams, raising his trembling hand. "All be quiet for a moment, Agatha!" he called as loudly as he could: "Listen to me." During the following silence they could just hear the faint sound of the child wildly shrieking in the dark vault in a panic of terror.

"My precious darling!" wailed the mother. "She will die of fright! Open the door! Oh, break it open! Can't you men do something?"

"There isn't a man nearer than Little Rock who can open that door," said Mr. Adams, in a shaky voice. "My God! Spencer, what shall we do? That child—she can't stand it long in there. There isn't enough air, and, besides, she'll go into convulsions from fright."

Agatha's mother, frantic now, beat the door of the vault with her hands. Somebody wildly suggested dynamite. Annabel turned to Jimmy, her large eyes full of anguish, but not yet despairing. To a woman nothing seems quite impossible to the powers of the man she worships.

"Can't you do something, Ralph—*try*, won't you?"

He looked at her with a queer, soft smile on his lips and in his keen eyes.

"Annabel," he said, "give me that rose you are wearing, will you?"

Hardly believing that she heard him aright, she unpinned the bud from the bosom of her dress, and placed it in his hand. Jimmy stuffed it into his vest-pocket, threw off his coat and pulled up his shirt-sleeves. With that act Ralph D. Spencer passed away and Jimmy Valentine took his place.

"Get away from the door, all of you," he commanded, shortly.

He set his suitcase on the table, and opened it out flat. From that time on he seemed to be unconscious of the presence of any one else. He laid out the shining, queer implements swiftly and orderly, whistling softly to himself as he always did when at work. In a deep silence and immovable, the others watched him as if under a spell.

In a minute Jimmy's pet drill was biting smoothly into the steel door. In ten minutes—breaking his own burglarious record—he threw back the bolts and opened the door.

Agatha, almost collapsed, but safe, was gathered into her mother's arms.

Jimmy Valentine put on his coat, and walked outside the railings toward the front door. As he went he thought he heard a far-away voice that he once knew call "Ralph!" But he never hesitated.

At the door a big man stood somewhat in his way.

"Hello, Ben!" said Jimmy, still with his strange smile. "Got around at last, have you? Well, let's go. I don't know that it makes much difference, now."

And then Ben Price acted rather strangely.

"Guess you're mistaken, Mr. Spencer," he said. "Don't believe I recognize you. Your buggy's waiting for you, ain't it?"

And Ben Price turned and strolled down the street.

The Higher Pragmatism

Where to go for wisdom has become a question of serious import. The ancients are discredited; Plato is boiler-plate; Aristotle is tottering; Marcus Aurelius is reeling; Æsop has been copyrighted by Indiana; Solomon is too solemn; you couldn't get anything out of Epictetus with a pick.

The ant, which for many years served as a model of intelligence and industry in the school-readers, has been proven to be a doddering idiot and a waster of time and effort. The owl to-day is hooted at. Chautauqua conventions have abandoned culture and adopted diabolo. Graybeards give glowing testimonials to the venders of patent hair-restorers. There are typographical errors in the almanacs published by the daily newspapers. College professors have become——

But there shall be no personalities.

To sit in classes, to delve into the encyclopedia or the past-performances page, will not make us wise. As the poet says, "Knowledge comes, but wisdom lingers." Wisdom is due, which, while we know it not, soaks into us, refreshes us, and makes us grow. Knowledge is a strong stream of water turned on us through a hose. It disturbs our roots.

Then, let us rather gather wisdom. But how to do so requires knowledge. If we know a thing, we know it; but very often we are not wise to it that we are wise, and——

But let's go on with the story.

II   Once upon a time I found a ten-cent magazine lying on a bench in a little city park. Anyhow, that was the amount he asked me for when I sat on the bench next to him. He was a musty, dingy, and tattered magazine, with some queer stories bound in him, I was sure. He turned out to be a scrap-book.

"I am a newspaper reporter," I said to him, to try him. "I have been detailed to write up some of the experiences of the unfortunate ones who spend their evenings in this park. May I ask you to what you attribute your downfall in——"

I was interrupted by a laugh from my purchase—a laugh so rusty and unpractised that I was sure it had been his first for many a day.

"Oh, no, no," said he. "You ain't a reporter. Reporters don't talk that way. They pretend to be one of us, and say they've just got on the blind baggage from St. Louis. I can tell a reporter on sight. Us park bums get to be fine judges of human nature. We sit here all day and watch the people go by. I can size up anybody who walks past my bench in a way that would surprise you."

"Well," I said, "go on and tell me. How do you size me up?"

"I should say," said the student of human nature with unpardonable hesitation, "that you was, say, in the contracting business—or maybe worked in a store—or was a sign-painter. You stopped in the park to finish your cigar, and thought you'd get a little free monologue out of me. Still, you might be a plasterer or a lawyer—it's getting kind of dark, you see. And your wife won't let you smoke at home."

I frowned gloomily.

"But, judging again," went on the reader of men, "I'd say you ain't got a wife."

"No," said I, rising restlessly. "No, no, no, I ain't. But I *will* have, by the arrows of Cupid. That is if——"

My voice must have trailed away and muffled itself in uncertainty and despair.

"I see you have a story yourself," said the dusty vagrant—imprudently, it seemed to me. "Suppose you take your dime back and spin your yarn for me. I'm interested myself in the ups and downs of unfortunate ones who spend their evenings in the park."

Somehow, that amused me. I looked at the frowsy derelict with more interest. I did have a story. Why not tell it to him? I had told none of my friends. I had always been a reserved and bottled-up man. It was psychical timidity or sensitiveness—perhaps both. And I smiled to myself in wonder when I felt an impulse to confide in this stranger and vagabond.

"Jack," said I.

"Mack," said he.

"Mack," said I, "I'll tell you."

"Do you want the dime back in advance?" said he. I handed him a dollar.

"The dime," said I, "was the price of listening to *your* story."

"Right on the point of the jaw," said he. "Go on."

And then, incredible as it may seem to the lovers in the world who confide their sorrows only to the night wind and the gibbous moon, I laid bare my secret to that wreck of all things that you would have supposed to be in sympathy with love.

I told him of the days and weeks and months that I had spent in adoring Mildred Telfair. I spoke of my despair, my grievous days and wakeful nights, my dwindling hopes and distress of mind. I even pictured to this night-prowler her beauty and dignity, the great sway she had in society, and the magnificence of her life as the elder daughter of an ancient race whose pride overbalanced the dollars of the city's millionaires.

"Why don't you cop the lady out?" asked Mack, bringing me down to earth and dialect again.

I explained to him that my worth was so small, my income so minute, and my fears so large that I hadn't the courage to speak to her of my worship. I told him that in her presence I could only blush and stammer, and that she looked upon me with a wonderful, maddening smile of amusement.

"She kind of moves in the professional class, don't she?" asked Mack.

"The Telfair family——" I began, haughtily.

"I mean professional beauty," said my hearer.

"She is greatly and widely admired," I answered, cautiously.

"Any sisters?"

"One."

"You know any more girls?"

"Why, several," I answered. "And a few others."

"Say," said Mack, "tell me one thing—can you hand out the dope to other girls? Can you chin 'em and make matinée eyes at 'em and squeeze 'em? You know what I mean. You're just shy when it comes to this particular dame—the professional beauty—ain't that right?"

"In a way you have outlined the situation with approximate truth," I admitted.

"I thought so," said Mack, grimly. "Now, that reminds me of my own case. I'll tell you about it."

I was indignant, but concealed it. What was this loafer's case or anybody's case compared with mine? Besides, I had given him a dollar and ten cents.

"Feel my muscle," said my companion, suddenly flexing his biceps. I did so mechanically. The fellows in gyms are always asking you to do that. His arm was as hard as cast-iron.

"Four years ago," said Mack, "I could lick any man in New York outside of the professional ring. Your case and mine is just the same. I come from the West Side—between Thirtieth and Fourteenth—and I won't give the number on the door. I was a scrapper when I was ten, and when I was twenty no amateur in the city could stand up four rounds with me. 'S a fact. You know Bill McCarty? No? He managed the smokers for some of them swell clubs. Well, I knocked out everything Bill brought up before me. I was a middle-weight, but could train down to a welter when necessary. I boxed all over the West Side at bouts and benefits and private entertainments, and was never put out once.

"But, say, the first time I put my foot in the ring with a professional I was no more than a canned lobster. I dunno how it was—I seemed to lose heart. I guess I got too much imagination. There was a formality and publicness about it that kind of weakened my nerve. I never won a fight in the ring. Light-weights and all kinds of scrubs used to sign up with my manager and then walk up and tap me on the wrist and see me fall. The minute I seen the crowd and a lot of gents in evening clothes down in front, and seen a professional come inside the ropes, I got as weak as ginger-ale.

"Of course, it wasn't long till I couldn't get no backers, and I didn't have any more chances to fight a professional—or many amateurs, either. But lemme tell you—I was as good as most men inside the ring or out. It was just that dumb, dead feeling I had when I was up against a regular that always done me up.

"Well, sir, after I had got out of the business, I got a mighty grouch on. I used to go round town licking private citizens and all kinds of unprofessionals just to please myself. I'd lick cops in dark streets and car-conductors and cab-drivers and draymen whenever I could start a row with 'em. It didn't make any difference how big they were, or how much science they had, I got away with 'em. If I'd only just have had the confidence in the ring that I had beating up the best men outside of it, I'd be wearing black pearls and heliotrope silk socks to-day.

"One evening I was walking along near the Bowery, thinking about things, when along comes a slumming-party. About six or seven they was, all in sallowtails, and these silk hats that don't shine. One of the gang kind of shoves me off the sidewalk. I hadn't had a scrap in three days, and I just says, 'De-light-ed' and hits him back of the ear.

"Well, we had it. That Johnnie put up as decent a little fight as you'd want to see in the moving pictures. It was on a side street, and no cops around. The other guy had a lot of science, but it only took me about six minutes to lay him out.

"Some of the swallowtails dragged him up against some steps and began to fan him. Another one of 'em comes over to me and says:

" 'Young man, do you know what you've done?'

" 'Oh, beat it,' says I. 'I've done nothing but a little punching-bag work. Take Freddy back to Yale and tell him to quit studying sociology on the wrong side of the sidewalk.'

" 'My good fellow,' says he, 'I don't know who you are, but I'd like to. You've knocked out Reddy Burns, the champion middle-weight of the world! He came to New York yesterday, to try to get a match on with Jim Jeffries. If you—'

"But when I come out of my faint I was laying on the floor in a drugstore saturated with aromatic spirits of ammonia. If I'd known that was Reddy Burns, I'd have got down in the gutter and crawled past him instead of handing him one like I did. Why, if I'd ever been in a ring and seen him climbing over the ropes, I'd have been all to the sal-volatile.

"So that's what imagination does," concluded Mack. "And as I said, your case and mine is simultaneous. You'll never win out. You can't go up against the professionals. I tell you, it's a park bench for yours in this romance business."

Mack, the pessimist, laughed harshly.

"I'm afraid I don't see the parallel," I said, coldly. "I have only a very slight acquaintance with the prize ring."

The derelict touched my sleeve with his fore-finger, for emphasis, as he explained his parable.

"Every man," said he, with some dignity, "has got his lamps on something that looks good to him. With you, it's this dame that you're afraid to say your say to. With me, it was to win out in the ring. Well, you'll lose just like I did."

"Why do you think I shall lose?" I asked, warmly.

" 'Cause," said he, "you're afraid to go in the ring. You dassen't stand up before a professional. Your case and mine is just the same. You're a amateur; and that means that you'd better keep outside of the ropes."

"Well, I must be going," I said, rising and looking with elaborate care at my watch.

When I was twenty feet away the park-bencher called to me.

"Much obliged for the dollar," he said. "And for the dime. But you'll never get 'er. You're in the amateur class."

"Serves you right," I said to myself, "for hobnobbing with a tramp. His impudence!"

But, as I walked, his words seemed to repeat themselves over and over again in my brain. I think I even grew angry at the man.

"I'll show him!" I finally said, aloud. "I'll show him that I can fight Reddy Burns, too—even knowing who he is."

I hurried to a telephone-booth and rang up the Telfair residence.

A soft, sweet voice answered. Didn't I know that voice? My hand holding the receiver shook.

"Is that *you?*" said I, employing the foolish words that form the vocabulary of every talker through the telephone.

"Yes, this is I," came back the answer in the low, clear-cut tones that are an inheritance of Telfairs. "Who is it, please?"

"It's me," said I, less ungrammatically than egotistically. "It's me, and I've got a few things that I want to say to you right now and immediately and straight to the point."

"*Dear* me," said the voice. "Oh, it's you, Mr. Arden!"

I wondered if any accent on the first word was intended. Mildred was fine at saying things that you had to study out afterward.

"Yes," said I, "I hope so. And now to come down to brass tacks." I thought that rather a vernacularism, if there is such a word, as soon as I had said it; but I didn't stop to apologize. "You know, of course, that I love you, and that I have been in that idiotic state for a long time. I don't want any more foolishness about it—that is, I mean I want an answer from you right now. Will you marry me or not? Hold the wire, please. Keep out, Central. Hello, hello! Will you, or will you *not?*"

That was just the uppercut for Reddy Burns' chin. The answer came back:

"Why, Phil, dear, of course I will! I didn't know that you—that is, you never said—oh, come up to the house, please—I can't say what I want to over the 'phone. You are so importunate. But please come up to the house, won't you?"

Would I?

I rang the bell of the Telfair house violently. Some sort of a human came to the door and shooed me into the drawing-room.

"Oh, well," said I to myself, looking at the ceiling, "any one can learn from any one. That was a pretty good philosophy of Mack's, anyhow. He didn't take advantage of his experience, but I get the benefit of it. If you want to get into the professional class, you've got to——"

I stopped thinking then. Someone was coming down the stairs. My knees began to shake. I knew then how Mack had felt when a professional began to climb over the ropes. I looked around foolishly for a door or a window by which I might escape. If it had been any other girl approaching, I mightn't have——

But just then the door opened, and Bess, Mildred's younger sister, came in. I'd never seen her look so much like a glorified angel. She walked straight up to me, and—and——

I'd never noticed before what perfectly wonderful eyes and hair Elizabeth Telfair had.

"Phil," she said, in the Telfair sweet, thrilling tones, "why didn't you tell me about it before? I thought it was sister you wanted all the time, until you telephoned to me a few minutes ago!"

I suppose Mack and I always will be hopeless amateurs. But, as the thing has turned out in my case, I'm mighty glad of it.

Conscience in Art

"I never could hold my partner, Andy Tucker, down to legitimate ethics of pure swindling," said Jeff Peters to me one day.

"Andy had too much imagination to be honest. He used to devise schemes of money-getting so fraudulent and high-financial that they wouldn't have been allowed in the bylaws of a railroad rebate system.

"Myself, I never believed in taking any man's dollars unless I gave him something for it—something in the way of rolled gold jewelry, garden seeds, lumbago lotion, stock certificates, stove polish or a crack on the head to show for his money. I guess I must have had New England ancestors away back and inherited some of their stanch and rugged fear of the police.

"But Andy's family tree was in different kind. I don't think he could have traced his descent any further back than a corporation.

"One summer while we was in the middle West, working down the Ohio valley with a line of family albums, headache powders and roach destroyer, Andy takes one of his notions of high and actionable financiering.

" 'Jeff,' says he, 'I've been thinking that we ought to drop these rutabaga fanciers and give our attention to something more nourishing and prolific. If we keep on snapshooting these hinds for their egg money we'll be classed as nature fakers. How about plunging into the fastnesses of the sky-scraper country and biting some big bull caribous in the chest?'

" 'Well,' says I, 'you know my idiosyncrasies. I prefer a

square, nonillegal style of business such as we are carrying on now. When I take money I want to leave some tangible object in the other fellow's hands for him to gaze at and to distract his attention from my spoor, even if it's only a Komical Kuss Trick Finger Ring for Squirting Perfume in a Friend's Eye. But if you've got a fresh idea, Andy,' says I, 'let's have a look at it. I'm not so wedded to petty graft that I would refuse something better in the way of a subsidy.'

" 'I was thinking,' says Andy, 'of a little hunt without horn, hound or camera among the great herd of the Midas Americanus, commonly known as the Pittsburg millionaires.'

" 'In New York?' I asks.

" 'No, sir,' says Andy, 'in Pittsburg. That's their habitat. They don't like New York. They go there now and then just because it's expected of 'em.'

" 'A Pittsburg Millionaire in New York is like a fly in a cup of hot coffee—he attracts attention and comment, but he don't enjoy it. New York ridicules him for "blowing" so much money in that town of sneaks and snobs, and sneers. The truth is, he don't spend anything while he is true. I saw a memorandum of expenses for a ten days' trip to Bunkum Town made by a Pittsburg man worth $15,000,000 once. Here's the way he set it down:

R. R. fare to and from	$ —	21 00
Cab fare to and from hotel		2 00
Hotel bill $5 per day		50 00
Tips		5,750 00
TOTAL	$	5,823 00

" 'That's the voice of New York,' goes on Andy. 'The town's nothing but a head waiter. If you tip it too much it'll go and stand by the door and make fun of you to the hat check boy. When a Pittsburger wants to spend money and have a good time he stays at home. That's where we'll go to catch him.'

"Well, to make a dense story more condensed, me and Andy cached our paris green and antipyrine powders and albums in a friend's cellar, and took the trail to Pittsburg. Andy didn't have any especial prospectus of chicanery and violence drawn up, but he always had plenty of confidence that his immoral nature would rise to any occasion that presented itself.

"As a concession to my ideas of self-preservation and rectitude he promised that if I should take an active and incriminating part in any little business venture that we might work up, there should be something actual and cognizant to the senses of touch, sight, taste or smell to transfer to the victim for the money so my conscience might rest easy. After that I felt better and entered more cheerfully into the foul play.

" 'Andy,' says I, as we strayed through the smoke along the cinderpath they call Smithfield Street, 'had you figured out how we are going to get acquainted with these coke kings and pig iron squeezers? Not that I would decry my own worth or system of drawing-room deportment, and work with the olive fork and pie knife,' says I, 'but isn't the entree nous into the salons of the stogie smokers going to be harder than you imagined?'

" 'If there's any handicap at all,' says Andy, 'it's our own refinement and inherent culture. Pittsburg millionaires are a fine body of plain, wholehearted, unassuming, democratic men.

" 'They are rough but uncivil in their manners, and though their ways are boisterous and unpolished, under it all they have a great deal of impoliteness and discourtesy. Nearly every one of 'em rose from obscurity,' says Andy, 'and they'll live in it till the town gets to using smoke consumers. If we act simple and unaffected and don't go too far from the saloons and keep making a noise like an import duty on steel rails we won't have any trouble in meeting some of 'em socially.'

"Well, Andy and me drifted about town three or four days getting our bearings. We got to knowing several millionaires by sight.

"One used to stop his automobile in front of our hotel and have a quart of champagne brought out to him. When the waiter opened it he'd turn it up to his mouth and drink it out of the bottle. That showed he used to be a glass-blower before he made his money.

"One evening Andy failed to come to the hotel for dinner. About 11 o'clock he came into my room.

" 'Landed one, Jeff,' says he. 'Twelve millions. Oil, rolling mills, real estate and natural gas. He's a fine man; no airs about him. Made all his money in the last five years. He's got professors posting him up now on education—art and literature and haberdashery and such things.

" 'When I saw him he'd just won a bet of $10,000 with a Steel Corporation man that there'd be four suicides in the Allegheny rolling mills to-day. So everybody in sight had to walk up and have drinks on him. He took a fancy to me and asked me to dinner with him. We went to a restaurant in Diamond Alley and sat on stools and had sparkling Moselle and clam chowder and apple fritters.

" 'Then he wanted to show me his bachelor apartment on Liberty Street. He's got ten rooms over a fish market with privilege of the bath on the next floor above. He told me it cost him $18,000 to furnish his apartment, and I believe it.

" 'He's got $40,000 worth of pictures in one room, and $20,000 worth of curios and antiques in another. His name's Scudder, and he's 45, and taking lessons on the piano and 15,000 barrels of oil a day out of his wells.'

" 'All right,' says I. 'Preliminary canter satisfactory. But, kay vooly, voo? What good is the art junk to us? And the oil?'

" 'Now, that man,' says Andy, sitting thoughtfully on the bed, 'ain't what you would call an ordinary scutt. When he was showing me his cabinet of art curios his face lighted up like the door of a coke oven. He says that if some of his big deals go through he'll make J. P. Morgan's collection of sweatshop tapestry and Augusta, Me., beadwork look like the contents of an ostrich's craw thrown on a screen by a magic lantern.

" 'And then he showed me a little carving,' went on Andy, 'that anybody could see was a wonderful thing. It was something like 2,000 years old, he said. It was a lotus flower with a woman's face in it carved out of a solid piece of ivory.

" 'Scudder looks it up in a catalogue and describes it. An Egyptian carver named Khafra made two of 'em for King Rameses II about the year B.C. The other one can't be found. The junkshops and antique bugs have rubbered all Europe for it, but it seems to be out of stock. Scudder paid $2,000 for the one he has.'

" 'Oh, well,' says I, 'this sounds like the purling of a rill to me. I thought we came here to teach the millionaires business, instead of learning art from 'em?'

" 'Be patient,' says Andy, kindly. 'Maybe we will see a rift in the smoke ere long.'

"All the next morning Andy was out. I didn't see him until about noon. He came to the hotel and called me into his room across the hall. He pulled a roundish bundle about as big as a goose egg out of his pocket and unwrapped it. It was an ivory carving just as he had described the millionaire's to me.

" 'I went in an old second-hand store and pawnshop a while ago,' says Andy, 'and I see this half hidden under a lot of old daggers and truck. The pawnbroker said he'd had it several years and thinks it was soaked by some Arabs or Turks or some foreign dubs that used to live down by the river.

" 'I offered him $2 for it, and I must have looked like I wanted it, for he said it would be taking the pumpernickel out of his children's mouths to hold any conversation that did not lead up to a price of $335. I finally got it for $25.

" 'Jeff,' goes on Andy, 'this is the exact counterpart of Scudder's carving. It's absolutely a dead ringer for it. He'll pay $2,000 for it as quick as he'd tuck a napkin under his chin. And why shouldn't it be the genuine other one, anyhow, that the old gypsy whittled out?'

" 'Why not, indeed?' says I. 'And how shall we go about compelling him to make a voluntary purchase of it?'

"Andy had his plan all ready, and I'll tell you how we carried it out.

"I got a pair of blue spectacles, put on my black frock coat, rumpled my hair up and became Prof. Pickleman. I went to another hotel, registered, and sent a telegram to Scudder to come to see me at once on important art business. The elevator dumped him on me in less than an hour. He was a foggy man with a clarion voice, smelling of Connecticut wrappers and naphtha.

" 'Hello, Profess!' he shouts. 'How's your conduct?'

"I rumpled my hair some more and gave him a blue glass stare.

" 'Sir,' says I. 'Are you Cornelius T. Scudder? Of Pittsburg, Pennsylvania?'

" 'I am,' says he. 'Come out and have a drink.'

" 'I have neither the time nor the desire,' says I, 'for such harmful and deleterious amusements. I have come from New York,' says I, 'on a matter of busi—on a matter of art.

" 'I learned there that you are the owner of an Egyptian ivory carving of the time of Rameses II., representing the head of Queen Isis in a lotus flower. There were only two of such carvings made. One has been lost for many years. I recently discovered and purchased the other in a pawn—in an obscure museum in Vienna. I wish to purchase yours. Name your price.'

" 'Well, the great ice jams, Profess!' says Scudder. 'Have you found the other one? Me sell? No. I don't guess Cornelius Scudder needs to sell anything that he wants to keep. Have you got the carving with you, Profess?'

"I shows it to Scudder. He examines it careful all over.

" 'It's the article,' says he. 'It's a duplicate of mine, every line and curve of it. Tell you what I'll do,' he says. 'I won't sell, but I'll buy. Give you $2,500 for yours.'

" 'Since you won't sell, I will,' says I. 'Large bills please. I'm a man of few words. I must return to New York to-night. I lecture to-morrow at the aquarium.'

"Scudder sends a check down and the hotel cashes it. He goes off with the piece of antiquity and I hurry back to Andy's hotel, according to arrangement.

"Andy is walking up and down the room looking at his watch.

" 'Well?' he says.

" 'Twenty-five hundred,' says I. 'Cash.'

" 'We've got just eleven minutes,' says Andy, 'to catch the B. & O. westbound. Grab your baggage.'

" 'What's the hurry?' says I. 'It was a square deal. And even if it was only an imitation of the original carving it'll take him some time to find it out. He seemed to be sure it was the genuine article.'

" 'It was,' says Andy. 'It was his own. When I was looking at his curios yesterday he stepped out of the room for a moment and I pocketed it. Now, will you pick up your suit case and hurry?'

" 'Then,' says I, 'why was that story about finding another one in the pawn—'

" 'Oh,' says Andy, 'out of respect for that conscience of yours. Come on.' "

The Ethics of Pig

On an east-bound train I went into the smoker and found Jefferson Peters, the only man with a brain west of the Wabash River who can use his cerebrum and cerebellum, and medulla oblongata at the same time.

Jeff is in the line of unillegal graft. He is not to be dreaded by widows and orphans; he is a reducer of surplusage. His favorite disguise is that of the target-bird at which the spendthrift or the rockless investor may shy a few inconsequentional dollars. He is readily vocalized by tobacco; so, with the aid of two thick and easy-burning brevas, I got the story of his latest Autolycan adventure.

"In my line of business," said Jeff, "the hardest thing is to find an upright, trustworthy, strictly honorable partner to work a graft with. Some of the best men I ever worked with in a swindle would resort to trickery at times.

"So, last summer, I thinks I will go over into this section of country where I hear the serpent has not yet entered, and see if I can find a partner naturally gifted with a talent for crime, but not yet contaminated by success.

"I found a village that seemed to show the right kind of a layout. The inhabitants hadn't found out that Adam had been dispossessed, and were going right along naming the animals and killing snakes just as if they were in the Garden of Eden. They call this town Mount Nebo, and it's up near the spot where Kentucky and West Virginia and North Carolina corner together. Them States don't meet? Well, it was in that neighborhood, anyway.

"After putting in a week proving I wasn't a revenue officer, I went over to the store where the rude fourflushers of the hamlet lied, to see if I could get a line on the kind of man I wanted.

" 'Gentlemen,' says I, after we had rubbed noses and gathered 'round the dried-apple barrel. 'I don't suppose there's another community in the whole world into which sin and chicanery has less extensively permeated than this. Life here, where all the women are brave and propitious and all the men honest and expedient, must, indeed, be an idol. It reminds me,' says I, 'of Goldstein's beautiful ballad entitled "The Deserted Village," which says:

'Ill fares the land, to hastening ills a prey;
    What art can drive its charms away?
The judge rode slowly down the lane, mother.
    For I'm to be Queen of the May.'

" 'Why, yes, Mr. Peters,' says the storekeeper. 'I reckon we air about as moral and torpid a community as there be on the mounting, according to censuses of opinion; but I reckon you ain't ever met Rufe Tatum.'

" 'Why, no,' says the town constable, 'he can't hardly have ever. That air Rufe is shore the monstrousest scalawag that has escaped hangin' on the galluses. And that puts me in mind that I ought to have turned Rufe out of the lockup day before yesterday. The thirty days he got for killin' Yance Goodloe was up then. A day or two more won't hurt Rufe any, though.'

" 'Shucks, now,' says I, in the mountain idiom, 'don't tell me there's a man in Mount Nebo as bad as that.'

" 'Worse,' says the storekeeper. 'He steals hogs.'

"I think I will look up this Mr. Tatum; so a day or two after the constable turned him out I got acquainted with him and invited him out on the edge of town to sit on a log and talk business.

"What I wanted was a partner with a natural rural make-up to play a part in some little one-act outrages that I was going to book with the Pitfall & Gin circuit in some of the Western towns; and this R. Tatum was born for the rôle as sure as nature cast Fairbanks for the stuff that kept *Eliza* from sinking into the river.

"He was about the size of a first baseman; and he had ambiguous blue eyes like the china dog on the mantelpiece that Aunt Harriet used to play with when she was a child. His hair waved a little bit like the statue of the dinkus-thrower in the vacation at Rome, but the color of it reminded you of the 'Sunset in the Grand Cañon, by an American Artist,' that they hang over the stove-pipe holes in the salongs. He was the Reub, without needing a touch. You'd have known him for one, even if you'd seen him on the vaudeville stage with one cotton suspender and a straw over his ear.

"I told him what I wanted, and found him ready to jump at the job.

" 'Overlooking such a trivial little peccadillo as the habit of manslaughter,' says I, 'what have you accomplished in the way of indirect brigandage or non-actionable thriftiness that you could point to, with or without pride, as an evidence of your qualifications for the position?'

" 'Why,' says he, in his kind of Southern system of procrastinated accents, 'hain't you heard tell? There ain't any man, black or white, in the Blue Ridge that can tote off a shoat as easy as I can without bein' heard, seen, or cotched. I can lift a shoat,' he goes on, 'out of a pen, from under a porch, at the trough, in the woods, day or night, anywhere or anyhow, and I guarantee nobody won't hear a squeal. It's all in the way you grab hold of 'em and carry 'em afterwards. Some day,' goes on this gentle despoiler of pig-pens, 'I hope to become reckernized as the champion shoat-stealer of the world.'

" 'It's proper to be ambitious,' says I; 'and hog-stealing will do very well for Mount Nebo; but in the outside world, M. Tatum, it would be considered as crude a piece of business as a bear raid on Bay State Gas. However, it will do as a guarantee of good faith. We'll go into partnership. I've got a thousand dollars cash capital; and with that homeward-plods atmosphere of yours we ought to be able to win out a few shares of Soon Parted, preferred, in the money market.'

"So I attaches Rufe, and we go away from Mount Nebo down into the lowlands. And all the way I coach him for his part in the grafts I had in mind. I had idled away two months on the Florida coast, and was feeling all to the Ponce de Leon, besides having so many new schemes up my sleeve that I had to wear kimonos to hold 'em.

"I intended to assume a funnel shape and mow a path nine miles wide through the farming belt of the Middle West; so we headed in that direction. But when we got as far as Lexington we found Binkley Brothers' circus there, and the blue-grass peasantry romping into town and pounding the Belgian blocks with their hand-pegged sabots as artless and arbitrary as an extra session of a Datto Bryan duma. I never pass a circus without pulling the valve-cord and coming down for a little Key West money; so I engaged a couple of rooms and board for Rufe and me at a house near the circus grounds run by a widow lady named Peevy. Then I took Rufe to a clothing store and gent's-outfitted him. He showed up strong, as I knew he would, after he was rigged up in the ready-made rutabaga regalia. Me and old Misfitzky stuffed him into a bright blue suit with a Nile-green visible plaid effect, and riveted on a fancy vest of a light Tuskegee Normal tan color, a red necktie, and the yellowest pair of shoes in town.

"They were the first clothes Rufe had ever worn except the gingham layette and the butternut top-dressing of his native kraal, and he looked as self-conscious as an Igorrote with a new nose-ring.

"That night I went down to the circus tents and opened a small shell game. Rufe was to be the capper. I gave him a roll of phony currency to bet with and kept a bunch of it in a special pocket to pay his winnings out of. No; I didn't mistrust him; but I simply can't manipulate the ball to lose when I see real money bet. My fingers go on a strike every time I try it.

"I set up my little table and began to show them how easy it was to guess which shell the little pea was under. The unlettered hinds gathered in a thick semicircle and began to nudge elbows and banter one another to bet. Then was when Rufe ought to have single-footed up and called the turn on the little joker for a few tens and fives to get them started. But, no Rufe. I'd seen him two or three times walking about and looking at the side-show pictures with his mouth full of peanut candy; but he never came nigh.

"The crowd piked a little; but trying to work the shells

without a capper is like fishing without bait. I closed the game with only forty-two dollars of the unearned increment, while I had been counting on yanking the yeomen for two hundred at least. I went home at eleven and went to bed. I supposed that the circus had proved too alluring for Rufe, and that he had succumbed to it, concert and all; but I meant to give him a lecture on general business principles in the morning.

"Just after Morpheus had got both my shoulders to the shuck mattress I hears a houseful of unbecoming and ribald noises like a youngster screeching with green-apple colic. I opens my door and calls out in the hall for the widow lady, and when she sticks her head out, I says: 'Mrs. Peevy, ma'am, would you mind choking off that kid of yours so that honest people can get their rest?'

" 'Sir,' says she, 'it's no child of mine. It's the pig squealing that your friend Mr. Tatum brought home to his room a couple of hours ago. And if you are uncle or second cousin or brother to it, I'd appreciate your stopping its mouth, sir, yourself, if you please.'

"I put on some of the polite outside habiliments of external society and went into Rufe's room. He had gotten up and lit his lamp, and was pouring some milk into a tin pan on the floor for a dingy-white, half-grown, squealing pig.

" 'How is this, Rufe?' says I. 'You flimflammed in your part of the work to-night and put the game on crutches. And how do you explain the pig? It looks like back-sliding to me.'

" 'Now, don't be too hard on me, Jeff,' says he. 'You know how long I've been used to stealing shoats. It's got to be a habit with me. And to-night, when I see such a fine chance, I couldn't help takin' it.'

" 'Well,' says I, 'maybe you've really got kleptopigia. And maybe when we get out of the pig belt you'll turn your mind to higher and more remunerative misconduct. Why you should want to stain your soul with such a distasteful, feeble-minded, perverted, roaring beast as that I can't understand.'

" 'Why, Jeff,' says he, 'you ain't in sympathy with shoats. You don't understand 'em like I do. This here seems to me to be an animal of more than common powers of ration and intelligence. He walked half across the room on his hind legs a while ago.'

" 'Well, I'm going back to bed,' says I. 'See if you can impress it upon your friend's ideas of intelligence that he's not to make so much noise.'

" 'He was hungry,' says Rufe. 'He'll go to sleep and keep quiet now.'

"I always get up before breakfast and read the morning paper whenever I happen to be within the radius of a Hoe cylinder or a Washington hand-press. The next morning I got up early, and found a Lexington daily on the front porch where the carrier had thrown it. The first thing I saw in it was a double-column ad. on the front page that read like this:

FIVE THOUSAND DOLLARS REWARD

The above amount will be paid, and no questions asked, for the return, alive and uninjured, of Beppo, the famous European educated pig, that strayed or was stolen from the side-show tents of Binkley Bros.' circus last night.

GEO. B. TAPLEY, Business Manager
At the circus grounds.

"I folded up the paper flat, put it into my inside pocket, and went to Rufe's room. He was nearly dressed, and was feeding the pig the rest of the milk and some apple-peelings.

" 'Well, well, well, good-morning all,' I says, hearty and amiable. 'So we are up? And piggy is having his breakfast. What had you intended doing with that pig, Rufe?'

" 'I'm going to crate him up,' says Rufe, 'and express him to ma in Mount Nebo. He'll be company for her while I am away.'

" 'He's a mighty fine pig,' says I, scratching him on the back.

" 'You called him a lot of names last night,' says Rufe.

" 'Oh, well,' says I, 'he looks better to me this morning. I was raised on a farm, and I'm very fond of pigs. I used to go to bed at sundown, so I never saw one by lamplight before. Tell you what I'll do, Rufe,' I says. 'I'll give you ten dollars for that pig.'

" 'I reckon I wouldn't sell this shoat,' says he. 'If it was any other one I might.'

" 'Why not this one?' I asked, fearful that he might know something.

" 'Why, because,' says he, 'it was the grandest achievement of my life. There ain't airy other man that could have done it. If I ever have a fireside and children, I'll sit beside it and tell 'em how their daddy toted off a shoat from a whole circus full of people. And maybe my grandchildren, too. They'll certainly be proud a whole passel. Why,' says he, 'there was two tents, one openin' into the other. This shoat was on a platform, tied with a little chain. I seen a giant and a lady with a fine chance of bushy white hair in the other tent. I got the shoat and crawled out from under the canvas again without him squeakin' as loud as a mouse. I put him under my coat, and I must have passed a hundred folks before I got out where the streets was dark. I reckon I wouldn't sell that shoat, Jeff. I'd want ma to keep it, so there'd be a witness to what I done.'

" 'The pig won't live long enough,' I says, 'to use as an exhibit in your senile fireside mendacity. Your grandchildren will have to take your word for it. I'll give you one hundred dollars for the animal.'

"Rufe looked at me astonished.

" 'The shoat can't be worth anything like that to you,' he says. 'What do you want him for?'

" 'Viewing me casuistically,' says I, with a rare smile, 'you wouldn't think that I've got an artistic side to my temper. But I have. I'm a collector of pigs. I've scoured the world of unusual pigs. Over in the Wabash Valley I've got a hog ranch with most every specimen on it, from a Merino to a Poland China. This looks like a blooded pig to me, Rufe,' say I. 'I believe it's a genuine Berkshire. That's why I'd like to have it.'

" 'I'd shore like to accommodate you,' says he, 'but I've got the artistic tenement, too. I don't see why it ain't art when you can steal a shoat better than anybody else can. Shoats is a kind of inspiration and genius with me. Specially this one. I wouldn't take two hundred and fifty for that animal.'

" 'Now, listen,' says I, wiping off my forehead, it's not so much a matter of business with me as it is art; and not so much art as it is philanthropy. Being a connoisseur and disseminator of pigs, I wouldn't feel like I'd done my duty to the world unless I added that Berkshire to my collection. Not intrinsically, but according to the ethics of pigs as friends and coadjutors of mankind, I offer you five hundred dollars for the animal.'

" 'Jeff,' says this pork esthete, 'it ain't money; it's sentiment with me.'

" 'Seven hundred,' says I.

" 'Make it eight hundred,' says Rufe, 'and I'll crush the sentiment out of my heart.'

"I went under my clothes for my money-belt, and counted him out forty twenty-dollar gold certificates.

" 'I'll just take him into my own room,' says I, 'and lock him up till after breakfast.'

"I took the pig by the hind leg. He turned on a squeal like the steam calliope at the circus.

" 'Let me tote him in for you,' says Rufe; and he picks up the beast under one arm, holding his snout with the other hand, and packs him into my room like a sleeping baby.

"After breakfast Rufe, who had a chronic case of haberdashery ever since I got his trousseau, says he believes he will amble down to Misfitzky's and look over some royal-purple socks. And then I got as busy as a one-armed man with the nettle-rash pasting on wall-paper. I found an old negro man with an express wagon to hire; and we tied the pig in a sack and drove down to the circus grounds.

"I found George B. Tapley in a little tent with a window flap open. He was a fattish man with an immediate eye, in a black skull-cap with a four-ounce diamond screwed into the bosom of his red sweater.

" 'Are you George B. Tapley?' I asks.

" 'I swear it,' says he.

" 'Well, I've got it,' says I.

" 'Designate,' says he. 'Are you the guinea pigs for the Asiatic python or the alfalfa for the sacred buffalo?'

" 'Neither,' says I. 'I've got Beppo, the educated hog, in a sack in that wagon. I found him rooting up the flowers in my front yard this morning. I'll take the five thousand in large bills, if it's handy.'

"George B. hustles out of his tent, and asks me to follow. We went into one of the side-shows. In there was a jet black pig with a pink ribbon around his neck lying on some hay and eating carrots that a man was feeding him.

" 'Hey, Mac,' calls G. B. 'Nothing wrong with the world-wide this morning, is there?'

" 'Him? No,' says the man. 'He's got an appetite like a chorus girl at 1 A. M.'

" 'How'd you get this pipe?' says Tapley to me. 'Eating too many pork chops last night?'

"I pulls out the paper and shows him the ad.

" 'Fake,' says he. 'Don't know anything about it. You've beheld with your own eyes the marvelous, world-wide porcine wonder of the four-footed kingdom eating with preternatural sagacity his matutinal meal, unstrayed and unstole. Good-morning.'

"I was beginning to see. I got in the wagon and told Uncle Ned to drive to the most adjacent orifice of the nearest alley. There I took out my pig, got the range carefully for the other opening, set his sights, and gave him such a kick that he went out the other end of the alley twenty feet ahead of his squeal.

"Then I paid Uncle Ned his fifty cents, and walked down to the newspaper office. I wanted to hear it in cold syllables. I got the advertising man to his window.

" 'To decide a bet,' says I, 'wasn't the man who had this ad. put in last night short and fat, with long black whiskers and a club-foot?'

" 'He was not,' says the man. 'He would measure about six feet by four and a half inches, with corn-silk hair, and dressed like the pansies of the conservatory.'

"At dinner time I went back to Mrs. Peevy's.

" 'Shall I keep some soup hot for Mr. Tatum till he comes back?' she asks.

" 'If you do, ma'am,' says I, 'you'll more than exhaust for firewood all the coal in the bosom of the earth and all the forests on the outside of it.'

"So there, you see," said Jefferson Peters, in conclusion, "how hard it is ever to find a fair-minded and honest business-partner."

"But," I began, with the freedom of long acquaintance, "the rule should work both ways. If you had offered to divide the reward you would not have lost——"

Jeff's look of dignified reproach stopped me.

"That don't involve the same principles at all," said he.

"Mine was a legitimate and moral attempt at speculation. Buy low and sell high—don't Wall Street indorse it? Bulls and bears and pigs—what's the difference? Why not bristles as well as horns and fur?"

Jeff Peters as a Personal Magnet

Jeff Peters has been engaged in as many schemes for making money as there are recipes for cooking rice in Charleston, S.C.

Best of all I like to hear him tell of his earlier days when he sold liniments and cough cures on street corners, living hand to mouth, heart to heart with the people, throwing heads or tails with fortune for his last coin.

"I struck Fisher Hill, Arkansaw," said he, "in buckskin suit, moccasins, long hair and a thirty-carat diamond ring that I got from an actor in Texarkana. I don't know what he ever did with the pocket knife I swapped him for it.

"I was Dr. Waugh-hoo, the celebrated Indian medicine man. I carried only one best bet just then, and that was Resurrection Bitters. It was made of life-giving plants and herbs accidentally discovered by Ta-qua-la, the beautiful wife of the chief of the Choctaw Nation, while gathering truck to garnish a platter of boiled dog for the annual corn dance.

"Business hadn't been good at the last town, so I only had five dollars. I went to the Fisher Hill druggist and he credited me for a half gross of eight ounce bottles and corks. I had the labels and ingredients in my valise, left over from the last town. Life began to look rosy again after I got in my hotel room with the water running from the tap, and the Resurrection Bitters lining up on the table by the dozen.

"Fake? No, sir. There was two dollars' worth of fluid extract of cinchona and a dime's worth of aniline in that half-gross of bitters. I've gone through towns years afterwards and had folks ask for 'em again.

"I hired a wagon that night and commenced selling the bitters on Main Street. Fisher Hill was a low, malarial town; and a compound hypothetical pneumo-cardiac anti-scorbutic tonic was just what I diagnosed the crowd as needing. The bitters started off like sweetbreads-on-toast at a vegetarian dinner. I had sold two dozen at fifty cents apiece when I felt somebody pull my coat tail. I knew what that meant; so I climbed down and sneaked a five-dollar bill into the hand of a man with a German silver star on his lapel.

" 'Constable,' says I, 'it's a fine night.'

" 'Have you got a city license,' he asks, 'to sell this illegitimate essence of spooju that you flatter by the name of medicine?'

" 'I have not,' says I. 'I didn't know you had a city. If I can find it to-morrow I'll take one out if it's necessary.'

" 'I'll have to close you up till you do,' says the constable.

"I quit selling and went back to the hotel. I was talking to the landlord about it.

" 'Oh, you won't stand no show in Fisher Hill,' says he. 'Dr. Hoskins, the only doctor here, is a brother-in-law of the Mayor, and they won't allow no fake doctors to practice in town.'

"I don't practice medicine,' says I, 'I've got a State peddler's license, and I take out a city one wherever they demand it.'

"I went to the Mayor's office the next morning and they told me he hadn't showed up yet. They didn't know when he'd be down. So Doc Waugh-hoo hunches down again in a hotel chair and lights a jimpson-weed regalia, and waits.

"By and by a young man in a blue necktie slips into the chair next to me and asks the time.

" 'Half-past ten,' says I, 'and you are Andy Tucker. I've seen you work. Wasn't it you that put up the Great Cupid Combination package on the Southern States? Let's see, it was a Chilian diamond engagement ring, a wedding ring, a potato masher, a bottle of soothing syrup and Dorothy Vernon—all for fifty cents.'

"Andy was pleased to hear that I remembered him. He was

a good street man; and he was more than that—he respected his profession, and he was satisfied with 300 per cent. profit. He had plenty of offers to go into the illegitimate drug and garden seed business; but he was never to be tempted off of the straight path.

"I wanted a partner, so Andy and me agreed to go out together. I told him about the situation on Fisher Hill and how finances was low on account of the local mixture of politics and jalap. Andy had just got in on the train that morning. He was pretty low himself, and was going to canvass the town for a few dollars to build a new battleship by popular subscription at Eureka Springs. So we went out and sat on the porch and talked it over.

"The next morning at eleven o'clock when I was sitting there alone, an Uncle Tom shuffles into the hotel and asked for the doctor to come and see Judge Banks, who, it seems, was the mayor and a mighty sick man.

" 'I'm no doctor,' says I. 'Why don't you go and get the doctor?'

" 'Boss,' says he. 'Doc Hoskin am done gone twenty miles in the country to see some sick persons. He's de only doctor in de town, and Massa Banks am powerful bad off. He sent me to ax you to please, suh, come.'

" 'As man to man,' says I, 'I'll go and look him over.' So I put a bottle of Resurrection Bitters in my pocket and goes up on the hill to the mayor's mansion, the finest house in town, with a mansard roof and two cast-iron dogs on the lawn.

"This Mayor Banks was in bed all but his whiskers and feet. He was making internal noises that would have had everybody in San Francisco hiking for the parks. A young man was standing by the bed holding a cup of water.

" 'Doc,' says the Mayor. 'I'm awful sick. I'm about to die. Can't you do nothing for me?'

" 'Mr. Mayor,' says I, 'I'm not a regular preordained disciple of S. Q. Lapius, I never took a course in a medical college,' says I. 'I've just come as a fellow man to see if I could be of any assistance.'

" 'I'm deeply obliged,' says he. 'Doc Waugh-hoo, this is my nephew, Mr. Biddle. He has tried to alleviate my distress, but without success. Oh, Lordy! Ow-ow-ow!!' he sings out.

"I nods at Mr. Biddle and sets down by the bed and feels the mayor's pulse. 'Let me see your liver—your tongue, I mean,' says I. Then I turns up the lids of his eyes and looks close at the pupils of 'em.

" 'How long have you been sick?' I asked.

" 'I was taken down—ow-ouch—last night,' says the Mayor. 'Gimme something for it, Doc, won't you?'

" 'Mr. Fiddle,' says I, 'raise the window shade a bit, will you?'

" 'Biddle,' says the young man. 'Do you feel like you could eat some ham and eggs, Uncle James?'

" 'Mr. Mayor,' says I, after laying my ear to his right shoulder blade and listening, 'you've got a bad attack of super-inflammation of the right clavicle of the harpsichord!'

" 'Good Lord!' says he, with a groan. 'Can't you rub something on it, or set it or anything?'

"I picks up my hat and starts for the door.

" 'You ain't going, Doc?' says the Mayor with a howl. 'You ain't going away and leave me to die with this— superfluity of the clapboards, are you?'

" 'Common humanity, Dr. Whoa-ha,' says Mr. Biddle, 'ought to prevent your deserting a fellow-human in distress.'

" 'Dr. Waugh-hoo, when you get through plowing,' says I. And then I walks back to the bed and throws back my long hair.

" 'Mr. Mayor,' says I, 'there is only one hope for you. Drugs will do you no good. But there is another power higher yet, although drugs are high enough,' says I.

" 'And what is that?' says he.

" 'Scientific demonstrations,' says I. 'The triumph of mind over sarsaparilla. The belief that there is no pain and sickness except what is produced when we ain't feeling well. Declare yourself in arrears. Demonstrate.'

" 'What is this paraphernalia you speak of, Doc?' says the Mayor. 'You ain't a Socialist, are you?'

" 'I am speaking,' says I, 'of the great doctrine of psychic financiering—of the enlightened school of long-distance, sub-conscientious treatment of fallacies and meningitis—of that wonderful in-door sport known as personal magnetism.'

" 'Can you work it, Doc?' asks the Mayor.

" 'I'm one of the Sole Sanhedrims and Ostensible Hooplas

of the Inner Pulpit,' says I. 'The lame talk and the blind
rubber whenever I make a pass at 'em. I am a medium, a
coloratura hypnotist and a spirituous control. It was only
through me at the recent seances at Ann Arbor that the late
president of the Vinegar Bitters Company could revisit the
earth to communicate with his sister Jane. You see me ped-
dling medicine on the streets,' says I, 'to the poor. I don't
practice personal magnetism on them. I do not drag it in the
dust,' says I, 'because they haven't got the dust.'

" 'Will you treat my case?' asks the Mayor.

" 'Listen,' says I. 'I've had a good deal of trouble with
medical societies everywhere I've been. I don't practice
medicine. But, to save your life, I'll give you the psychic
treatment if you'll agree as mayor not to push the license
question.'

" 'Of course I will,' says he. 'And now get to work, Doc,
for them pains are coming on again.'

" 'My fee will be $250.00, cure guaranteed in two
treatments,' says I.

" 'All right,' says the Mayor. 'I'll pay it. I guess my life's
worth that much.'

"I sat down by the bed and looked him straight in the eye.

" 'Now,' says I, 'get your mind off the disease. You ain't
sick. You haven't got a heart or a clavicle or a funny bone or
brains or anything. You haven't got any pain. Declare error.
Now you feel the pain that you didn't have leaving, don't
you?'

" 'I do feel some little better, Doc,' says the Mayor,
'darned if I don't. Now state a few lies about my not having
this swelling in my left side, and I think I could be propped
up and have some sausage and buckwheat cakes.'

"I made a few passes with my hands.

" 'Now,' says I, 'the inflammation's gone. The right lobe
of the perihelion has subsided. You're getting sleepy. You
can't hold your eyes open any longer. For the present the
disease is checked. Now, you are asleep.'

"The Mayor shut his eyes slowly and began to snore.

" 'You observe, Mr. Tiddle,' says I, 'the wonders of
modern science.'

" 'Biddle,' says he. 'When will you give uncle the rest of
the treatment, Dr. Pooh-pooh?'

" 'Waugh-hoo,' says I. 'I'll come back at eleven to-morrow. When he wakes up give him eight drops of turpentine and three pounds of steak. Good morning.'

"The next morning I went back on time. 'Well, Mr. Riddle,' says I, when he opened the bedroom door, 'and how is uncle this morning?'

" 'He seems much better,' says the young man.

"The Mayor's color and pulse was fine. I gave him another treatment, and he said the last of the pain left him.

" 'Now,' says I, 'you'd better stay in bed for a day or two, and you'll be all right. It's a good thing I happened to be in Fisher Hill, Mr. Mayor,' says I, 'for all the remedies in the cornucopia that the regular schools of medicine use couldn't have saved you. And now that error has flew and pain proved a perjurer, let's allude to a cheerfuller subject—say the fee of $250. No checks, please, I hate to write my name on the back of a check almost as bad as I do on the front.'

" 'I've got the cash here,' says the Mayor, pulling a pocket book from under his pillow.

"He counts out five fifty-dollar notes and holds 'em in his hand.

" 'Bring the receipt,' he says to Biddle.

"I signed the receipt and the Mayor handed me the money. I put it in my inside pocket careful.

" 'Now do your duty, officer,' says the Mayor, grinning much unlike a sick man.

"Mr. Biddle lays his hand on my arm.

" 'You're under arrest, Dr. Waugh-hoo, alias Peters,' says he, 'for practising medicine without authority under the State law.'

" 'Who are you?' I asks.

" 'I'll tell you who he is,' says the Mayor, sitting up in bed. 'He's a detective employed by the State Medical Society. He's been following you over five counties. He came to me yesterday and we fixed up this scheme to catch you. I guess you won't do any more doctoring around these parts, Mr. Fakir. What was it you said I had, Doc?' the Mayor laughs, 'compound—well it wasn't softening of the brain, I guess, anyway.'

" 'A detective,' says I.

" 'Correct,' says Biddle. 'I'll have to turn you over to the sheriff.'

" 'Let's see you do it,' says I, and I grabs Biddle by the throat and half throws him out the window, but he pulls a gun and sticks it under my chin, and I stand still. Then he puts handcuffs on me, and takes the money out of my pocket.

" 'I witness,' says he, 'that they're the same bills that you and I marked, Judge Banks. I'll turn them over to the sheriff when we get to his office, and he'll send you a receipt. They'll have to be used as evidence in the case.'

" 'All right, Mr. Biddle,' says the Mayor. 'And now, Doc Waugh-hoo,' he goes on, 'why don't you demonstrate? Can't you pull the cork out of your magnetism with your teeth and hocus-pocus them handcuffs off?'

" 'Come on, officer,' says I, dignified. 'I may as well make the best of it.' And then I turns to old Banks and rattles my chains.

" 'Mr. Mayor,' says I, 'the time will come soon when you'll believe that personal magnetism is a success. And you'll be sure that it succeeded in this case, too.'

"And I guess it did.

"When we got nearly to the gate, I says: 'We might meet somebody now, Andy. I reckon you better take 'em off, and——' Hey? Why, of course it was Andy Tucker. That was his scheme; and that's how we got the capital to go into business together.''

A Tempered Wind

The first time my optical nerves was disturbed by the side of Buckingham Skinner was in Kansas City. I was standing on a corner when I see Buck stick his straw-colored head out of a third-story window of a business block and holler, "Whoa, there! Whoa!'' like you would in endeavoring to assuage a team of runaway mules.

I looked around; but all the animals I see in sight is a policeman, having his shoes shined, and a couple of delivery wagons hitched to posts. Then in a minute downstairs tumbles this Buckingham Skinner, and runs to the corner, and stands and gazes down the other street at the imaginary dust kicked up by the fabulous hoofs of the fictitious team of chimerical quadrupeds. And then B. Skinner goes back up to the third-story room again, and I see that the lettering on the window is "The Farmers' Friend Loan Company."

By and by Straw-top comes down again, and I crossed the street to meet him, for I had my ideas. Yes, sir, when I got close I could see where he overdone it. He was Reub all right as far as his blue jeans and cowhide boots went, but he had a matinée actor's hands, and the rye straw stuck over his ear looked like it belonged to the property man of the Old Homestead Co. Curiosity to know what his graft was got the best of me.

"Was that your team broke away and run just now?" I asks him, polite. "I tried to stop 'em," says I, "but I couldn't. I guess they're halfway back to the farm by now."

"Gosh blame them darned mules," says Straw-top, in a voice so good that I nearly apologized; "they're a'lus bustin' loose." And then he looks at me close, and then he takes off his hayseed hat, and says, in a different voice:

"I'd like to shake hands with Parleyvoo Pickens, the greatest street man in the West, barring only Montague Silver, which you can no more than allow."

I let him shake hands with me.

"I learned under Silver," I said; "I don't begrudge him the lead. But what's your graft, son? I admit that the phantom flight of the non-existing animals at which you remarked 'Whoa!' has puzzled me somewhat. How do you win out on the trick?"

Buckingham Skinner blushed.

"Pocket money," says he; "that's all. I am temporarily unfinanced. This little coup de rye straw is good for forty dollars in a town of this size. How do I work it? Why, I involve myself, as you perceive, in the loathsome apparel of the rural dub. Thus embalmed I am Jonas Stubblefield—a name impossible to improve upon. I repair nosily to the office of some loan company conveniently located in the third-floor, front. There I lay my hat and yarn gloves on the floor and ask to mortgage my farm for $2,000 to pay for my sister's musical education in Europe. Loans like that always suit the loan companies. It's ten to one that when the note falls due the foreclosure will be leading the semiquavers by a couple of lengths.

"Well, sir, I reach in my pocket for the abstract of title; but I suddenly hear my team running away. I run to the window and emit the word—or exclamation, whichever it may be—viz, 'Whoa!' Then I rush downstairs and down the street, returning in a few minutes. 'Dang them mules,' I says; 'they done run away and busted the double tree and two traces. Now I got to hoof it home, for I never brought no money along. Reckon we'll talk about that loan some other time, gen'lemen.'

"Then I spreads out my tarpaulin, like the Israelites, and waits for the manna to drop.

" 'Why, no, Mr. Stubblefield,' says the lobster-colored party in the specs and dotted piqué vest; 'oblige us by accepting this ten-dollar bill until to-morrow. Get your harness repaired and call in at ten. We'll be pleased to accommodate you in the matter of this loan.'

"It's a slight thing," says Buckingham Skinner, modest, "but, as I said, only for temporary loose change."

"It's nothing to be ashamed of," says I, in respect for his mortification; "in case of an emergency. Of course, it's small compared to organizing a trust or bridge whist, but even the Chicago University had to be started in a small way."

"What's your graft these days?" Buckingham Skinner asks me.

"The legitimate," says I. "I'm handling rhinestones and Dr. Oleum Sinapi's Electric Headache Battery and the Swiss Warbler's Bird Call, a small lot of the new queer ones and twos, and the Bonanza Budget, consisting of a rolled-gold wedding and engagement ring, six Egyptian lily bulbs, a combination pickle fork and nail-clipper, and fifty engraved visiting cards—no two names alike—all for the sum of 38 cents."

"Two months ago," says Buckingham Skinner, "I was doing well down in Texas with a patent instantaneous fire kindler, made of compressed wood ashes and benzine. I sold loads of 'em in towns where they like to burns niggers quick, without having to ask somebody for a light. And just when I was doing the best they strikes oil down there and puts me out of business. 'Your machine's too slow, now, pardner,' they tells me. 'We can have a coon in hell with this here petroleum before your old flint-and-tinder truck can get him warm enough to perfess religion.' And so I gives up the kindler and drifts up here to K. C. This little curtain-raiser you seen me doing, Mr. Pickens, with the simulated farm and the hypothetical team, ain't in my line at all, and I'm ashamed you found me working it.''

"No man," says I, kindly, "need to be ashamed of putting the skibunk on a loan corporation for even so small a sum as ten dollars, when he is financially abashed. Still, it wasn't quite the proper thing. It's too much like borrowing money without paying it back."

I liked Buckingham Skinner from the start, for as good a man as ever stood over the axles and breathed gasoline smoke. And pretty soon we gets thick, and I let him in on a scheme I'd had in mind for some time, and offers to go partners.

"Anything," says Buck, "that is not actually dishonest will find me willing and ready. Let us perforate into the inwardness of your proposition. I feel degraded when I am forced to wear property straw in my hair and assume a bucolic air for the small sum of ten dollars. Actually, Mr. Pickens, it makes me feel like the Ophelia of the Great Occidental All-Star One-Night Consolidated Theatrical Aggregation."

This scheme of mine was one that suited my proclivities. By nature I am some sentimental, and have always felt gentle toward the mollifying elements of existence. I am disposed to be lenient with the arts and sciences; and I find time to instigate a cordiality for the more human works of nature, such as romance and the atmosphere and grass and poetry and the Seasons. I never skin a sucker without admiring the prismatic beauty of his scales. I never sell a little auriferous trifle to the man with the hoe without noticing the beautiful harmony there is between gold and green. And that's why I liked this scheme; it was so full of outdoor air and landscapes and easy money.

We had to have a young lady assistant to help us work this graft; and I asked Buck if he knew of one to fill the bill.

"One," says I, "that is cool and wise and strictly business from her pompadour to her Oxfords. No ex-toe-dancers or gum-chewers or crayon portrait canvassers for this."

Buck claimed he knew a suitable feminine and he takes me around to see Miss Sarah Malloy. The minute I see her I am pleased. She looked to be the goods as ordered. No sign of the three p's about her—no peroxide, patchouli, nor peau de soie; about twenty-two, brown hair, pleasant ways—the kind of a lady for the place.

"A description of the sandbag, if you please," she begins.

"Why, ma'am," says I, "this graft of ours is so nice and refined and romantic, it would make the balcony scene in 'Romeo and Juliet' look like second-story work."

We talked it over, and Miss Malloy agreed to come in as a business partner. She said she was glad to get a chance to give up her place as stenographer and secretary to a suburban lot company, and go into something respectable.

This is the way we worked our scheme. First, I figured it out by a kind of a proverb. The best grafts in the world are built up on copybook maxims and psalms and proverbs and Esau's fables. They seem to kind of hit off human nature. Our peaceful little swindle was constructed on the old saying: "The whole push loves a lover."

One evening Buck and Miss Malloy drives up like blazes in a buggy to a farmer's door. She is pale but affectionate, clinging to his arm—always clinging to his arm. Anyone can see that she is a peach and of the cling variety. They claim they are eloping for to be married on account of cruel parents. They ask where they can find a preacher. Farmer says, "B'gum there ain't any preacher nigher than Reverend Abels, four miles over on Caney Creek." Farmeress wipes her hand on her apron and rubbers through her specs.

Then, lo and look ye! Up the road from the other way joggs Parleyvoo Pickens in a gig, dressed in black, white necktie, long face, sniffing his nose, emitting a spurious kind of noise resembling the long-meter doxology.

"B'jinks!" says farmer, "if thar ain't a preacher now!"

It transpires that I am Rev. Abijah Green, travelling over to Little Bethel school-house for to preach next Sunday.

The young folks will have it they must be married, for pa is pursuing them with the plow mules and the buckboard. So the Reverend Green, after hesitation, marries 'em in farmer's parlor. And farmer grins and has in cider, and says "B'gum!" and farmeress sniffles a bit and pats the bride on the shoulder. And Parleyvoo Pickens, the wrong reverend, writes out a marriage certificate, and farmer and farmeress sign it as witnesses. And the parties of the first, second, and third part gets in their vehicles and rides away. Oh, that was an idyllic graft! True love and the lowing kine and the sun shining on the red barns—it certainly had all other impostures I know about beat to a batter.

I suppose I happened along in time to marry Buck and Miss Malloy at about twenty farm-houses. I hated to think how the romance was going to fade later on when all them marriage certificates turned up in banks where we'd discounted 'em, and the farmers had to pay them notes of hand they'd signed, running from $300 to $500.

On the 15th day of May us three divided about $6,000. Miss Malloy nearly cried with joy. You don't often see a tenderhearted girl or one that was so bent on doing right.

"Boys," says she, dabbing her eyes with a little handkerchief, "this stake comes in handier than a powder rag at a fat men's ball. It gives me a chance to reform. I was trying to get out of the real estate business when you fellows came along. But if you hadn't taken me in on this neat little proposition for removing the cuticle of the rutabaga propagators I'm afraid I'd have got into something worse. I was about to accept a place in one of these Women's Auxiliary Bazaars, where they build a parsonage by selling a spoonful of chicken salad and a cream-puff for seventy-five cents and calling it a Business Men's Lunch.

"Now I can go into a square, honest business and give all them queer jobs the shake. I'm going to Cincinnati and start a palm reading and clairvoyant joint. As Madame Saramaloi, Egyptian Sorceress, I shall give everybody a dollar's worth of good honest prognostication. Good-by, boys. Take my advice and go into some decent fake. Get friendly with the police and newspapers and you'll be all right."

So then we all shook hands, and Miss Malloy left us. Me and Buck also rose up and sauntered off a few hundred miles;

for we didn't care to be around when them marriage certificates fell due.

With about $4,000 between us we hit that bumptious little town off the New Jersey coast they call New York.

If there ever was an aviary overstocked with jays it is that Yaptown-on-the-Hudson. Cosmopolitan they call it. You bet. So's a piece of flypaper. You listen close when they're buzzing and trying to pull their feet out of the sticky stuff. "Little old New York's good enough for us"—that's what they sing.

There's enough Reubs walk down Broadway in one hour to buy up a week's output of the factory in Augusta, Maine, that makes Knaughty Knovelties and the little Phine Phun oroide gold finger ring that sticks a needle in your friend's hand.

You'd think New York people was all wise; but no. They don't get a chance to learn. Everything's too compressed. Even the hayseeds are baled hayseeds. But what else can you expect from a town that's shut off from the world by the ocean on one side and New Jersey on the other?

It's no place for an honest grafter with a small capital. There's too big a protective tariff on bunco. Even when Giovanni sells a quart of warm worms and chestnut hulls he has to hand out a pint to an insectivorous cop. And the hotel man charges double for everything in the bill that he sends by the patrol wagon to the altar where the duke is about to marry the heiress.

But old Badville-near-Coney is the ideal burg for a refined piece of piracy if you can pay the bunco duty. Imported grafts come pretty high. The custom-house officers that look after it carry clubs, and it's hard to smuggle in even a bib-and-tucker swindle to work Brooklyn with unless you can pay the toll. But now, me and Buck, having capital, descends upon New York to try and trade the metropolitan backwoodsmen a few glass beads for real estate just as the Vans did a hundred or two years ago.

At an East Side hotel we gets acquainted with Romulus G. Atterbury, a man with the finest head for financial operations I ever saw. It was all bald and glossy except for gray side whiskers. Seeing that head behind an office railing, and you'd deposit a million with it without a receipt. This Atterbury was well dressed, though he ate seldom; and the synopsis of his talk would make the conversation of a siren sound like a cab driver's kick. He said he used to be a member of the Stock Exchange, but some of the big capitalists got jealous and formed a ring that forced him to sell his seat.

Atterbury got to liking me and Buck and he begun to throw on the canvas for us some of the schemes that had caused his hair to evacuate. He had one scheme for starting a National Bank on $45 that made the Mississippi Bubble look as solid as a glass marble. He talked this to us for three days, and when his throat was good and sore we told him about the roll we had. Atterbury borrowed a quarter from us and went out and got a box of throat lozenges and started all over again. This time he talked bigger things, and he got us to see 'em as he did. The scheme he laid out looked like a sure winner, and he talked me and Buck into putting our capital against his burnished dome of thought. It looked all right for a kid-gloved graft. It seemed to be just about an inch and a half outside of the reach of the police, and as money-making as a mint. It was just what me and Buck wanted—a regular business at a permanent stand, with an open air spieling with tonsillitis on the street corners every evening.

So, in six weeks you see a handsome furnished set of offices down in the Wall Street neighborhood, with "The Golconda Gold Bond and Investment Company" in gilt letters on the door. And you see in his private room, with the door open, the secretary and treasurer, Mr. Buckingham Skinner, costumed like the lilies of the conservatory, with his high silk hat close to his hand. Nobody yet ever saw Buck outside of an instantaneous reach for his hat.

And you might perceive the president and general manager, Mr. R. G. Atterbury, with his priceless polished poll, busy in the main office room dictating letters to a shorthand countess, who has got pomp and a pompadour that is no less than a guarantee to investors.

There is a bookkeeper and an assistant, and a general atmosphere of varnish and culpability.

At another desk the eye is relieved by the sight of an ordinary man, attired with unscrupulous plainness, sitting with his feet up, eating apples, with his obnoxious hat on the back of his head. That man is no other than Colonel Tecumseh (once "Parleyvoo") Pickens, the vice-president of the company.

"No recherché rags for me," I says to Atterbury when we was organizing the stage properties of the robbery. "I'm a plain man," says I, "and I do not use pajamas, French, or military hair-brushes. Cast me for the rôle of the rhinestone-in-the-rough or I don't go on exhibition. If you can use me in my natural, though displeasing form, do so."

"Dress you up?" says Atterbury; "I should say not! Just as you are you're worth more to the business than a whole roomful of the things they pin chrysanthemums on. You're to play the part of the solid but disheveled capitalist from the Far West. You despise the conventions. You've got so many stocks you can afford to shake socks. Conservative, homely, rough, shrewd, saving—that's your pose. It's a winner in New York. Keep your feet on the desk and eat apples. Whenever anybody comes in eat an apple. Let 'em see you stuff the peelings in a drawer of your desk. Look as economical and rich and rugged as you can."

I followed out Atterbury's instructions. I played the Rocky Mountain capitalist without ruching or frills. The way I deposited apple peelings to my credit in a drawer when any customers came in made Hetty Green look like a spendthrift. I could hear Atterbury saying to victims, as he smiled at me, indulgent and venerating, "That's our vice-president, Colonel Pickens . . . fortune in Western investments . . . delightfully plain manners, but . . . could sign his check for half a million . . . simple as a child . . . wonderful head . . . conservative and careful almost to a fault."

Atterbury managed the business. Me and Buck never quite understood all of it, though he explained it to us in full. It seems the company was a kind of coöperative one, and everybody that bought stock shared in the profits. First, we officers bought up a controlling interest—we had to have that—of the shares at 50 cents a hundred—just what the printer charged us—and the rest went to the public at a dollar each. The company guaranteed the stockholders a profit of ten per cent each month, payable on the last day thereof.

When any stockholder had paid in as much as $100, the company issued him a Gold Bond and he became a bondholder. I asked Atterbury one day what benefits and appurtenances these Gold Bonds was to an investor more so than the immunities and privileges enjoyed by the common sucker who only owned stock. Atterbury picked up one of them Gold Bonds, all gilt and lettered up with flourishes and a big red seal tied with a blue ribbon in a bowknot, and he looked at me like his feelings was hurt.

"My dear Colonel Pickens," says he, "you have no soul for Art. Think of a thousand homes made happy by possessing one of these beautiful gems of the lithographer's skill! Think of the joy in the household where one of these Gold Bonds hangs by a pink cord to the what-not, or is chewed by the baby, caroling gleefully upon the floor! Ah, I see your eye growing moist, Colonel—I have touched you, have I not?"

"You have not," says I, "for I've been watching you. The moisture you see is apple juice. You can't expect one man to act as a human cider-press and an art connoisseur too."

Atterbury attended to the details of the concern. As I understand it, they was simple. The investors in stock paid in their money, and—well, I guess that's all they had to do. The company received it, and—I don't call to mind anything else. Me and Buck knew more about selling corn salve than we did about Wall Street, but even we could see how the Golconda Gold Bond Investment Company was making money. You take in money and pay back ten per cent of it; it's plain enough that you make a clean, legitimate profit of 90 per cent, less expenses as long as the fish bite.

Atterbury wanted to be president and treasurer too, but Buck winks an eye at him and says: "You was to furnish the brains. Do you call it good brain work when you propose to take in money at the door, too? Think again. I hereby nominate myself treasurer ad valorem, sine die, and by acclamation. I chip in that much brain work free. Me and Pickens, we furnished the capital, and we'll handle the unearned increment as it incremates."

It costs us $500 for office rent and first payment on furniture; $1,500 more went for printing and advertising. Atterbury knew his business. "Three months to a minute we'll last," says he. "A day longer than that and we'll have to either go under or go under an alias. By that time we ought to clean up $60,000. And then a money belt and a lower berth for me, and the yellow journals and the furniture men can pick the bones."

Our ads. done the work. "Country weeklies and Washington hand-press dailies of course," says I when we was ready to make contracts.

"Man," says Atterbury, "as its advertising manager you would cause a Limburger cheese factory to remain undiscovered during a hot summer. The game we're after is right here in New York and Brooklyn and the Harlem reading-rooms. They're the people that the street-car fenders and the Answers to Correspondents columns and the pickpocket notices are made for. We want our ads, in the biggest city dailies, top of column, next to editorials on radium and pictures of the girl doing health exercises."

Pretty soon the money begins to roll in. Buck didn't have to pretend to be busy; his desk was piled high up with money orders and checks and greenbacks. People began to drop in the office and buy stock every day.

Most of the shares went in small amounts—$10 and $25 and $50, and a good many $2 and $3 lots. And the bald and inviolate cranium of President Atterbury shines with enthusiasm and demerit, while Colonel Tecumseh Pickens, the rude but reputable Crœsus of the West, consumes so many apples that the peelings hang to the floor from the mahogany garbage chest that he calls his desk.

Just as Atterbury said, we ran along about three months without being troubled. Buck cashed the paper as fast as it came in and kept the money in a safe deposit vault a block or so away. Buck never thought much of banks for such purposes. We paid the interest regular on the stock we'd sold, so there was nothing for anybody to squeal about. We had nearly $50,000 on hand and all three of us had been living as high as prize fighters out of training.

One morning, as me and Buck sauntered into the office, fat and flippant, from our noon grub, we met an easy-looking fellow, with a bright eye and a pipe in his mouth, coming out. We found Atterbury looking like he'd been caught a mile from home in a wet shower.

"Know that man?" he asked us.

We said we didn't.

"I don't either," says Atterbury, wiping off his head; "but I'll bet enough Gold Bonds to paper a cell in the Tombs that he's a newspaper reporter."

"What did he want?" asks Buck.

"Information," says our president. "Said he was thinking of buying some stock. He asked me about nine hundred questions, and every one of 'em hit some sore place in the business. I know he's on a paper. You can't fool me. You see a man about half shabby, with an eye like a gimlet, smoking cut plug, with dandruff on his coat collar, and knowing more than J. P. Morgan and Shakespeare put together—if that ain't a reporter I never saw one. I was afraid of this. I don't mind detectives and post-office inspectors—I talk to 'em eight minutes and then sell 'em stock—but them reporters take the starch out of my collar. Boys, I recommend that we declare a dividend and fade away. The signs point that way."

Me and Buck talked to Atterbury and got him to stop swearing and stand still. That fellow didn't look like a reporter to us. Reporters always pull out a pencil and tablet on you, and tell you a story you've heard, and strikes you for the drinks. But Atterbury was shaky and nervous all day.

The next day me and Buck comes down from the hotel about ten-thirty. On the way we buys the papers, and the first thing we see is a column on the front page about our little imposition. It was a shame the way that reporter intimated that we were no blood relatives of the late George W. Childs. He tells all about the scheme as he sees it, in a rich, racy kind of guying style that might amuse most anybody except a stockholder. Yes, Atterbury was right; it behooveth the gaily clad treasurer and the pearly pated president and the rugged vice-president of the Golconda Gold Bond and Investment Company to go away real sudden and quick that their days might be longer upon the land.

Me and Buck hurries down to the office. We finds on the stairs and in the hall a crowd of people trying to squeeze into our office, which is already jammed full inside to the railing. They've nearly all got Golconda stock and Gold Bonds in their hands. Me and Buck judged they'd been reading the papers, too.

We stopped and looked at our stockholders, some surprised. It wasn't quite the kind of a gang we supposed had been investing. They all looked like poor people; there was plenty of old women and lots of young girls that you'd say worked in factories and mills. Some was old men that looked like war veterans, and some was crippled, and a good many was just kids—bootblacks and newsboys and messengers. Some was workingmen in overalls, with their sleeves rolled up. No one of the gang looked like a stockholder in anything unless it was a peanut stand. But they all had Golconda stock and looked as sick as you please.

I saw a queer kind of pale look come on Buck's face when he sized up the crowd. He stepped up to a sickly looking woman and says: "Madam, do you own any of this stock?"

"I put in a hundred dollars," says the woman, faint like. "It was all I had saved in a year. One of my children is dying at home now and I haven't a cent in the house. I came to see if I could draw out some. The circulars said you could draw it at any time. But they say now I will lose it all."

There was a smart kind of a kid in the gang—I will guess he was a newsboy. "I got in twenty-fi' mister," he says, looking hopeful at Buck's silk hat and clothes. "Dey paid me two-fifty a mont' on it. Say, a man tells me dey can't do dat and be on the square? Is dat straight? Do you guess I can get out my twenty-fi'?"

Some of the old women was crying. The factory girls was plumb distracted. They'd lost all their savings and they'd be docked for the time they lost coming to see about it.

There was one girl—a pretty one—in a red shawl, crying in the corner like her heart would dissolve. Buck goes over and asks her about it.

"It ain't so much losing the money, mister," says she, shaking all over, "though I've been two years saving it up; but Jakey won't marry me now. He'll take Rosa Steinfeld. I know J—J—Jakey. She's got $400 in the savings bank. Ai, ai, ai——" she sings out.

Buck looks all around with that same funny look on his face. And then we see leaning against the wall, puffing at his pipe, with his eye shining at us, this newspaper reporter. Buck and me walks over to him.

"You're a real interesting writer," says Buck. "How far do you mean to carry it? Anything more up your sleeve?"

"Oh, I'm just waiting around," says the reporter, smoking away, "in case any news turns up. It's up to your stockholders now. Some of them might complain, you know. Isn't that

the patrol wagon now?" he says, listening to a sound outside.
"No," he goes on, "that's Doc Whittleford's old cadaver
coupé from the Roosevelt. I ought to know that gong. Yes, I
suppose I've written some interesting stuff at times."

"You wait," says Buck; "I'm going to throw an item of
news in your way."

Buck reaches in his pocket and hands me a key. I knew
what he meant before he spoke. Confounded old buccaneer—I
knew what he meant. They don't make them any better than
Buck.

"Pick," says he looking at me hard, "ain't this graft a little
out of our line? Do we want Jakey to marry Rosa Steinfeld?"

"You've got my vote," says I. "I'll have it here in ten
minutes." And I starts for the safe deposit vaults.

I comes back with the money done up in a big bundle, and
then Buck and me takes the journalist reporter around to
another door and we let ourselves into one of the office
rooms.

"Now, my literary friend," says Buck, "take a chair, and
keep still, and I'll give you an interview. You see before you
two grafters from Graftersville, Grafter County, Arkansas.
Me and Pick have sold brass jewelry, hair tonic, song books,
marked cards, patent medicines, Connecticut Smyrna rugs,
furniture polish, and albums in every town from Old Point
Comfort to the Golden Gate. We've grafted a dollar whenever we saw one that had a surplus look to it. But we never
went after the simoleon in the toe of the sock under the loose
brick in the corner of the kitchen hearth. There's an old
saying you may have heard—'fussily decency averni'—which
means it's an easy slide from the street faker's dry goods box
to a desk in Wall Street. We've took that slide, but we didn't
know exactly what was at the bottom of it. Now, you ought
to be wise, but you ain't. You've got New York wiseness,
which means that you judge a man by the outside of his
clothes. That ain't right. You ought to look at the lining and
seams and the button-holes. While we are waiting for the
patrol wagon you might get out your little stub pencil and
take notes for another funny piece in the paper."

And then Buck turns to me and says: "I don't care what
Atterbury thinks. He only put in brains, and if he gets his
capital out he's lucky. But what do you say, Pick?"

"Me?" says I. "You ought to know me, Buck. I didn't know who was buying the stock."

"All right," says Buck. And then he goes through the inside door into the main office and looks at the gang trying to squeeze through the railing. Atterbury and his hat was gone. And Buck makes 'em a short speech.

"All you lambs get in line. You're going to get your wool back. Don't shove so. Get in a line—a *line*—not a pile. Lady, will you please stop bleating? Your money's waiting for you. Here, sonny, don't climb over that railing; your dimes are safe. Don't cry, sis; you ain't out a cent. Get in *line*, I say. Here, Pick, come and straighten 'em out and let 'em through and out by the other door."

Buck takes off his coat, pushes his silk hat on the back of his head, and lights up a reina victoria. He sits at the table with the boodle before him, all done up in neat packages. I gets the stockholders strung out and marches 'em, single file, through from the main room; and the reporter passes 'em out of the side door into the hall again. As they go by, Buck takes up the stock and the Gold Bonds, paying 'em cash, dollar for dollar, the same as they paid in. The shareholders of the Golconda Gold Bond and Investment Company can't hardly believe it. They almost grabs the money out of Buck's hands. Some of the women keep on crying, for it's a custom of the sex to cry when they have sorrow, to weep when they have joy, and to shed tears whenever they find themselves without either.

The old women's fingers shake when they stuff the skads in the bosoms of their rusty dresses. The factory girls just stoop over and flap their dry goods a second, and you hear the elastic go "pop" as the currency goes down in the ladies' department of the "Old Domestic Lisle-Thread Bank."

Some of the stockholders that had been doing the Jeremiah act the loudest outside had spasms of restored confidence and wanted to leave the money invested. "Salt away that chicken feed in your duds and skip along," says Buck. "What business have you got investing in bonds? The tea-pot or the crack in the wall behind the clock for your hoard of pennies."

When the pretty girl in the red shawl cashes in Buck hands her an extra twenty.

"A wedding present," says our treasurer, "from the

Golconda Company. And say—if Jakey ever follows his nose, even at a respectful distance, around the corner where Rosa Steinfeld lives, you are hereby authorized to knock a couple inches of it off.''

When they was all paid off and gone, Buck calls the newspaper reporter and shoves the rest of the money over to him.

"You begun this," says Buck; "now finish it. Over there are the books, showing every share and bond issued. Here's the money to cover, except what we've spent to live on. You'll have to act as receiver. I guess you'll do the square thing on account of your paper. This is the best way we know how to settle it. Me and our substantial but apple-weary vice-president are going to follow the example of our revered president, and skip. Now, have you got enough news for to-day, or do you want to interview us on etiquette and the best way to make over an old taffeta skirt?"

"News!" says the newspaper man, taking his pipe out; "do you think I could use this? I don't want to lose my job. Suppose I go around to the office and tell 'em this happened. What'll the managing editor say? He'll just hand me a pass to Bellevue and tell me to come back when I get cured. I might turn in a story about a sea serpent wiggling up Broadway, but I haven't got the nerve to try 'em with a pipe like this. A get-rich-quick—excuse me—gang giving back the boodle! Oh, no. I'm not on the comic supplement."

"You can't understand it, of course," says Buck, with his hand on the door knob. "Me and Pick ain't Wall Streeters like you know 'em. We never allowed to swindle sick old women and working girls and take nickels off of kids. In the lines of graft we worked we took money from the people the Lord made to be buncoed—sports and rounders and smart Alecks and street crowds, that always have a few dollars to throw away, and farmers that wouldn't ever be happy if the grafters didn't come around and play with 'em when they sold their crops. We never cared to fish for the kind of suckers that bite here. No, sir. We got too much respect for the profession and for ourselves. Good-by to you, Mr. Receiver."

"Here!" says the journalist reporter; "wait a minute. There's a broker I know on the next floor. Wait till I put this truck in his safe. I want you fellows to take a drink on me before you go.''

"On you?'' says Buck, winking solemn. "Don't you go and try to make 'em believe at the office you said that. Thanks. We can't spare the time, I reckon. So long.''

And me and Buck slides out the door; and that's the way the Golconda Company went into involuntary liquefaction.

If you had seen me and Buck the next night you'd have had to go to a little bum hotel over near the West Side ferry landings. We was in a little back room, and I was filling up a gross of six-ounce bottles with hydrant water colored red with aniline and flavored with cinnamon. Buck was smoking, contented, and he wore a decent brown derby in place of his silk hat.

"It's a good thing, Pick,'' says he, as he drove in the corks, "that we got Brady to loan us his horse and wagon for a week. We'll rustle up a stake by then. This hair tonic'll sell right along over in Jersey. Bald heads ain't popular over there on account of the mosquitoes.''

Directly I dragged out my valise and went down in it for labels.

"Hair tonic labels are out,'' says I. "Only about a dozen on hand.''

"Buy some more,'' says Buck.

We investigated our pockets and found we had just enough money to settle our hotel bill in the morning and pay our passage over the ferry.

"Plenty of the 'Shake-the-Shakes Chill Cure' labels,'' says I, after looking.

"What more do you want?'' says Buck. "Slap 'em on. The chill season is just opening up in the Hackensack low grounds. What's hair, anyway, if you have to shake it off?''

We posted on the Chill Cure labels about half an hour and Buck says:

"Making an honest livin's better than that Wall Street, anyhow; ain't it, Pick?''

"You bet,'' says I.

The Wild West and the Tame West

~

Telemachus, Friend

Returning from a hunting trip, I waited at the little town of Los Piños, in New Mexico, for the south-bound train, which was one hour late. I sat on the porch of the Summit House and discussed the functions of life with Telemachus Hicks, the hotel proprietor.

Perceiving that personalities were not out of order, I asked him what species of beast had long ago twisted and mutilated his left ear. Being a hunter, I was concerned in the evils that may befall one in the pursuit of game.

"That ear," says Hicks, "is the relic of true friendship."

"An accident?" I persisted.

"No friendship is an accident," said Telemachus; and I was silent.

"The only perfect case of true friendship I ever knew," went on my host, "was a cordial intent between a Connecticut man and a monkey. The monkey climbed palms in Barranquilla and threw down cocoanuts to the man. The man sawed them in two and made dippers, which he sold for two *reales* each and bought rum. The monkey drank the milk of the nuts. Through each being satisfied with his own share of the graft, they lived like brothers.

"But in the case of human beings, friendship is a transitory act, subject to discontinuance without further notice.

"I had a friend once, of the entitlement of Paisley Fish, that I imagined was sealed to me for an endless space of time. Side by side for seven years we had mined, ranched, sold patent churns, herded sheep, took photographs and other things, built wire fences, and picked prunes. Thinks I, neither homicide nor flattery nor riches nor sophistry nor drink can make trouble between me and Paisley Fish. We was friends an amount you could hardly guess at. We was friends in business, and we let our amicable qualities lap over and season our hours of recreation and folly. We certainly had days of Damon and nights of Pythias.

"One summer me and Paisley gallops down into these San Andrés mountains for the purpose of a month's surcease and levity, dressed in the natural store habiliments of man. We hit this town of Los Piños, which certainly was a roof-garden spot of the world, and flowing with condensed milk and honey. It had a street or two, and air, and hens, and a eating-house; and that was enough for us.

"We strikes the town after supper-time, and we concludes to sample whatever efficacy there is in this eating-house down by the railroad tracks. By the time we had set down and pried up our plates with a knife from the red oil-cloth, along intrudes Widow Jessup with the hot biscuit and fried liver.

"Now, there was a woman that would have tempted an anchovy to forget his vows. She was not so small as she was large; and a kind of welcome air seemed to mitigate her vicinity. The pink of her face was the *in hoc signo* of a culinary temper and a warm disposition, and her smile would have brought out the dogwood blossoms in December.

"Widow Jessup talks to us a lot of garrulousness about the climate and history and Tennyson and prunes and the scarcity of mutton, and finally wants to know where we came from.

" 'Spring Valley,' says I.

" 'Big Spring Valley,' chips in Paisley, out of a lot of potatoes and knuckle-bone of ham in his mouth.

"That was the first sign I noticed that the old *fidus Diogenes* business between me and Paisley Fish was ended forever. He knew how I hated a talkative person, and yet he stampedes into the conversation with his amendments and addendums of syntax. On the map it was Big Spring Valley; but I had heard Paisley himself call it Spring Valley a thousand times.

"Without saying any more, we went out after supper and set on the railroad track. We had been pardners too long not to know what was going on in each other's mind.

" 'I reckon you understand,' says Paisley, 'that I've made up my mind to accrue that widow woman as part and parcel in and to my hereditaments forever, both domestic, sociable, legal, and otherwise, until death us do part.'

" 'Why, yes,' says I, 'I read it between the lines, though you only spoke one. And I suppose you are aware,' says I, 'that I have a movement on foot that leads up to the widow's changing her name to Hicks, and leaves you writing to the society column to inquire whether the best man wears a japonica or seamless socks at the wedding!'

" 'There'll be some hiatuses in your program,' says Paisley, chewing up a piece of a railroad tie. 'I'd give in to you,' says he, 'in 'most any respect if it was secular affairs, but this is not so. The smiles of woman,' goes on Paisley, 'is the whirlpool of Squills and Chalybeates, into which vortex the good ship Friendship is often drawn and dismembered. I'd assault a bear that was annoying you,' says Paisley, 'or I'd indorse your note, or rub the place between your shoulder-blades with opodeldoc the same as ever; but there my sense of etiquette ceases. In this fracas with Mrs. Jessup we play it alone. I've notified you fair.'

"And then I collaborates with myself, and offers the following resolutions and by-laws:

" 'Friendship between man and man,' says I, 'is an ancient historical virtue enacted in the days when men had to protect each other against lizards with eighty-foot tails and flying turtles. And they've kept up the habit to this day, and stand by each other till the bellboy comes up and tells them the animals are not really there. I've often heard,' I says, 'about ladies stepping in and breaking up a friendship between men. Why should that be? I'll tell you, Paisley, the first sight and hot biscuit of Mrs. Jessup appears to have inserted a oscillation into each of our bosoms. Let the best man of us have her. I'll play you a square game, and won't do any underhanded work. I'll do all of my courting of her in your presence, so you will have an equal opportunity. With that arrangement I don't see why our steamboat of friendship should fall overboard in the medicinal whirlpools you speak of, whichever of us wins out.'

" 'Good old hoss!' says Paisley, shaking my hand. 'And I'll do the same,' says he. 'We'll court the lady synonymously, and without any of the prudery and bloodshed usual to such occasions. And we'll be friends still, win or lose.'

"At one side of Mrs. Jessup's eating-house was a bench under some trees where she used to sit in the breeze after the south-bound had been fed and gone. And there me and Paisley used to congregate after supper and make partial payments on our respects to the lady of our choice. And we was so honorable and circuitous in our calls that if one of us got there first we waited for the other before beginning any gallivantery.

"The first evening that Mrs. Jessup knew about our arrangement I got to the bench before Paisley did. Supper was just over, and Mrs. Jessup was out there with a fresh pink dress on, and almost cool enough to handle.

"I sat down by her and made a few specifications about the moral surface of nature as set forth by the landscape and the contiguous perspective. That evening was surely a case in point. The moon was attending to business in the section of sky where it belonged, and the trees was making shadows on the ground according to science and nature, and there was a kind of conspicuous hullabaloo going on in the bushes between the bull-bats and the orioles and the jack-rabbits and other feathered insects of the forest. And the wind out of the mountains was singing like a jew's-harp in the pile of old tomato-cans by the railroad track.

"I felt a kind of sensation in my left side—something like dough rising in a crock by the fire. Mrs. Jessup had moved up closer.

" 'Oh, Mr. Hicks,' says she, 'when one is alone in the world, don't they feel it more aggravated on a beautiful night like this?'

"I rose up off the bench at once.

" 'Excuse me, ma'am,' says I, 'but I'll have to wait till Paisley comes before I can give a audible hearing to leading questions like that.'

"And then I explained to her how we was friends cinctured by years of embarrassment and travel and complicity, and how we had agreed to take no advantage of each other in any of the more mushy walks of life, such as might be fomented by sentiment and proximity. Mrs. Jessup appears to think serious about the matter for a minute, and then she breaks into a species of laughter that makes the wildwood resound.

"In a few minutes Paisley drops around, with oil of bergamot on his hair, and sits on the other side of Mrs. Jessup, and inaugurates a sad tale of adventure in which him and Pieface Lumley has a skinning-match of dead cows in '95 for a silver-mounted saddle in the Santa Rita valley during the nine months' drought.

"Now, from the start of that courtship I had Paisley Fish hobbled and tied to a post. Each one of us had a different system of reaching out for the easy places in the female heart. Paisley's scheme was to petrify 'em with wonderful relations of events that he had either come across personally or in large print. I think he must have got his idea of subjugation from one of Shakespeare's shows I see once called 'Othello.' There is a colored man in it who acquires a duke's daughter by disbursing to her a mixture of the talk turned out by Rider Haggard, Lew Dockstader, and Dr. Parkhurst. But that style of courting don't work well off the stage.

"Now, I give you my own recipe for inveigling a woman into that state of affairs when she can be referred to as 'née Jones.' Learn how to pick up her hand and hold it, and she's yours. It ain't so easy. Some men grab at it so much like they was going to set a dislocation of the shoulder that you can smell the arnica and hear 'em tearing off bandages. Some take it up like a hot horseshoe, and hold it off at arm's length like a druggist pouring tincture of asafœtida in a bottle. And most of 'em catch hold of it and drag it right out before the lady's eyes like a boy finding a baseball in the grass, without giving her a chance to forget that the hand is growing on the end of her arm. Them ways are all wrong.

"I'll tell you the right way. Did you ever see a man sneak out in the backyard and pick up a rock to throw at a tomcat that was sitting on a fence looking at him? He pretends he hasn't got a thing in his hand, and that the cat don't see him, and that he don't see the cat. That's the idea. Never drag her hand out where she'll have to take notice of it. Don't let her know that you think she knows you have the least idea she is aware you are holding her hand. That was my rule of tactics; and as far as Paisley's serenade about hostilities and misadventure went, he might as well have been reading to her a time-table of the Sunday trains that stop at Ocean Grove, New Jersey.

"One night when I beat Paisley to the bench by one pipeful,

my friendship gets subsidized for a minute, and I asks Mrs. Jessup if she didn't think a 'H' was easier to write than a 'J.' In a second her head was mashing the oleander flower in my button-hole, and I leaned over and—but I didn't.

" 'If you don't mind,' says I, standing up, 'we'll wait for Paisley to come before finishing this. I've never done anything dishonorable yet to our friendship, and this won't be quite fair.'

" 'Mr. Hicks,' says Mrs. Jessup, looking at me peculiar in the dark, 'if it wasn't for but one thing, I'd ask you to hike yourself down the gulch and never disresume your visits to my house.'

" 'And what is that, ma'am?' I asks.

" 'You are too good a friend not to make a good husband,' says she.

"In five minutes Paisley was on his side of Mrs. Jessup.

" 'In Silver City, in the summer of '98,' he begins, 'I see Jim Bartholomew chew off a Chinaman's ear in the Blue Light Saloon on account of a crossbarred muslin shirt that— what was that noise?'

"I had resumed matters again with Mrs. Jessup right where we had left off.

" 'Mrs. Jessup,' says I, 'has promised to make it Hicks. And this is another of the same sort.'

"Paisley winds his feet around a leg of the bench and kind of groans.

" 'Lem,' says he, 'we been friends for seven years. Would you mind not kissing Mrs. Jessup quite so loud? I'd do the same for you.'

" 'All right,' says I. 'The other kind will do as well.'

" 'This Chinaman,' goes on Paisley, 'was the one that shot a man named Mullins in the spring of '97, and that was——'

"Paisley interrupted himself again.

" 'Lem,' says he, 'if you was a true friend you wouldn't hug Mrs. Jessup quite so hard. I felt the bench shake all over just then. You know you told me you would give me an even chance as long as there was any.'

" 'Mr. Man,' says Mrs. Jessup, turning around to Paisley, 'if you was to drop in to the celebration of mine and Mr. Hicks's silver wedding, twenty-five years from now, do you think you could get it into that Hubbard squash you call your head that you are *nix cum rous* in this business? I've put up with you a long time because you was Mr. Hicks's friend; but it seems to me it's time for you to wear the willow and trot off down the hill.'

" 'Mrs. Jessup,' says I, without losing my grasp on the situation as fiancé, 'Mr. Paisley is my friend, and I offered him a square deal and a equal opportunity as long as there was a chance.'

" 'A chance!' says she. 'Well, he may think he has a chance; but I hope he won't think he's got a cinch, after what he's been next to all the evening.'

"Well, a month afterwards me and Mrs. Jessup was married in the Los Piños Methodist Church; and the whole town closed up to see the performance.

"When we lined up in front and the preacher was beginning to sing out his rituals and observances, I looks around and misses Paisley. I calls time on the preacher. 'Paisley ain't here,' says I. 'We've got to wait for Paisley. A friend once, a friend always—that's Telemachus Hicks,' says I. Mrs. Jessup's eyes snapped some; but the preacher holds up the incantations according to instructions.

"In a few minutes Paisley gallops up the aisle, putting on a cuff as he comes. He explains that the only dry-goods store in town was closed for the wedding, and he couldn't get the kind of a boiled shirt that his taste called for until he had broke open the back window of the store and helped himself. Then he ranges up on the other side of the bride, and the wedding goes on. I always imagined that Paisley calculated as a last chance that the preacher might marry him to the widow by mistake.

"After the proceedings was over we had tea and jerked antelope and canned apricots, and then the populace hiked itself away. Last of all Paisley shook me by the hand and told me I'd acted square and on the level with him and he was proud to call me a friend.

"The preacher had a small house on the side of the street that he'd fixed up to rent; and he allowed me and Mrs. Hicks to occupy it till the ten-forty train the next morning, when we was going on a bridal tour to El Paso. His wife had decorated it all up with hollyhocks and poison ivy, and it looked real festal and bowery.

"About ten o'clock that night I sets down in the front door and pulls off my boots a while in the cool breeze, while Mrs. Hicks was fixing around in the room. Right soon the light went out inside; and I sat there a while, reverberating over old times and scenes. And then I heard Mrs. Hicks call out, 'Ain't you coming in soon, Lem?'

" 'Well, well!' says I, kind of rousing up. 'Durn me if I wasn't waiting for old Paisley to——'

"But when I got that far," concluded Telemachus Hicks, "I thought somebody had shot this left ear of mine off with a forty-five. But it turned out to be only a lick from a broomhandle in the hands of Mrs. Hicks."

The Caballero's Way

The Cisco Kid had killed six men in more or less fair scrimmages, had murdered twice as many (mostly Mexicans), and had winged a larger number whom he modestly forebore to count. Therefore a woman loved him.

The Kid was twenty-five, looked twenty; and a careful insurance company would have estimated the probable time of his demise at, say, twenty-six. His habitat was anywhere between the Frio and the Rio Grande. He killed for the love of it—because he was quick-tempered—to avoid arrest—for his own amusement—any reason that came to his mind would suffice. He had escaped capture because he could shoot five-sixths of a second sooner than any sheriff or ranger in the service, and because he rode a speckled roan horse that knew every cowpath in the mesquite and pear thickets from San Antonio to Matamoras.

Tonia Perez, the girl who loved the Cisco Kid, was half Carmen, half Madonna, and the rest—oh, yes, a woman who is half Carmen and half Madonna can always be something more—the rest, let us say, was humming-bird. She lived in a grass-roofed *jacal* near a little Mexican settlement at the Lone Wolf Crossing of the Frio. With her lived a father or grandfather, a lineal Aztec, somewhat less than a thousand years old, who herded a hundred goats and lived in a continuous drunken dream from drinking *mescal*. Back of the *jacal* a tremendous forest of bristling pear, twenty feet high at its worst, crowded almost to its door. It was along the bewildering maze of this spinous thicket that the speckled roan would bring the Kid to see his girl. And once, clinging like a lizard to the ridge-pole, high up under the peaked grass roof, he had heard Tonia, with her Madonna face and Carmen beauty and humming-bird soul, parley with the sheriff's posse, denying knowledge of her man in her soft *mélange* of Spanish and English.

One day the adjutant-general of the State, who is, *ex officio,* commander of the ranger forces, wrote some sarcastic lines to Captain Duval of Company X, stationed at Laredo, relative to the serene and undisturbed existence led by murderers and desperadoes in the said captain's territory.

The captain turned the color of brick dust under his tan, and forwarded the letter, after adding a few comments, per ranger Private Bill Adamson, to ranger Lieutenant Sandridge, camped at a water hole on the Nueces with a squad of five men in preservation of law and order.

Lieutenant Sandridge turned a beautiful *couleur de rose* through his ordinary strawberry complexion, tucked the letter in his hip pocket, and chewed off the end of his gamboge moustache.

The next morning he saddled his horse and rode alone to the Mexican settlement at the Lone Wolf Crossing of the Frio, twenty miles away.

Six feet two, blond as a Viking, quiet as a deacon, dangerous as a machine gun, Sandridge moved among the *Jacales,* patiently seeking news of the Cisco Kid.

Far more than the law, the Mexicans dreaded the cold and certain vengeance of the lone rider that the ranger sought. It had been one of the Kid's pastimes to shoot Mexicans "to see them kick": if he demanded from them moribund Terpsichorean feats, simply that he might be entertained, what terrible and extreme penalties would be certain to follow should they anger him! One and all they lounged with upturned palms and shrugging shoulders, filling the air with *"quién sabes"* and denials of the Kid's acquaintance.

But there was a man named Fink who kept a store at the Crossing—a man of many nationalities, tongues, interests, and ways of thinking.

"No use to ask them Mexicans," he said to Sandridge. "They're afraid to tell. This *hombre* they call the Kid—Goodall is his name, ain't it?—he's been in my store once or twice. I have an idea you might run across him at—but I guess I don't keer to say, myself. I'm two seconds later in pulling a gun than I used to be and the difference is worth thinking about. But this Kid's got a half-Mexican girl at the Crossing that he comes to see. She lives in that *jacal* a hundred yards down the arroyo at the edge of the pear. Maybe she—no, I don't suppose she would, but that *jacal* would be a good place to watch, anyway."

Sandridge rode down to the *jacal* of Perez. The sun was low, and the broad shade of the great pear thicket already covered the grass-thatched hut. The goats were enclosed for the night in a brush corral near by. A few kids walked the top of it, nibbling the chaparral leaves. The old Mexican lay upon a blanket on the grass, already in a stupor from his mescal, and dreaming, perhaps, of the nights when he and Pizarro touched glasses to their New World fortunes—so old his wrinkled face seemed to proclaim him to be. And in the door of the *jacal* stood Tonia. And Lieutenant Sandridge sat in his saddle staring at her like a gannet agape at a sailorman.

The Cisco Kid was a vain person, as all eminent and successful assassins are, and his bosom would have been ruffled had he known that at a simple exchange of glances two persons, in whose minds he had been looming large, suddenly abandoned (at least for the time) all thought of him.

Never before had Tonia seen such a man as this. He seemed to be made of sunshine and blood-red tissue and clear weather. He seemed to illuminate the shadow of the pear when he smiled, as though the sun were rising again. The men she had known had been small and dark. Even the Kid, in spite of his achievements, was a stripling no larger than herself, with black straight hair and a cold marble face that chilled the noonday.

As for Tonia, though she sends description to the poorhouse, let her make a millionaire of your fancy. Her blue-black hair, smoothly divided in the middle and bound close to her head, and her large eyes full of the Latin melancholy, gave her the Madonna touch. Her motions and air spoke of the concealed fire and the desire to charm that she had inherited from the *gitanas* of the Basque province. As for the humming-bird part of her, that dwelt in her heart; you could not perceive it unless her bright red skirt and dark blue blouse gave you a symbolic hint of the vagarious bird.

The newly lighted sun-god asked for a drink of water. Tonia brought it from the red jar hanging under the brush shelter. Sandridge considered it necessary to dismount so as to lessen the trouble of her ministrations.

I play no spy; not do I assume to master the thoughts of any human heart; but I assert, by the chronicler's right, that before a quarter of an hour had sped, Sandridge was teaching her how to plait a six-strand rawhide stake-rope, and Tonia had explained to him that were it not for her little English book that the peripatetic *padre* had given her and the little crippled *chivo,* that she fed from a bottle, she would be very, very lonely indeed.

Which leads to a suspicion that the Kid's fences needed repairing, and that the adjutant-general's sarcasm had fallen upon unproductive soil.

In his camp by the water hole Lieutenant Sandbridge announced and reiterated his intention of either causing the Cisco Kid to nibble the black loam of the Frio country prairies or of hailing him before a judge and jury. That sounded business-like. Twice a week he rode over to the Lone Wolf Crossing of the Frio, and directed Tonia's slim, slightly lemon-tinted fingers among the intricacies of the slowly growing lariat. A six-strand plait is hard to learn and easy to teach.

The ranger knew that he might find the Kid there at any visit. He kept his armament ready, and had a frequent eye for the pear thicket at the rear of the *jacal.* Thus he might bring down the kite and the humming-bird with one stone.

While the sunny-haired ornithologist was pursuing his studies the Cisco Kid was also attending to his professional duties. He moodily shot up a saloon in a small cow village on Quintana Creek, killed the town marshal (plugging him neatly in the centre of his tin badge), and then rode away, morose and unsatisfied. No true artist is uplifted by shooting an aged man carrying an old-style .38 bulldog.

On his way the Kid suddenly experienced the yearning that all men feel when wrong-doing loses its keen edge of delight. He yearned for the woman he loved to reassure him that she was his in spite of it. He wanted her to call his bloodthirstiness bravery and his cruelty devotion. He wanted Tonia to bring him water from the red jug under the brush shelter, and tell him how the *chivo* was thriving on the bottle.

The Kid turned the speckled roan's head up the ten-mile pear flat that stretches along the Arroyo Hondo until it ends at the Lone Wolf Crossing of the Frio. The roan whickered; for he had a sense of locality and direction equal to that of a belt-line street-car horse; and he knew he would soon be nibbling the rich mesquite grass at the end of a forty-foot stake rope while Ulysses rested his head in Circe's straw-roofed hut.

More weird and lonesome than the journey of an Amazonian explorer is the ride of one through a Texas pear flat. With dismal monotony and startling variety the uncanny and multiform shapes of the cacti lift their twisted trunks and fat, bristly hands to encumber the way. The demon plant, appearing to live without soil or rain, seems to taunt the parched traveler with its lush gray greenness. It warps itself a thousand times about what look to be open and inviting paths, only to lure the rider into blind and impassable spine-defended "bottoms of the bag," leaving him to retreat if he can, with the points of the compass whirling in his head.

To be lost in the pear is to die almost the death of the thief on the cross, pierced by nails and with grotesque shapes of all the fiends hovering about.

But it was not so with the Kid and his mount. Winding, twisting, circling, tracing the most fantastic and bewildering trail ever picked out, the good roan lessened the distance to the Lone Wolf Crossing with every coil and turn that he made.

While they fared the Kid sang. He knew but one tune and he sang it, as he knew but one code and lived it, and but one girl and loved her. He was a single-minded man of conventional ideas. He had a voice like a coyote with bronchitis, but whenever he chose to sing his song he sang it. It was a conventional song of the camps and trail, running at its beginning as near as may be to these words:

Don't you monkey with my Lulu girl
Or I'll tell you what I'll do——

and so on. The roan was inured to it, and did not mind.

But even the poorest singer will, after a certain time, gain his own consent to refrain from contributing to the world's noises. So the Kid, by the time he was within a mile or two of Tonia's *jacal*, had reluctantly allowed his song to die away—not because his vocal performance had become less charming to his own ears, but because his laryngeal muscles were aweary.

As though he were in a circus ring the speckled roan wheeled and danced through the labyrinth of pear until at length his rider knew by certain landmarks that the Lone Wolf Crossing was close at hand. Then, where the pear was thinner, he caught sight of the grass roof of the *jacal* and the hackberry tree on the edge of the arroyo. A few yards farther the Kid stopped the roan and gazed intently through the prickly openings. Then he dismounted, dropped the roan's reins, and proceeded on foot, stooping and silent, like an Indian. The roan, knowing his part, stood still, making no sound.

The kid crept noiselessly to the very edge of the pear thicket and reconnoitered between the leaves of a clump of cactus.

Ten yards from his hiding-place, in the shade of the *jacal*, sat his Tonia calmly plaiting a raw-hide lariat. So far she might surely escape condemnation; women have been known, from time to time, to engage in more mischievous occupations. But if all must be told, there is to be added that her head reposed against the broad and comfortable chest of a tall red-and-yellow man, and that his arm was about her, guiding her nimble small fingers that required so many lessons at the intricate six-strand plait.

Sandridge glanced quickly at the dark mass of pear when he heard a slight squeaking sound that was not altogether unfamiliar. A gun-scabbard will make that sound when one grasps the handle of a six-shooter suddenly. But the sound was not repeated; and Tonia's fingers needed close attention.

And then, in the shadow of death, they began to talk of their love; and in the still July afternoon every word they uttered reached the ears of the Kid.

"Remember, then," said Tonia, "you must not come again until I send for you. Soon he will be here. A *vaquero* at the *tienda* said to-day he saw him on the Guadalupe three days ago. When he is that near he always comes. If he comes and finds you here he will kill you. So, for my sake, you must come no more until I send you the word."

"All right," said the ranger. "And then what?"

"And then," said the girl, "you must bring your men here and kill him. If not, he will kill you."

"He ain't a man to surrender, that's sure," said Sandridge. "It's kill or be killed for the officer that goes up against Mr. Cisco Kid."

"He must die," said the girl. "Otherwise there will not be any peace in the world for thee and me. He has killed many. Let him so die. Bring your men, and give him no chance to escape."

"You used to think right much of him," said Sandridge.

Tonia dropped the lariat, twisted herself around, and curved a lemon-tinted arm over the ranger's shoulder.

"But then," she murmured in liquid Spanish, "I had not beheld thee, thou great, red mountain of a man! And thou art kind and good, as well as strong. Could one choose him, knowing thee? Let him die; for then I will not be filled with fear by day and night lest he hurt thee or me."

"How can I know when he comes?" asked Sandridge.

"When he comes," said Tonia, "he remains two days, sometimes three. Gregorio, the small son of old Luisa, the *lavandera,* has a swift pony. I will write a letter to thee and send it by him, saying how it will be best to come upon him. By Gregorio will the letter come. And bring many men with thee, and have much care, oh, dear red one, for the rattle-snake is not quicker to strike than is 'El Chivato,' as they call him, to send a ball from his *pistola.*"

"The Kid's handy with his gun, sure enough," admitted Sandridge, "but when I come for him I shall come alone. I'll get him by myself or not at all. The Cap wrote one or two things to me that make me want to do the trick without any help. You let me know when Mr. Kid arrives, and I'll do the rest.''

"I will send you the message by the boy Gregorio," said the girl. "I knew you were braver than that small slayer of men who never smiles. How could I ever have thought I cared for him?"

It was time for the ranger to ride back to his camp on the water hole. Before he mounted his horse he raised the slight form of Tonia with one arm high from the earth for a parting salute. The drowsy stillness of the torpid summer air still lay thick upon the dreaming afternoon. The smoke from the fire in the *jacal,* where the *frijoles* blubbered in the iron pot, rose straight as a plumb-line above the clay-daubed chimney. No sound or movement disturbed the serenity of the dense pear thicket ten yards away.

When the form of Sandridge had disappeared, loping his big dun down the steep banks of the Frio crossing, the Kid crept back to his own horse, mounted him, and rode back along the tortuous trail he had come.

But not far. He stopped and waited in the silent depths of the pear until half an hour had passed. And then Tonia heard the high, untrue notes of his unmusical singing coming nearer and nearer; and she ran to the edge of the pear to meet him.

The Kid seldom smiled; but he smiled and waved his hat when he saw her. He dismounted, and his girl sprang into his arms. The Kid looked at her fondly. His thick black hair clung to his head like a wrinkled mat. The meeting brought a slight ripple of some undercurrent of feeling to his smooth, dark face that was usually as motionless as a clay mask.

"How's my girl?" he asked, holding her close.

"Sick of waiting so long for you, dear one," she answered. "My eyes are dim with always gazing into that devil's pin-cushion through which you come. And I can see into it such a little way, too. But you are here, beloved one, and I will not scold. *Qué mal muchacho!* not to come to see your *alma* more often. Go in and rest, and let me water your horse and stake him with the long rope. There is cool water in the jar for you."

The Kid kissed her affectionately.

"Not if the court knows itself do I let a lady stake my horse for me," said he. "But if you'll run in, *chica,* and throw a pot of coffee together while I attend to the *caballo,* I'll be a good deal obliged."

Besides his marksmanship the Kid had another attribute for which he admired himself greatly. He was *muy caballero,* as the Mexicans express it, where the ladies were concerned. For them he had always gentle words and consideration. He could not have spoken a harsh word to a woman. He might ruthlessly slay their husbands and brothers, but he could not have laid the weight of a finger in anger upon a woman. Wherefore many of that interesting division of humanity who had come under the spell of his politeness declared their disbelief in the stories circulated about Mr. Kid. One shouldn't believe everything one heard, they said. When confronted by their indignant men folk with proof of the *caballero's* deeds of infamy, they said maybe he had been driven to it, and that he knew how to treat a lady, anyhow.

Considering this extremely courteous idiosyncrasy of the Kid and the pride that he took in it, one can perceive that the solution of the problem that was presented to him by what he saw and heard from his hiding-place in the pear that afternoon (at least as to one of the actors) must have been obscured by difficulties. And yet one could not think of the Kid overlooking little matters of that kind.

At the end of the short twilight they gathered around a supper of *frijoles,* goat steaks, canned peaches, and coffee, by the light of a lantern in the *jacal.* Afterward, the ancestor, his flock corralled, smoked a cigarette and became a mummy in a gray blanket. Tonia washed the few dishes while the Kid dried them with the flour-sacking towel. Her eyes shone; she chatted volubly of the inconsequent happenings of her small world since the Kid's last visit; it was as all his other homecomings had been.

Then outside Tonia swung in a grass hammock with her guitar and sang sad *canciones de amor.*

"Do you love me just the same, old girl?" asked the Kid, hunting for his cigarette papers.

"Always the same, little one," said Tonia, her dark eyes lingering upon him.

"I must go over to Fink's," said the Kid, rising, "for

some tobacco. I thought I had another sack in my coat. I'll be back in a quarter of an hour."

"Hasten," said Tonia, "and tell me—how long shall I call you my own this time? Will you be gone again to-morrow, leaving me to grieve, or will you be longer with your Tonia?"

"Oh, I might stay two or three days this trip," said the Kid, yawning. "I've been on the dodge for a month, and I'd like to rest up."

He was gone half an hour for his tobacco. When he returned Tonia was still lying in the hammock.

"It's funny," said the Kid, "how I feel. I feel like there was somebody lying behind every bush and tree waiting to shoot me. I never had mully-grubs like them before. Maybe it's one of them presumptions. I've got half a notion to light out in the morning before day. The Guadalupe country is burning up about that old Dutchman I plugged down there."

"You are not afraid—no one could make my brave little one fear."

"Well, I haven't been usually regarded as a jack-rabbit when it comes to scrapping; but I don't want a posse smoking me out when I'm in your *jacal*. Somebody might get hurt that oughtn't to."

"Remain with your Tonia; no one will find you here."

The Kid looked keenly into the shadows up and down the arroyo and toward the dim lights of the Mexican village.

"I'll see how it looks later on," was his decision.

At midnight a horseman rode into the rangers' camp, blazing his way by noisy "halloes" to indicate a pacific mission. Sandridge and one or two others turned out to investigate the row. The rider announced himself to be Domingo Sales, from the Lone Wolf Crossing. He bore a letter for Señor Sandridge. Old Luisa, the *lavandera,* had persuaded him to bring it, he said, her son Gregorio being too ill of a fever to ride.

Sandridge lighted the camp lantern and read the letter. These were its words:

Dear One: He has come. Hardly had you ridden away when he came out of the pear. When he first talked he said he would stay three days or more. Then as it grew later he was like a wolf or a fox, and walked about without rest, looking and listening. Soon he said he must leave before daylight when it is dark and stillest. And then he seemed to suspect that I be not true to him. He looked at me so strange that I am frightened. I swear to him that I love him, his own Tonia. Last of all he said I must prove to him I am true. He thinks that even now men are waiting to kill him as he rides from my house. To escape he says he will dress in my clothes, my red skirt and the blue waist I wear and the brown mantilla over the head, and thus ride away. But before that he says that I must put on his clothes, his *pantalones* and *camisa* and hat, and ride away on his horse from the *jacal* as far as the big road beyond the crossing and back again. This before he goes, so he can tell if I am true and if men are hidden to shoot him. It is a terrible thing. An hour before daybreak this is to be. Come, my dear one, and kill this man and take me for your Tonia. Do not try to take hold of him alive, but kill him quickly. Knowing all, you should do that. You must come long before the time and hide yourself in the little shed near the *jacal* where the wagon and saddles are kept. It is dark in there. He will wear my red skirt and blue waist and brown mantilla. I send you a hundred kisses. Come surely and shoot quickly and straight.

Thine Own Tonia

Sandridge quickly explained to his men the official part of the missive. The rangers protested against his going alone.

"I'll get him easy enough," said the lieutenant. "The girl's got him trapped. And don't even think he'll get the drop on me."

Sandridge saddled his horse and rode to the Lone Wolf Crossing. He tied his big dun in a clump of brush on the arroyo, took his Winchester from its scabbard, and carefully approached the Perez *jacal*. There was only the half of a high moon drifted over by ragged, milk-white gulf clouds.

The wagon-shed was an excellent place for ambush; and the ranger got inside it safely. In the black shadow of the brush shelter in front of the *jacal* he could see a horse tied and hear him impatiently pawing the hard-trodden earth.

He waited almost an hour before two figures came out of

the *jacal*. One, in man's clothes, quickly mounted the horse and galloped past the wagon-shed toward the crossing and village. And then the other figure, in skirt, waist, and mantilla over its head, stepped out into the faint moonlight, gazing after the rider. Sandridge thought he would take his chance then before Tonia rode back. He fancied she might not care to see it.

"Throw up your hands," he ordered, loudly, stepping out of the wagon-shed with his Winchester at his shoulder.

There was a quick turn of the figure, but no movement to obey, so the ranger pumped in the bullets—one—two—three—and then twice more; for you never could be too sure of bringing down the Cisco Kid. There was no danger of missing at ten paces, even in that half moonlight.

The old ancestor, asleep on his blanket, was awakened by the shots. Listening further, he heard a great cry from some man in mortal distress or anguish, and rose up grumbling at the disturbing ways of moderns.

The tall, red ghost of a man burst into the *jacal,* reaching one hand, shaking like a *tule* reed, for the lantern hanging on its nail. The other spread a letter on the table.

"Look at this letter, Perez," cried the man. "Who wrote it?"

"*Ah, Dios!* it is Señor Sandridge," mumbled the old man, approaching. "*Pues, señor,* that letter was written by '*El Chivato,*' as he is called—by the man of Tonia. They say he is a bad man; I do not know. While Tonia slept he wrote the letter and sent it by this old hand of mine to Domingo Sales to be brought to you. Is there anything wrong in the letter? I am very old; and I did not know. *Valgame Dios!* it is a very foolish world; and there is nothing in the house to drink—nothing to drink."

Just then all that Sandridge could think of to do was to go outside and throw himself face downward in the dust by the side of his humming-bird, of whom not a feather fluttered. He was not a *caballero* by instinct, and he could not understand the niceties of revenge.

A mile away the rider who had ridden past the wagon-shed struck up a harsh, untuneful song, the words of which began:

Don't you monkey with my Lulu girl
Or I'll tell you what I'll do——

Friends in San Rosario

The west-bound stopped at San Rosario on time at 8:20 A.M. A man with a thick black-leather wallet under his arm left the train and walked rapidly up the main street of the town. There were other passengers who also got off at San Rosario, but they either slouched limberly over to the railroad eating-house or the Silver Dollar saloon, or joined the groups of idlers about the station.

Indecision had no part in the movements of the man with the wallet. He was short in stature, but strongly built, with very light, closely trimmed hair, smooth, determined face, and aggressive, gold-rimmed nose glasses. He was well dressed in the prevailing Eastern style. His air denoted a quiet but conscious reserve force, if not actual authority.

After walking a distance of three squares he came to the center of the town's business area. Here another street of importance crossed the main one, forming the hub of San Rosario's life and commerce. Upon one corner stood the postoffice. Upon another Rubensky's Clothing Emporium. The other two diagonally opposing corners were occupied by the town's two banks, the First National and the Stockmen's National. Into the First National Bank of San Rosario the newcomer walked, never slowing his brisk step until he stood at the cashier's window. The bank opened for business at nine, and the working force was already assembled, each member preparing his department for the day's business. The cashier was examining the mail when he noticed the stranger standing at his window.

"Bank doesn't open 'til nine," he remarked, curtly, but without feeling. He had had to make that statement so often to early birds since San Rosario adopted city banking hours.

"I am well aware of that," said the other man, in cool, brittle tones. "Will you kindly receive my card?"

The cashier drew the small, spotless parallelogram inside the bars of his wicket, and read:

> ## J. F. C. NETTLEWICK
> ### NATIONAL BANK EXAMINER

"Oh—er—will you walk around inside, Mr.—er—Nettlewick. Your first visit—didn't know your business, of course. Walk right around, please."

The examiner was quickly inside the sacred precincts of the bank, where he was ponderously introduced to each employee in turn by Mr. Edlinger, the cashier—a middle-aged gentleman of deliberation, discretion, and method.

"I was kind of expecting Sam Turner round again, pretty soon," said Mr. Edlinger. "Sam's been examining us now for about four years. I guess you'll find us all right, though considering the tightness in business. Not overly much money on hand, but able to stand the storms, sir, stand the storms."

"Mr. Turner and I have been ordered by the Comptroller to exchange districts," said the examiner, in his decisive, formal tones. "He is covering my old territory in southern Illinois and Indiana. I will take the cash first, please."

Perry Dorsey, the teller, was already arranging his cash on the counter for the examiner's inspection. He knew it was right to a cent, and he had nothing to fear, but he was nervous and flustered. So was every man in the bank. There was something so icy and swift, so impersonal and uncompromising about this man that his very presence seemed an accusation. He looked to be a man who would never make nor overlook an error.

Mr. Nettlewick first seized the currency, and with a rapid, almost juggling motion, counted it by packages. Then he spun the sponge cup toward him and verified the count by bills. His thin, white fingers flew like some expert musician's upon the keys of a piano. He dumped the gold upon the counter with a crash, and the coins whined and sang as they skimmed across the marble slab from the tips of his nimble digits. The air was full of fractional currency when he came to the halves and quarters. He counted the last nickel and dime. He had the scales brought, and he weighed every sack of silver in the vault. He questioned Dorsey concerning each of the cash memoranda—certain checks, charge slips, etc., carried over from the previous day's work—with unimpeachable courtesy, yet with something so mysteriously momentous in his frigid manner, that the teller was reduced to pink cheeks and a stammering tongue.

This newly imported examiner was so different from Sam Turner. It had been Sam's way to enter the bank with a shout, pass the cigars, and tell the latest stories he had picked up on his rounds. His customary greeting to Dorsey had been, "Hello, Perry! Haven't skipped out with the boodle yet, I see." Turner's way of counting the cash had been different too. He would finger the packages of bills in a tired kind of way, and then go into the vault and kick over a few sacks of silver, and the thing was done. Halves and quarters and dimes? Not for Sam Turner. "No chicken feed for me," he would say when they were set before him. "I'm not in the agricultural department." But, then, Turner was a Texan, an old friend of the bank's president, and had known Dorsey since he was a baby.

While the examiner was counting the cash, Major Thomas B. Kingman—known to every one as "Major Tom"—the president of the First National, drove up to the side door with his old dun horse and buggy, and came inside. He saw the examiner busy with the money, and going into the little "pony corral," as he called it, in which his desk was railed off, he began to look over his letters.

Earlier, a little incident had occurred that even the sharp eyes of the examiner had failed to notice. When he had begun his work at the cash counter, Mr. Edlinger had winked significantly at Roy Wilson, the youthful bank messenger, and nodded his head slightly toward the front door. Roy understood, got his hat and walked leisurely out, with his collector's book under his arm. Once outside, he made a beeline for the Stockmen's National. That bank was also getting ready to open. No customers had, as yet, presented themselves.

"Say, you people!" cried Roy, with the familiarity of

youth and long acquaintance, "you want to get a move on you. There's a new bank examiner over at the first, and he's a stem-winder. He's counting nickels on Perry, and he's got the whole outfit bluffed. Mr. Edlinger gave me the tip to let you know."

Mr. Buckley, president of the Stockmen's National—a stout, elderly man, looking like a farmer dressed for Sunday—heard Roy from his private office at the rear and called him.

"Has Major Kingman come down to the bank yet?" he asked of the boy.

"Yes, sir, he was just driving up as I left," said Roy.

"I want you to take him a note. Put it into his own hands as soon as you get back."

Mr. Buckley sat down and began to write.

Roy returned and handed to Major Kingman the envelope containing the note. The major read it, folded it, and slipped it into his vest pocket. He leaned back in his chair for a few moments as if he were meditating deeply, and then rose and went into the vault. He came out with the bulky, old-fashioned leather note case stamped on the back in gilt letters, "Bills Discounted." In this were the notes due the bank with their attached securities, and the major, in his rough way, dumped the lot upon his desk and began to sort them over.

By this time Nettlewick had finished his count of the cash. His pencil fluttered like a swallow over the sheet of paper on which he had set his figures. He opened his black wallet, which seemed to be also a kind of secret memorandum book, made a few rapid figures in it, wheeled and transfixed Dorsey with the glare of his spectacles. That look seemed to say: "You're safe this time, but——"

"Cash all correct," snapped the examiner. He made a dash for the individual bookkeeper, and, for a few minutes there was a fluttering of ledger leaves and a sailing of balance sheets through the air.

"How often do you balance your pass-books?" he demanded, suddenly.

"Er—once a month," faltered the individual bookkeeper, wondering how many years they would give him.

"All right," said the examiner, turning and charging upon the general bookkeeper, who had the statements of his foreign banks and their reconcilement memoranda ready. Everything there was found to be all right. Then the stub book of the certificates of deposit. Flutter—flutter—zip—zip—check! All right, list of over-drafts, please. Thanks. H'm-m. Unsigned bills of the bank next. All right.

Then came the cashier's turn, and easy-going Mr. Edlinger rubbed his nose and polished his glasses nervously under the quick fire of questions concerning the circulation, undivided profits, bank real estate, and stock ownership.

Presently Nettlewick was aware of a big man towering above him at his elbow—a man sixty years of age, rugged and hale, with a rough, grizzled beard, a mass of gray hair, and a pair of penetrating blue eyes that confronted the formidable glasses of the examiner without a flicker.

"Er—Major Kingman, our president—er—Mr. Nettlewick," said the cashier.

Two men of very different types shook hands. One was a finished product of the world of straight lines, conventional methods, and formal affairs. The other was something freer, wider, and nearer to nature. Tom Kingman had not been cut to any pattern. He had been mule-driver, cowboy, ranger, soldier, sheriff, prospector and cattleman. Now, when he was bank president, his old comrades from the prairies, of the saddle, tent, and trail, found no change in him. He had made his fortune when Texas cattle were at the high tide of value, and had organized the First National Bank of San Rosario. In spite of his largeness of heart and sometimes unwise generosity toward his old friends, the bank had prospered, for Major Tom Kingman knew men as well as he knew cattle. Of late years the cattle business had known a depression, and the major's bank was one of the few whose losses had not been great.

"And now," said the examiner, briskly, pulling out his watch, "the last thing is the loans. We will take them up now, if you please."

He had gone through the First National at almost record-breaking speed—but thoroughly, as he did everything. The running order of the bank was smooth and clean, and that had facilitated his work. There was but one other bank in the town. He received from the Government a fee of twenty-five dollars for each bank that he examined. He should be able to go over those loans and discounts in half an hour. If so, he could examine the other bank immediately afterward, and catch the 11:45, the only other train that day in the direction he was working. Otherwise, he would have to spend the night and Sunday in this uninteresting Western town. That was why Mr. Nettlewick was rushing matters.

"Come with me, sir," said Major Kingman, in his deep voice, that united the Southern drawl with the rhythmic twang of the West. "We will go over them together. Nobody in the bank knows those notes as I do. Some of 'em are a little wobbly on their legs, and some are mavericks without extra many brands on their backs, but they'll 'most all pay out at the round-up."

The two sat down at the president's desk. First, the examiner went through the notes at lightning speed, and added up their total, finding it to agree with the amount of loans carried on the book of daily balances. Next, he took up the larger loans, inquiring scrupulously into the condition of their endorsers or securities. The new examiner's mind seemed to course and turn and make unexpected dashes hither and thither like a bloodhound seeking a trail. Finally he pushed aside all the notes except a few, which he arranged in a neat pile before him, and began a dry, formal little speech.

"I find, sir, the condition of your bank to be very good, considering the poor crops and the depression in the cattle interests of your state. The clerical work seems to be done accurately and punctually. Your past-due paper is moderate in amount, and promises only a small loss. I would recommend the calling in of your large loans, and the making of only sixty and ninety day or call loans until general business revives. And now, there is one thing more, and I will have finished with the bank. Here are six notes aggregating something like $40,000. They are secured, according to their faces, by various stocks, bonds, shares, etc., to the value of $70,000. Those securities are missing from the notes to which they should be attached. I suppose you have them in the safe or vault. You will permit me to examine them."

Major Tom's light-blue eyes turned unflinchingly toward the examiner.

"No, sir," he said, in a low but steady tone; "those securities are neither in the safe nor the vault. I have taken them. You may hold me personally responsible for their absence.''

Nettlewick felt a slight thrill. He had not expected this. He had struck a momentous trail when the hunt was drawing to a close.

"Ah!" said the examiner. He waited a moment, and then continued: "May I ask you to explain more definitely?"

"The securities were taken by me," repeated the major. "It was not for my own use, but to save an old friend in trouble. Come in here, sir, and we'll talk it over."

He led the examiner into the bank's private office at the rear, and closed the door. There was a desk, and a table, and half-a-dozen leather-covered chairs. On the wall was the mounted head of a Texas steer with horns five feet from tip to tip. Opposite hung the major's old cavalry saber that he had carried at Shiloh and Fort Pillow.

Placing a chair for Nettlewick, the major seated himself by the window, from which he could see the post-office and the carved limestone front of the Stockmen's National. He did not speak at once, and Nettlewick felt, perhaps, that the ice should be broken by something so near its own temperature as the voice of official warning.

"Your statement," he began, "since you have failed to modify it, amounts, as you must know, to a very serious thing. You are aware, also, of what my duty must compel me to do. I shall have to go before the United States Commissioner and make——"

"I know, I know," said Major Tom, with a wave of his hand. "You don't suppose I'd run a bank without being posted on national banking laws and the revised statutes! Do your duty. I'm not asking any favors. But I spoke of my friend. I did want you to hear me tell about Bob."

Nettlewick settled himself in his chair. There would be no leaving San Rosario for him that day. He would have to telegraph to the Comptroller of the Currency; he would have to swear out a warrant before the United States Commissioner for the arrest of Major Kingman; perhaps he would be ordered to close the bank on account of the loss of the securities. It was not the first crime the examiner had unearthed. Once or twice the terrible upheaval of human emotions that his investigations had loosed had almost caused a ripple in his official calm. He had seen bank men kneel and plead and cry like women for a chance—an hour's time—the overlooking of a single error. One cashier had shot himself at his desk before him. None of them had taken it with the dignity and coolness of this stern old Westerner. Nettlewick felt that he owed it to him at least to listen if he wished to talk. With his elbow on the arm of his chair, and his square chin resting upon the fingers of his right hand, the bank examiner waited to hear the confession of the president of the First National Bank of San Rosario.

"When a man's your friend," began Major Tom, somewhat didactically, "for forty years, and tried by water, fire, earth, and cyclones, when you can do him a little favor you feel like doing it."

("Embezzle for him $70,000 worth of securities," thought the examiner.)

"We were cowboys together, Bob and I," continued the major, speaking slowly, and deliberately, and musingly, as if his thoughts were rather with the past than the critical present, "and we prospected together for gold and silver over Arizona, New Mexico, and a good part of California. We were both in the war of sixty-one, but in different commands. We've fought Indians and horse thieves side by side; we've starved for weeks in a cabin in the Arizona mountains, buried twenty feet deep in snow; we've ridden herd together when the wind blew so hard the lightning couldn't strike—well, Bob and I have been through some rough spells since the first time we met in the branding camp of the old Anchor-Bar ranch. And during that time we've found it necessary more than once to help each other out of tight places. In those days it was expected of a man to stick to his friend, and he didn't ask any credit for it. Probably next day you'd need him to get at your back and help stand off a band of Apaches, or put a tourniquet on your leg above a rattlesnake bite and ride for whisky. So, after all, it was give and take, and if you didn't stand square with your pardner, why, you might be shy one when you needed him. But Bob was a man who was willing to go further than that. He never played a limit.

"Twenty years ago I was sheriff of this county and I made Bob my chief deputy. That was before the boom in cattle when we both made our stake. I was sheriff and collector, and it was a big thing for me then. I was married, and we had a boy and a girl—a four and a six year old. There was a comfortable house next to the courthouse, furnished by the county, rent free, and I was saving some money. Bob did most of the office work. Both of us had seen rough times and plenty of rustling and danger, and I tell you it was great to hear the rain and the sleet dashing against the windows of nights, and be warm and safe and comfortable, and know you could get up in the morning and be shaved and have folks call you 'mister.' And then, I had the finest wife and kids that ever struck the range, and my old friend with me enjoying the first fruits of prosperity and white shirts, and I guess I was happy. Yes, I was happy about that time.''

The major sighed and glanced casually out of the window. The bank examiner changed his position, and leaned his chin upon his other hand.

"One winter," continued the major, "the money for the county taxes came pouring in so fast that I didn't have time to take the stuff to the bank for a week. I just shoved the checks into a cigar box and the money into a sack, and locked them in the big safe that belonged in the sheriff's office.

"I had been overworked that week, and was about sick, anyway. My nerves were out of order, and my sleep at night didn't seem to rest me. The doctor had some scientific name for it, and I was taking medicine. And so, added to the rest, I went to bed at night with that money on my mind. Not that there was much need of being worried, for the safe was a good one, and nobody but Bob and I knew the combination. On Friday night there was about $6,500 in cash in the bag. On Saturday morning I went to the office as usual. The safe was locked, and Bob was writing at his desk. I opened the safe, and the money was gone. I called Bob, and roused everybody in the courthouse to announce the robbery. It struck me that Bob took it pretty quiet, considering how much it reflected upon both him and me.

"Two days went by and we never got a clew. It couldn't have been burglars, for the safe had been opened by the combination in the proper way. People must have begun to talk, for one afternoon in comes Alice—that's my wife—and the boy and girl, and Alice stamps her foot, and her eyes flash, and she cries out, 'The lying wretches—Tom, Tom!'

and I catch her in a faint, and bring her 'round little by little, and she lays her head down and cries and cries for the first time since she took Tom Kingman's name and fortunes. And Jack and Zilla—the youngsters—they were always wild as tigers cubs to rush at Bob and climb all over him whenever they were allowed to come to the courthouse—they stood and kicked their little shoes, and herded together like scared partridges. They were having their first trip down into the shadows of life. Bob was working at his desk, and he got up and went out without a word. The grand jury was in session then, and the next morning Bob went before them and confessed that he stole the money. He said he lost it in a poker game. In fifteen minutes they had found a true bill and sent me the warrant to arrest the man with whom I'd been closer than a thousand brothers for many a year.

"I did it, and then I said to Bob, pointing: 'There's my house, and here's my office, and up there's Maine, and out that way is California, and over there is Florida—and that's your range 'til court meets. You're in my charge, and I take the responsibility. You be here when you're wanted.'

" 'Thanks, Tom,' he said, kind of carelessly; 'I was sort of hoping you wouldn't lock me up. Court meets next Monday, so, if you don't object, I'll just loaf around the office until then. I've got one favor to ask, if it isn't too much. If you'd let the kids come out in the yard once in a while and have a romp I'd like it.'

" 'Why not?' I answered him. 'They're welcome, and so are you. And come to my house the same as ever.' You see, Mr. Nettlewick, you can't make a friend of a thief, but neither can you make a thief of a friend, all at once."

The examiner made no answer. At that moment was heard the shrill whistle of a locomotive pulling into the depot. That was the train on the little, narrow-gauge road that struck into San Rosario from the south. The major cocked his ear and listened for a moment, and looked at his watch. The narrow-gauge was in on time—10:35. The major continued.

"So Bob hung around the office, reading the papers and smoking. I put another deputy to work in his place, and, after a while, the first excitement of the case wore off.

"One day when we were alone in the office Bob came over to where I was sitting. He was looking sort of grim and blue—the same look he used to get when he'd been up watching for Indians all night or herd-riding.

" 'Tom,' says he, 'it's harder than standing off redskins; it's harder than lying in the lava desert forty miles from water; but I'm going to stick it out to the end. You know that's been my style. But if you'd tip me the smallest kind of a sign—if you'd just say, "Bob I understand," why, it would make it lots easier.'

"I was surprised. 'I don't know what you mean, Bob,' I said. 'Of course, you know that I'd do anything under the sun to help you that I could. But you've got me guessing.'

" 'All right, Tom,' was all he said, and he went back to his newspaper and lit another cigar.

"It was the night before the court met when I found out what he meant. I went to bed that night with the same old, light-headed, nervous feeling come back upon me. I dropped off to sleep about midnight. When I woke I was standing half dressed in one of the courthouse corridors. Bob was holding one of my arms, our family doctor the other and Alice was shaking me and half crying. She had sent for the doctor without my knowing it, and when he came they had found me out of bed and missing, and had begun a search.

" 'Sleep-walking,' said the doctor.

"All of us went back to the house, and the doctor told us some remarkable stories about the strange things people had done while in that condition. I was feeling rather chilly after my trip out, and, as my wife was out of the room at the time, I pulled open the door of an old wardrobe that stood in the room and dragged out a big quilt I had seen in there. With it tumbled out the bag of money for stealing which Bob was to be tried—and convicted—in the morning.

" 'How the jumping rattlesnakes did that get there?' I yelled, and all hands must have seen how surprised I was. Bob knew in a flash.

" 'You darned old snoozer,' he said, with the old-time look on his face, 'I saw you put it there. I watched you open the safe and take it out, and I followed you. I looked through the window and saw you hide it in that wardrobe.'

" 'Then, you blankety-blank, flop-eared, sheep-headed coyote, what did you say you took it for?'

" 'Because,' said Bob, simply, 'I didn't know you were asleep.'

"I saw him glance toward the door of the room where Jack and Zilla were, and I knew then what it meant to be a man's friend from Bob's point of view."

Major Tom paused, and again directed his glance out of the window. He saw someone in the Stockmen's National Bank reach and draw a yellow shade down the whole length of its plate-glass, big front window, although the position of the sun did not seem to warrant such a defensive movement against its rays.

Nettlewick sat up straight in his chair. He had listened patiently, but without consuming interest, to the major's story. It had impressed him as irrelevant to the situation, and it could certainly have no effect upon the consequences. Those Western people, he thought, had an exaggerated sentimentality. They were not business-like. They needed to be protected from their friends. Evidently the major had concluded. And what he had said amounted to nothing.

"May I ask," said the examiner, "if you have anything further to say that bears directly upon the question of those abstracted securities?"

"Abstracted securities, sir!" Major Tom turned suddenly in his chair, his blue eyes flashing upon the examiner. "What do you mean, sir?"

He drew from his coat pocket a batch of folded papers held together by a rubber band, tossed them into Nettlewick's hands, and rose to his feet.

"You'll find those securities there, sir, every stock, bond, and share of 'em. I took them from the notes while you were counting the cash. Examine and compare them for yourself."

The major led the way back into the banking room. The examiner, astounded, perplexed, nettled, at sea, followed. He felt that he had been made the victim of something that was not exactly a hoax, but that left him in the shoes of one who had been played upon, used, and then discarded, without even an inkling of the game. Perhaps, also, his official position had been irreverently juggled with. But there was nothing he could take hold of. An official report of the matter would be an absurdity. And, somehow, he felt that he would never know anything more about the matter than he did then.

Frigidly, mechanically, Nettlewick examined the securities, found them to tally with the notes, gathered his black wallet, and rose to depart.

"I will say," he protested, turning the indignant glare of his glasses upon Major Kingman, "that your statements—your misleading statements, which you have not condescended to explain—do not appear to be quite the thing, regarded either as business or humor. I do not understand such motives or actions."

Major Tom looked down at him serenely and not unkindly.

"Son," he said, "there are plenty of things in the chaparral, and on the prairies, and up the cañons that you don't understand. But I want to thank you for listening to a garrulous old man's prosy story. We old Texans love to talk about our adventures and our old comrades, and the home folks have long ago learned to run when we begin with 'Once upon a time,' so we have to spin our yarns to the stranger within our gates."

The major smiled, but the examiner only bowed coldly, and abruptly quitted the bank. They saw him travel diagonally across the street in a straight line and enter the Stockmen's National Bank.

Major Tom sat down at his desk and drew from his vest pocket the note Roy had given him. He had read it once, but hurriedly, and now, with something like a twinkle in his eyes, he read it again. These were the words he read:

Dear Tom:

I hear there's one of Uncle Sam's greyhounds going through you, and that means that we'll catch him inside of a couple of hours, maybe. Now, I want you to do something for me. We've got just $2,200 in the bank, and the law requires that we have $20,000. I let Ross and Fisher have $18,000 late yesterday afternoon to buy up that Gibson bunch of cattle. They'll realize $40,000 in less than thirty days on the transaction, but that won't make my cash on hand look any prettier to that bank examiner. Now, I can't show him those notes, for they're just plain notes of hand without any security in sight, but you know very well that Pink Ross and Jim Fisher are two of the finest white men God ever made, and they'll do the square thing. You remember Jim Fisher—he was the one who shot that faro dealer in El Paso. I wired Sam Bradshaw's bank to send me $20,000, and it will get in on the narrow-gauge at 10:35. You can't let a bank examiner in to count $2,200 and close your doors. Tom, you hold that examiner. Hold him. Hold him if you have to rope him and sit on his head. Watch our front window after the narrow-gauge gets in, and when we've got the cash inside we'll pull down the shade for a signal. Don't turn him loose till then. I'm counting on you, Tom.

                              Your Old Pard,
                              Bob Buckley,
                        Prest. Stockmen's National

The major began to tear the note into small pieces and throw them into his waste basket. He gave a satisfied little chuckle as he did so.

"Confounded old reckless cowpuncher!" he growled, contentedly, "that pays him some on account for what he tried to do for me in the sheriff's office twenty years ago."

The Sphinx Apple

Twenty miles out from Paradise, and fifteen miles short of Sunrise City, Bildad Rose, the stage-driver, stopped his team. A furious snow had been falling all day. Eight inches it measured now, on a level. The remainder of the road was not without peril in daylight, creeping along the ribs of a bijou range of ragged mountains. Now, when both snow and night masked its dangers, further travel was not to be thought of, said Bildad Rose. So he pulled up his four stout horses, and delivered to his five passengers oral deductions of his wisdom.

Judge Menefee, to whom men granted leadership and the initiatory as upon a silver salver, sprang from the coach at once. Four of his fellow-passengers followed, inspired by his example, ready to explore, to objurgate, to resist, to submit, to proceed, according as their prime factor might be inclined to sway them. The fifth passenger, a young woman, remained in the coach.

Bildad had halted upon the shoulder of the first mountain spur. Two rail-fences, ragged-black, hemmed the road. Fifty yards above the upper fence, showing a dark blot in the white drifts, stood a small house. Upon this house descended—or rather ascended—Judge Menefee and his cohorts with boyish whoops born of the snow and stress. They called; they pounded at window and door. At the inhospitable silence they waxed restive; they assaulted and forced the pregnable barriers, and invaded the premises.

The watches from the coach heard stumblings and shoutings from the interior of the ravaged house. Before long a light within flickered, glowed, flamed high and bright and cheerful. Then came running back through the driving flakes the exuberant explorers. More deeply pitched than the clarion—even orchestral in volume—the voice of Judge Menefee proclaimed the succor that lay in apposition with their state of travail. The one room of the house was uninhabited, he said, and bare of furniture; but it contained a great fireplace; and they had discovered an ample store of chopped wood in a lean-to at the rear. Housing and warmth against the shivering night were thus assured. For the placation of Bildad Rose there was news of a stable, not ruined beyond service, with hay in a loft, near the house.

"Gentlemen," cried Bildad Rose from his seat, swathed in coats and robes, "tear me down two panels of that fence, so I can drive in. That is old man Redruth's shanty. I thought we must be nigh it. They took him to the foolish house in August."

Cheerfully the four passengers sprang at the snow-capped rails. The exhorted team tugged the coach up the slant to the door of the edifice from which a mid-summer madness had ravished its proprietor. The driver and two of the passengers began to unhitch. Judge Menefee opened the door of the coach, and removed his hat.

"I have to announce, Miss Garland," said he, "the enforced suspension of our journey. The driver asserts that the risk in traveling the mountain road by night is too great even to consider. It will be necessary to remain in the shelter of this house until morning. I beg that you will feel that there is nothing to fear beyond a temporary inconvenience. I have personally inspected the house, and find that there are means to provide against the rigor of the weather, at least. You shall be made as comfortable as possible. Permit me to assist you to alight."

To the Judge's side came the passenger whose pursuit in life was the placing of the Little Goliath windmill. His name was Dunwoody; but that matters not much. In traveling merely from Paradise to Sunrise City one needs little or no name. Still, one who would seek to divide honors with Judge Madison L. Menefee deserves a cognominal peg upon which Fame may hang a wreath. Thus spake, loudly and buoyantly, the aërial miller:

"Guess you'll have to climb out of the ark, Mrs. McFarland. This wigwam ain't exactly the Palmer House, but it turns snow, and they won't search your grip for souvenir spoons when you leave. *We've* got a fire going; and *we'll* fix you up with dry Trilbys and keep the mice away, anyhow, all right, all right."

One of the two passengers who were struggling in a *mêlée* of horses, harness, snow, and the sarcastic injunctions of Bildad Rose, called loudly from the whirl of his volunteer duties: "Say! some of you fellows get Miss Solomon into the house, will you? Whoa, there! you confounded brute!"

Again must it be gently urged that in traveling from Paradise to Sunrise City an accurate name is prodigality. When Judge Menefee—sanctioned to the act by his grey hair and widespread repute—had introduced himself to the lady passenger, she had, herself, sweetly breathed a name, in response, that the hearing of the male passengers had variously interpreted. In the not unjealous spirit of rivalry that eventuated, each clung stubbornly to his own theory. For the lady passenger to have reasseverated or corrected would have seemed didactic if not unduly solicitous of a specific acquaintance. Therefore the lady passenger permitted herself to be Garlanded and McFarlanded and Solomoned with equal and discreet complacency. It is thirty-five miles from Paradise to Sunrise City. *Compagnon de voyage* is name enough, by the gripsack of the Wandering Jew! for so brief a journey.

Soon the little party of wayfarers were happily seated in a cheerful arc before the roaring fire. The robes, cushions, and removable portions of the coach had been brought in and put to service. The lady passenger chose a place near the hearth at one end of the arc. There she graced almost a throne that her subjects had prepared. She sat upon cushions and leaned against an empty box and barrel, robe bespread, which formed a defence from the invading draughts. She extended her feet, delectably shod, to the cordial heat. She ungloved her hands, but retained about her neck her long fur boa. The unstable flames half revealed, while the warding boa half submerged, her face—a youthful face, altogether feminine, clearly moulded and calm with beauty's unchallenged confidence. Chivalry and manhood were here vying to please and comfort her. She seemed to accept their devoirs—not piquantly, as one courted and attended; not preeningly, as many of her sex unworthily reap their honors; nor yet stolidly, as the ox receives his hay; but concordantly with nature's own plan—as the lily ingests the drop of dew foreordained to its refreshment.

Outside the wind roared mightily, the fine snow whizzed through the cracks, the cold besieged the backs of the immolated six; but the elements did not lack a champion that night. Judge Menefee was attorney for the storm. The weather was his client, and he strove by special pleading to convince his companions in that frigid jury-box that they sojourned in a bower of roses, beset only by benignant zephyrs. He drew upon a fund of gaiety, wit, and anecdote, sophistical, but crowned with success. His cheerfulness communicated itself irresistibly. Each one hastened to contribute his quota toward the general optimism. Even the lady passenger was moved to expression.

"I think it is quite charming," she said, in her slow, crystal tones.

At intervals some one of the passengers would rise and humorously explore the room. There was little evidence to be collected of its habitation by old man Redruth.

Bildad Rose was called upon vivaciously for the ex-hermit's history. Now, since the stage-driver's horses were fairly comfortable and his passengers appeared to be so, peace and comity returned to him.

"The old didapper," began Bildad, somewhat irreverently, "infested this here house about twenty year. He never allowed nobody to come nigh him. He'd duck his head inside and slam the door whenever a team drove along. There was spinning-wheels up in his loft, all right. He used to buy his groceries and tobacco at Sam Tilly's store, on the Little Muddy. Last August he went up there dressed in a red bedquilt, and told Sam he was King Solomon, and that the Queen of Sheba was coming to visit him. He fetched along all the money he had—a little bag full of silver—and dropped it in Sam's well. 'She won't come,' says old man Redruth to Sam, 'if she knows I've got any money.'

"As soon as folks heard he had that sort of a theory about women and money they knowed he was crazy; so they sent down and packed him to the foolish asylum."

"Was there a romance in his life that drove him to a solitary existence?" asked one of the passengers, a young man who had an Agency.

"No," said Bildad, "not that I ever heard spoke of. Just ordinary trouble. They say he had had unfortunateness in the way of love derangements with a young lady when he was young; before he contracted red bedquilts and had his financial conclusions disqualified. I never heard of no romance."

"Ah!" exclaimed Judge Menefee, impressively; "a case of unrequited affection, no doubt."

"No, sir," returned Bildad, "not at all. She never married him. Marmaduke Mulligan, down at Paradise, seen a man once that come from old Redruth's town. He said Redruth was a fine young man, but when you kicked him on the pocket all you could hear jingle was a cuff-fastener and a bunch of keys. He was engaged to this young lady—Miss Alice—something was her name; I've forgot. This man said she was the kind of a girl you like to have reach across you in a car to pay the fare. Well, there come to the town a young chap all affluent and easy, and fixed up with buggies and mining stock and leisure time. Although she was a staked claim, Miss Alice and the new entry seemed to strike a mutual kind of a clip. They had calls and coincidences of going to the post office and such things as sometimes make a girl send back the engagement ring and other presents—'a rift within the loot,' the poetry man calls it.

"One day folks seen Redruth and Miss Alice standing talking at the gate. Then he lifts his hat and walks away, and that was the last anybody in that town seen of him, as far as this man knew."

"What about the young lady?" asked the young man who had an Agency.

"Never heard," answered Bildad. "Right there is where my lode of information turns to an old spavined crowbait, and folds its wings, for I've pumped it dry."

"A very sad—" began Judge Menefee, but his remark was curtailed by a higher authority.

"What a charming story!" said the lady passenger, in flute-like tones.

A little silence followed, except for the wind and the crackling of the fire.

The men were seated upon the floor, having slightly mitigated its inhospitable surface with wraps and stray pieces of boards. The man who was placing Little Goliath windmills arose and walked about to ease his cramped muscles.

Suddenly a triumphant shout came from him. He hurried back from a dusky corner of the room, bearing aloft something in his hand. It was an apple—a large, red-mottled, firm pippin, pleasing to behold. In a paper bag on a high shelf in that corner he had found it. It could have been no relic of the love-wrecked Redruth, for its glorious soundness repudiated the theory that it had laid on that musty shelf since August. No doubt some recent bivouackers, lunching in the deserted house, had left it there.

Dunwoody—again his exploits demand for him the honors of nomenclature—flaunted his apple in the faces of his fellow-marooners. "See what I found, Mrs. McFarland!" he cried, vaingloriously. He held the apple high up in the light of the fire, where it glowed a still richer red. The lady passenger smiled calmly—always calmly.

"What a charming apple!" she murmured, clearly.

For a brief space Judge Menefee felt crushed, humiliated, relegated. Second place galled him. Why had this blatant, obtrusive, unpolished man of windmills been selected by Fate instead of himself to discover the sensational apple? He could have made of the act a scene, a function, a setting for some impromptu fanciful discourse or piece of comedy—and have retained the rôle of cynosure. Actually, the lady passenger was regarding this ridiculous Dunboddy or Woodbundy with an admiring smile, as if the fellow had performed a feat! And the windmill man swelled and gyrated like a sample of his own goods, puffed up with the wind that ever blows from the chorus land toward the domain of the star.

While the transported Dunwoody, with his Aladdin's apple, was receiving the fickle attentions of all, the resourceful jurist formed a plan to recover his own laurels.

With his courtliest smile upon his heavy but classic features, Judge Menefee advanced, and took the apple, as if to examine it, from the hand of Dunwoody. In his hand it became Exhibit A.

"A fine apple," he said, approvingly. "Really, my dear Mr. Dunwindy, you have eclipsed all of us as a forager. But I have an idea. This apple shall become an emblem, a token, a symbol, a prize bestowed by the mind and heart of beauty upon the most deserving."

The audience, except one, applauded. "Good on the stump, ain't he?" commented the passenger who was nobody in particular to the young man who had an Agency.

The unresponsive one was the windmill man. He saw himself reduced to the ranks. Never would the thought have occurred to him to declare his apple an emblem. He had intended after it had been divided and eaten, to create diversion by sticking the seeds against his forehead and naming them for young ladies of his acquaintance. One he was going to name Mrs. McFarland. The seed that fell off first would be—but 'twas too late now.

"The apple," continued Judge Menefee, charging his jury, "in modern days occupies, though undeservedly, a lowly place in our esteem. Indeed, it is so constantly associated with the culinary and the commercial that it is hardly to be classed among the polite fruits. But in ancient times this was not so. Biblical, historical, and mythological lore abounds with evidences that the apple was the aristocrat of fruits. We still say 'the apple of the eye' when we wish to describe something superlatively precious. We find in Proverbs the comparison to 'apples of silver.' No other product of tree or vine has been so utilized in figurative speech. Who has not heard of and longed for the 'apples of the Hesperides'? I need not call your attention to the most tremendous and significant instance of the apple's ancient prestige when its consumption by our first parents occasioned the fall of man from his state of goodness and perfection.''

"Apples like them," said the windmill man, lingering with the objective article, "are worth $3.50 a barrel in the Chicago market."

"Now, what I have to propose," said Judge Menefee, conceding an indulgent smile to his interrupter, "is this: We must remain here, perforce, until morning. We have wood in plenty to keep us warm. Our next need is to entertain ourselves as best we can, in order that the time shall not pass too slowly. I propose that we place this apple in the hands of Miss Garland. It is no longer a fruit, but, as I said, a prize, in award, representing a great human idea. Miss Garland, herself, shall cease to be an individual—but only temporarily, I am happy to add''—(a low bow, full of the old-time grace). "She shall represent her sex; she shall be the embodiment, the epitome of womankind—the heart and brain, I may say, of God's masterpiece of creation. In this guise she shall judge and decide the question which follows:

"But a few minutes ago our friend, Mr. Rose, favored us with an entertaining but fragmentary sketch of the romance in the life of the former possessor of this habitation. The few facts that we have learned seem to me to open up a fascinating field for conjecture, for the study of human hearts, for the exercise of the imagination—in short, for story-telling. Let us make use of the opportunity. Let each one of us relate his own version of the story of Redruth, the hermit, and his lady-love, beginning where Mr. Rose's narrative ends—at the parting of the lovers at the gate. This much should be assumed and conceded—that the young lady was not necessarily to blame for Redruth's becoming a crazed and world-hating hermit. When we have done, Miss Garland shall render the JUDGMENT OF WOMAN. As the Spirit of her Sex she shall decide which version of the story best and most truly depicts human and love interest, and most faithfully estimates the character and acts of Redruth's betrothed according to the feminine view. The apple shall be bestowed upon him who is awarded the decision. If you are all agreed, we shall be pleased to hear the first story from Mr. Dinwiddie.''

The last sentence captured the windmill man. He was not one to linger in the dumps.

"That's a first-rate scheme, Judge," he said, heartily. "Be a regular short-story vaudeville, won't it? I used to be correspondent for a paper in Springfield, and when there wasn't any news I faked it. Guess I can do my turn all right."

"I think the idea is charming," said the lady passenger, brightly. "It will be almost like a game."

Judge Menefee stepped forward and placed the apple in her hand impressively.

"In olden days," he said, profoundly, "Paris awarded the golden apple to the most beautiful."

"I was at the Exposition," remarked the windmill man, now cheerful again, "but I never heard of it. And I was on the Midway, too, all the time I wasn't at the machinery exhibit."

"But now," continued the Judge, "the fruit shall translate to us the mystery and wisdom of the feminine heart. Take the apple, Miss Garland. Hear our modest tales of romance, and then award the prize as you may deem it just."

The lady passenger smiled sweetly. The apple lay in her lap beneath her robes and wraps. She reclined against her protecting bulwark, brightly and cosily at ease. But for the voices and the wind one might have listened hopefully to hear her purr. Someone cast fresh logs upon the fire. Judge Menefee nodded suavely. "Will you oblige us with the initial story?" he asked.

The windmill man sat as sits a Turk, with his hat well back on his head on account of the draughts.

"Well," he began, without any embarrassment, "this is about the way I size up the difficulty: Of course Redruth was jostled a good deal by this duck who had money to play ball with who tried to cut him out of his girl. So he goes around, naturally, and asks her if the game is still square. Well, nobody wants a guy cutting in with buggies and gold bonds when he's got an option on a girl. Well, he goes around to see her. Well, maybe he's hot, and talks like the proprietor, and forgets that an engagement ain't always a lead-pipe cinch.

Well, I guess that makes Alice warm under the lace yoke. Well, she answers back sharp. Well, he——''

"Say!" interrupted the passenger who was nobody in particular, "if you could put up a windmill on every one of them 'wells' you're using, you'd be able to retire from business, wouldn't you?"

The windmill man grinned good-naturedly.

"Oh, I ain't no *Guy de Mopassong*," he said, cheerfully. "I'm giving it to you in straight American. Well, she says something like this: 'Mr. Gold Bonds is only a friend,' says she; 'but he takes me riding and buys me theatre tickets, and that's what you never do. Ain't I to never have any pleasure in life while I can?' 'Pass this chatfield-chatfield thing along,' says Redruth;—'hand out the mitt to the Willie with creases in it or you don't put your slippers under my wardrobe.'

"Now that kind of train orders don't go with a girl that's got any spirit. I bet that girl loved her honey all the time. Maybe she only wanted, as girls do, to work the good thing for a little fun and caramels before she settled down to patch George's other pair, and be a good wife. But he is glued to the high horse, and won't come down. Well, she hands him back the ring, proper enough; and George goes away and hits the booze. Yep. That's what done it. I bet that girl fired the cornucopia with the fancy vest two days after her steady left. George boards a freight and checks his bag of crackers for parts unknown. He sticks to Old Booze for a number of years; and then the aniline and aquafortis gets the decision. 'Me for the hermit's hut,' says George, 'and the long whiskers, and the buried can of money that isn't there.'

"But that Alice, in my mind, was on the level. She never married, but took up typewriting as soon as the wrinkles began to show, and kept a cat that came when you said 'weeny—weeny—weeny!' I got too much faith in good women to believe they throw down the fellow they're stuck on every time for the dough." The windmill man ceased.

"I think," said the lady passenger, slightly moving upon her lowly throne, "that that is a char——"

"Oh, Miss Garland!" interposed Judge Menefee, with uplifted hand, "I beg of you, no comments! It would not be fair to the other contestants. Mr.—er—will you take the next turn?'' The Judge addressed the young man who had the Agency.

"My version of the romance," began the young man, diffidently clasping his hands, "would be this: They did not quarrel when they parted. Mr. Redruth bade her good-bye and went out into the world to seek his fortune. He knew his love would remain true to him. He scorned the thought that his rival could make an impression upon a heart so fond and faithful. I would say that Mr. Redruth went out to the Rocky Mountains in Wyoming to seek for gold. One day a crew of pirates landed and captured him while at work, and——"

"Hey! what's that?" sharply called the passenger who was nobody in particular—"a crew of pirates landed in the Rocky Mountains! Will you tell us how they sailed——"

"Landed from a train," said the narrator, quietly and not without some readiness. "They kept him prisoner in a cave for months, and then they took him hundreds of miles away to the forests of Alaska. There a beautiful Indian girl fell in love with him, but he remained true to Alice. After another year of wandering in the woods, he set out with the diamonds——"

"What diamonds?" asked the unimportant passenger, almost with acerbity.

"The ones the saddlemaker showed him in the Peruvian temple," said the other, somewhat obscurely. "When he reached home, Alice's mother led him, weeping, to a green mound under a willow tree. 'Her heart was broken when you left,' said her mother. 'And what of my rival—of Chester McIntosh?' asked Mr. Redruth, as he knelt sadly by Alice's grave. 'When he found out,' she answered, 'that her heart was yours, he pined away day by day until, at length, he started a furniture store in Grand Rapids. We heard lately that he was bitten to death by an infuriated moose near South Bend, Ind., where he had gone to try to forget scenes of civilization.' With which, Mr. Redruth forsook the face of mankind and became a hermit, as we have seen.

"My story," concluded the young man with an Agency, "may lack the literary quality; but what I want it to show is that the young lady remained true. She cared nothing for wealth in comparison with true affection. I admire and believe in the fair sex too much to think otherwise."

The narrator ceased, with a sidelong glance at the corner where reclined the lady passenger.

Bildad Rose was next invited by Judge Menefee to contribute his story in the contest for the apple of judgment. The stage-driver's essay was brief.

"I'm not one of them lobo wolves," he said, "who are always blaming on women the calamities of life. My testimony in regards to the fiction story you ask for, Judge, will be about as follows: What ailed Redruth was pure laziness. If he had up and slugged this Percival De Lacey that tried to give him the outside of the road, and had kept Alice in the grape-vine swing with the blind-bridle on, all would have been well. The woman you want is sure worth taking pains for.

" 'Send for me if you want me again,' says Redruth, and hoists his Stetson, and walks off. He'd have called it pride, but the nixycomlogical name for it is laziness. No woman don't like to run after a man. 'Let him come back, hisself,' says the girl; and I'll be bound she tells the boy with the pay ore to trot; and then spends her time watching out the window for the man with the empty pocket-book and the tickly moustache.

"I reckon Redruth waits about nine year expecting her to send him a note by a nigger asking him to forgive her. But she don't. 'This game won't work,' says Redruth; 'then so won't I.' And he goes in the hermit business and raises whiskers. Yes; laziness and whiskers was what done the trick. They travel together. You ever hear of a man with long whiskers and hair striking a bonanza? No. Look at the Duke of Marlborough and this Standard Oil snoozer. Have they got 'em?

"Now, this Alice didn't never marry, I'll bet a hoss. If Redruth had married somebody else she might have done so, too. But he never turns up. She has these here things they call fond memories, and maybe a lock of hair and a corset steel that he broke, treasured up. Them sort of articles is as good as a husband to some women. I'd say she played out a lone hand. I don't blame no woman for old man Redruth's abandonment of barber shops and clean shirts."

Next in order came the passenger who was nobody in

particular. Nameless to us, he travels the road from Paradise to Sunrise City.

But him you shall see, if the firelight be not too dim, as he responds to the Judge's call.

A lean form, in rusty-brown clothing, sitting like a frog, his arms wrapped about his legs, his chin resting upon his knees. Smooth, oakum-colored hair; long nose; mouth like a satyr's, with upturned, tobacco-stained corners. An eye like a fish's; a red necktie with a horseshoe pin. He began with a rasping chuckle that gradually formed itself into words.

"Everybody wrong so far. What! A romance without any orange blossoms! Ho, ho! My money on the lad with the butterfly tie and the certified checks in his trouserings.

"Take 'em as they parted at the gate? All right. 'You never loved me,' says Redruth, wildly, 'or you wouldn't speak to a man who can buy you the ice cream.' 'I hate him,' says she. 'I loathe his side-bar buggy; I despise the elegant cream bonbons he sends me in gilt boxes covered with real lace; I feel that I could stab him to the heart when he presents me with a solid medallion locket with turquoises and pearls running in a vine around the border. Away with them! 'Tis only you I love.' 'Back to the cosy corner!' says Redruth. 'Was I bound and lettered in East Aurora? Get platonic, if you please. No jack-pots for mine. Go and hate your friend some more. For me the Nickerson girl on Avenue B, and gum, and a trolley ride.'

"Around that night comes John W. Crœsus. 'What! tears?' says he, arranging his pearl pin. 'You have driven my lover away,' says little Alice sobbing: 'I hate the sight of you.' 'Marry me, then,' says John W., lighting a Henry Clay. 'What!' she cries, indignantly, 'marry you! Never,' she says, 'until this blows over, and I can do some shopping, and you see about the license. There's a telephone next door if you want to call up the county clerk.' "

The narrator paused to give vent to his cynical chuckle.

"Did they marry?" he continued. "Did the duck swallow the June-bug? And then I take up the case of Old Boy Redruth. There's where you are all wrong again, according to my theory. What turned him into a hermit? One says laziness; one says remorse; one says booze. I say women did it. How old is the old man now?'' asked the speaker, turning to Bildad Rose.

"I should say about sixty-five."

"All right. He conducted his hermit shop here for twenty years. Say he was twenty-five when he took off his hat at the gate. That leaves twenty years for him to account for, or else be docked. Where did he spend that ten and two fives? I'll give you my idea. Up for bigamy. Say there was the fat blonde in Saint Jo, and the panatela brunette at Skillet Ridge, and the gold tooth down in the Kaw valley. Redruth gets his cases mixed, and they send him up the road. He gets out after they are through with him, and says: 'Any line for me except the crinoline. The hermit trade is not overdone, and the stenographers never apply to 'em for work. The jolly hermit's life for me. No more long hairs in the comb or dill pickles lying around in the cigar tray.' You tell me they pinched old Redruth for the noodle villa just because he said he was King Solomon? Figs! He *was* Solomon. That's all of mine. I guess it don't call for any apples. Enclosed find stamps. It don't sound much like a prize winner.''

Respecting the stricture laid by Judge Menefee against comments upon the stories, all were silent when the passenger who was nobody in particular had concluded. And then the ingenious originator of the contest cleared his throat to begin the ultimate entry for the prize. Though seated with small comfort upon the floor, you might search in vain for any abatement of dignity in Judge Menefee. The now diminishing firelight played softly upon his face, as clearly chiselled as a Roman emperor's on some old coin, and upon the thick waves of his honorable gray hair.

"A woman's heart!" he began, in even but thrilling tones—"who can hope to fathom it? The ways and desires of men are various. I think that the hearts of all women beat with the same rhythm, and to the same old tune of love. Love, to a woman, means sacrifice. If she be worthy of the name, no gold or rank will outweigh with her a genuine devotion.

"Gentlemen of the—er—I should say, my friends, the case of Redruth *versus* love and affection has been called. Yet, who is on trial? Not Redruth, for he has been punished. Not those immortal passions that clothe our lives with the joy of the angels. Then who? Each man of us here to-night stands at the bar to answer if chivalry or darkness inhabits his bosom. To judge us sits womankind in the form of one of its fairest flowers. In her hand she holds the prize, intrinsically insignificant, but worthy of our noblest efforts to win as a guerdon of approval from so worthy a representative of feminine judgment and taste.

"In taking up the imaginary history of Redruth and the fair being to whom he gave his heart, I must, in the beginning, raise my voice against the unworthy insinuation that the selfishness or perfidy or love of luxury of any woman drove him to renounce the world. I have not found woman to be so unspiritual or venal. We must seek elsewhere, among man's baser nature and lower motives for the cause.

"There was, in all probability, a lovers' quarrel as they stood at the gate on that memorable day. Tormented by jealousy, young Redruth vanished from his native haunts. But had he just cause to do so? There is no evidence for or against. But there is something higher than evidence: there is the grand, eternal belief in woman's goodness, in her steadfastness against temptation, in her loyalty even in the face of proffered riches.

"I picture to myself the rash lover, wandering, self-tortured, about the world. I picture his gradual descent, and, finally, his complete despair when he realizes that he has lost the most precious gift life had to offer him. Then his withdrawal from the world of sorrow and the subsequent derangement of his faculties becomes intelligible.

"But what do I see on the other hand? A lonely woman fading away as the years roll by; still faithful, still waiting, still watching for a form and listening for a step that will come no more. She is old now. Her hair is white and smoothly banded. Each day she sits at the door and gazes longingly down the dusty road. In spirit she is waiting there at the gate, just as he left her—his forever, but not here below. Yes; my belief in woman paints that picture in my mind. Parted forever on earth, but waiting! She in anticipation of a meeting in Elysium; he in the Slough of Despond."

"I thought he was in the bughouse," said the passenger who was nobody in particular.

Judge Menefee stirred, a little impatiently. The men sat, drooping, in grotesque attitudes. The wind had abated its violence; coming now in fitful, virulent puffs. The fire had burned to a mass of red coals which shed but a dim light within the room. The lady passenger in her cosy nook looked to be but a formless dark bulk, crowned by a mass of coiled, sleek hair and showing but a small space of snowy forehead above her clinging boa.

Judge Menefee got stiffly to his feet.

"And now, Miss Garland," he announced, "we have concluded. It is for you to award the prize to the one of us whose argument—especially, I may say, in regard to his estimate of true womanhood—approaches nearest to your own conception."

No answer came from the lady passenger. Judge Menefee bent over solicitously. The passenger who was nobody in particular laughed low and harshly. The lady was sleeping sweetly. The Judge essayed to take her hand to awaken her. In doing so he touched a small, cold, round, irregular something in her lap.

"She has eaten the apple," announced Judge Menefee, in awed tones, as he held up the core for them to see.

The Princess and the Puma

There had to be a king and queen, of course. The king was a terrible old man who wore six-shooters and spurs, and shouted in such a tremendous voice that the rattlers on the prairie would run into their holes under the prickly pear. Before there was a royal family they called the man "Whispering Ben." When he came to own 50,000 acres of land and more cattle than he could count, they called him O'Donnell "the Cattle King."

The queen had been a Mexican girl from Laredo. She made

a good, mild, Coloradoclaro wife, and even succeeded in teaching Ben to modify his voice sufficiently while in the house to keep the dishes from being broken. When Ben got to be king she would sit on the gallery of Espinosa Ranch and weave rush mats. When wealth became so irresistible and oppressive that upholstered chairs and a centre table were brought down from San Antone in the wagons, she bowed her smooth, dark head, and shared the fate of the Danaë.

To avoid *lèse-majesté* you have been presented first to the king and queen. They do not enter the story, which might be called "The Chronicle of the Princess, the Happy Thought, and the Lion that Bungled his Job."

Josefa O'Donnell was the surviving daughter, the princess. From her mother she inherited warmth of nature and a dusky, semi-tropic beauty. From Ben O'Donnell the royal she acquired a store in intrepidity, common sense, and the faculty of ruling. The combination was worth going miles to see. Josefa while riding her pony at a gallop could put five out of six bullets through a tomato-can swinging at the end of a string. She could play for hours with a white kitten she owned, dressing it in all manner of absurd clothes. Scorning a pencil, she could tell you out of her head what 1545 two-year-olds would bring on the hoof, at $8.50 per head. Roughly speaking, the Espinosal Ranch is forty miles long and thirty broad—but mostly leased land. Josefa, on her pony, had prospected over every mile of it. Every cow-puncher on the range knew her by sight and was a loyal vassal. Ripley Givens, foreman of one of the Espinosal outfits, saw her one day, and made up his mind to form a royal matrimonial alliance. Presumptuous? No. In those days in the Nueces country a man was a man. And, after all, the title of cattle king does not presuppose blood royal. Often it only signifies that its owner wears the crown in token of his magnificent qualities in the art of cattle stealing.

One day Ripley Givens rode over to the Double Elm Ranch to inquire about a bunch of strayed yearlings. He was late in setting out on his return trip, and it was sundown when he struck the White Horse Crossing of the Nueces. From there to his own camp it was sixteen miles. To the Espinosal ranch-house it was twelve. Givens was tired. He decided to pass the night at the Crossing.

There was a fine water hole in the river-bed. The banks were thickly covered with great trees, undergrown with brush. Back from the water hole fifty yards was a stretch of curly mesquite grass—supper for his horse and bed for himself. Givens staked his horse, and spread out his saddle blankets to dry. He sat down with his back against a tree and rolled a cigarette. From somewhere in the dense timber along the river came a sudden, rageful, shivering wail. The pony danced at the end of his rope and blew a whistling snort of comprehending fear. Givens puffed at his cigarette, but he reached leisurely for his pistol-belt, which lay on the grass, and twirled the cylinder of his weapon tentatively. A great gar plunged with a loud splash into the water hole. A little brown rabbit skipped around a bunch of catclaw and sat twitching his whiskers and looking humorously at Givens. The pony went on eating grass.

It is well to be reasonably watchful when a Mexican lion sings soprano along the arroyos at sundown. The burden of his song may be that young calves and fat lambs are scarce, and that he has a carnivorous desire for your acquaintance.

In the grass lay an empty fruit can, cast there by some former sojourner. Givens caught sight of it with a grunt of satisfaction. In his coat pocket tied behind his saddle was a handful or two of ground coffee. Black coffee and cigarettes! What ranchero could desire more?

In two minutes he had a little fire going clearly. He started, with his can, for the water hole. When within fifteen yards of its edge he saw, between the bushes, a side-saddled pony with down-dropped reins cropping grass a little distance to his left. Just rising from her hands and knees on the brink of the water hole was Josefa O'Donnell. She had been drinking water, and she brushed the sand from the palms of her hands. Ten yards away, to her right, half concealed by a clump of sacuista, Givens saw the crouching form of the Mexican lion. His amber eyelids glared hungrily; six feet from them was the tip of the tail stretched straight, like a pointer's. His hind-quarters rocked with the motion of the cat tribe preliminary to leaping.

Givens did what he could. His six-shooter was thirty-five yards away lying on the grass. He gave a loud yell, and dashed between the lion and the princess.

The "rucus," as Givens called it afterward, was brief and

somewhat confused. When he arrived on the line of attack he saw a dim streak in the air, and heard a couple of faint cracks. Then a hundred pounds of Mexican lion plumped down upon his head and flattened him, with a heavy jar, to the ground. He remembered calling out: "Let up, now—no fair gouging!" and then he crawled from under the lion like a worm, with his mouth full of grass and dirt, and a big lump on the back of his head where it had struck the root of a water-elm. The lion lay motionless. Givens, feeling aggrieved, and suspicious of fouls, shook his fist at the lion, and shouted: "I'll rastle you again for twenty——" and then he got back to himself.

Josefa was standing in her tracks, quietly reloading her silver-mounted .38. It had not been a difficult shot. The lion's head made an easier mark than a tomato-can swinging at the end of a string. There was a provoking, teasing, maddening smile upon her mouth and in her dark eyes. The would-be-rescuing knight felt the fire of his fiasco burn down to his soul. Here had been his chance, the chance that he had dreamed of; and Momus, and not Cupid, had presided over it. The satyrs in the wood were, no doubt, holding their sides in hilarious, silent laughter. There had been something like vaudeville—say Signor Givens and his funny knockabout act with the stuffed lion.

"Is that you, Mr. Givens?" said Josefa, in her deliberate, saccharine contralto. "You nearly spoiled my shot when you yelled. Did you hurt your head when you fell?"

"Oh, no," said Givens, quietly; "that didn't hurt." He stooped ignominiously and dragged his best Stetson hat from under the beast. It was crushed and wrinkled to a fine comedy effect. Then he knelt down and softly stroked the fierce, open-jawed head of the dead lion.

"Poor old Bill!" he exclaimed, mournfully.

"What's that?" asked Josefa, sharply.

"Of course you didn't know, Miss Josefa," said Givens, with an air of one allowing magnanimity to triumph over grief. "Nobody can blame you. I tried to save him, but I couldn't let you know in time."

"Save who?"

"Why, Bill. I've been looking for him all day. You see, he's been our camp pet for two years. Poor old fellow, he wouldn't have hurt a cottontail rabbit. It'll break the boys all up when they hear about it. But you couldn't tell, of course, that Bill was just trying to play with you.''

Josefa's black eyes burned steadily upon him. Ripley Givens met the test successfully. He stood rumpling the yellow-brown curls on his head pensively. In his eyes was regret, not unmingled with a gentle reproach. His smooth features were set to a pattern of indisputable sorrow. Josefa wavered.

"What was your pet doing here?" she asked, making a last stand. "There's no camp near the White Horse Crossing."

"The old rascal ran away from camp yesterday," answered Givens, readily. "It's a wonder the coyotes didn't scare him to death. You see, Jim Webster, our horse wrangler, brought a little terrier pup into camp last week. The pup made life miserable for Bill—he used to chase him around and chew his hind legs for hours at a time. Every night when bedtime came Bill would sneak under one of the boys' blankets and sleep to keep the pup from finding him. I reckon he must have been worried pretty desperate or he wouldn't have run away. He was always afraid to get out of sight of camp."

Josefa looked at the body of the fierce animal. Givens gently patted one of the formidable paws that could have killed a yearling calf with one blow. Slowly a red flush widened upon the dark olive face of the girl. Was it the signal of shame of the true sportsman who has brought down ignoble quarry? Her eyes grew softer, and the lowered lids drove away all their bright mockery.

"I'm very sorry," she said, humbly; "but he looked so big, and jumped so high that—"

"Poor old Bill was hungry," interrupted Givens, in quick defence of the deceased. "We always made him jump for his supper in camp. He would lie down and roll over for a piece of meat. When he saw you he thought he was going to get something to eat from you."

Suddenly Josefa's eyes opened wide.

"I might have shot you!" she exclaimed. "You ran right in between. You risked your life to save your pet! That was fine, Mr. Givens. I like a man who is kind to animals."

Yes; there was even admiration in her gaze now. After all, there was a hero rising out of the ruins of the anti-climax.

The look on Givens's face would have secured him a high position in the S. P. C. A.

"I always loved 'em," said he; "horses, dogs, Mexican lions, cows, alligators—"

"I hate alligators," instantly demurred Josefa; "crawly, muddy things!"

"Did I say alligators?" said Givens. "I meant antelopes, of course."

Josefa's conscience drove her to make further amends. She held out her hand penitently. There was a bright, unshed drop in each of her eyes.

"Please forgive me, Mr. Givens, won't you? I'm only a girl, you know, and I was frightened at first. I'm very, very sorry I shot Bill. You don't know how ashamed I feel. I wouldn't have done it for anything."

Givens took the proffered hand. He held it for a time while he allowed the generosity of his nature to overcome his grief at the loss of Bill. At last it was clear that he had forgiven her.

"Please don't speak of it any more, Miss Josefa. 'Twas enough to frighten any young lady the way Bill looked. I'll explain it all right to the boys."

"Are you really sure you don't hate me?" Josefa came closer to him impulsively. Her eyes were sweet—oh, sweet and pleading with gracious penitence. "I would hate any one who would kill my kitten. And how daring and kind of you to risk being shot when you tried to save him! How very few men would have done that!" Victory wrested from defeat! Vaudeville turned into drama! Bravo, Ripley Givens!

It was now twilight. Of course Miss Josefa could not be allowed to ride on to the ranch-house alone. Givens resaddled his pony in spite of that animal's reproachful glances, and rode with her. Side by side they galloped across the smooth grass, the princess and the man who was kind to animals. The prairie odors of fruitful earth and delicate bloom were thick and sweet around them. Coyotes yelping over there on the hill! No fear. And yet—

Josefa rode closer. A little hand seemed to grope. Givens found it with his own. The ponies kept an even gait. The hands lingered together, and the owner of one explained.

"I never was frightened before, but just think! How terrible it would be to meet a really wild lion! Poor Bill! I'm so glad you came with me!''

O'Donnell was sitting on the ranch gallery.

"Hello, Rip!" he shouted—"that you?"

"He rode in with me," said Josefa. "I lost my way and was late."

"Much obliged," called the cattle king. "Stop over, Rip, and ride to camp in the morning."

But Givens would not. He would push on to camp. There was a bunch of steers to start off on the trail at daybreak. He said good-night, and trotted away.

An hour later, when the lights were out, Josefa, in her night-robe, came to her door and called to the king in his own room across the brick-paved hallway:

"Say, Pop, you know that old Mexican lion they call the 'Gotch-eared Devil'—the one that killed Gonzales, Mr. Martin's sheep herder, and about fifty calves on the Salada range? Well, I settled his hash this afternoon over at the White Horse Crossing. Put two balls in his head with my .38 while he was on the jump. I knew him by the slice gone from his left ear that old Gonzales cut off with his machete. You couldn't have made a better shot yourself, Daddy."

"Bully for you!" thundered Whispering Ben from the darkness of the royal chamber.

A Chaparral Prince

Nine o'clock at last, and the drudging toil of the day was ended. Lena climbed to her room in the third half-story of the Quarrymen's Hotel. Since daylight she had slaved, doing the work of a full-grown woman, scrubbing the floors, washing the heavy ironstone plates and cups, making the beds, and supplying the insatiate demands for wood and water in that turbulent and depressing hostelry.

The din of the day's quarrying was over—the blasting and drilling, the creaking of the great cranes, the shouts of the foremen, the backing and shifting of the flat-cars hauling the heavy blocks of limestone. Down in the hotel office three or four of the laborers were growling and swearing over a belated game of checkers. Heavy odors of stewed meat, hot grease, and cheap coffee hung like a depressing fog about the house.

Lena lit the stump of a candle and sat limply upon her wooden chair. She was eleven years old, thin and ill-nourished. Her back and limbs were sore and aching. But the ache in her heart made the biggest trouble. The last straw had been added to the burden upon her small shoulders. They had taken away Grimm. Always at night, however tired she might be, she had turned to Grimm for comfort and hope. Each time had Grimm whispered to her that the prince or the fairy would come and deliver her out of the wicked enchantment. Every night she had taken fresh courage and strength from Grimm.

To whatever tale she read she found an analogy in her own condition. The woodcutter's lost child, the unhappy goose girl, the persecuted step-daughter, the little maiden imprisoned in the witch's hut—all these were but transparent disguises for Lena, the overworked kitchenmaid in the Quarrymen's Hotel. And always when the extremity was direst came the good fairy or the gallant prince to the rescue.

So, here in the ogre's castle, enslaved by a wicked spell, Lena had leaned upon Grimm and waited, longing for the powers of goodness to prevail. But on the day before Mrs. Maloney had found the book in her room and had carried it away, declaring sharply that it would not do for servants to read at night; they lost sleep and did not work briskly the next day. Can one only eleven years old, living away from one's mamma, and never having any time to play, live entirely deprived of Grimm? Just try it once and you will see what a difficult thing it is.

Lena's home was in Texas, away up among the little mountains on the Pedernales River, in a little town called Fredericksburg. They are all German people who live in Fredericksburg. Of evenings they sit at little tables along the sidewalk and drink beer and play pinochle and scat. They are very thrifty people.

Thriftiest among them was Peter Hildesmuller, Lena's father. And that is why Lena was sent to work in the hotel at the quarries, thirty miles away. She earned three dollars every week there, and Peter added her wages to his well-guarded store. Peter had an ambition to become as rich as his neighbor, Hugo Heffelbauer, who smoked a meerschaum pipe three feet long and had wiener schnitzel and hassenpfeffer for dinner every day in the week. And now Lena was quite old enough to work and assist in the accumulation of riches. But conjecture, if you can, what it means to be sentenced at eleven years of age from a home in the pleasant little Rhine village to hard labor in the ogre's castle, where you must fly to serve the ogres, while they devour cattle and sheep, growling fiercely as they stamp white limestone dust from their great shoes for you to sweep and scour with your weak, aching fingers. And then—to have Grimm taken away from you!

Lena raised the lid of an old empty case that had once contained canned corn and got out a sheet of paper and a piece of pencil. She was going to write a letter to her mamma. Tommy Ryan was going to post it for her at Ballinger's. Tommy was seventeen, worked in the quarries, went home to Ballinger's every night, and was now waiting in the shadows under Lena's window for her to throw the letter out to him. That was the only way she could send a letter to Fredericksburg. Mrs. Maloney did not like for her to write letters.

The stump of candle was burning low, so Lena hastily bit the wood from around the lead of her pencil and began. This is the letter she wrote:

Dearest Mamma:—I want so much to see you. And Gretel and Claus and Heinrich and little Adolf. I am so tired. I want to see you. To-day I was slapped by Mrs. Maloney and had no supper. I could not bring in enough wood, for my hand hurt. She took my book yesterday. I mean "Grimms's Fairy Tales," which Uncle Leo gave me. It did not hurt any one for me to read the book. I try to work as well as I can, but there is so much to do. I read only a little bit every night. Dear Mamma, I shall tell you what I am going to do. Unless you send for me

to-morrow to bring me home I shall go to a deep place I
know in the river and drown. It is wicked to drown, I
suppose, but I wanted to see you, and there is no one
else. I am very tired, and Tommy is waiting for the
letter. You will excuse me, mamma, if I do it.

> Your respectful and loving daughter,
> Lena

Tommy was still waiting faithfully when the letter was
concluded, and when Lena dropped it out she saw him pick it
up and start up the steep hillside. Without undressing she
blew out the candle and curled herself upon the mattress on
the floor.

At 10:30 o'clock old man Ballinger came out of his house
in his stocking feet and leaned over the gate, smoking his
pipe. He looked down the big road, white in the moonshine,
and rubbed one ankle with the toe of his other foot. It was
time for the Fredericksburg mail to come pattering up the
road.

Old man Ballinger had waited only a few minutes when he
heard the lively hoofbeats of Fritz's team of little black
mules, and very soon afterward his covered spring wagon
stood in front of the gate. Fritz's big spectacles flashed in the
moonlight and his tremendous voice shouted a greeting to the
postmaster of Ballinger's. The mail-carrier jumped out and
took the bridles from the mules, for he always fed them oats
at Ballinger's.

While the mules were eating from their feed bags old man
Ballinger brought out the mail sack and threw it into the
wagon.

Fritz Bergmann was a man of three sentiments—or to be
more accurate—four, the pair of mules deserving to be reckoned individually. Those mules were the chief interest and
joy of his existence. Next came the Emperor of Germany and
Lena Hildesmuller.

"Tell me," said Fritz, when he was ready to start, "contains
the sacks a letter to Frau Hildesmuller from the little Lena at
the quarries? One came in the last mail to say that she is a
little sick, already. Her mamma is very anxious to hear
again."

"Yes," said old man Ballinger, "thar's a letter for Mrs.

Helterskelter, or some sich name. Tommy Ryan brung it over when he come. Her little gal workin' over thar, you say?''

"In the hotel," shouted Fritz, as he gathered up the lines; "eleven years old and not bigger as a frankfurter. The close-fist of a Peter Hildesmuller!—some day shall I with a big club pound that man's dummkopf—all in and out the town. Perhaps in this letter Lena will say that she is yet feeling better. So, her mamma will be glad. *Auf wiedersehen,* Herr Ballinger—your feets will take cold out in the night air."

"So long, Fritzy," said old man Ballinger. "You got a nice cool night for your drive."

Up the road went the little black mules at their steady trot, while Fritz thundered at them occasional words of endearment and cheer.

These fancies occupied the mind of the mailcarrier until he reached the big post-oak forest, eight miles from Ballinger's. Here his ruminations were scattered by the sudden flash and report of pistols and a whooping as if from a whole tribe of Indians. A band of galloping centaurs closed in around the mail wagon. One of them leaned over the front wheel, covered the driver with his revolver, and ordered him to stop. Others caught at the bridles of Donder and Blitzen.

"Donnerwetter!" shouted Fritz, with all his tremendous voice—"wass ist? Release your hands from dose mules. Ve vas der United States mail!"

"Hurry up, Dutch!" drawled a melancholy voice. "Don't you know when you're in a stick-up? Reverse your mules and climb out of the cart."

It is due to the breadth of Hondo Bill's demerit and the largeness of his achievements to state that the holding up of the Fredericksburg mail was not perpetrated by way of an exploit. As the lion while in the pursuit of prey commensurate to his prowess might set a frivolous foot upon a casual rabbit in his path, so Hondo Bill and his gang had swooped sportively upon the pacific transport of Meinherr Fritz.

The real work of their sinister night ride was over. Fritz and his mail bag and his mules came as a gentle relaxation, grateful after the arduous duties of their profession. Twenty miles to the southeast stood a train with a killed engine, hysterical passengers, and a looted express and mail car. That represented the serious occupation of Hondo Bill and his gang. With a fairly rich prize of currency and silver the robbers were making a wide detour to the west through the less populous country, intending to seek safety in Mexico by means of some fordable spot on the Rio Grande. The booty from the train had melted the desperate bushrangers to jovial and happy skylarkers.

Trembling with outraged dignity and no little personal apprehension, Fritz climbed out to the road after replacing his suddenly removed spectacles. The band had dismounted and were singing, capering, and whooping, thus expressing their satisfied delight in the life of a jolly outlaw. Rattlesnake Rogers, who stood at the heads of the mules, jerked a little too vigorously at the rein of the tender-mouthed Donder, who reared and emitted a loud, protesting snort of pain. Instantly Fritz, with a scream of anger, flew at the bulky Rogers and began assiduously to pommel that surprised free-booter with his fists.

"Villain!" shouted Fritz, "dog, bigstiff! Dot mule he has a soreness by his mouth. I vill knock off your shoulders mit your head—robber-mans!"

"Yi-yi!" howled Rattlesnake, roaring with laughter and ducking his head, "somebody git this here sourkrout off'n me!"

One of the band jerked Fritz back by the coat-tail, and the woods rang with Rattlesnake's vociferous comments.

"The dog-goned little wienerwurst," he yelled, amiably. "He's not so much of a skunk, for a Dutchman. Took up for his animile plum quick, didn't he? I like to see a man like his hoss, even if it is a mule. The dad-blamed little Limburger he went for me, didn't he! Whoa, now, muley—I ain't a-goin' to hurt your mouth agin any more."

Perhaps the mail would not have been tampered with had not Ben Moody, the lieutenant, possessed certain wisdom that seemed to promise more spoils.

"Say, Cap," he said, addressing Hondo Bill, "there's liable to be good pickings in these mail sacks. I've done some hoss tradin' with these Dutchmen around Fredericksburg, and I know the style of the varmints. There's big money goes through the mails to that town. Them Dutch risk a thousand dollars sent wrapped in a piece of paper before they'd pay the banks to handle the money."

Hondo Bill, six feet two, gentle of voice and impulsive in action, was dragging the sacks from the rear of the wagon before Moody had finished his speech. A knife shone in his hand, and they heard the ripping sound as it bit through the tough canvas. The outlaws crowded around and began tearing open letters and packages, enlivening their labors by swearing affably at the writers, who seemed to have conspired to confute the prediction of Ben Moody. Not a dollar was found in the Fredericksburg mail.

"You ought to be ashamed of yourself," said Hondo Bill to the mail-carrier in solemn tones, "to be packing around such a lot of old, trashy paper as this. What d'you mean by it, anyhow? Where do you Dutchers keep your money at?"

The Ballinger mail sack opened like a cocoon under Hondo's knife. It contained but a handful of mail. Fritz had been fuming with terror and excitement until this sack was reached. He now remembered Lena's letter. He addressed the leader of the band, asking him that that particular missive be spared.

"Much obliged, Dutch," he said to the disturbed carrier. "I guess that's the letter we want. Got spondulicks in it, ain't it? Here she is. Make a light, boys."

Hondo found and tore open the letter to Mrs. Hildesmuller. The others stood about, lighting twisted-up letters one from another. Hondo gazed with mute disapproval at the single sheet of paper covered with the angular German script.

"Whatever is this you've humbugged us with, Dutchy? You call this here a valuable letter? That's a mighty low-down trick to play on your friends what come along to help you distribute your mail."

"That's Chiny writin'," said Sandy Grundy, peering over Hondo's shoulder.

"You're off your kazip," declared another of the gang, an effective youth, covered with silk handkerchiefs and nickel plating. "That's shorthand. I seen 'em do it once in court."

"Ach, no, no, no—dot is German," said Fritz. "It is no more as a little girl writing a letter to her mamma. One poor little girl, sick and vorking hard avay from home. Ach! it is a shame. Good Mr. Robber-man, you vill please let me have dot letter?"

"What the devil do you take us for, old Pretzels?" said Hondo with sudden and surprising severity. "You ain't presumin' to insinuate that we gents ain't possessed of sufficient politeness for to take an interest in the miss's health, are you? Now, you go on, and you read that scratchin' out loud and in plain United States language to this here company of educated society."

Hondo twirled his six-shooter by its trigger guard and stood towering above the little German, who at once began to read the letter, translating the simple words into English. The gang of rovers stood in absolute silence, listening intently.

"How old is that kid?" asked Hondo when the letter was done.

"Eleven," said Fritz.

"And where is she at?"

"At dose rock quarries—working. Ach, mein Gott—little Lena, she speak of drowning. I do not know if she vill do it, but if she shall I schwear I vill dot Peter Hildesmuller shoot mit a gun."

"You Dutchers," said Hondo Bill, his voice swelling with fine contempt, "make me plenty tired. Hirin' out your kids to work when they ought to be playin' dolls in the sand. You're a hell of a sect of people. I reckon we'll fix your clock for a while just to show what we think of your old cheesy nation. Here, boys!"

Hondo Bill parleyed aside briefly with his band, and then they seized Fritz and conveyed him off the road to one side. Here they bound him fast to a tree with a couple of lariats. His team they tied to another tree near by.

"We ain't going to hurt you bad," said Hondo, reassuringly. " 'Twon't hurt you to be tied up for a while. We will now pass you the time of day, as it is up to us to depart. Ausgespielt—nixcumrous, Dutchy. Don't get any more impatience."

Fritz heard a great squeaking of saddles as the men mounted their horses. Then a loud yell and a great clatter of hoofs as they galloped pell-mell back along the Fredericksburg road.

For more than two hours Fritz sat against his tree, tightly but not painfully bound. Then from the reaction after his exciting adventure he sank into slumber. How long he slept he knew not, but he was at last awakened by a rough shake. Hands were untying his ropes. He was lifted to his feet, dazed, confused in mind, and weary of body. Rubbing his eyes, he looked and saw that he was again in the midst of the same band of terrible bandits. They shoved him up to the seat of his wagon and placed the lines in his hands.

"Hit it out for home, Dutch," said Hondo Bill's voice, commandingly. "You've given us lots of trouble and we're pleased to see the back of your neck. Spiel! Zwei bier! Vamoose!"

Hondo reached out and gave Blitzen a smart cut with his quirt.

The little mules sprang ahead, glad to be moving again. Fritz urged them along, himself dizzy and muddled over his fearful adventure.

According to schedule time, he should have reached Fredericksburg at daylight. As it was, he drove down the long street of the town at eleven o'clock A.M. He had to pass Peter Hildesmuller's house on his way to the post-office. He stopped his team at the gate and called. But Frau Hildesmuller was watching for him. Out rushed the whole family of Hildesmullers.

Frau Hildesmuller, fat and flushed, inquired if he had a letter from Lena, and then Fritz raised his voice and told the tale of his adventure. He told the contents of the letter that the robber had made him read, and then Frau Hildesmuller broke into wild weeping. Her little Lena drown herself! Why had they sent her from home? What could be done? Perhaps it would be too late by the time they could send for her now. Peter Hildesmuller dropped his meerschaum on the walk and it shivered into pieces.

"Woman!" he roared at his wife, "why did you let that child go away? It is your fault if she comes home to us no more."

Every one knew that it was Peter Hildesmuller's fault, so they paid no attention to his words.

A moment afterward a strange, faint voice was heard to call: "Mamma!" Frau Hildesmuller at first thought it was Lena's spirit calling, and then she rushed to the rear of Fritz's covered wagon, and, with a loud shriek of joy, caught up Lena herself, covering her pale little face with kisses and smothering her with hugs. Lena's eyes were heavy with the deep slumber of exhaustion, but she smiled and lay close to the one she had longed to see. There among the mail sacks, covered in a nest of strange blankets and comforters, she had lain asleep until wakened by the voices around her.

Fritz stared at her with eyes that bulged behind his spectacles.

"Gott in Himmel!" he shouted. "How did you get in that wagon? Am I going crazy as well as to be murdered and hanged by robbers this day?"

"You brought her to us, Fritz," cried Frau Hildesmuller. "How can we ever thank you enough?"

"Tell mamma how you came in Fritz's wagon," said Frau Hildesmuller.

"I don't know," said Lena. "But I know how I got away from the hotel. The Prince brought me."

"By the Emperor's crown!" shouted Fritz, "we are all going crazy."

"I always knew he would come," said Lena, sitting down on her bundle of bedclothes on the sidewalk. "Last night he came with his armed knights and captured the ogre's castle. They broke the dishes and kicked down the doors. They pitched Mr. Maloney into a barrel of rain water and threw flour all over Mrs. Maloney. The workmen in the hotel jumped out of the windows and ran into the woods when the knights began firing their guns. They wakened me up and I peeped down the stair. And then the Prince came up and wrapped me in the bedclothes and carried me out. He was so tall and strong and fine. His face was as rough as a scrubbing brush, and he talked soft and kind and smelled of schnapps. He took me on his horse before him and we rode away among the knights. He held me close and I went to sleep that way, and didn't wake up till I got home."

"Rubbish!" cried Fritz Bergmann. "Fairy tales! How did you come from the quarries to my wagon?"

"The Prince brought me," said Lena, confidently.

And to this day the good people of Fredericksburg haven't been able to make her give any other explanation.

The Enchanted Kiss

But a clerk in the Cut-rate Drug Store was Samuel Tansey, yet his slender frame was a pad that enfolded the passion of Romeo, the gloom of Lara, the romance of D'Artagnan, and the desperate inspiration of Melnotte. Pity, then, that he had been denied expression, that he was doomed to the burden of utter timidity and diffidence, that Fate had set him tongue-tied and scarlet before the muslin-clad angels whom he adored and vainly longed to rescue, clasp, comfort, and subdue.

The clock's hands were pointing close upon the hour of ten while Tansey was playing billiards with a number of his friends. On alternate evenings he was released from duty at the store after seven o'clock. Even among his fellow men Tansey was timorous and constrained. In his imagination he had done valiant deeds and performed acts of distinguished gallantry; but in fact he was a shallow youth of twenty-three, with an over-modest demeanor and scant vocabulary.

When the clock struck ten, Tansey hastily laid down his cue and struck sharply upon the show-case with a coin for the attendant to come and receive the pay for his score.

"What's your hurry, Tansey?" called one. "Got another engagement?"

"Tansey got an engagement!" echoed another. "Not on your life. Tansey's got to get home at ten by Mother Peek's orders."

"It's no such thing," chimed in a pale youth, taking a large cigar from his mouth; "Tansey's afraid to be late because Miss Katie might come downstairs to unlock the door, and kiss him in the hall."

This delicate piece of raillery sent a fiery tingle into Tansey's blood, for the indictment was true—barring the kiss. That was a thing to dream of; to wildly hope for; but too remote and sacred a thing to think of lightly.

Casting a cold and contemptuous look at the speaker—a punishment commensurate with his own diffident spirit—Tansey left the room, descending the stairs into the street.

For two years he had silently adored Miss Peek, worshiping her from a spiritual distance through which her attractions took on stellar brightness and mystery. Mrs. Peek kept a few choice boarders, among whom was Tansey. The other young men romped with Katie, chased her with crickets in their fingers, and "jollied" her with an irreverent freedom that turned Tansey's heart into cold lead in his bosom. The signs of his adoration were few—a tremulous "Good morning," stealthy glances at her during meals, and occasionally (Oh, rapture!) a blushing, delirious game of cribbage with her in the parlor on some rare evening when a miraculous lack of engagement kept her at home. Kiss him in the hall! Aye, he feared it, but it was an ecstatic fear such as Elijah must have felt when the chariot lifted him into the unknown.

But to-night the gibes of his associates had stung him to a feeling of forward, lawless mutiny; a defiant, challenging, atavistic recklessness. Spirit of corsair, adventurer, lover, poet, Bohemian, possessed him. The stars he saw above him seemed no more unattainable, no less high, than the favor of Miss Peek or the fearsome sweetness of her delectable lips. His fate seemed to him strangely dramatic and pathetic, and to call for a solace consonant with its extremity. A saloon was near by, and to this he flitted, calling for absinthe—beyond doubt the drink most adequate to his mood—the tipple of the roué, the abandoned, the vainly sighing lover.

Once he drank of it, and again, and then again until he felt a strange, exalted sense of non-participation in worldly affairs pervade him. Tansey was no drinker; his consumption of three absinthe anisettes within almost as few minutes proclaimed his unproficiency in the art; Tansey was merely flooding with unproven liquor his sorrows; which record and tradition alleged to be drownable.

Coming out upon the sidewalk, he snapped his fingers defiantly in the direction of the Peek homestead, turned the other way, and voyaged, Columbus-like, into the wilds of an enchanted street. Nor is the figure exorbitant, for, beyond his store the foot of Tansey had scarcely been set for years—store and boarding-house; between these ports he was chartered to run, and contrary currents had rarely deflected his prow.

Tansey aimlessly protracted his walk, and, whether it was his unfamiliarity with the district, his recent accession of audacious errantry, or the sophistical whisper of a certain green-eyed fairy, he came at last to tread a shuttered, blank, and echoing thoroughfare, dark and unpeopled. And, suddenly, this way came to an end (as many streets do in the Spanish-built, archaic town of San Antone), butting its head against an imminent, high, brick wall. No—the street still lived! To the right and to the left it breathed through slender tubes of exit—narrow, somnolent ravines, cobble paved and unlighted. Accommodating a rise in the street to the right was reared a phantom flight of five luminous steps of limestone, flanked by a wall of the same height and of the same material.

Upon one of these steps Tansey seated himself and bethought him of his love, and how she might never know she was his love. And of Mother Peek, fat, vigilant and kind; not unpleased, Tansey thought, that he and Katie should play cribbage in the parlor together. For the Cut-rate had not cut his salary, which, sordidly speaking, ranked him star boarder at the Peeks'. And he thought of Captain Peek, Katie's father, a man he dreaded and abhorred; a genteel loafer and spendthrift, battening upon the labor of his women-folk; a very queer fish, and, according to repute, not of the freshest.

The night had turned chill and foggy. The heart of the town, with its noises, was left behind. Reflected from the high vapors, its distant lights were manifest in quivering, cone-shaped streamers, in questionable blushes of unnamed colors, in unstable, ghostly waves of far, electric flashes. Now that the darkness was become more friendly, the wall against which the street splintered developed a stone coping topped with an armature of spikes. Beyond it loomed what appeared to be the acute angles of mountain peaks, pierced here and there by little lambent parallelograms. Considering this vista, Tansey at length persuaded himself that the seeming mountains were, in fact, the convent of Santa Mercedes, with which ancient and bulky pile he was better familiar from different coigns of view. A pleasant noise of singing in his ears reënforced his opinion. High, sweet, holy carolling, far and harmonious and uprising, as of sanctified nuns at their responses. At what hour did the Sisters sing? He tried to think—was it six, eight, twelve? Tansey leaned his back against the limestone wall and wondered. Strange things followed. The air was full of white, fluttering pigeons that circled about, and settled upon the convent wall. The wall blossomed with a quantity of shining green eyes that blinked and peered at him from the solid masonry. A pink, classic nymph came from an excavation in the cavernous road and danced, barefoot and airy, upon the ragged flints. The sky was traversed by a company of beribboned cats, marching in stupendous, aërial procession. The noise of singing grew louder; an illumination of unseasonable fire-flies danced past, and strange whispers came out of the dark without meaning or excuse.

Without amazement Tansey took note of these phenomena. He was on some new plane of understanding, though his mind seemed to him clear and, indeed, happily tranquil.

A desire for movement and exploration seized him: he rose and turned into the black gash of street to his right. For a time the high wall formed one of its boundaries, but farther on, two rows of black-windowed houses closed it in.

Here was the city's quarter once given over to the Spaniard. Here were still his forbidding abodes of concrete and adobe, standing cold and indomitable against the century. From the murky fissure, the eye saw, flung against the sky, the tangled filigree of his Moorish balconies. Through stone archways breaths of dead, vault-chilled air coughed upon him; his feet struck jingling iron rings in staples stone-buried for half a cycle. Along these paltry avenues had swaggered the arrogant Don, had caracoled and serenaded and blustered while the tomahawk and the pioneer's rifle were already uplifted to expel him from a continent. And Tansey, stumbling through this old-world dust, looked up, dark as it was, and saw Andalusian beauties glimmering on the balconies. Some of them were laughing and listening to the goblin music that still followed; others harked fearfully through the night, trying to catch the hoof beats of caballeros whose last echoes from those stones had died away a century ago. Those women were silent, but Tansey heard the jangle of horseless bridle-bits, the whirr of riderless rowels, and, now and then, a muttered malediction in a foreign tongue. But he was not frightened. Shadows, nor shadows of sounds could daunt him. Afraid? No. Afraid of Mother Peek? Afraid to face the girl of his heart? Afraid of tipsy Captain Peek? Nay! nor of these apparitions, nor of that spectral singing that always pursued him. Singing! He would show them! He lifted up a strong and untuneful voice:

"When you hear them bells go tingalingling,"

serving notice upon those mysterious agencies that if it should come to a face-to-face encounter

"There'll be a hot time
In the old town
To-night!"

How long Tansey consumed in treading this haunted by-way was not clear to him, but in time he emerged into a more commodious avenue. When within a few yards of the corner he perceived, through a window, that a small confectionery of mean appearance was set in the angle. His same glance that estimated its meagre equipment, its cheap soda-water fountain and stock of tobacco and sweets, took cognizance of Captain Peek within lighting a cigar at a swinging gaslight.

As Tansey rounded the corner Captain Peek came out, and they met *vis-à-vis*. An exultant joy filled Tansey when he found himself sustaining the encounter with implicit courage. Peek, indeed! He raised his hand, and snapped his fingers loudly.

It was Peek himself who quailed guiltily before the valiant mien of the drug clerk. Sharp surprise and a palpable fear bourgeoned upon the Captain's face. And, verily, that face was one to rather call up such expressions upon the faces of others. The face of a libidinous heathen idol, small eyed, with carven folds in the heavy jowls, and a consuming, pagan license in its expression. In the gutter just beyond the store Tansey saw a closed carriage standing with its back toward him and a motionless driver perched in his place.

"Why, it's Tansey!" exclaimed Captain Peek. "How are you, Tansey? H-have a cigar, Tansey?"

"Why, it's Peek!" cried Tansey, jubilant at his own temerity. "What deviltry are you up to now, Peek? Back streets and a closed carriage! Fie! Peek!"

"There's no one in the carriage," said the Captain, smoothly.

"Everybody out of it is in luck," continued Tansey, aggressively. "I'd love for you to know, Peek, that I'm not stuck on you. You're a bottle-nosed scoundrel."

"Why, the little rat's drunk!" cried the Captain, joyfully; "only drunk, and I thought he was on! Go home, Tansey, and quit bothering grown persons on the street."

But just then a white-clad figure sprang out of the carriage, and a shrill voice—Katie's voice—sliced the air: "Sam! Sam! —help me, Sam!"

Tansey sprang toward her, but Captain Peek interposed his bulky form. Wonder of wonders! the whilom spiritless youth struck out with his right, and the hulking Captain went over in a swearing heap. Tansey flew to Katie, and took her in his arms like a conquering knight. She raised her face, and he kissed her—violets! electricity! caramels! champagne! Here was the attainment of a dream that brought no disenchantment.

"Oh, Sam," cried Katie, when she could, "I knew you would come to rescue me. What do you suppose the mean things were going to do with me?"

"Have your picture taken," said Tansey, wondering at the foolishness of his remark.

"No, they were going to eat me. I heard them talking about it."

"Eat you!" said Tansey, after pondering a moment. "That can't be; there's no plates."

But a sudden noise warned him to turn. Down upon him were bearing the Captain and a monstrous long-bearded dwarf in a spangled cloak and red trunk-hose. The dwarf leaped twenty feet and clutched him. The Captain seized Katie and hurled her, shrieking, back into the carriage, himself followed, and the vehicle dashed away. The dwarf lifted Tansey high above his head and ran with him into the store. Holding him with one hand, he raised the lid of an enormous chest half filled with cakes of ice, flung Tansey inside, and closed down the cover.

The force of the fall must have been great, for Tansey lost consciousness. When his faculties revived his first sensation was one of severe cold along his back and limbs. Opening his eyes, he found himself to be seated upon the lime-stone steps still facing the wall and convent of Santa Mercedes. His first thought was of the ecstatic kiss from Katie. The outrageous villainy of Captain Peek, the unnatural mystery of the situation, his preposterous conflict with the improbable dwarf—these things roused and angered him, but left no impression of the unreal.

"I'll go back there to-morrow," he grumbled aloud, "and knock the head off that comic-opera squab. Running out and picking up perfect strangers, and shoving them into cold storage!"

But the kiss remained uppermost in his mind. "I might have done that long ago," he mused. "She liked it, too. She called me 'Sam' four times. I'll not go up that street again. Too much scrapping. Guess I'll move down the other way. Wonder what she meant by saying they were going to eat her!"

Tansey began to feel sleepy, but after a while he decided to move along again. This time he ventured into the street to his left. It ran level for a distance, and then dipped gently downward, opening into a vast, dim, barren space—the old Military Plaza. To his left, some hundred yards distant, he saw a cluster of flickering lights along the Plaza's border. He knew the locality at once.

Huddled within narrow confines were the remnants of the once-famous purveyors of the celebrated Mexican national cookery. A few years before, their nightly encampments upon the historic Alamo Plaza, in the heart of the city, had been a carnival, a saturnalia that was renowned throughout the land. Then the caterers numbered hundreds; the patrons thousands. Drawn by the coquettish *señoritas,* the music of the weird Spanish minstrels, and the strange piquant Mexican dishes served at a hundred competing tables, crowds thronged the Alamo Plaza all night. Travellers, rancheros, family parties, gay gasconading rounders, sight-seers and prowlers of polyglot, owlish San Antone mingled there at the centre of the city's fun and frolic. The popping of corks, pistols, and questions; the glitter of eyes, jewels, and daggers; the ring of laughter and coin—these were the order of the night.

But now no longer. To some half-dozen tents, fires, and

tables had dwindled the picturesque festival, and these had been relegated to an ancient disused plaza.

Often had Tansey strolled down to these stands at night to partake of the delectable *chili-con-carne,* a dish evolved by the genius of Mexico, composed of delicate meats minced with aromatic herbs and the poignant *chili colorado*—a compound full of singular savor and a fiery zest delightful to the Southron's palate.

The titillating odor of this concoction came now, on the breeze, to the nostrils of Tansey, awakening in him hunger for it. As he turned in that direction he saw a carriage dash up to the Mexicans' tents out of the gloom of the Plaza. Some figures moved back and forward in the uncertain light of the lanterns, and then the carriage was driven swiftly away.

Tansey approached, and sat at one of the tables covered with gaudy oilcloth. Traffic was dull at the moment. A few half-grown boys noisily fared at another table; the Mexicans hung listless and phlegmatic about their wares. And it was still. The night hum of the city crowded to the wall of dark buildings surrounding the Plaza, and subsided to an indefinite buzz through which sharply perforated the crackle of the languid fires and the rattle of fork and spoon. A sedative wind blew from the southeast. The starless firmament pressed down upon the earth like a leaden cover.

In all that quiet Tansey turned his head suddenly, and saw, without disquietude, a troop of spectral horsemen deploy into the Plaza and charge a luminous line of infantry that advanced to sustain the shock. He saw the fierce flame of cannon and small arms, but heard no sound. The careless victuallers lounged vacantly, not deigning to view the conflict. Tansey mildly wondered to what nations these mute combatants might belong; turned his back to them and ordered his *chili* and coffee from the Mexican woman who advanced to serve him. This woman was old and careworn; her face was lined like the rind of a cantaloupe. She fetched the viands from a vessel set by the smouldering fire, and then retired to a tent, dark within, that stood near by.

Presently Tansey heard a turmoil in the tent; a wailing, broken-hearted pleading in the harmonious Spanish tongue, and then two figures tumbled out into the light of the lanterns. One was the old woman; the other was a man clothed with a sumptuous and flashing splendor. The woman seemed to clutch and beseech from him something against his will. The man broke from her and struck her brutally back into the tent, where she lay, whimpering and invisible. Observing Tansey, he walked rapidly to the table where he sat. Tansey recognized him to be Ramon Torres, a Mexican, the proprietor of the stand he was patronizing.

Torres was a handsome, nearly full-blooded descendant of the Spanish, seemingly about thirty years of age, and of a haughty, but extremely courteous demeanor. To-night he was dressed with signal magnificence. His costume was that of a triumphant *matador*, made of purple velvet almost hidden by jeweled embroidery. Diamonds of enormous size flashed upon his garb and his hands. He reached for a chair, and, seating himself at the opposite side of the table, began to roll a finical cigarette.

"Ah, Meester Tansee," he said, with a sultry fire in his silky, black eye, "I give myself pleasure to see you this evening. Meester Tansee, you have many times come to eat at my table. I theenk you a safe man—a verree good friend. How much would it please you to leeve forever?"

"Not come back any more?" inquired Tansey.

"No; not leave—*leeve;* the not-to-die."

"I would call that," said Tansey, "a snap."

Torres leaned his elbows upon the table, swallowed a mouthful of smoke, and spake—each word being projected in a little puff of gray.

"How old do you theenk I am, Meester Tansee?"

"Oh, twenty-eight or thirty."

"Thees day," said the Mexican, "ees my birthday. I am four hundred and three years of old to-day."

"Another proof," said Tansey, airily, "of the healthfulness of our climate."

"Eet is not the air. I am to relate to you a secret of verree fine value. Listen me, Meester Tansee. At the age of twenty-three I arrive in Mexico from Spain. When? In the year fifteen hundred nineteen, with the *soldados* of Hernando Cortez. I come to thees country seventeen fifteen. I saw your Alamo reduced. It was like yesterday to me. Three hundred ninety-six year ago I learn the secret always to leeve. Look at these clothes I wear—at these *diamantes*. Do you theenk I buy them with the money I make with selling the *chili-con-carne,* Meester Tansee?''

"I should think not," said Tansey, promptly. Torres laughed loudly.

"*Válgame Dios!* but I do. But it not the kind you eating now. I make a deeferent kind, the eating of which makes men to always leeve. What do you think! One thousand people I supply—*diez pesos* each one pays me the month. You see! ten thousand *pesos* everee month! *Qué diablos!* how not I wear the fine *ropo!* You see that old woman try to hold me back a little while ago? That ees my wife. When I marry her she is young—seventeen years—*bonita*—. Like the rest she ees become old and—what you say!—tough? I am the same—young all the time. To-night I resolve to dress myself and find another wife befitting my age. This old woman try to scr-r-ratch my face. Ha! Ha! Meester Tansee—same way they do *entre los Americanos.*''

"And this health-food you spoke of?" said Tansey.

"Hear me," said Torres, leaning over the table until he lay flat upon it; "eet is the *chili-con-carne* made not from the beef or the chicken, but from the flesh of the *señorita*—young and tender. That ees the secret. Everee month you must eat it, having care to do so before the moon is full, and you will not die any times. See how I trust you, friend Tansee! To-night I have bought one young ladee—veree pretty—so *fina, gorda, blandita!* To-morrow the *chili* will be ready. *Ahora si!* One thousand dollars I pay for thees young ladee. From an *Americano* I have bought—a veree tip-top man—*el Capitan Peek—Qué es, Señor?*''

For Tansey had sprung to his feet, upsetting the chair. The words of Katie reverberated in his ears: "They're going to eat me, Sam." This, then, was the monstrous fate to which she had been delivered by her unnatural parent. The carriage he had seen drive up from the Plaza was Captain Peek's. Where was Katie? Perhaps already——

Before he could decide what to do a loud scream came from the tent. The old Mexican woman ran out, a flashing knife in her hand. "I have released her," she cried. "You shall kill no more. They will hang you—*ingrato-encantador!*''

Torres, with a hissing exclamation, sprang at her.

"Ramoncito!" she shrieked; "once you loved me."

The Mexican's arm raised and descended. "You are old," he cried; and she fell and lay motionless.

Another scream; the flaps of the tent were flung aside, and there stood Katie, white with fear, her wrists still bound with a cruel cord.

"Sam!" she cried, "save me again!"

Tansey rounded the table, and flung himself, with superb nerve, upon the Mexican. Just then a clangor began; the clocks of the city were tolling the midnight hour. Tansey clutched at Torres, and, for a moment, felt in his grasp the crunch of velvet and the cold facets of the glittering gems. The next instant, the bedecked caballero turned in his hands to a shrunken, leather-visaged, white-bearded, old, old screaming mummy, sandalled, ragged, four hundred and three. The Mexican woman was crawling to her feet, and laughing. She shook her brown hand in the face of the whining *viejo*.

"Go, now," she cried, "and seek your señorita. It was I, Ramoncito, who brought you to this. Within each moon you eat of the life-giving *chili*. It was I that kept the wrong time for you. You should have eaten *yesterday* instead of *to-morrow*. It is too late. Off with you, *hombre!* You are too old for me!"

"This," decided Tansey, releasing his hold of the graybeard, "is a private family matter concerning age, and no business of mine."

With one of the table knives he hastened to saw asunder the fetters of the fair captive; and then, for the second time that night he kissed Katie Peek—tasted again the sweetness, the wonder, the thrill of it, attained once more the maximum of his incessant dreams.

The next instant an icy blade was driven deep between his shoulders; he felt his blood slowly congeal; heard the senile cackle of the perennial Spaniard; saw the Plaza rise and reel till the zenith crashed into the horizon—and knew no more.

When Tansey opened his eyes again he was sitting upon those self-same steps gazing upon the dark bulk of the sleeping convent. In the middle of his back was still the acute, chilling pain. How had he been conveyed back there again? He got stiffly to his feet and stretched his cramped limbs. Supporting himself against the stonework he revolved in his mind the extravagant adventures that had befallen him each time he had strayed from the steps that night. In reviewing them certain features strained his credulity. Had he really met Captain Peek or Katie or the unparalleled Mexican in his wanderings—had he really encountered them under commonplace conditions and his over-stimulated brain had supplied the incongruities? However that might be, a sudden, elating thought caused him an intense joy. Nearly all of us have, at some point in our lives—either to excuse our own stupidity or placate our consciences—promulgated some theory of fatalism. We have set up an intelligent Fate that works by codes and signals. Tansey had done likewise; and now he read, through the night's incidents, the finger-prints of destiny. Each excursion that he had made had led to the one paramount finale—to Katie and that kiss, which survived and grew strong and intoxicating in his memory. Clearly, Fate was holding up to him the mirror that night, calling him to observe what awaited him at the end of whichever road he might take. He immediately turned, and hurried homeward.

Clothed in an elaborate, pale blue wrapper, cut to fit, Miss Katie Peek reclined in an arm-chair before a waning fire in her room. Her little, bare feet were thrust into house-shoes rimmed with swan's down. By the light of a small lamp she was attacking the society news of the latest Sunday paper. Some happy substance, seemingly indestructible, was being rhythmically crushed between her small white teeth. Miss Katie read of functions and furbelows, but she kept a vigilant ear for outside sounds and a frequent eye upon the clock over the mantel. At every footstep upon the asphalt sidewalk her smooth, round chin would cease for a moment its regular rise and fall, and a frown of listening would pucker her pretty brows.

At last she heard the latch of the iron gate click. She sprang up, tripped swiftly to the mirror, where she made a few of those feminine, flickering passes at her front hair and throat which are warranted to hypnotize the approaching guest.

The door-bell rang. Miss Katie, in her haste, turned the blaze of the lamp lower instead of higher, and hastened noiselessly downstairs into the hall. She turned the key, the door opened, and Mr. Tansey sidestepped in.

"Why, the i-de-a!" exclaimed Miss Katie, "is this you,

Mr. Tansey? It's after midnight. Aren't you ashamed to wake me up at such an hour to let you in? You're just *awful!*''

"I was late," said Tansey, brilliantly.

"I should think you were! Ma was awfully worried about you. When you weren't in by ten, that hateful Tom McGill said you were out calling on another—said you were out calling on some young lady. I just despise Mr. McGill. Well, I'm not going to scold you any more, Mr. Tansey, if it *is* a little late—Oh! I turned it the wrong way!''

Miss Katie gave a little scream. Absent-mindedly she had turned the blaze of the lamp entirely out instead of higher. It was very dark.

Tansey heard a musical, soft giggle, and breathed an entrancing odor of heliotrope. A groping light hand touched his arm.

"How awkward I was! Can you find your way—Sam?''

"I—I think I have a match, Miss K-Katie.''

A scratching sound; a flame; a glow of light held at arm's length by the recreant follower of Destiny illuminating a tableau which shall end the ignominious chronicle—a maid with unkissed, curling, contemptuous lips slowly lifting the lamp chimney and allowing the wick to ignite; then waving a scornful and abjuring hand toward the staircase—the unhappy Tansey erstwhile champion in the prophetic lists of fortune, ingloriously ascending to his just and certain doom, while (let us imagine) half within the wings stands the imminent figure of Fate jerking wildly at the wrong strings, and mixing things up in her usual able manner.

The Lonesome Road

Brown as a coffee-berry, rugged, pistoled, spurred, wary, indefeasible, I saw my old friend, Deputy-Marshal Buck Caperton, stumble, with jingling rowels, into a chair in the marshal's outer office.

And because the courthouse was almost deserted at that hour, and because Buck would sometimes relate to me things that were out of print, I followed him in and tricked him into talk through knowledge of a weakness he had. For, cigarettes rolled with sweet corn husk were as honey to Buck's palate; and though he could finger the trigger of a forty-five with skill and suddenness, he never could learn to roll a cigarette.

It was through no fault of mine (for I rolled the cigarettes tight and smooth), but the upshot of some whim of his own, that instead of to an Odyssey of the chaparral, I listened to—a dissertation upon matrimony! This from Buck Caperton! But I maintain that the cigarettes were impeccable, and crave absolution for myself.

"We just brought in Jim and Bud Granberry," said Buck. "Train robbing, you know. Held up the Aransas Pass last month. We caught 'em in the Twenty-Mile pear flat, south of the Nueces."

"Have much trouble coralling them?" I asked, for here was the meat that my hunger for epics craved.

"Some," said Buck; and then, during a little pause, his thoughts stampeded off the trail. "It's kind of queer about women," he went on, "and the place they're supposed to occupy in botany. If I was asked to classify them I'd say they was a human loco weed. Ever see a bronc that had been chewing loco? Ride him up to a puddle of water two feet wide, and he'll give a snort and fall back on you. It looks as big as the Mississippi River to him. Next trip he'd walk into a cañon a thousand feet deep thinking it was a prairie-dog hole. Same way with a married man.

"I was thinking of Perry Rountree, that used to be my sidekicker before he committed matrimony. In them days me and Perry hated indisturbances of any kind. We roamed around considerable, stirring up the echoes and making 'em attend to business. Why, when me and Perry wanted to have some fun in a town it was a picnic for the census takers. They just counted the marshal's posse that it took to subdue us, and there was your population. But then there came along this Mariana Good-night girl and looked at Perry sideways, and he was all bridle-wise and saddle-broke before you could skin a yearling.

"I wasn't even asked to the wedding. I reckon the bride had my pedigree and the front elevation of my habits all mapped out, and she decided that Perry would trot better in double harness without any unconverted mustang like Buck Caperton whickering around on the matrimonial range. So it was six months before I saw Perry again.

"One day I was passing on the edge of town, and I see something like a man in a little yard by a little house with a sprinkling-pot squirting water on a rosebush. Seemed to me, I'd seen something like it before, and I stopped at the gate, trying to figure out its brands. 'Twas not Perry Rountree, but 'twas the kind of a curdled jellyfish matrimony had made out of him.

"Homicide was what that Mariana had perpetrated. He was looking well enough, but he had on a white collar and shoes, and you could tell in a minute that he'd speak polite and pay taxes and stick his little finger out while drinking, just like a sheep man or a citizen. Great skyrockets! but I hated to see Perry all corrupted and Willie-ized like that.

"He came out to the gate and shook hands; and I says, with scorn, and speaking like a paroquet with the pip: 'Beg pardon—Mr. Rountree, I believe. Seems to me I sagatiated in your associations once, if I am not mistaken.'

" 'Oh, go to the devil, Buck,' says Perry, polite, as I was afraid he'd be.

" 'Well, then,' says I, 'you poor, contaminated adjunct of

a sprinkling-pot and degraded household pet, what did you go and do it for? Look at you, all decent and unriotous, and only fit to sit on juries and mend the wood-house door. You was a man once. I have hostility for all such acts. Why don't you go in the house and count the tidies or set the clock, and not stand out here in the atmosphere? A jackrabbit might come along and bite you.'

" 'Now, Buck,' says Perry, speaking mild, and some sorrowful, 'you don't understand. A married man has got to be different. He feels different from a tough old cloudburst like you. It's sinful to waste time pulling up towns just to look at their roots, and playing faro and looking upon red liquor, and such restless policies as them.'

" 'There was a time,' I says, and I expect I sighed when I mentioned it, 'when a certain domesticated little Mary's lamb I could name was some instructed himself in the line of pernicious sprightliness. I never expected, Perry, to see you reduced down from a full-grown pestilence to such a frivolous fraction of a man. Why,' says I, 'you've got a necktie on; and you speak a senseless kind of indoor drivel, that reminds me of a storekeeper or a lady. You look to me like you might tote an umbrella and wear suspenders, and go home of nights.'

" 'The little woman,' says Perry, 'has made some improvements, I believe. You can't understand, Buck. I haven't been away from the house at night since we was married.'

"We talked on a while, me and Perry, and, as sure as I live, that man interrupted me in the middle of my talk to tell me about six tomato plants he had growing in his garden. Shoved his agricultural degradation right up under my nose while I was telling him about the fun we had tarring and feathering that faro dealer at California Pete's layout! But by and by Perry shows a flicker of sense.

" 'Buck,' says he, 'I'll have to admit that it is a little dull at times. Not that I'm not perfectly happy with the little woman, but a man seems to require some excitement now and then. Now, I'll tell you: Mariana's gone visiting this afternoon, and she won't be home till seven o'clock. That's the limit for both of us—seven o'clock. Neither of us ever stays out a minute after that time unless we are together. Now, I'm glad you came along, Buck,' says Perry, 'for I'm feeling just like having one more rip-roaring razoo with you for the sake of old times. What you say to us putting in the afternoon having fun?—I'd like it fine,' says Perry.

"I slapped that old captive range-rider half across his little garden.

" 'Get your hat, you old dried-up alligator,' I shouts, 'you ain't dead yet. You're part human, anyhow, if you did get all bogged up in matrimony. We'll take this town to pieces and see what makes it tick. We'll make all kinds of profligate demands upon the science of cork pulling. You'll grow horns yet, old muley cow,' says I, punching Perry in the ribs, 'if you trot around on the trail of vice with your Uncle Buck.'

" 'I'll have to be home by seven, you know,' says Perry again.

" 'Oh, yes,' says I, winking to myself, for I knew the kind of seven o'clocks Perry Rountree got back by after he once got to passing repartee with the bartenders.

"We goes down to the Gray Mule saloon—that old 'dobe building by the depot.

" 'Give it a name,' says I, as soon as we got one hoof on the footrest.

" 'Sarsaparilla,' says Perry.

"You could have knocked me down with a lemon peeling.

" 'Insult me as much as you want to,' I says to Perry, 'but don't startle the bartender. He may have heart-disease. Come on, now; your tongue got twisted. The tall glasses,' I orders, 'and the bottle in the left hand corner of the ice-chest.'

" 'Sarsaparilla,' repeats Perry, and then his eyes get animated, and I see he's got some great scheme in his mind he wants to emit.

" 'Buck,' he says, all interested, 'I'll tell you what! I want to make this a red-letter day. I've been keeping close at home, and I want to turn myself a-loose. We'll have the highest old time you ever saw. We'll go in the back room here and play checkers till half-past six.'

"I leaned against the bar, and I says to Gotch-eared Mike, who was on watch:

" 'For God's sake don't mention this. You know what Perry used to be. He's had the fever, and the doctor says we must humor him.'

" 'Give us the checker-board and the men, Mike,' says Perry. 'Come on, Buck, I'm just wild to have some excitement.'

"I went in the back room with Perry. Before we closed the door, I says to Mike:

" 'Don't ever let it straggle out from under your hat that you seen Buck Caperton fraternal with sarsaparilla or *persona grata* with a checkerboard, or I'll make a swallow-fork in your other ear.'

"I locked the door and me and Perry played checkers. To see that poor old humiliated piece of household bric-à-brac sitting there and sniggering out loud whenever he jumped a man, and all obnoxious with animation when he got into my king row, would have made a sheep-dog sick with mortification. Him that was once satisfied only when he was pegging six boards at keno or giving the faro dealers nervous prostration—to see him pushing them checkers about like Sally Louisa at a school-children's party—why, I was all smothered up with mortification.

"And I sits there playing the black men, all sweating for fear somebody I knew would find it out. And I thinks to myself some about this marrying business, and how it seems to be the same kind of a game as that Mrs. Delilah played. She give her old man a hair cut, and everybody knows what a man's head looks like after a woman cuts his hair. And then when the Pharisees came around to guy him he was so 'shamed he went to work and kicked the whole house down on top of the whole outfit. 'Them married men,' thinks I, 'lose all their spirit and instinct for riot and foolishness. They won't drink, they won't buck the tiger, they won't even fight. What do they want to go and stay married for?' I asks myself.

"But Perry seems to be having hilarity in considerable quantities.

" 'Buck old hoss,' says he, 'isn't this just the hell-roaringest time we ever had in our lives? I don't know when I've been stirred up so. You see, I've been sticking pretty close to home since I married, and I haven't been on a spree in a long time.'

" 'Spree!' Yes, that's what he called it. Playing checkers in the back room of the Gray Mule! I suppose it did seem to him a little immoral and nearer to a prolonged debauch than standing over six tomato plants with a sprinkling pot.

"Every little bit Perry looks at his watch and says:

" 'I got to be home, you know, Buck, at seven.'

" 'All right,' I'd say. 'Romp along and move. This here excitement's killing me. If I don't reform some, and loosen up the strain of this checkered dissipation I won't have a nerve left.'

"It might have been half-past six when commotions began to go on outside in the street. We heard a yelling and a six-shooting, and a lot of galloping and maneuvers.

" 'What's that?' I wonders.

" 'Oh, some nonsense outside,' says Perry. 'It's your move. We just got time to play this game.'

" 'I'll just take a peep through the window,' says I, 'and see. You can't expect a mere mortal to stand the excitement of having a king jumped and listen to an unidentified conflict going on at the same time.'

"The Gray Mule saloon was one of them old Spanish 'dobe buildings, and the back room only had two little windows a foot wide, with iron bars in 'em. I looked out one, and I see the cause of the rucus.

"There was the Trimble gang—ten of 'em—the worst outfit of desperadoes and horse-thieves in Texas, coming up the street shooting right and left. They was coming right straight for the Gray Mule. Then they got past the range of my sight, but we heard 'em ride up to the front door, and then they socked the place full of lead. We heard the big looking-glass behind the bar knocked all to pieces and the bottles crashing. We could see Gotch-eared Mike in his apron running across the plaza like a coyote, with the bullets puffing up the dust all around him. Then the gang went to work in the saloon, drinking what they wanted and smashing what they didn't.

"Me and Perry both knew that gang, and they knew us. The year before Perry married, him and me was in the same ranger company—and we fought that outfit down on the San Miguel, and brought back Ben Trimble and two others for murder.

" 'We can't get out,' says I. 'We'll have to stay in here till they leave.'

"Perry looked at his watch.

" 'Twenty-five to seven,' says he. 'We can finish that

game. I got two men on you. It's your move, Buck. I got to be home at seven, you know.'

"We sat down and went on playing. The Trimble gang had a roughhouse for sure. They were getting good and drunk. They'd drink a while and holler a while, and then they'd shoot up a few bottles and glasses. Two or three times they came and tried to open our door. Then there was some more shooting outside, and I looked out the window again. Ham Gossett, the town marshal, had a posse in the houses and stores across the street, and was trying to bag a Trimble or two through the windows.

"I lost that game of checkers. I'm free in saying that I lost three kings that I might have saved if I had been corralled in a more peaceful pasture. But that drivelling married man sat there and cackled when he won a man like an unintelligent hen picking up a grain of corn.

"When the game was over Perry gets up and looks at his watch.

" 'I've had a glorious time, Buck,' says he, 'but I'll have to be going now. It's a quarter to seven, and I got to be home by seven, you know.'

"I thought he was joking.

" 'They'll clear out or be dead drunk in half an hour or an hour,' says I. 'You ain't that tired of being married that you want to commit any more sudden suicide, are you?' says I, giving him the laugh.

" 'One time,' says Perry, 'I was half an hour late getting home. I met Mariana on the street looking for me. If you could have seen her, Buck—but you don't understand. She knows what a wild kind of a snoozer I've been, and she's afraid something will happen. I'll never be late getting home again. I'll say good-bye to you now, Buck.'

"I got between him and the door.

" 'Married man,' says I, 'I know you was christened a fool the minute the preacher tangled you up, but don't you never sometimes think one little think on a human basis? There's ten of that gang in there, and they're pizen with whisky and desire for murder. They'll drink you up like a bottle of booze before you get halfway to the door. Be intelligent, now, and use at least wild-hog sense. Sit down and wait till we have some chance to get out without being carried in baskets.'

" 'I got to be home by seven, Buck,' repeats this henpecked thing of little wisdom, like an unthinking poll parrot. 'Mariana,' says he, ' 'll be looking out for me.' And he reaches down and pulls a leg out of the checker table. 'I'll go through this Trimble outfit,' says he, 'like a cottontail through a brush corral. I'm not pestered any more with a desire to engage in rucuses, but I got to be home by seven. You lock the door after me, Buck. And don't you forget—I won three out of them five games. I'd play longer, but Mariana——'

" 'Hush up, you old locoed road runner,' I interrupts. 'Did you ever notice your Uncle Buck locking doors against trouble? I'm not married,' says I, 'but I'm as big a d—n fool as any Mormon. One from four leaves three,' says I, and I gathers out another leg of the table. 'We'll get home by seven,' says I, 'whether it's the heavenly one or the other. May I see you home?' says I, 'you sarsaparilla-drinking, checker-playing glutton for death and destruction.'

"We opened the door easy, and then stampeded for the front. Part of the gang was lined up at the bar; part of 'em was passing over the drinks, and two or three was peeping out the door and window taking shots at the marshal's crowd. The room was so full of smoke we got halfway to the front door before they noticed us. Then I heard Berry Trimble's voice somewhere yell out:

" 'How'd that Buck Caperton get in here?' and he skinned the side of my neck with a bullet. I reckon he felt bad over that miss, for Berry's the best shot south of the Southern Pacific Railroad. But the smoke in the saloon was some too thick for good shooting.

"Me and Perry smashed over two of the gang with our table legs, which didn't miss like the guns did, and as we run out the door I grabbed a Winchester from a fellow who was watching the outside, and I turned and regulated the account of Mr. Berry.

"Me and Perry got out and around the corner all right. I never much expected to get out, but I wasn't going to be intimidated by that married man. According to Perry's idea, checkers was the event of the day, but if I am any judge of gentle recreations that little table-leg parade through the Gray Mule saloon deserved the head-lines in the bill of particulars.

" 'Walk fast,' says Perry, 'it's two minutes to seven, and I got to be home by——'

" 'Oh, shut up,' says I. 'I had an appointment as chief performer at an inquest at seven, and I'm not kicking about not keeping it.'

"I had to pass by Perry's little house. His Mariana was standing at the gate. We got there at five minutes past seven. She had on a blue wrapper, and her hair was pulled back smooth like little girls do when they want to look grown-folksy. She didn't see us till we got close, for she was gazing up the other way. Then she backed around, and saw Perry, and a kind of look scooted around over her face—danged if I can describe it. I heard her breathe long, just like a cow when you turn her calf in the lot, and she says: 'You're late, Perry.'

" 'Five minutes,' says Perry, cheerful. 'Me and old Buck was having a game of checkers.'

"Perry introduces me to Mariana, and they ask me to come in. No, sir-ee. I'd had enough truck with married folks for that day. I says I'll be going along, and that I've spent a very pleasant afternoon with my old partner—'especially,' says I, just to jostle Perry, 'during that game when the table legs came all loose.' But I'd promised him not to let her know anything.

"I've been worrying over that business ever since it happened," continued Buck. "There's one thing about it that's got me all twisted up, and I can't figure it out."

"What was that?" I asked, as I rolled and handed Buck the last cigarette.

"Why, I'll tell you: When I saw the look that little woman give Perry when she turned round and saw him coming back to the ranch safe—why was it I got the idea all in a minute that that look of hers was worth more than the whole caboo-dle of us—sarsaparilla, checkers, and all, and that the d—n fool in the game wasn't named Perry Rountree at all?"

The Hiding of Black Bill

A lank, strong, red-faced man with a Wellington beak and small, fiery eyes tempered by flaxen lashes, sat on the station platform at Los Pinos swinging his legs to and fro. At his side sat another man, fat, melancholy, and seedy, who seemed to be his friend. They had the appearance of men to whom life had appeared as a reversible coat—seamy on both sides.

"Ain't seen you in about four years, Ham," said the seedy man. "Which way you been travelling?"

"Texas," said the red-faced man. "It was too cold in Alaska for me. And I found it warm in Texas. I'll tell you about one hot spell I went through there.

"One morning I steps off the International at a water-tank and lets it go on without me. 'Twas a ranch country, and fuller of spitehouses than New York City. Only out there they build 'em twenty miles away so you can't smell what they've got for dinner, instead of running 'em up two inches from their neighbors' windows.

"There wasn't any roads in sight, so I footed it 'cross country. The grass was shoe-top deep, and the mesquite timber looked just like a peach orchard. It was so much like a gentleman's private estate that every minute you expected a kennelful of bulldogs to run out and bite you. But I must have walked twenty miles before I came in sight of a ranch-house. It was a little one, about as big as an elevated railroad station.

"There was a little man in a white shirt and brown overalls and pink handkerchief around his neck rolling cigarettes under a tree in front of the door.

" 'Greetings,' says I. 'Any refreshments, welcome, emoluments, or even work for a comparative stranger?'

266

" 'Oh, come in,' says he, in a refined tone. 'Sit down on that stool, please. I didn't hear your horse coming.'

" 'He isn't near enough yet,' says I. 'I walked. I don't want to be a burden, but I wonder if you have three or four gallons of water handy.'

" 'You do look pretty dusty,' says he; 'but our bathing arrangements—'

" 'It's a drink I want,' says I. 'Never mind the dust that's on the outside.'

"He gets me a dipper of water out of a red jar hanging up, and then goes on:

" 'Do you want work?'

" 'For a time,' says I. 'This is a rather quiet section of the country, isn't it?'

" 'It is,' says he. 'Sometimes—so I have been told—one sees no human being pass for weeks at a time. I've been here only a month. I bought the ranch from an old settler who wanted to move farther west.'

" 'It suits me,' says I. 'Quiet and retirement are good for a man sometimes. And I need a job. I can tend bar, salt mines, lecture, float stock, do a little middle-weight slugging, and play the piano.'

" 'Can you herd sheep?' asks the little ranchman.

" 'Do you mean *have* I heard sheep?' says I.

" 'Can you herd 'em—take charge of a flock of 'em?' says he.

" 'Oh,' says I, 'now I understand. You mean chase 'em around and bark at 'em like collie dogs. Well, I might,' says I. 'I've never exactly done any sheep-herding, but I've often seen 'em from car windows masticating daisies, and they don't look dangerous.'

" 'I'm short a herder,' says the ranchman. 'You never can depend on the Mexicans. I've only got two flocks. You may take out my bunch of muttons—there are only eight hundred of 'em—in the morning, if you like. The pay is twelve dollars a month and your rations furnished. You camp in a tent on the prairie with your sheep. You do your own cooking, but wood and water are brought to your camp. It's an easy job.'

" 'I'm on,' says I. 'I'll take the job even if I have to garland my brow and hold on to a crook and wear a loose effect and play on a pipe like the shepherds do in pictures.'

"So the next morning the little ranchman helps me drive the flock of muttons from the corral to about two miles out and let 'em graze on a little hillside on the prairie. He gives me a lot of instructions about not letting bunches of them stray off from the herd, and driving 'em down to a water-hole to drink at noon.

" 'I'll bring out your tent and camping outfit and rations in the buckboard before night,' says he.

" 'Fine,' says I. 'And don't forget the rations. Nor the camping outfit. And be sure to bring the tent. Your name's Zollicoffer, ain't it?'

" 'My name,' said he, 'is Henry Ogden.'

" 'All right, Mr. Ogden,' says I. 'Mine is Mr. Percival Saint Clair.'

"I herded sheep for five days on the Rancho Chiquito; and then the wool entered my soul. That getting next to Nature certainly got next to me. I was lonesomer than Crusoe's goat. I've seen a lot of persons more entertaining as companions than those sheep were. I'd drive 'em to the corral and pen 'em every evening, and then cook my corn-bread and mutton and coffee, and lie down in a tent the size of a tablecloth, and listen to the coyotes and whip-poor-wills singing around the camp.

"The fifth evening, after I had corralled my costly but uncongenial muttons, I walked over to the ranch-house and stepped in the door.

" 'Mr. Ogden,' says I, 'you and me have got to get sociable. Sheep are all very well to dot the landscape and furnish eight-dollar cotton suitings for man, but for table-talk and fireside companions they rank along with five-o'clock teazers. If you've got a deck of cards, or a parcheesi outfit, or a game of authors, get 'em out, and let's get on a mental basis. I've got to do something in an intellectual line, if it's only to knock somebody's brains out.'

"This Henry Ogden was a peculiar kind of ranchman. He wore finger-rings and a big gold watch and careful neckties. And his face was calm, and his nose-spectacles was kept very shiny. I saw once, in Muscogee, an outlaw hung for murdering six men, who was a dead ringer for him. But I knew a preacher in Arkansas that you would have taken to be his brother. I didn't care much for him either way; what I wanted was some fellowship and communion with holy saints or lost sinners—anything sheepless would do.

" 'Well, Saint Clair,' says he, laying down the book he was reading, 'I guess it must be pretty lonesome for you at first. And I don't deny that it's monotonous for me. Are you sure you corralled your sheep so they won't stray out?'

" 'They're shut up as tight as the jury of a millionaire murderer,' says I. 'And I'll be back with them long before they'll need their trained nurse.

"So Ogden digs up a deck of cards, and we play casino. After five days and nights of my sheep-camp it was like a toot on Broadway. When I caught big casino I felt as excited as if I had made a million in Trinity. And when H. O. loosened up a little and told the story about the lady in the Pullman car I laughed for five minutes.

"That showed what a comparative thing life is. A man may see so much that he'd be bored to turn his head to look at a $3,000,000 fire for Joe Weber or the Adriatic Sea. But let him herd sheep for a spell, and you'll see him splitting his ribs laughing at 'Curfew Shall Not Ring To-night,' or really enjoying himself playing cards with ladies.

"By-and-by Ogden gets out a decanter of Bourbon, and there is a total eclipse of sheep.

" 'Do you remember reading in the papers about a month ago,' says he, 'about a train hold-up on the M. K. & T.? The express agent was shot through the shoulder and about $15,000 in currency taken. And it's said that only one man did the job.'

" 'Seems to me I do,' says I. 'But such things happen so often they don't linger long in the human Texas mind. Did they overtake, overhaul, seize, or lay hands upon the despoiler?'

" 'He escaped,' says Ogden. 'And I was just reading in a paper to-day that the officers have tracked him down into this part of the country. It seems the bills the robbers got were all the first issue of currency to the Second National Bank of Espinosa City. And so they've followed the trail where they've been spent, and it leads this way.'

"Ogden pours out some more Bourbon, and shoves me the bottle.

" 'Imagine,' says I, after ingurgitating another modicum of the royal booze, 'that it wouldn't be at all a disingenuous

idea for a train-robber to run down into this part of the
country to hide for a spell. A sheep-ranch, now,' says I,
'would be the finest kind of a place. Who'd ever expect to
find such a desperate character among these song-birds and
muttons and wild flowers? And, by the way,' says I, kind of
looking H. Ogden over, 'was there any description mentioned
to this single-handed terror? Was his lineaments or height and
thickness or teeth fillings or style of habiliments set forth in
print?'

" 'Why, no,' says Ogden; 'because they say nobody got a
good sight of him because he wore a mask. But they know it
was a train-robber called Black Bill, because he always works
alone and because he dropped a handkerchief in the express-
car that had his name on it.'

" 'All right,' says I. 'I approve of Black Bill's retreat to
the sheep-ranges. I guess they won't find him.'

" 'There's one thousand dollars reward for his capture,'
says Ogden.

" 'I don't need that kind of money,' says I, looking Mr.
Sheepman straight in the eye. 'The twelve dollars a month
you pay me is enough. I need a rest, and I can save up until I
get enough to pay my fare to Texarkana, where my widowed
mother lives. If Black Bill,' I goes on, looking significantly
at Ogden, 'was to have come down this way—say, a month
ago—and bought a little sheep-ranch and—'

" 'Stop,' says Ogden, getting out of his chair and looking
pretty vicious. 'Do you mean to insinuate—'

" 'Nothing,' says I; 'no insinuations. I'm stating a hypo-
dermical case. I say, if Black Bill had come down here and
bought a sheep-ranch and hired me to Little-Boy-Blue 'em
and treated me square and friendly, as you've done, he'd
never have anything to fear from me. A man is a man,
regardless of any complications he may have with sheep or
railroad trains. Now you know where I stand.'

"Ogden looks black as camp-coffee for nine seconds, and
then he laughs, amused.

" 'You'll do, Saint Clair,' says he. 'If I *was* Black Bill I
wouldn't be afraid to trust you. Let's have a game or two of
seven-up to-night. That is, if you don't mind playing with a
train-robber.'

" 'I've told you,' says I, 'my oral sentiments, and there's no strings to 'em.'

"While I was shuffling after the first hand, I asked Ogden, as if the idea was a kind of a casualty, where he was from.

" 'Oh,' says he, 'from the Mississippi Valley.'

" 'That's a nice little place,' says I. 'I've often stopped over there. But didn't you find the sheets a little damp and the food poor? Now, I hail,' says I, 'from the Pacific Slope. Ever put up there?'

" 'Too draughty,' says Ogden. 'But if you're ever in the Middle West just mention my name, and you'll get foot-warmers and dripped coffee.'

" 'Well,' says I, 'I wasn't exactly fishing for your private telephone number and the middle name of your aunt that carried off that Cumberland Presbyterian minister. It don't matter. I just want you to know you are safe in the hands of your shepherd. Now, don't play hearts on spades, and don't get nervous.'

" 'Still harping,' says Ogden, laughing again. 'Don't you suppose that if I was Black Bill and thought you suspected me, I'd put a Winchester bullet into you and stop my nervousness if I had any?'

" 'Not any,' says I. 'A man who's got the nerve to hold up a train single-handed wouldn't do a trick like that. I've knocked about enough to know that them are the kind of men who put a value on a friend. Not that I can claim being a friend of yours, Mr. Ogden,' says I, 'being only your sheep-herder; but under more expeditious circumstances we might have been.'

" 'Forget the sheep temporarily, I beg,' says Ogden, 'and cut for deal.'

"About four days afterwards, while my muttons was nooning on the water-hole and I deep in the interstices of making a pot of coffee, up rides softly on the grass a mysterious person in the garb of the being he wished to represent. He was dressed somewhere between a Kansas City detective, Buffalo Bill, and the town dog-catcher of Baton Rouge. His chin and eye wasn't moulded on fighting lines, so I knew he was only a scout.

" 'Herdin' sheep?' he asks me.

" 'Well,' says I, 'to a man of your evident gumptional

endowments, I wouldn't have the nerve to state that I am engaged in decorating old bronzes or oiling bicycle sprockets.'

" 'You don't talk or look like a sheep-herder to me,' says he.

" 'But you talk like what you look like to me,' says I.

"And then he asks me who I was working for, and I shows him Rancho Chiquito, two miles away, in the shadow of a low hill, and he tells me he's a deputy sheriff.

" 'There's a train-robber called Black Bill supposed to be somewhere in these parts,' says the scout. 'He's been traced as far as San Antonio, and may be farther. Have you seen or heard of any strangers around here during the past month?'

" 'I have not,' says I, 'except a report of one over at the Mexican quarters of Loomis' ranch, on the Frio.'

" 'What do you know about him?' asks the deputy.

" 'He's three days old,' says I.

" 'What kind of a looking man is the man you work for?' he asks. 'Does old George Ramey own this place yet? He's run sheep here for the last ten years, but never had no success.'

" 'The old man had sold out and gone West,' I tells him. 'Another sheep-fancier bought him out about a month ago.'

" 'What kind of a looking man is he?' asks the deputy again.

" 'Oh,' says I, 'a big, fat kind of a Dutchman with long whiskers and blue specs. I don't think he knows a sheep from a ground-squirrel. I guess old George soaked him pretty well on the deal,' says I.

"After indulging himself in a lot more non-communicative information and two thirds of my dinner, the deputy rides away.

"That night I mentions the matter to Ogden.

" 'They're drawing the tendrils of the octopus around Black Bill,' says I. And then I told him about the deputy sheriff, and how I'd described him to the deputy, and what the deputy said about the matter.

" 'Oh, well,' says Ogden, 'let's don't borrow any of Black Bill's troubles. We've a few of our own. Get the Bourbon out of the cupboard and we'll drink to his health—unless,' says he, with his little cackling laugh, 'you're prejudiced against train-robbers.'

" 'I'll drink,' says I, 'to any man who's a friend to a friend. And I believe that Black Bill,' I goes on, 'would be that. So here's to Black Bill, and may he have good luck.'

"And both of us drank.

"About two weeks later comes shearing-time. The sheep had to be driven up to the ranch, and a lot of frowzy-headed Mexicans would snip the fur off them with back-action scissors. So the afternoon before the barbers were to come I hustled my underdone muttons over the hill, across the dell, down by the winding brook, and up to the ranch-house, when I penned 'em in a corral and bade 'em my nightly adieus.

"I went from there to the ranch-house. I find H. Ogden, Esquire, lying asleep on his little cot bed. I guess he had been overcome by anti-insomnia or diswakefulness or some of the diseases peculiar to the sheep business. His mouth and vest were open, and he breathed like a second-hand bicycle pump. I looked at him and gave vent to just a few musings. 'Imperial Cæsar,' says I, 'asleep in such a way, might shut his mouth and keep the wind away.'

"A man asleep is certainly a sight to make angels weep. What good is all his brain, muscle, backing, nerve, influence, and family connections? He's at the mercy of his enemies, and more so of his friends. And he's about as beautiful as a cab-horse leaning against the Metropolitan Opera House at 12:30 A.M. dreaming of the plains of Arabia. Now, a woman asleep you regard as different. No matter how she looks, you know it's better for all hands for her to be that way.

"Well, I took a drink of Bourbon and one for Ogden, and started in to be comfortable while he was taking his nap. He had some books on his table on indigenous subjects, such as Japan and drainage and physical culture—and some tobacco, which seemed more to the point.

"After I'd smoked a few, and listened to the sartorial breathing of H.O., I happened to look out the window toward the shearing-pens, where there was a kind of a road coming up from a kind of a road across a kind of a creek farther away.

"I saw five men riding up to the house. All of 'em carried guns across their saddles, and among 'em was the deputy that had talked to me at my camp.

"They rode up careful, in open formation, with their guns

ready. I set apart with my eye the one I opinionated to be the boss muckraker of this law-and-order cavalry.

" 'Good-evening, gents,' says I. 'Won't you 'light and tie your horses?'

"The boss rides up close, and swings his gun over till the opening in it seems to cover my whole front elevation.

" 'Don't you move your hands none,' says he, 'till you and me indulge in a adequate amount of necessary conversation.'

" 'I will not,' says I. 'I am no deaf-mute, and therefore will not have to disobey your injunctions in replying.'

" 'We are on the lookout,' says he, 'for Black Bill, the man that held up the Katy for $15,000 in May. We are searching the ranches and everybody on 'em. What is your name, and what do you do on this ranch?'

" 'Captain,' says I, 'Percival Saint Clair is my occupation, and my name is sheep-herder. I've got my flock of veals—no, muttons—penned here to-night. The searchers are coming to-morrow to give them a haircut—with baa-a-rum, I suppose.'

" 'Where's the boss of this ranch?' the captain of the gang asks me.

" 'Wait just a minute, cap'n,' says I. 'Wasn't there a kind of a reward offered for the capture of this desperate character you have referred to in your preamble?'

" 'There's a thousand dollars reward offered,' says the captain, 'but it's for his capture and conviction. There don't seem to be no provision made for an informer.'

" 'It looks like it might rain in a day or so,' says I, in a tired way, looking up at the cerulean blue sky.

" 'If you know anything about the locality, disposition, or secretiveness of this here Black Bill,' says he, in a severe dialect, 'you are amiable to the law in not reporting it.'

" 'I heard a fence-rider say,' says I, in a desultory kind of voice, 'that a Mexican told a cowboy named Jake over at Pidgin's store on the Nueces that he heard that Black Bill had been seen in Matamoras by a sheepman's cousin two weeks ago.'

" 'Tell you what I'll do, Tight Mouth,' says the captain, after looking me over for bargains. 'If you put us on so we can scoop Black Bill, I'll pay you a hundred dollars out of my own—out of our own—pockets. That's liberal,' says he. 'You ain't entitled to anything. Now, what do you say?'

" 'Cash down now?' I ask.

"The captain has a sort of discussion with his helpmates, and they all produce the contents of their pockets for analysis. Out of the general results they figured up $102.30 in cash and $31 worth of plug tobacco.

" 'Come nearer, captain meeo,' says I, 'and listen.' He so did.

" 'I am mighty poor and low down in the world,' says I. 'I am working for twelve dollars a month trying to keep a lot of animals together whose only thought seems to be to get asunder. Although,' says I, 'I regard myself as some better than the State of South Dakota, it's a come-down to a man who has heretofore regarded sheep only in the form of chops. I'm pretty far reduced in the world on account of foiled ambitions and rum and a kind of cocktail they make along the P. R. R. all the way from Scranton to Cincinnati—dry gin, French vermouth, one squeeze of a lime, and a good dash of orange bitters. If you're ever up that way, don't fail to let one try you. And, again,' says I, 'I have never yet went back on a friend. I've stayed by 'em when they had plenty, and when adversity's overtaken me I've never forsook 'em.

" 'But,' I goes on, 'this is not exactly the case of a friend. Twelve dollars a month is only bowing-acquaintance money. And I do not consider brown beans and cornbread the food of friendship. I am a poor man,' says I, 'and I have a widowed mother in Texarkana. You will find Black Bill,' says I, 'lying asleep in this house on a cot in the room to your right. He's the man you want, as I know from his words and conversation. He was in a way a friend,' I explains, 'and if I was the man I once was the entire product of the mines of Gondola would not have tempted me to betray him. But,' says I, 'every week half of the beans was wormy, and not nigh enough wood in camp.'

" 'Better go in careful, gentlemen,' says I. 'He seems impatient at times, and when you think of his late professional pursuits one would look for abrupt actions if he was come upon sudden.'

"So the whole posse unmounts and ties their horses, and unlimbers their ammunition and equipments, and tiptoes into the house. And I follows, like Delilah when she set the Philip Steins on to Samson.

"The leader of the posse shakes Ogden and wakes him up. And then he jumps up and two more of the reward-hunters grab him. Ogden was mighty tough with all his slimness, and gives 'em as neat a single-footed tussle against odds as I ever see.

" 'What does this mean?' he says, after they had him down.

" 'You're scooped in, Mr. Black Bill,' says the captain. 'That's all.'

" 'It's an outrage,' says H. Ogden, madder yet.

" 'It was,' says the peace-and-good-will man. 'The Katy wasn't bothering you, and there's a law against monkeying with express packages.'

"And he sits on H. Ogden's stomach and goes through his pockets symptomatically and careful.

" 'I'll make you perspire for this,' says Ogden, perspiring some himself. 'I can prove who I am.'

" 'So can I,' says the captain, as he draws from H. Ogden's inside coat-pocket a handful of new bills of the Second National Bank of Espinosa City. 'Your regular engraved Tuesdays-and-Fridays visiting-card wouldn't have a louder voice in proclaiming your indemnity than this here currency. You can get up now and prepare to go with us and expatriate your sins.'

"H. Ogden gets up and fixes his necktie. He says no more after they have taken the money off of him.

" 'A well-greased idea,' says the sheriff captain, admiring, 'to slip off down here and buy a little sheep-ranch where the hand of man is seldom heard. It was the slickest hide-out I ever see,' says the captain.

"So one of the men goes to the shearing-pen and hunts up the other herder, a Mexican they call John Sallies, and he saddles Ogden's horse, and the sheriffs all ride up close around him with their guns in hand, ready to take their prisoner to town.

"Before starting, Ogden puts the ranch in John Sallies' hands and gives him orders about the shearing and where to graze the sheep, just as if he intended to be back in a few days. And a couple of hours afterward one Percival Saint Clair, an ex-sheep-herder of the Rancho Chiquito, might have been seen, with a hundred and nine dollars—wages and blood money—in his pocket, riding south on another horse belonging to said ranch.''

The red-faced man paused and listened. The whistle of a coming freight-train sounded far away among the low hills.

The fat, seedy man at his side sniffed, and shook his frowzy head slowly and disparagingly.

"What is it, Snipy?" asked the other. "Got the blues again?"

"No, I ain't," said the seedy one, sniffing again. "But I don't like your talk. You and me have been friends, off and on, for fifteen year; and I never yet knew or heard of you giving anybody up to the law—not no one. And here was a man whose saleratus you had et and at whose table you had played games of cards—if casino can be so called. And yet you inform him to the law and take money for it. It never was like you, I say."

"This H. Ogden," resumed the red-faced man, "through a lawyer, proved himself free by alibis and other legal terminalities, as I so heard afterward. He never suffered no harm. He did me favors, and I hated to hand him over."

"How about the bills they found in his pocket?" asked the seedy man.

"I put 'em there," said the red-faced man, "while he was asleep, when I saw the posse riding up. I was Black Bill. Look out, Snipy, here she comes! We'll board her on the bumpers when she takes water."

Hygeia at the Solito

If you are knowing in the chronicles of the ring you will recall to mind an event in the early 'nineties when, for a minute and sundry odd seconds, a champion and a "would-be" faced each other on the alien side of an international river. So brief a conflict had rarely imposed upon the fair promise of true sport. The reporters made what they could of it, but, divested of padding, the action was sadly fugacious. The champion merely smote his victim, turned his back upon him, remarking, "I know what I done to dat stuff," and extended an arm like a ship's mast for his glove to be removed.

Which accounts for a trainload of extremely disgusted gentlemen in uproar of fancy vests and neckwear being spilled from their Pullman in San Antonio in the early morning following the fight. Which also partly accounts for the unhappy predicament in which "Cricket" McGuire found himself as he tumbled from his car and sat upon the depot platform, torn by a spasm of that hollow, racking cough so familiar to San Antonian ears. At that time, in the uncertain light of dawn, that way passed Curtis Raidler, the Nueces County cattleman—may his shadow never measure under six feet two.

The cattleman, out this early to catch the south-bound for his ranch station, stopped at the side of the distressed patron of sport and spoke in the kindly drawl of his ilk and region, "Got it pretty bad, bud?"

"Cricket" McGuire, exfeather-weight prize-fighter, tout, jockey, follower of the "ponies," all-around sport, and manipulator of the gum balls and walnut shells, looked up pugnaciously at the imputation cast by "bud."

278

"G'wan," he rasped, "telegraph pole. I didn't ring for yer."

Another paroxysm wrung him, and he leaned limply against a convenient baggage truck. Raidler waited patiently, glancing around at the white hats, short overcoats, and big cigars thronging the platform. "You're from the No'th, ain't you, bud?" he asked when the other was partially recovered. "Come down to see the fight?"

"Fight!" snapped McGuire. "Puss-in-the-corner! 'Twas a hypodermic injection. Handed him just one like a squirt of dope, and he's asleep, and no tanbark needed in front of his residence. Fight!" He rattled a bit, coughed, and went on, hardly addressing the cattleman, but rather for the relief of voicing his troubles. "No more dead sure t'ings for me. But Rus Sage himself would have snatched at it. Five to one dat de boy from Cork wouldn't stay t'ree rounds is what I invested in. Put my last cent on, and could already smell the sawdust in dat all-night joint of Jimmy Delaney's on T'irty-seventh Street I was goin' to buy. And den—say, telegraph pole, what a gazaboo a guy is to put his whole roll on one turn of the gaboozlum!"

"You're plenty right," said the big cattleman; "more 'specially when you lose. Son, you get up and light out for a hotel. You got a mighty bad cough. Had it long?"

"Lungs," said McGuire comprehensively. "I got it. The croaker says I'll come to time for six months longer—maybe a year if I hold my gait. I wanted to settle down and take care of myself. Dat's why I speculated on dat five to one perhaps. I had a t'ousand iron dollars saved up. If I winned I was goin' to buy Delaney's café. Who'd a t'ought dat stiff would take a nap in de foist round—say?"

"It's a hard deal," commented Raidler, looking down at the diminutive form of McGuire crumpled against the truck. "But you go to a hotel and rest. There's the Menger and the Maverick, and——"

"And the Fi'th Av'noo, and the Waldorf-Astoria," mimicked McGuire. "Told you I went broke. I'm on de bum proper. I've got one dime left. Maybe a trip to Europe or a sail in me private yacht would fix me up—pa'per!"

He flung his dime at a newsboy, got his *Express*, propped

his back against the truck, and was at once rapt in the account of his Waterloo, as expanded by the ingenious press.

Curtis Raidler interrogated an enormous gold watch, and laid his hand on McGuire's shoulder.

"Come on, bud," he said. "We got three minutes to catch a train."

Sarcasm seemed to be McGuire's vein.

"You ain't seen me cash in any chips or call a turn since I told you I was broke, a minute ago, have you? Friend, chase yourself away."

"You're going down to my ranch," said the cattleman, "and stay till you get well. Six months'll fix you good as new." He lifted McGuire with one hand, and half-dragged him in the direction of the train.

"What about the money?" said McGuire, struggling weakly to escape.

"Money for what?" asked Raidler, puzzled. They eyed each other, not understanding, for they touched only as at the gear of bevelled cog-wheels—at right angles, and moving upon different axes.

Passengers on the south-bound saw them seated together, and wondered at the conflux of two such antipodes. McGuire was five feet one, with a countenance belonging to either Yokohama or Dublin. Bright-beady of eye, bony of cheek and jaw, scarred, toughened, broken and reknit, indestructible, grisly, gladiatorial as a hornet, he was a type neither new nor unfamiliar. Raidler was the product of a different soil. Six feet two in height, miles broad, and no deeper than a crystal brook, he represented the union of the West and South. Few accurate pictures of his kind have been made, for art galleries are so small and the mutoscope is as yet unknown in Texas. After all, the only possible medium of portrayal of Raidler's kind would be the fresco—something high and simple and cool and unframed.

They were rolling southward on the International. The timber was huddling into little, dense green motts at rare distances before the inundation of the downright, vert prairies. This was the land of the ranches; the domain of the kings of the kine.

McGuire sat, collapsed into his corner of the seat, receiving with acid suspicion the conversation of the cattleman.

What was the "game" of this big "geezer" who was carrying him off? Altruism would have been McGuire's last guess. "He ain't no farmer," thought the captive, "and he ain't no con man, for sure. W'at's his lay? You trail in, Cricket, and see how many cards he draws. You're up against it, anyhow. You get a nickel and gallopin' consumption, and you better lay low. Lay low and see w'at's his game."

At Rincon, a hundred miles from San Antonio, they left the train for a buckboard which was waiting there for Raidler. In this they travelled the thirty miles between the station and their destination. If anything could, this drive should have stirred the acrimonious McGuire to a sense of his ransom. They sped upon velvet wheels across an exhilarant savanna. The pair of Spanish ponies struck a nimble, tireless trot, which gait they occasionally relieved by a wild, untrammelled gallop. The air was wine and seltzer, perfumed, as they absorbed it, with the delicate redolence of prairie flowers. The road perished, and the buckboard swam the uncharted billows of the grass itself, steered by the practical hand of Raidler, to whom each tiny distant mott of trees was a signboard, each convolution of the low hills a voucher of course and distance. But McGuire reclined upon his spine, seeing nothing but a desert, and receiving the cattleman's advances with sullen distrust. "W'at's he up to?" was the burden of his thoughts; "w'at kind of a gold brick has the big guy got to sell?" McGuire was only applying the measure of the streets he had walked to a range bounded by the horizon and the fourth dimension.

A week before, while riding the prairies, Raidler had come upon a sick and weakling calf deserted and bawling. Without dismounting he had reached and slung the distressed bossy across his saddle, and dropped it at the ranch for the boys to attend to. It was impossible for McGuire to know or comprehend that, in the eyes of the cattleman, his case and that of the calf were identical in interest and demand upon his assistance. A creature was ill and helpless; he had the power to render aid—these were the only postulates required for the cattleman to act. They formed his system of logic and the most of his creed. McGuire was the seventh invalid whom Raidler had picked up thus casually in San Antonio, where so many thousand go for the ozone that is said to linger about its contracted streets. Five of them had been guests of Solito Ranch until they had been able to leave, cured or better, and exhausting the vocabulary of tearful gratitude. One came too late, but rested very comfortably, at last, under a ratama tree in the garden.

So, then, it was no surprise to the ranchhold when the buckboard spun to the door, and Raidler took up his debile *protégé* like a handful of rags and set him down upon the gallery.

McGuire looked upon things strange to him. The ranch-house was the best in the country. It was built of brick hauled one hundred miles by wagon, but it was of but one story, and its four rooms were completely encircled by a mud floor "gallery." The miscellaneous setting of horses, dogs, saddles, wagons, guns, and cow-punchers' paraphernalia oppressed the metropolitan eye of the wrecked sportsman.

"Well, here we are at home," said Raidler, cheeringly.

"It's a h—l of a looking place," said McGuire promptly, as he rolled upon the gallery floor, in a fit of coughing.

"We'll try to make it comfortable for you, buddy," said the cattleman, gently. "It ain't fine inside; but it's the outdoors, anyway, that'll do you the most good. This'll be your room, in here. Anything we got, you ask for it."

He led McGuire into the east room. The floor was bare and clean. White curtains waved in the gulf breeze through the open windows. A big willow rocker, two straight chairs, a long table covered with newspapers, pipes, tobacco, spurs, and cartridges stood in the centre. Some well-mounted heads of deer and one of an enormous black javeli projected from the walls. A wide, cool cot-bed stood in a corner. Nueces County people regarded this guest chamber as fit for a prince. McGuire showed his eye teeth at it. He took out his nickel and spun it up to the ceiling.

"T'ought I was lyin' about the money, did ye? Well, you can frisk me if you wanter. Dat's the last simoleon in the treasury. Who's goin' to pay?"

The cattleman's clear gray eyes looked steadily from under his grizzly brows into the huckleberry optics of his guest. After a little he said simply, and not ungraciously, "I'll be much obliged to you, son, if you won't mention money any more. Once was quite a plenty. Folks I ask to my ranch don't have to pay anything, and they very scarcely ever offers it. Supper'll be ready in half an hour. There's water in the pitcher, and some, cooler, to drink in that red jar hanging on the gallery.''

"Where's the bell?" asked McGuire, looking about.

"Bell for what?"

"Bell to ring for things. I can't—see here," he exploded in a sudden weak fury, "I never asked you to bring me here. I never held you up for a cent. I never gave you a hard-luck story till you asked me. Here I am fifty mile from a bellboy or a cocktail. I'm sick. I can't hustle. Gee! but I'm up against it!" McGuire fell upon the cot and sobbed shiveringly.

Raidler went to the door and called. A slender, bright-complexioned Mexican youth about twenty came quickly. Raidler spoke to him in Spanish.

"Ylario, it is in my mind that I promised you the position of *vaquero* on the San Carlos range at the fall *rodeo*."

"*Sí señor*, such was your goodness."

"Listen. This *señorito* is my friend. He is very sick. Place yourself at his side. Attend to his wants at all times. Have much patience and care with him. And when he is well, or—and when he is well, instead of *vaquero* I will make you *mayordomo* of the Rancho de las Piedras. *Está bueno?*"

"*Sí, sí—mil gracias, señor*." Ylario tried to kneel upon the floor in his gratitude, but the cattleman kicked at him benevolently, growling, "None of your opery-house antics, now."

Ten minutes later Ylario came from McGuire's room and stood before Raidler.

"The little *señor*," he announced, "presents his compliments" (Raidler credited Ylario with the preliminary) "and desires some pounded ice, one hot bath, one gin feez-z, that the windows be all closed, toast, one shave, one Newyorkheral', cigarettes, and to send one telegram."

Raidler took a quart bottle of whisky from his medicine cabinet. "Here, take him this," he said.

Thus was instituted the reign of terror at the Solito Ranch. For a few weeks McGuire blustered and boasted and swaggered before the cow-punchers who rode in for miles around to see this latest importation of Raidler's. He was an absolutely new experience to them. He explained to them all the intricate points of sparring and the tricks of training and defence. He opened to their minds' view all the indecorous life of a tagger after professional sports. His jargon of slang was a continuous joy and surprise to them. His gestures, his strange poses, his frank ribaldry of tongue and principle fascinated them. He was like a being from a new world.

Strange to say, this new world he had entered did not exist to him. He was an utter egoist of bricks and mortar. He had dropped out, he felt, into open space for a time, and all it contained was an audience for his reminiscences. Neither the limitless freedom of the prairie days nor the grand hush of the close-drawn, spangled nights touched him. All the hues of Aurora could not win him from the pink pages of a sporting journal. "Get something for nothing," was his mission in life; "T'irty-seventh" Street was his goal.

Nearly two months after his arrival he began to complain that he felt worse. It was then that he became the ranch's incubus, its harpy, its Old Man of the Sea. He shut himself in his room like some venomous kobold or flibbertigibbet, whining, complaining, cursing, accusing. The keynote of his plaint was that he had been inveigled into a gehenna against his will; that he was dying of neglect and lack of comforts. With all his dire protestations of increasing illness, to the eye of others he remained unchanged. His currant-like eyes were as bright and diabolic as ever; his voice was as rasping; his callous face, with the skin drawn tense as a drum-head, had no flesh to lose. A flush on his prominent cheek bones each afternoon hinted that a clinical thermometer might have revealed a symptom, and percussion might have established the fact that McGuire was breathing with only one lung, but his appearance remained the same.

In constant attendance upon him was Ylario, whom the coming reward of the *mayordomoship* must have greatly stimulated, for McGuire chained him to a bitter existence. The air—the man's only chance for life—he commanded to be kept out by closed windows and drawn curtains. The room was always blue and foul with cigarette smoke; whosoever entered it must sit, suffocating, and listen to the imp's interminable gasconade concerning his scandalous career.

The oddest thing of all was the relation existing between McGuire and his benefactor. The attitude of the invalid toward the cattleman was something like that of a peevish, perverse child toward an indulgent parent. When Raidler would leave the ranch McGuire would fall into a fit of malevolent, silent sullenness. When he returned, he would be met by a string of violent and stinging reproaches. Raidler's attitude toward his charge was quite inexplicable in its way. The cattleman seemed actually to assume and feel the character assigned him by McGuire's intemperate accusations—the character of tyrant and guilty oppressor. He seemed to have adopted the responsibility of the fellow's condition, and he always met his tirades with a pacific, patient, and even remorseful kindness that never altered.

One day Raidler said to him, "Try more air, son. You can have the buckboard and a driver every day if you'll go. Try a week or two in one of the cow camps. I'll fix you up plum comfortable. The ground, and the air next to it—them's the things to cure you. I knowed a man from Philadelphy, sicker than you are, got lost on the Guadalupe, and slept on the bare grass in sheep camps for two weeks. Well, sir, it started him getting well, which he done. Close to the ground—that's where the medicine in the air stays. Try a little hossback riding now. There's a gentle pony—"

"What've I done to yer?" screamed McGuire. "Did I ever double-cross yer? Did I ask you to bring me here? Drive me out to your camps if you wanter; or stick a knife in me and save trouble. Ride! I can't lift my feet. I couldn't sidestep a jar from a five-year-old kid. That's what you d—d ranch has done for me. There's nothing to eat, nothing to see, and nobody to talk to but a lot of Reubens who don't know a punching bag from a lobster salad."

"It's a lonesome place, for certain," apologized Raidler abashedly. "We got plenty, but it's rough enough. Anything you think of you want, the boys'll ride up and fetch it down for you."

It was Chad Murchison, a cow-puncher from the Circle Bar outfit, who first suggested that McGuire's illness was fraudulent. Chad had brought a basket of grapes for him thirty miles, and four out of his way, tied to his saddle-horn. After remaining in the smoke-tainted room for a while, he emerged and bluntly confided his suspicions to Raidler.

"His arm," said Chad, "is harder'n a diamond. He

interduced me to what he called a shore-perplexus punch, and 'twas like being kicked twice by a mustang. He's playin' it low down on you, Curt. He ain't no sicker'n I am. I hate to say it, but the runt's workin' you for range and shelter.''

The cattleman's ingenuous mind refused to entertain Chad's view of the case, and when, later, he came to apply the test, doubt entered not into his motives.

One day, about noon, two men drove up to the ranch, alighted, hitched, and came in to dinner; standing and general invitations being the custom of the country. One of them was a great San Antonio doctor, whose costly services had been engaged by a wealthy cowman who had been laid low by an accidental bullet. He was now being driven to the station to take the train back to town. After dinner Raidler took him aside, pushed a twenty-dollar bill against his hand, and said:

"Doc, there's a young chap in that room I guess has got a bad case of consumption. I'd like for you to look him over and see just how bad he is, and if we can do anything for him."

"How much was that dinner I just ate, Mr. Raidler?" said the doctor bluffly, looking over his spectacles. Raidler returned the money to his pocket. The doctor immediately entered McGuire's room, and the cattleman seated himself upon a heap of saddles on the gallery, ready to reproach himself in the event the verdict should be unfavorable.

In ten minutes the doctor came briskly out. "Your man," he said promptly, "is as sound as a new dollar. His lungs are better than mine. Respiration, temperature, and pulse normal. Chest expansion four inches. Not a sign of weakness anywhere. Of course I didn't examine for the bacillus, but it isn't there. You can put my name to the diagnosis. Even cigarettes and a vilely close room haven't hurt him. Coughs, does he? Well, you tell him it isn't necessary. You asked if there is anything we could do for him. Well, I advise you to set him digging post-holes or breaking mustangs. There's our team ready. Good-day, sir." And like a puff of wholesome, blustery wind the doctor was off.

Raidler reached out and plucked a leaf from a mesquite bush by the railing, and began chewing it thoughtfully.

The branding season was at hand, and the next morning Ross Hargis, foreman of the outfit, was mustering his force of some twenty-five men at the ranch, ready to start for the San Carlos range, where the work was to begin. By six o'clock the horses were all saddled, the grub wagon ready, and the cow-punchers were swinging themselves upon their mounts, when Raidler bade them wait. A boy was bringing up an extra pony, bridled and saddled, to the gate. Raidler walked to McGuire's room and threw open the door. McGuire was lying on his cot, not yet dressed, smoking.

"Get up," said the cattleman, and his voice was clear and brassy, like a bugle.

"How's that?" asked McGuire, a little startled.

"Get up and dress. I can stand a rattlesnake, but I hate a liar. Do I have to tell you again?" He caught McGuire by the neck and stood him on the floor.

"Say, friend," cried McGuire wildly, "are you bug-house? I'm sick—see? I'll croak if I got to hustle. What've I done to yer?"—he began his chronic whine—"I never asked yer to——"

"Put on your clothes," called Raidler, in a rising tone.

Swearing, stumbling, shivering, keeping his amazed, shiny eyes upon the now menacing form of the aroused cattleman, McGuire managed to tumble into his clothes. Then Raidler took him by the collar and shoved him out and across the yard to the extra pony hitched at the gate. The cow-punchers lolled in their saddles, open-mouthed.

"Take this man," said Raidler to Ross Hargis, "and put him to work. Make him work hard, sleep hard, and eat hard. You boys know I done what I could for him, and he was welcome. Yesterday the best doctor in San Antone examined him, and says he's got the lungs of a burro and the constitution of a steer. You know what to do with him, Ross."

Ross Hargis only smiled grimly.

"Aw," said McGuire, looking intently at Raidler, with a peculiar expression upon his face, "the croaker said I was all right, did he? Said I was fakin', did he? You put him onto me. You t'ought I wasn't sick. You said I was a liar. Say, friend, I talked rough, I know, but I didn't mean most of it. If you felt like I did—aw! I forgot—I ain't sick, the croaker says. Well, friend, now I'll go work for yer. Here's where you play even."

He sprang into the saddle easily as a bird, got the quirt

from the horn, and gave his pony a slash with it. "Cricket," who once brought in Good Boy by a neck at Hawthorne—and a 10 to 1 shot—had his foot in the stirrups again.

McGuire led the cavalcade as they dashed away from San Carlos, and the cow-punchers gave a yell of applause as they closed in behind his dust.

But in less than a mile he had lagged to the rear, and was last man when they struck the patch of high chaparral below the horse pens. Behind a clump of this he drew rein, and held a handkerchief to his mouth. He took it away drenched with bright, arterial blood, and threw it carefully into a clump of prickly pear. Then he slashed with his quirt again, gasped "G'wan" to his astonished pony, and galloped after the gang.

That night Raidler received a message from his old home in Alabama. There had been a death in the family; an estate was to divide, and they called for him to come. Daylight found him in the buckboard, skimming the prairies for the station. It was two months before he returned. When he arived at the ranch-house he found it well-nigh deserted save for Ylario, who acted as a kind of steward during his absence. Little by little the youth made him acquainted with the work done while he was away. The branding camp, he was informed, was still doing business. On account of many severe storms the cattle had been badly scattered, and the branding had been accomplished but slowly. The camp was now in the valley of the Guadalupe, twenty miles away.

"By the way," said Raidler, suddenly remembering, "that fellow I sent along with them—McGuire—is he working yet?"

"I do not know," said Ylario. "Man's from the camp come verree few times to the ranch. So plentee work with the leetle calves. They no say. Oh, I think that fellow McGuire he dead much time ago."

"Dead!" said Raidler. "What you talking about?"

"Verree sick fellow, McGuire," replied Ylario, with a shrug of his shoulder. "I theenk he no live one, two month when he go away."

"Shucks!" said Raidler. "He humbugged you, too, did he? The doctor examined him and said he was sound as a mesquite knot."

"That doctor," said Ylario, smiling, "he tell you so? That doctor no see McGuire."

"Talk up," ordered Raidler. "What the devil do you mean?"

"McGuire," continued the boy tranquilly, "he getting drink water outside when that doctor come in room. That doctor take me and pound me all over here with his fingers" —putting his hand to his chest—"I not know for what. He put his ear here and here and here, and listen—I not know for what. He put his little glass stick in my mouth. He feel my arm here. He make me count like whisper—so—twenty, *treinta, cuarenta.* Who knows," concluded Ylario, with a deprecating spread of his hands, "for what that doctor do those verree droll and such-like things?"

"What horses are up?" asked Raidler, shortly.

"Paisano is grazing out behind the little corral, *señor.*"

"Saddle him for me at once."

Within a very few minutes the cattleman was mounted and away. Paisano, well named after that ungainly but swift-running bird, struck into his long lope that ate up the road like a strip of macaroni. In two hours and a quarter Raidler, from a gentle swell, saw the branding camp by a water hole in the Guadalupe. Sick with expectancy of the news he feared, he rode up, dismounted, and dropped Paisano's reins. So gentle was his heart that at that moment he would have pleaded guilty to the murder of McGuire.

The only being in the camp was the cook, who was just arranging the hunks of barbecued beef, and distributing the tin coffee cups for supper. Raidler evaded a direct question concerning the one subject in his mind.

"Everything all right in camp, Pete?" he managed to inquire.

"So, so," said Pete, conservatively. "Grub give out twice. Wind scattered the cattle, and we've had to rake the brush for forty mile. I need a new coffee-pot. And the mosquitoes is some more hellish than common."

"The boys—all well?"

Pete was no optimist. Besides, inquiries concerning the health of cow-punchers were not only superfluous, but bordered on flaccidity. It was not like the boss to make them.

"What's left of 'em don't miss no calls to grub," the cook conceded.

"What's left of 'em?" repeated Raidler in a husky voice. Mechanically he began to look around for McGuire's grave. He had in his mind a white slab such as he had seen in the Alabama church-yard. But immediately he knew that was foolish.

"Sure," said Pete; "what's left. Cow camps change in two months. Some's gone."

Raidler nerved himself.

"That—chap—I sent along—McGuire—did—he—"

"Say," interrupted Pete, rising with a chunk of corn bread in each hand, "that was a dirty shame, sending that poor, sick kid to a cow camp. A doctor that couldn't tell he was graveyard meat ought to be skinned with a cinch buckle. Game as he was, too—it's a scandal among snakes—lemme tell you what he done. First night in camp the boys started to initiate him in the leather breeches degree. Ross Hargis busted him one swipe with his chaparreras, and what do you reckon the poor child did? Got up, the little skeeter, and licked Ross. Licked Ross Hargis. Licked him good. Hit him plenty and everywhere and hard. Ross'd just get up and pick out a fresh place to lay down on agin.

"Then that McGuire goes off there and lays down with his head in the grass and bleeds. A hem'ridge they calls it. He lays there eighteen hours by the watch, and they can't budge him. Then Ross Hargis, who loves any man who can lick him, goes to work and damns the doctors from Greenland to Poland Chiny; and him and Green Branch Johnson they gets McGuire in a tent, and spells each other feedin' him chopped raw meat and whisky.

"But it looks like the kid ain't got no appetite to git well, for they misses him from the tent in the night and finds him rootin' in the grass, and likewise a drizzle fallin'. 'Gwan,' he says, 'lemme go and die like I wanter. He said I was a liar and a fake and I was playin' sick. Lemme alone.'

"Two weeks," went on the cook, "he laid around, not noticin' nobody, and then——"

A sudden thunder filled the air, and a score of galloping centaurs crashed through the brush into camp.

"Illustrious rattlesnakes!" exclaimed Pete, springing all

ways at once; "here's the boys come, and I'm an assassinated man if supper ain't ready in three minutes."

But Raidler saw only one thing. A little brown-faced, grinning chap, springing from his saddle in the full light of the fire. McGuire was not like that, and yet——

In another instant the cattleman was holding him by the hand and shoulder.

"Son, son, how goes it?" was all he found to say.

"Close to the ground, says you," shouted McGuire, crunching Raidler's fingers in a grip of steel; "and dat's where I found it—healt' and strengt', and tumbled to what a cheap skate I been actin'. T'anks fer kickin' me out, old man. And—say! de joke's on dat croaker, ain't it? I looked t'rough the window and see him playin' tag on dat Dago kid's solar plexus."

"You son of a tinker," growled the cattleman, "whyn't you talk up and say the doctor never examined you?"

"Aw—g'wan!" said McGuire, with a flash of his old asperity, "nobody can't bluff me. You never ast me. You made your spiel, and you t'rowed me out, and I let it go at dat. And, say, friend, dis chasin' cows is outer sight. Dis is de whitest bunch of sports I ever travelled with. You'll let me stay, won't yer, old man?"

Raidler looked wonderingly toward Ross Hargis.

"That cussed little runt," remarked Ross tenderly, "is the Jo-dartin'est hustler—and the hardest hitter in anybody's cow camp."

Our Neighbors to the South

Domestic

~

"The Rose of Dixie"

When *The Rose of Dixie* magazine was started by a stock company in Toombs City, Georgia, there was never but one candidate for its chief editorial position in the minds of its owners. Col. Aquila Telfair was the man for the place. By all the rights of learning, family, reputation, and Southern traditions, he was its foreordained, fit, and logical editor. So, a committee of the patriotic Georgia citizens who had subscribed the founding fund of $100,000 called upon Colonel Telfair at his residence, Cedar Heights, fearful lest the enterprise and the South should suffer by his possible refusal.

The colonel received them in his great library, where he spent most of his days. The library had descended to him from his father. It contained ten thousand volumes, some of which had been published as late as the year 1861. When the deputation arrived, Colonel Telfair was seated at his massive white-pine centre-table, reading Burton's "Anatomy of Melancholy." He arose and shook hands punctiliously with each member of the committee. If you were familiar with *The Rose of Dixie* you will remember the colonel's portrait, which appeared in it from time to time. You could not forget the long, carefully brushed white hair, the hooked, high-bridged nose, slightly twisted to the left; the keen eyes under the still black eyebrows; the classic mouth beneath the drooping white mustache, slightly frazzled at the ends.

The committee solicitously offered him the position of managing editor, humbly presenting an outline of the feld that the publication was designed to cover and mentioning a comfortable salary. The colonel's lands were growing poorer each

year and were much cut up by red gullies. Besides, the honor
was not one to be refused.

In a forty-minute speech of acceptance, Colonel Telfair
gave an outline of English literature from Chaucer to Macaulay,
re-fought the battle of Chancellorsville, and said that, God
helping him, he would so conduct *The Rose of Dixie* that its
fragrance and beauty would permeate the entire world, hurling
back into the teeth of the Northern minions their belief that
no genius or good could exist in the brains and hearts of the
people whose property they had destroyed and whose rights
they had curtailed.

Offices for the magazine were partitioned off and furnished
in the second floor of the First National Bank building; and it
was for the colonel to cause *The Rose of Dixie* to blossom and
flourish or to wilt in the balmy air of the land of flowers.

The staff of assistants and contributors that Editor-Colonel
Telfair drew about him was a peach. It was a whole crate of
Georgia peaches. The first assistant editor, Tolliver Lee Fairfax,
had had a father killed during Pickett's charge. The second
assistant, Keats Unthank, was the nephew of one of Morgan's
Raiders. The book reviewer, Jackson Rockingham, had been
the youngest soldier in the Confederate army, having appeared on the field of battle with a sword in one hand and a
milk-bottle in the other. The art editor, Roncesvalles Sykes,
was a third cousin to a nephew of Jefferson Davis. Miss
Lavinia Terhune, the colonel's stenographer and typewriter,
had an aunt who had once been kissed by Stonewall Jackson.
Tommy Webster, the head office boy, got his job by having
recited Father Ryan's poems, complete, at the commence-
ment exercises of the Toombs City High School. The girls
who wrapped and addressed the magazines were members of
old Southern families in Reduced Circumstances. The cashier
was a scrub named Hawkins, from Ann Arbor, Michigan,
who had recommendations and a bond from a guarantee
company filed with the owners. Even Georgia stock compa-
nies sometimes realize that it takes live ones to bury the dead.

Well, sir, if you believe me, *The Rose of Dixie* blossomed
five times before anybody heard of it except the people who
buy their hooks and eyes in Toombs City. Then Hawkins
climbed off his stool and told on 'em to the stock company.
Even in Ann Arbor he had been used to having his business

propositions heard of at least as far away as Detroit. So an advertising manager was engaged—Beauregard Fitzhugh Banks—a young man in a lavender necktie, whose grandfather had been the Exalted High Pillow-slip of the Kuklux Klan.

In spite of which *The Rose of Dixie* kept coming out every month. Although in every issue it ran photos of either the Taj Mahal or the Luxembourg Gardens, or Carmencita or La Follette, a certain number of people bought it and subscribed for it. As a boom for it, Editor-Colonel Telfair ran three different views of Andrew Jackson's old home, "The Hermitage," a full-page engraving of the second battle of Manasses, entitled "Lee to the Rear!" and a five-thousand-word biography of Belle Boyd in the same number. The subscription list that month advanced 118. Also there were poems in the same issue by Leonina Vashti Haricot (pen-name), related to the Haricots of Charleston, South Carolina, and Bill Thompson, nephew of one of the stockholders. And an article from a special society correspondent describing a tea-party given by the swell Boston and English set, where a lot of tea was spilled overboard by some of the guests masquerading as Indians.

One day a person whose breath would easily cloud a mirror, he was so much alive, entered the office of *The Rose of Dixie*. He was a man about the size of a real-estate agent, with a self-tied tie and a manner that he must have borrowed conjointly from W. J. Bryan, Hackenschmidt, and Hetty Green. He was shown into the editor-colonel's *pons asinorum*. Colonel Telfair rose and began a Prince Albert bow.

"I'm Thacker," said the intruder, taking the editor's chair—"T. T. Thacker, of New York."

He dribbled hastily upon the colonel's desk some cards, a bulk manila envelope, and a letter from the owners of *The Rose of Dixie*. This letter introduced Mr. Thacker, and politely requested Colonel Telfair to give him a conference and whatever information about the magazine he might desire.

"I've been corresponding with the secretary of the magazine owners for some time," said Thacker, briskly. "I'm a practical magazine man myself, and a circulation booster as good as any, if I do say it. I'll guarantee an increase of anywhere from ten thousand to a hundred thousand a year for any publication that isn't printed in a dead language. I've had my eye on *The Rose of Dixie* ever since it started. I know every end of the business from editing to setting up the classified ads. Now, I've come down here to put a good bunch of money in the magazine, if I can see my way clear. It ought to be made to pay. The secretary tells me it's losing money. I don't see why a magazine in the South, if it's properly handled, shouldn't get a good circulation in the North, too."

Colonel Telfair leaned back in his chair and polished his gold-rimmed glasses.

"Mr. Thacker," said he, courteously but firmly, "*The Rose of Dixie* is a publication devoted to the fostering and the voicing of Southern genius. Its watchword, which you may have seen on the cover, is 'Of, For, and By the South.' "

"But you wouldn't object to a Northern circulation, would you?" asked Thacker.

"I suppose," said the editor-colonel, "that it is customary to open the circulation lists to all. I do not know. I have nothing to do with the business affairs of the magazine. I was called upon to assume editorial control of it, and I have devoted to its conduct such poor literary talents as I may possess and whatever store of erudition I may have acquired."

"Sure," said Thacker. "But a dollar is a dollar anywhere, North, South, or West—whether you're buying codfish, goober peas, or Rocky Ford cantaloupes. Now, I've been looking over your November number. I see one here on your desk. You don't mind running over it with me?

"Well, your leading article is all right. A good write-up of the cottonbelt with plenty of photographs is a winner any time. New York is always interested in the cotton crop. And this sensational account of the Hatfield-McCoy feud, by a schoolmate of a niece of the Governor of Kentucky, isn't such a bad idea. It happened so long ago that most people have forgotten it. Now, here's a poem three pages long called 'The Tyrant's Foot,' by Lorella Lascelles. I've pawed around a good deal over manuscripts, but I never saw her name on a rejection slip."

"Miss Lascelles," said the editor, "is one of our most widely recognized Southern poetesses. She is closely related to the Alabama Lascelles family, and made with her own hands the silken Confederate banner that was presented to the governor of that state at his inauguration."

"But why," persisted Thacker, "is the poem illustrated with a view of the M. & O. Railroad depot at Tuscaloosa?"

"The illustration," said the colonel, with dignity, "shows a corner of the fence surrounding the old homestead where Miss Lascelles was born."

"All right," said Thacker. "I read the poem, but I couldn't tell whether it was about the depot or the battle of Bull Run. Now, here's a short story called 'Rosie's Temptation,' by Fosdyke Piggott. It's rotten. What is a Piggott, anyway?"

"Mr. Piggott," said the editor, "is a brother of the principal stockholder of the magazine."

"All's right with the world—Piggott passes," said Thacker. "Well, this article on Arctic exploration and the one on tarpon fishing might go. But how about this write-up of the Atlanta, New Orleans, Nashville, and Savannah breweries? It seems to consist mainly of statistics about their output and the quality of their beer. What's the chip over the bug?"

"If I understand your figurative language," answered Colonel Telfair, "it is this: the article you refer to was handed to me by the owners of the magazine with instructions to publish it. The literary quality of it did not appeal to me. But, in a measure, I feel impelled to conform, in certain matters, to the wishes of the gentlemen who are interested in the financial side of *The Rose*."

"I see," said Thacker. "Next we have two pages of selections from 'Lalla Rookh,' by Thomas Moore. Now, what Federal prison did Moore escape from, or what's the name of the F.F.V. family that he carries as a handicap?"

"Moore was an Irish poet who died in 1852," said Colonel Telfair, pityingly. "He is a classic. I have been thinking of reprinting his translation of Anacreon serially in the magazine."

"Look out for the copyright laws," said Thacker, flippantly. "Who's Bessie Belleclair, who contributes the essay on the newly completed waterworks plant in Milledgeville?"

"The name, sir," said Colonel Telfair, "is the *nom de guerre* of Miss Elvira Simpkins. I have not the honor of knowing the lady; but her contribution was sent us by Congressman Brower, of her native state. Congressman Brower's mother was related to the Polks of Tennessee."

"Now, see here, Colonel," said Thacker, throwing down the magazine, "this won't do. You can't successfully run a magazine for one particular section of the country. You've got to make a universal appeal. Look how the Northern publications have catered to the South and encouraged the Southern writers. And you've got to go far and wide for your contributors. You've got to buy stuff according to its quality, without any regard to the pedigree of the author. Now, I'll bet a quart of ink that this Southern parlor organ you've been running has never played a note that originated above Mason & Hamlin's line. Am I right?"

"I have carefully and conscientiously rejected all contributions from that section of the country—if I understand your figurative language aright," replied he colonel.

"All right. Now, I'll show you something."

Thacker reached for his thick manila envelope and dumped a mass of typewritten manuscript on the editor's desk.

"Here's some truck," said he, "that I paid cash for, and brought along with me."

One by one he folded back the manuscripts and showed their first pages to the colonel.

"Here are four short stories by four of the highest priced authors in the United States—three of 'em living in New York, and one commuting. There's a special article on Vienna-bred society by Tom Vampson. Here's an Italian serial by Captain Jack—no—it's the other Crawford. Here are three separate exposés of city governments by Sniffings, and here's a dandy entitled 'What Women Carry in Dress-Suit Cases'—a Chicago newspaper woman hired herself out for five years as a lady's maid to get that information. And here's a Synopsis of Preceding Chapters of Hall Caine's new serial to appear next June. And here's a couple of pounds of *vers de société* that I got at a rate from the clever magazines. That's the stuff that people everywhere want. And now here's a write-up with photographs at the ages of four, twelve, twenty-two, and thirty of George B. McClellan. It's a prognostication. He's bound to be elected Mayor of New York. It'll make a big hit all over the country. He——"

"I beg your pardon," said Colonel Telfair, stiffening in his chair. "What was the name?"

"Oh, I see," said Thacker, with half a grin. "Yes, he's a

son of the General. We'll pass that manuscript up. But, if you'll excuse me, Colonel, it's a magazine we're trying to make go off—not the first gun at Fort Sumter. Now, here's a thing that's bound to get next to you. It's an original poem by James Whitcomb Riley. J. W. himself. You know what that means to a magazine. I won't tell you what I had to pay for that poem; but I'll tell you this—Riley can make more money writing with a fountain-pen than you or I can with one that lets the ink run. I'll read you the last two stanzas:

"Pa lays around 'n' loafs all day,
  'N' reads and makes us leave him
  be.
He lets me do just like I please,
  'N' when I'm bad he laughs at me,
'N' when I holler loud 'n' say
  Bad words 'n' then begin to tease
The cat, 'n' pa just smiles, ma's mad
  'N' gives me Jesse crost her knees.
    I always wondered why that
    wuz—
    I guess it's cause
    Pa never does.

" 'N' after all the lights are out
  I'm sorry 'bout it; so I creep
Out of my trundle bed to ma's
  'N' say I love her a whole heap,
'N' kiss her, 'n' I hug her tight.
  'N' it's too dark to see her eyes,
But every time I do I know
  She cries 'n' cries 'n' cries 'n' cries.
    I always wondered why that
    wuz—
    I guess it's cause
    Pa never does.

"That's the stuff," continued Thacker. "What do you think of that?"

"I am not unfamiliar with the works of Mr. Riley," said the colonel deliberately. "I believe he lives in Indiana. For the last ten years I have been somewhat of a literary recluse, and am familiar with nearly all the books in the Cedar Heights library. I am also of the opinion that a magazine should contain a certain amount of poetry. Many of the sweetest singers of the South have already contributed to the pages of *The Rose of Dixie*. I, myself, have thought of translating from the original for publication in its pages the works of the great Italian poet Tasso. Have you ever drunk from the fountain of this immortal poet's lines, Mr. Thacker?"

"Not even a demi-Tasso," said Thacker. "Now, let's come to the point, Colonel Telfair. I've already invested some money in this as a flyer. That bunch of manuscripts cost me $4,000. My object was to try a number of them in the next issue—I believe you make up less than a month ahead—

and see what effect it has on the circulation. I believe that by printing the best stuff we can get in the North, South, East, or West we can make the magazine go. You have there the letter from the owning company asking you to coöperate with me in the plan. Let's chuck out some of this slush that you've been publishing just because the writers are related to the Skoop-doodles of Skoopdoodle County. Are you with me?''

''As long as I continue to be the editor of *The Rose*,'' said Colonel Telfair, with dignity, ''I shall be its editor. But I desire also to conform to the wishes of its owners if I can do so conscientiously.''

''That's the talk,'' said Thacker, briskly. ''Now, how much of this stuff I've brought can we get into the January number? We want to begin right away.''

''There is yet space in the January number,'' said the editor, ''for about eight thousand words, roughly estimated.''

''Great!'' said Thacker. ''It isn't much, but it'll give the readers some change from goobers, governors, and Gettysburg. I'll leave the selection of the stuff I brought to fill the space to you, as it's all good. I've got to run back to New York, and I'll be down again in a couple of weeks.''

Colonel Telfair slowly swung his eye-glasses by their broad, black ribbon.

''The space in the January number that I referred to,'' said he, measuredly, ''has been held open purposely, pending a decision that I have not yet made. A short time ago a contribution was submitted to *The Rose of Dixie* that is one of the most remarkable literary efforts that has ever come under my observation. None but a master mind and talent could have produced it. It would about fill the space that I have reserved for its possible use.''

Thacker looked anxious.

''What kind of stuff is it?'' he asked. ''Eight thousand words sounds suspicious. The oldest families must have been collaborating. It there going to be another secession?''

''The author of the article,'' continued the colonel, ignoring Thacker's allusions, ''is a writer of some reputation. He has also distinguished himself in other ways. I do not feel at liberty to reveal to you his name—at least not until I have decided whether or not to accept his contribution.''

''Well,'' said Thacker, nervously, ''is it a continued story, or an account of the unveiling of the new town pump in Whitmire, South Carolina, or a revised list of General Lee's body-servants, or what?''

"You are disposed to be facetious," said Colonel Telfair, calmly. "The article is from the pen of a thinker, a philosopher, a lover of mankind, a student, and a rhetorician of high degree.''

"It must have been written by a syndicate," said Thacker. "But, honestly, Colonel, you want to go slow. I don't know of any eight-thousand-word single doses of written matter that are read by anybody these days, except Supreme Court briefs and reports of murder trials. You haven't by any accident gotten hold of a copy of one of Daniel Webster's speeches, have you?''

Colonel Telfair swung a little in his chair and looked steadily from under his bushy eyebrows at the magazine promoter.

"Mr. Thacker," he said, gravely, "I am willing to segregate the somewhat crude expression of your sense of humor from the solicitude that your business investments undoubtedly have conferred upon you. But I must ask you to cease your jibes and derogatory comments upon the South and the Southern people. They, sir, will not be tolerated in the office of *The Rose of Dixie* for one moment. And before you proceed with more of your covert insinuations that I, the editor of this magazine, am not a competent judge of the merits of the matter submitted to its consideration, I beg that you will first present some evidence or proof that you are my superior in any way, shape, or form relative to the question in hand.''

"Oh, come, Colonel," said Thacker, good-naturedly. "I didn't do anything like that to you. It sounds like an indictment by the fourth assistant attorney-general. Let's get back to business. What's this 8,000 to 1 shot about?''

"The aricle," said Colonel Telfair, acknowledging the apology by a slight bow, "covers a wide area of knowledge. It takes up theories and questions that have puzzled the world for centuries, and disposes of them logically and concisely. One by one it holds up to view the evils of the world, points out the way of eradicating them, and then conscientiously and in detail commends the good. There is hardly a phase of human life that it does not discuss wisely, calmy, and equitably. The great policies of governments, the duties of private citizens, the obligations of home life, ethics, morality— all these important subjects are handled with a calm wisdom and confidence that I must confess has captured my admiration.''

"It must be a crackerjack," said Thacker, impressed.

"It is a great contribution to the world's wisdom," said the colonel. "The only doubt remaining in my mind as to the tremendous advantage it would be to us to give it publication in *The Rose of Dixie* is that I have not yet sufficient information about the author to give his work publicity in our magazine."

"I thought you said he is a distinguished man," said Thacker.

"He is," replied the colonel, "both in literary and in other more diversified and extraneous fields. But I am extremely careful about the matter that I accept for publication. My contributors are people of unquestionable repute and connections, which fact can be verified at any time. As I said, I am holding this article until I can acquire more information about its author. I do not know whether I will publish it or not. If I decide against it, I shall be much pleased, Mr. Thacker, to substitute the matter that you are leaving with me in its place."

Thacker was somewhat at sea.

"I don't seem to gather," said he, "much about the gist of this inspired piece of literature. It sounds more like a dark horse than Pegasus to me."

"It is a human document," said the colonel-editor, confidently, "from a man of great accomplishments who, in my opinion, has obtained a stronger grasp on the world and its outcomes than that of any man living to-day."

Thacker rose to his feet excitedly.

"Say!" he said. "It isn't possible that you've cornered John D. Rockefeller's memoirs, is it? Don't tell me that all at once."

"No, sir," said Colonel Telfair. "I am speaking of mentality and literature, not of the less worthy intricacies of trade."

"Well, what's the trouble about running the article," asked Thacker, a little impatiently, "if the man's well known and has got the stuff?"

Colonel Telfair sighed.

"Mr. Thacker," said he, "for once I have been tempted. Nothing has yet appeared in *The Rose of Dixie* that has not been from the pen of one of its sons or daughters. I know little about the author of this article except that he has acquired prominence in a section of the country that has always been inimical to my heart and mind. But I recognize his genius; and, as I have told you, I have instituted an investigation of his personality. Perhaps it will be futile. But I shall pursue the inquiry. Until that is finished, I must leave open the question of filling the vacant space in our January number."

Thacker arose to leave.

"All right, Colonel," he said, as cordially as he could. "You use your own judgment. If you've really got a scoop or something that will make 'em sit up, run it instead of my stuff. I'll drop in again in about two weeks. Good luck!"

Colonel Telfair and the magazine promoter shook hands.

Returning a fortnight later, Thacker dropped off a very rocky Pullman at Toombs City. He found the January number of the magazine made up and the forms closed.

The vacant space that had been yawning for type was filled by an article that was headed thus:

SECOND MESSAGE TO CONGRESS

Written for

THE ROSE OF DIXIE

BY

A Member of the Well-Known
BULLOCH FAMILY, OF GEORGIA
T. ROOSEVELT

Cherchez la Femme

Robbins, reporter for the *Picayune,* and Dumars, of *L'Abeille*—
the old French newspaper that has buzzed for nearly a century—
were good friends, well proven by years of ups and downs
together. They were seated where they had a habit of
meeting—in the little, Creole-haunted café of Madame Tibault,
in Dumaine Street. If you know the place, you will experience a thrill of pleasure in recalling it to mind. It is small and
dark, with six little polished tables, at which you may sit and
drink the best coffee in New Orleans, and concoctions of
absinthe equal to Sazerac's best. Madame Tibault, fat and
indulgent, presides at the desk, and takes your money. Nicolette
and Mémé, Madame's nieces, in charming bib aprons, bring
the desirable beverages.

Dumars, with true Creole luxury, was sipping his absinthe,
with half-closed eyes, in a swirl of cigarette smoke. Robbins
was looking over the morning *Pic.,* detecting, as young
reporters will, the gross blunders in the make-up, and the
envious blue-pencilling his own stuff had received. This item,
in the advertising columns, caught his eye, and with an
exclamation of sudden interest he read it aloud to his friend.

PUBLIC AUCTION.—At three o'clock this afternoon there
will be sold to the highest bidder all the common property of the Little Sisters of Samaria, at the home of the
Sisterhood, in Bonhomme Street. The sale will dispose
of the building, ground, and the complete furnishings of
the house and chapel, without reserve.

This notice stirred the two friends to a reminiscent talk
concerning an episode in their journalistic career that had

occurred about two years before. They recalled the incidents, went over the old theories, and discussed it anew from the different perspective time had brought.

There were no other customers in the café. Madame's fine ear had caught the line of their talk, and she came over to their table—for had it not been her lost money—her vanished twenty thousand dollars—that had set the whole matter going?

The three took up the long-abandoned mystery, threshing over the old, dry chaff of it. It was in the chapel of this house of the Little Sisters of Samaria that Robbins and Dumars had stood during that eager, fruitless news search of theirs, and looked upon the gilded statue of the Virgin.

"Thass so, boys," said Madame, summing up. "Thass ver' wicked man, M'sieur Morin. Everybody shall be cert' he steal those money I plaze in his hand to keep safe. Yes. He's boun' spend that money, somehow." Madame turned a broad and comprehensive smile upon Dumars. "I ond'stand you, M'sieur Dumars, those day you come ask me fo' tell ev'ything I know 'bout M'sieur Morin. Ah! yes, I know most time when those men lose money you say 'Cherchez la femme' —there is somewhere the woman. But not for M'sieur Morin. No, boys. Before he shall die, he is like one saint. You might's well, M'sieur Dumars, go try find those money in those statue of Virgin Mary that M'sieur Morin present at those *p'tite sœurs,* as try find one *femme.*"

At Madame Tibault's last words, Robbins started slightly and cast a keen sidelong glance at Dumars. The Creole sat, unmoved, dreamily watching the spirals of his cigarette smoke.

It was then nine o'clock in the morning and, a few minutes later, the two friends separated, going different ways to their day's duties. And now follows the brief story of Madame Tibault's vanished thousands:

New Orleans will readily recall to mind the circumstances attendant upon the death of Mr. Gaspard Morin, in that city. Mr. Morin was an artistic goldsmith and jeweller in the old French Quarter, and a man held in the highest esteem. He belonged to one of the oldest French families, and was of some distinction as an antiquary and historian. He was a bachelor, about fifty years of age. He lived in quiet comfort, at one of those rare old hostelries in Royal Street. He was found in his rooms, one morning, dead from unknown causes.

When his affairs came to be looked into, it was found that he was practically insolvent, his stock of goods and personal property barely—but nearly enough to free him from censure—covering his liabilities. Following came the disclosure that he had been intrusted with the sum of twenty thousand dollars by a former upper servant in the Morin family, one Madame Tibault, which she had received as a legacy from relatives in France.

The most searching scrutiny by friends and the legal authorities failed to reveal the disposition of the money. It had vanished, and left no trace. Some weeks before his death, Mr. Morin had drawn the entire amount, in gold coin, from the bank where it had been placed while he looked about (he told Madame Tibault) for a safe investment. Therefore, Mr. Morin's memory seemed doomed to bear the cloud of dishonesty, while Madame was, of course, disconsolate.

Then it was that Robbins and Dumars, representing their respective journals, began one of those pertinacious private investigations which, of late years, the press has adopted as a means to glory and the satisfaction of public curiosity.

"Cherchez la femme," said Dumars.

"That's the ticket!" agreed Robbins. "All roads lead to the eternal feminine. We will find the woman."

They exhausted the knowledge of the staff of Mr. Morin's hotel, from the bellboy down to the proprietor. They gently, but inflexibly, pumped the family of the deceased as far as his cousins twice removed. They artfully sounded the employees of the late jeweller, and dogged his customers for information concerning his habits. Like bloodhounds they traced every step of the supposed defaulter, as nearly as might be, for years along the limited and monotonous paths he had trodden.

At the end of their labors, Mr. Morin stood, an immaculate man. Not one weakness that might be served up as a criminal tendency, not one deviation from the path of rectitude, not even a hint of a predilection for the opposite sex, was found to be placed to his debit. His life had been as regular and austere as a monk's; his habits, simple and unconcealed.

Generous, charitable, and a model in propriety, was the verdict of all who knew him.

"What, now?" asked Robbins, fingering his empty notebook.

"*Cherchez la femme,*" said Dumars, lighting a cigarette. "Try Lady Bellairs."

This piece of femininity was the race-track favorite of the season. Being feminine, she was erratic in her gaits, and there were a few heavy losers about town who had believed she could be true. The reporters applied for information.

Mr. Morin? Certainly not. He was never ever a spectator at the races. Not that kind of a man. Surprised the gentlemen should ask.

"Shall we throw it up?" suggested Robbins, "and let the puzzle department have a try?"

"*Cherchez la femme,*" hummed Dumars, reaching for a match. "Try the Little Sisters of What-d'-you-call-'em."

It had developed, during the investigation, that Mr. Morin had held this benevolent order in particular favor. He had contributed liberally toward its support and had chosen its chapel as his favorite place of private worship. It was said that he went there daily to make his devotions at the altar. Indeed, toward the last of his life his whole mind seemed to have fixed itself upon religious matters, perhaps to the detriment of his worldly affairs.

Thither went Robbins and Dumars, and were admitted through the narrow doorway in the blank stone wall that frowned upon Bonhomme Street. An old woman was sweeping the chapel. She told them that Sister Félicité, the head of the order, was then at prayer at the altar in the alcove. In a few moments she would emerge. Heavy, black curtains screened the alcove. They waited.

Soon the curtains were disturbed, and Sister Félicité came forth. She was tall, tragic, bony, and plain-featured, dressed in the black gown and severe bonnet of the sisterhood.

Robbins, a good rough-and-tumble reporter, but lacking the delicate touch, began to speak.

They represented the press. The lady had, no doubt, heard of the Morin affair. It was necessary, in justice to that gentleman's memory, to probe the mystery of the lost money. It was known that he had come often to this chapel. Any information, now, concerning Mr. Morin's habits, tastes, the friends he had, and so on, would be of value in doing him posthumous justice.

Sister Félicité had heard. Whatever she knew would be willingly told, but it was very little. Monsieur Morin had been a good friend to the order, sometimes contributing as much as a hundred dollars. The sisterhood was an independent one, depending entirely upon private contributions for the means to carry on its charitable work. Mr. Morin had presented the chapel with silver candlesticks and an altar cloth. He came every day to worship in the chapel, sometimes remaining for an hour. He was a devout Catholic, consecrated to holiness. Yes, and also in the alcove was a statue of the Virgin that he had himself modeled, cast, and presented to the order. Oh, it was cruel to cast a doubt upon so good a man!

Robbins was also profoundly grieved at the imputation. But, until it was found what Mr. Morin had done with Madame Tibault's money, he feared the tongue of slander would not be stilled. Sometimes—in fact, very often—in affairs of the kind there was—er—as the saying goes—er—a lady in the case. In absolute confidence, now—if—perhaps——

Sister Félicité's large eyes regarded him solemnly.

"There was one woman," she said, slowly, "to whom he bowed—to whom he gave his heart."

Robbins fumbled rapturously for his pencil.

"Behold the woman!" said Sister Félicité, suddenly, in deep tones.

She reached a long arm and swept aside the curtain of the alcove. In there was a shrine, lit to a glow of soft color by the light pouring through a stained-glass window. Within a deep niche in the bare stone wall stood an image of the Virgin Mary, the color of pure gold.

Dumars, a conventional Catholic, succumbed to the dramatic in the act. He bowed his head for an instant and made the sign of the cross. The somewhat abashed Robbins, murmuring an indistinct apology, backed awkwardly away. Sister Félicité drew back the curtain, and the reporters departed.

On the narrow stone sidewalk of Bonhomme Street, Robbins turned to Dumars, with unworthy sarcasm.

"Well, what next? Churchy law fem?"

"Absinthe," said Dumars.

With the history of the missing money thus partially related, some conjecture may be formed of the sudden idea that Madame Tibault's words seemed to have suggested to Robbins's brain.

Was it so wild a surmise—that the religious fanatic had offered up his wealth—or, rather, Madame Tibault's—in the shape of a material symbol of his consuming devotion? Stranger things have been done in the name of worship. Was it not possible that the lost thousands were molded into that lustrous image? That the goldsmith had formed it of the pure and precious metal, and set it there, through some hope of a perhaps disordered brain to propitiate the saints and pave the way to his own selfish glory?

That afternoon, at five minutes to three, Robbins entered the chapel door of the Little Sisters of Samaria. He saw, in the dim light, a crowd of perhaps a hundred people gathered to attend the sale. Most of them were members of various religious orders, priests and churchmen, come to purchase the paraphernalia of the chapel, lest they fall into desecrating hands. Others were business men and agents come to bid upon the realty. A clerical-looking brother had volunteered to wield the hammer, bringing to the office of auctioneer the anomaly of choice diction and dignity of manner.

A few of the minor articles were sold, and then two assistants brought forward the image of the Virgin.

Robbins started the bidding at ten dollars. A stout man, in an ecclesiastical garb, went to fifteen. A voice from another part of the crowd raised to twenty. The three bid alternately, raising by bids of five, until the offer was fifty dollars. Then the stout man dropped out, and Robbins, as a sort of *coup de main,* went to a hundred.

"One hundred and fifty," said the other voice.

"Two hundred," bid Robbins, boldly.

"Two-fifty," called his competitor, promptly.

The reporter hesitated for the space of a lightning flash, estimating how much he could borrow from the boys in the office, and screw from the business manager from his next month's salary.

"Three hundred," he offered.

"Three-fifty," spoke up the other, in a louder voice—a voice that sent Robbins diving suddenly through the crowd in its direction to catch Dumars, its owner, ferociously by the collar.

"You unconverted idiot!" hissed Robbins, close to his ear—"fool!"

"Agreed!" said Dumars, coolly. "I couldn't raise three hundred and fifty dollars with a search-warrant, but I can stand half. What you come bidding against me for?"

"I thought I was the only fool in the crowd," explained Robbins.

No one else bidding, the statue was knocked down to the syndicate at their last offer. Dumars remained with the prize, while Robbins hurried forth to wring from the resources and credit of both the prize. He soon returned with the money, and the two musketeers loaded their precious package into a carriage and drove with it to Dumars's room, in old Chartres Street, near by. They lugged it, covered with a cloth, up the stairs, and deposited it on a table. A hundred pounds it weighed, if an ounce, and at that estimate, according to their calculation, if their daring theory were correct, it stood there, worth twenty thousand golden dollars.

Robbins removed the covering, and opened his pocket-knife.

"Sacré!" muttered Dumars, shuddering. "It is the Mother of Christ. What would you do?"

"Shut up, Judas!" said Robbins, coldly. "It's too late for you to be saved now."

With a firm hand, he clipped a slice from the shoulder of the image. The cut showed a dull, grayish metal, with a thin coating of gold leaf.

"Lead!" announced Robbins, hurling his knife to the floor—"gilded!"

"To the devil with it!" said Dumars forgetting his scruples. "I must have a drink."

Together they walked moodily to the café of Madame Tibault, two squares away.

It seemed that Madame's mind had been stirred that day to fresh recollections of the past services of the two young men in her behalf.

'You mustn't sit by those table," she interposed, as they were about to drop into their accustomed seats. "Thass so, boys. But no. I mek you come at this room, like my *très bons amis*. Yes. I goin' mek for you myself one *anisette* and one *café royale* ver' fine. Ah! I lak treat my fren' nize. Yes. Plis come in this way.''

Madame led them into the little back room, into which she sometimes invited the especially favored of her customers. In two comfortable armchairs, by a big window that opened upon the courtyard, she placed them, with a low table between. Bustling hospitably about, she began to prepare the promised refreshments.

It was the first time the reporters had been honored with admission to the sacred precincts. The room was in dusky twilight, flecked with gleams of the polished fine woods and burnished glass and metal that the Creoles love. From the little courtyard a tiny fountain sent in an insinuating sound of trickling waters, to which a banana plant by the window kept time with its tremulous leaves.

Robbins, an investigator by nature, sent a curious glance roving about the room. From some barbaric ancestor, Madame had inherited a *penchant* for the crude in decoration.

The walls were adorned with cheap lithographs—florid libels upon nature, addressed to the taste of the *bourgeoisie*—birthday cards, garish newspaper supplements, and specimens of art-advertising calculated to reduce the optic nerve to stunned submission. A patch of something unintelligible in the midst of the more candid display puzzled Robbins, and he rose and took a step nearer, to interrogate it at closer range. Then he leaned weakly against the wall, and called out:

''Madame Tibault! Oh, madame! Since when—oh! since when have you been in the habit of papering your walls with five thousand dollar United States four per cent. gold bonds? Tell me—is this a Grimm's fairy tale, or should I consult an oculist?''

At his words, Madame Tibault and Dumars approached.

''H'what you say?'' said Madame, cheerily. ''H'what you say, M'sieur Robbin'? *Bon!* Ah those nize li'l peezes papier! One tam I think those w'at you call calendair, wiz ze li'l day of mont' below. But, no. Those wall is broke in those plaze, M'sieur Robbin', and I plaze those li'l peezes papier to conceal ze crack. I did think the couleur harm'nize so well with the wall papier. Where I get them from? Ah, yes, I remem' ver' well. One day M'sieur Morin, he come at my house—thass 'bout one mont' before he shall die—thass 'long 'bout tam he promise fo' inves' those money fo' me. M'sieur Morin, he leave those li'l peezes papier in those table, and say ver' much 'bout money thass hard for me to ond'stan. *Mais* I never see those money again. Thass ver' wicked man, M'sieur Morin. H'what you call those peeze papier, M'sieur Robbin'—*bon!*''

Robbins explained.

''There's your twenty thousand dollars, with coupons attached,'' he said, running his thumb around the edge of the four bonds. ''Better get an expert to peel them off for you. Mister Morin was all right. I'm going out to get my ears trimmed.''

He dragged Dumars by the arm into the outer room. Madame was screaming for Nicolette and Mémé to come and observe the fortune returned to her by M'sieur Morin, that best of men, that saint in glory.

''Marsy,'' said Robbins. ''I'm going on a jamboree. For three days the esteemed *Pic*. will have to get along without my valuable services. I advise you to join me. Now, that green stuff you drink is no good. It stimulates thought. What we want to do is to forget to remember. I'll introduce you to the only lady in this case that is guaranteed to produce the desired results. Her name is Belle of Kentucky, twelve-year-old Bourbon. In quarts. How does the idea strike you?''

''*Allons!*'' said Dumars. ''*Cherchez la femme.*''

The Fool-Killer

Down South whenever any one perpetrates some particularly monumental piece of foolishness everybody says: ''Send for Jesse Holmes.''

Jesse Holmes is the Fool-Killer. Of course he is a myth,

like Santa Claus and Jack Frost and General Prosperity and all those concrete conceptions that are supposed to represent an idea that Nature had failed to embody. The wisest of the Southrons cannot tell you whence comes the Fool-Killer's name; but few and happy are the households from the Roanoke to the Rio Grande in which the name of Jesse Holmes has not been pronounced or invoked. Always with a smile, and often with a tear, is he summoned to his official duty. A busy man is Jesse Holmes.

I remember the clear picture of him that hung on the walls of my fancy during my barefoot days when I was dodging his oft-threatened devoirs. To me he was a terrible old man, in gray clothes, with a long, ragged, gray beard, and reddish, fierce eyes. I looked to see him come stumping up the road in a cloud of dust, with a white oak staff in his hand and his shoes tied with leather thongs. I may yet——

But this is a story, not a sequel.

I have taken notice with regret that few stories worth reading have been written that did not contain drink of some sort. Down go the fluids, from Arizona Dick's three fingers of red pizen to the inefficacious Oolong that nerves Lionel Monstresser to repartee in the "Dotty Dialogues." So, in such good company I may introduce an absinthe drip—one absinthe drip, dripped through a silver dripper, orderly, opalescent, cool, green-eyed—deceptive.

Kerner was a fool. Besides that, he was an artist and my good friend. Now, if there is one thing on earth utterly despicable to another, it is an artist in the eyes of an author whose story he has illustrated. Just try it once. Write a story about a mining camp in Idaho. Sell it. Spend the money, and then, six months later, borrow a quarter (or a dime), and buy the magazine containing it. You find a full-page wash drawing of your hero, Black Bill, the cowboy. Somewhere in your story you employed the word "horse." Aha! the artist has grasped the idea. Black Bill has on the regulation trousers of the M. F. H. of the Westchester County Hunt. He carries a parlor rifle, and wears a monocle. In the distance is a section of Forty-second Street during a search for a lost gas-pipe, and the Taj Mahal, the famous mausoleum in India.

Enough! I hated Kerner, and one day I met him and we became friends. He was young and gloriously melancholy because his spirits were so high and life had so much in store for him. Yes, he was almost riotously sad. That was his youth. When a man begins to be hilarious in a sorrowful way you can bet a million that he is dyeing his hair. Kerner's hair was plentiful and carefully matted as an artist's thatch should be. He was a cigaretteur, and he audited his dinners with red wine. But, most of all, he was a fool. And, wisely, I envied him, and listened patiently while he knocked Velasquez and Tintoretto. Once he told me that he liked a story of mine that he had come across in an anthology. He described it to me, and I was sorry that Mr. Fitz James O'Brien was dead and could not learn of the eulogy of his work. But mostly Kerner made few breaks and was a consistent fool.

I'd better explain what I mean by that. There was a girl. Now, a girl, as far as I am concerned, is a thing that belongs in a seminary or an album; but I conceded the existence of the animal in order to retain Kerner's friendship. He showed me her picture in a locket—she was a blonde or a brunette—I have forgotten which. She worked in a factory for eight dollars a week. Lest factories quote this wage by way of vindication, I will add that the girl had worked for five years to reach that supreme elevation of remuneration, beginning at $1.50 per week.

Kerner's father was worth a couple of millions. He was willing to stand for art, but he drew the line at the factory girl. So Kerner disinherited his father and walked out to a cheap studio and lived on sausages for breakfast and on Farroni for dinner. Farroni had the artistic soul and a line of credit for painters and poets, nicely adjusted. Sometimes Kerner sold a picture and bought some new tapestry, a ring and a dozen silk cravats, and paid Farroni two dollars on account.

One evening Kerner had me to dinner with himself and the factory girl. They were to be married as soon as Kerner could slosh paint profitably. As for the ex-father's two millions—pouf!

She was a wonder. Small and halfway pretty, and as much at her ease in that cheap café as though she were only in the Palmer House, Chicago, with a souvenir spoon already safely hidden in her shirt waist. She was natural. Two things I noticed about her especially. Her belt buckle was exactly in the middle of her back, and she didn't tell us that a large man with a ruby stick-pin had followed her up all the way from Fourteenth Street. Was Kerner such a fool? I wondered. And then I thought of the quantity of striped cuffs and blue glass beads that $2,000,000 can buy for the heathen, and I said to myself that he was. And then Elise—certainly that was her name—told us, merrily, that the brown spot on her waist was caused by her landlady knocking at the door while she (the girl—confound the English language) was heating an iron over the gas jet, and she hid the iron under the bedclothes until the coast was clear, and there was a piece of chewing gum stuck to it when she began to iron the waist and—well, I wondered how in the world the chewing gum came to be there—don't they ever stop chewing it?

A while after that—don't be impatient, the absinthe drip is coming now—Kerner and I were dining at Farroni's. A mandolin and a guitar were being attacked; the room was full of smoke in nice, long crinkly layers just like the artists draw the steam from a plum pudding on Christmas posters and a lady in a blue silk and gasolined gauntlets was beginning to hum an air from the Catskills.

"Kerner," said I, "you are a fool."

"Of course," said Kerner, "I wouldn't let her go on working. Not my wife. What's the use to wait? She's willing. I sold that water color of the Palisades yesterday. We could cook on a two-burner gas stove. You know the ragouts I can throw together? Yes, I think we will marry next week."

"Kerner," said I, "you are a fool."

"Have an absinthe drip?" said Kerner, grandly. "To-night you are a guest of Art in paying quantities. I think we will get a flat with a bath."

"I never tried one—I mean an absinthe drip," said I.

The waiter brought it and poured the water slowly over the ice in the dipper.

"It looks exactly like the Mississippi River water in the big bend below Natchez," said I, fascinated, gazing at the bemuddled drip.

"There are such flats for eight dollars a week," said Kerner.

"You are a fool," said I, and began to sip the filtration. "What you need," I continued, "is the official attention of one Jesse Holmes."

Kerner, not being a Southerner, did not comprehend, so he sat, sentimental, figuring on his flat in his sordid, artistic way, while I gazed into the green eyes of the sophisticated Spirit of Wormwood.

Presently I noticed casually that a procession of bacchantes limned on the wall immediately below the ceiling had begun to move, traversing the room from right to left in a gay and spectacular pilgrimage. I did not confide my discovery to Kerner. The artistic temperament is too highstrung to view deviations from the natural laws of the art of kalsomining. I sipped my absinthe drip and sawed wormwood.

One absinthe drip is not much—but I said again to Kerner, kindly: "You are a fool." And then, in the vernacular: "Jesse Holmes for yours."

And then I looked around and saw the Fool-Killer, as he had always appeared to my imagination, sitting at a nearby table, and regarding us with his reddish, fatal, relentless eyes. He was Jesse Holmes from top to toe; he had the long, gray, ragged beard, the gray clothes of ancient cut, the executioner's look, and the dusty shoes of one who had been called from afar. His eyes were turned fixedly upon Kerner. I shuddered to think that I had invoked him from his assiduous southern duties. I thought of flying, and then I kept my seat, reflecting that many men had escaped his ministrations when it seemed that nothing short of an appointment as Ambassador to Spain could save them from him. I had called my brother Kerner a fool and was in danger of hell fire. That was nothing; but I would try to save him from Jesse Holmes.

The Fool-Killer got up from his table and came over to ours. He rested his hands upon it, and turned his burning, vindictive eyes upon Kerner, ignoring me.

"You are a hopeless fool," he said to the artist. "Haven't you had enough of starvation yet? I offer you one more opportunity. Give up this girl and come back to your home. Refuse, and you must take the consequences."

The Fool-Killer's threatening face was within a foot of his victim's; but to my horror, Kerner made not the slightest sign of being aware of his presence.

"We will be married next week," he muttered absent-mindedly. "With my studio furniture and some second-hand stuff we can make out."

"You have decided your own fate," said the Fool-Killer, in a low but terrible voice. "You may consider yourself as one dead. You have had your last chance."

"In the moonlight," went on Kerner, softly, "we will sit under the skylight with our guitar and sing away the false delights of pride and money."

"On your own head be it," hissed the Fool-Killer, and my scalp prickled when I perceived that neither Kerner's eyes nor his ears took the slightest cognizance of Jesse Holmes. And then I knew that for some reason the veil had been lifted for me alone, and that I had been elected to save my friend from destruction at the Fool-Killer's hand. Something of the fear and wonder of it must have showed itself in my face.

"Excuse me," said Kerner, with his wan, amiable smile; "was I talking to myself? I think it is getting to be a habit with me."

The Fool-Killer turned and walked out of Farroni's.

"Wait here for me," said I, rising; "I must speak to that man. Had you no answer for him? Because you are a fool must you die like a mouse under his foot? Could you not utter one squeak in your own defence?"

"You are drunk," said Kerner, heartlessly. "No one addressed me."

"The destroyer of your mind," said I, "stood above you just now and marked you for his victim. You are not blind or deaf."

"I recognize no such person," said Kerner. "I have seen no one but you at this table. Sit down. Hereafter you shall have no more absinthe drips."

"Wait here," said I, furious; "if you don't care for your own life, I will save it for you."

I hurried out and overtook the man in gray halfway down the block. He looked as I had seen him in my fancy a thousand times—truculent, gray and awful. He walked with the white oak staff, and but for the street-sprinkler the dust would have been flying under his tread.

I caught him by the sleeve and steered him to a dark angle of a building. I knew he was a myth, and I did not want a cop to see me conversing with vacancy, for I might land in Bellevue minus my silver matchbox and diamond ring.

"Jesse Holmes," said I, facing him with apparent bravery,

"I know you. I have heard of you all my life. I know now what a scourge you have been to your country. Instead of killing fools you have been murdering the youth and genius that are necessary to make a people live and grow great. You are a fool yourself, Holmes; you began killing off the brightest and best of your countrymen three generations ago, when the old and obsolete standards of society and honor and orthodoxy were narrow and bigoted. You proved that when you put your murderous mark upon my friend Kerner—the wisest chap I ever knew in my life."

The Fool-Killer looked at me grimly and closely.

"You're a queer jag," said he curiously. "Oh, yes; I see who you are now. You were sitting with him at the table. Well, if I'm not mistaken, I heard you call him a fool, too."

"I did," said I. "I delight in doing so. It is from envy. By all the standards that you know he is the most egregious and grandiloquent and gorgeous fool in all the world. That's why you want to kill him."

"Would you mind telling me who or what you think I am?" asked the old man.

I laughed boisterously and then stopped suddenly, for I remembered that it would not do to be seen so hilarious in the company of nothing but a brick wall.

"You are Jesse Holmes, the Fool-Killer," I said, solemnly, "and you are going to kill my friend Kerner. I don't know who rang you up, but if you do kill him I'll see that you get pinched for it. That is," I added, despairingly, "if I can get a cop to see you. They have a poor eye for mortals, and I think it would take the whole force to round up a myth murderer."

"Well," said the Fool-Killer, briskly, "I must be going. You had better go home and sleep it off. Good-night."

At this I was moved at a sudden fear for Kerner to a softer and more pleading mood. I leaned against the gray man's sleeve and besought him:

"Good Mr. Fool-Killer, please don't kill little Kerner. Why can't you go back South and kill Congressmen and clay-eaters and let us alone? Why don't you go up on Fifth Avenue and kill millionaires that keep their money locked up and won't let young fools marry because one of 'em lives on the wrong street? Come and have a drink, Jesse. Will you never get on to your job?"

"Do you know this girl that your friend has made himself a fool about?" asked the Fool-Killer.

"I have the honor," said I, "and that's why I called Kerner a fool. He is a fool because he has waited so long before marrying her. He is a fool because he has been waiting in the hopes of getting the consent of some absurd two-million-dollar-fool parent or something of the sort."

"Maybe," said the Fool-Killer—"maybe I—I might have looked at it differently. Would you mind going back to the restaurant and bringing your friend Kerner here?"

"Oh, what's the use, Jesse," I yawned. "He can't see you. He didn't know you were talking to him at the table. You are a fictitious character, you know."

"Maybe he can this time. Will you go fetch him?"

"All right," said I, "but I've a suspicion that you're not strictly sober, Jesse. You seem to be wavering and losing your outlines. Don't vanish before I get back."

I went back to Kerner and said:

"There's a man with an invisible homicidal mania waiting to see you outside. I believe he wants to murder you. Come along. You won't see him, so there's nothing to be frightened about."

Kerner looked anxious.

"Why," said he, "I had no idea one absinthe would do that. You'd better stick to Wurzburger. I'll walk home with you."

I led him to Jesse Holmes's.

"Rudolph," said the Fool-Killer, "I'll give in. Bring her up to the house. Give me your hand, boy."

"Good for you, dad," said Kerner, shaking hands with the old man. "You'll never regret it after you know her."

"So, you did see him when he was talking to you at the table?" I asked Kerner.

"We hadn't spoken to each other in a year," said Kerner. "It's all right now."

I walked away.

"Where are you going?" called Kerner.

"I am going to look for Jesse Holmes," I answered, with dignity and reserve.

The Moment of Victory

Ben Granger is a war veteran aged twenty-nine—which should enable you to guess the war. He is also principal merchant and postmaster of Cadiz, a little town over which the breezes from the Gulf of Mexico perpetually blow.

Ben helped to hurl the Don from his stronghold in the Greater Antilles; and then, hiking across half the world, he marched as a corporal-usher up and down the blazing tropic aisles of the open-air college in which the Filipino was schooled. Now, with his bayonet beaten into a cheese slicer, he rallies his corporal's guard of cronies in the shade of his well-whittled porch, instead of in the matted jungles of Mindanao. Always have his interest and choice been for deeds rather than for words; but the consideration and digestion of motives is not beyond him, as this story, which is his, will attest.

"What is it," he asked me one moonlit eve, as we sat among his boxes and barrels, "that generally makes men go through dangers, and fire, and trouble, and starvation, and battle, and such recourses? What does a man do it for? Why does he try to outdo his fellow-humans, and be braver and stronger and more daring and showy than even his best friends are? What's his game? What does he expect to get out of it? He don't do it just for the fresh air and exercise. What would you say, now, Bill, that an ordinary man expects, generally speaking, for his efforts along the line of ambition and extraordinary hustling in the market-places, forums, shooting-galleries, lyceums, battlefields, links, cinder-paths, and arenas of the civilized and *vice versa* places of the world?"

"Well, Ben," said I, with judicial seriousness, "I think

we might safely limit the number of motives of a man who
seeks fame to three—to ambition, which is a desire for
popular applause; to avarice, which looks to the material side
of success; and to love of some woman whom he either
possesses or desires to possess.''

Ben pondered over my words while a mocking-bird on the
top of a mesquite by the porch trilled a dozen bars.

"I reckon," said he, "that your diagnosis about covers the
case according to the rules laid down in the copybooks and
historical readers. But what I had in my mind was the case of
Willie Robbins, a person I used to know. I'll tell you about
him before I close up the store, if you don't mind listening.

"Willie was one of our social set up in San Augustine. I
was clerking there then for Brady & Murchison, wholesale
dry-goods and ranch supplies. Willie and I belonged to the
same german club and athletic association and military
company. He played the triangle in our serenading and quartet crowd that used to ring the welkin three nights a week
somewhere in town.

"Willie jibed with his name considerable. He weighed
about as much as a hundred pounds of veal in his summer
suitings, and he had a Where-is-Mary? expression on his
features so plain that you could almost see the wool growing
on him.

"And yet you couldn't fence him away from the girls with
barbed wire. You know that kind of young fellows—a kind of
a mixture of fools and angels—they rush in and fear to tread
at the same time; but they never fail to tread when they get
the chance. He was always on hand when 'a joyful occasion
was had,' as the morning paper would say, looking as happy
as a king full, and at the same time as uncomfortable as a raw
oyster served with sweet pickles. He danced like he had hind
hobbles on; and he had a vocabulary of about three hundred
and fifty words that he made stretch over four germans a
week, and plagiarized from to get him through two ice-cream
suppers and a Sunday-night call. He seemed to me to be a
sort of a mixture of Maltese kitten, sensitive plant, and a
member of a stranded 'Two Orphans' company.

"I'll give you an estimate of his physiological and pictorial
make-up and then I'll stick spurs into the sides of my narrative.

"Willie inclined to the Caucasian in his coloring and manner of style. His hair was opalescent and his conversation fragmentary. His eyes were the same blue shade as the china dog's in the right-hand corner of your Aunt Ellen's mantelpiece. He took things as they came, and I never felt any hostility against him. I let him live, and so did others.

"But what does this Willie do but coax his heart out of his boots and lose it to Myra Allison, the liveliest, brightest, keenest, smartest, and prettiest girl in San Augustine. I tell you, she had the blackest eyes, the shiniest curls, and the most tantalizing—Oh, no you're off—I wasn't a victim. I might have been, but I knew better. I kept out. Joe Granberry was It from the start. He had everybody else beat a couple of leagues and thence east to a stake and mound. But, anyhow, Myra was a nine-pound, full-merino, fall-clip fleece, sacked and loaded on a four-horse team to San Antone.

"One night there was an ice-cream sociable at Mrs. Colonel Spraggins', in San Augustine. We fellows had a big room upstairs opened up for us to put our hats and things in, and to comb our hair and put on the clean collars we brought along inside the sweat-bands of our hats—in short, a room to fix up in just like they have everywhere at high-toned doings. A little farther down the hall was the girls' room, which they used to powder up in, and so forth. Downstairs we—that is, the San Augustine Social Cotillion and Merrymakers' Club— had a stretcher put down in the parlor where our dance was going on.

"Willie Robbins and me happened to be up in our—cloakroom, I believe we called it—when Myra Allison skipped through the hall on her way downstairs from the girl's room. Willie was standing before the mirror, deeply interested in smoothing down the blond grassplot on his head, which seemed to give him lots of trouble. Myra was always full of life and devilment. She stopped and stuck her head in our door. She certainly was good-looking. But I knew how Joe Granberry stood with her. So did Willie; but he kept on ba-a-a-ing after her and following her around. He had a system of persistence that didn't coincide with pale hair and light eyes.

" 'Hello, Willie!' says Myra. 'What are you doing to yourself in the glass?'

" 'I'm trying to look fly,' says Willie.

" 'Well, you never could *be* fly,' says Myra with her special laugh, which was the provokingest sound I ever heard except the rattle of an empty canteen against my saddle-horn.

"I looked around at Willie after Myra had gone. He had a kind of a lily-white look on him which seemed to show that her remark had, as you might say, disrupted his soul. I never noticed anything in what she said that sounded particularly destructive to a man's ideas of self-consciousness; but he was set back to an extent you could scarcely imagine.

"After we went downstairs with our clean collars on, Willie never went near Myra again that night. After all, he seemed to be a diluted kind of a skim-milk sort of a chap, and I never wondered that Joe Granberry beat him out.

"The next day the battleship *Maine* was blown up, and then pretty soon somebody—I reckon it was Joe Bailey, or Ben Tillman, or maybe the Government—declared war against Spain.

"Well, everybody south of Mason & Hamlin's line knew that the North by itself couldn't whip a whole country the size of Spain. So the Yankees commence to holler for help, and the Johnny Rebs answered the call. 'We're coming, Father William, a hundred thousand strong—and then some,' was the way they sang it. And the old party lines drawn by Sherman's march and the Kuklux and nine-cent cotton and the Jim Crow street-car ordinances faded away. We became one undivided country, with no North, very little East, a good-sized chunk of West, and a South that loomed up as big as the first foreign label in a new eight-dollar suitcase.

"Of course the dogs of war weren't a complete pack without a yelp from the San Augustine Rifles, Company D, of the Fourteenth Texas Regiment. Our company was among the first to land in Cuba and strike terror into the hearts of the foe. I'm not going to give you a history of the war; I'm just dragging it in to fill out my story about Willie Robbins, just as the Republican party dragged it in to help out the election in 1898.

"If anybody ever had heroitis, it was that Willie Robbins. From the minute he set foot on the soil of the tyrants of Castile he seemed to engulf danger as a cat laps up cream. He certainly astonished every man in our company, from the captain up. You'd have expected him to gravitate naturally to the job of an orderly to the colonel, or typewriter in the commissary—but not any. He created the part of the flaxen-haired boy hero who lives and gets back home with the goods, instead of dying with an important despatch in his hands at his colonel's feet.

"Our company got into a section of Cuban scenery where one of the messiest and most unsung portions of the campaign occurred. We were out every day capering around in the bushes, and having little skirmishes with the Spanish troops that looked more like kind of tired-out feuds than anything else. The war was a joke to us, and of no interest to them. We never could see it any other way than as a howling farce-comedy that the San Augustine Rifles were actually fighting to uphold the Stars and Stripes. And the blamed little señors didn't get enough pay to make them care whether they were patriots or traitors. Now and then somebody would get killed. It seemed like a waste of life to me. I was at Coney Island when I went to New York once, and one of them down-hill skidding apparatuses they call 'roller-coasters' flew the track and killed a man in a brown sack-suit. Whenever the Spaniards shot one of our men, it struck me as just about as unnecessary and regrettable as that was.

"But I'm dropping Willie Robbins out of the conversation.

"He was out for bloodshed, laurels, ambitions, medals, recommendations, and all other forms of military glory. And he didn't seem to be afraid of any of the recognized forms of military danger, such as Spaniards, cannon-balls, canned beef, gunpowder, or nepotism. He went forth with his pallid hair and china-blue eyes and ate up Spaniards like you would sardines *à la* canopy. Wars and rumbles of wars never flustered him. He would stand guard-duty, mosquitoes, hard-tack, treat, and fire with equally perfect unanimity. No blondes in history ever come in comparison distance of him except the Jack of Diamonds and Queen Catherine of Russia.

"I remember, one time, a little *caballard* of Spanish men sauntered out from behind a patch of sugar-cane and shot Bob Turner, the first sergeant of our company, while we were eating dinner. As required by the army regulations, we fellows went through the usual tactics of falling into line, saluting the enemy, and loading and firing, kneeling.

"That wasn't the Texas way of scrapping; but, being a

very important addendum and annex to the regular army, the San Augustine Rifles had to conform to the red-tape system of getting even.

"By the time we had got out our 'Upton's Tactics,' turned to page fifty-seven, said 'one—two—three—one—two—three' a couple of times, and got blank cartridges into our Springfields, the Spanish outfit had smiled repeatedly, rolled and lit cigarettes by squads, and walked away contemptuously.

"I went straight to Captain Floyd, and says to him: 'Sam, I don't think this war is a straight game. You know as well as I do that Bob Turner was one of the whitest fellows that ever threw a leg over a saddle, and now these wire-pullers in Washington have fixed his clock. He's politically and ostensibly dead. It ain't fair. Why should they keep this thing up? If they want Spain licked, why don't they turn the San Augustine Rifles and Joe Seely's ranger company and a carload of West Texas deputy-sheriffs on to these Spaniards, and let us exonerate them from the face of the earth? I never did,' says I, 'care much about fighting by the Lord Chesterfield ring rules. I'm going to hand in my resignation and go home if anybody else I am personally acquainted with gets hurt in this war. If you can get somebody in my place, Sam,' says I, 'I'll quit the first of next week. I don't want to work in an army that don't give its help a chance. Never mind my wages,' says I; 'let the Secretary of the Treasury keep 'em.'

" 'Well, Ben,' says the Captain to me, 'your allegations and estimations of the tactics of war, government, patriotism, guard-mounting, and democracy are all right. But I've looked into the system of international arbitration and the ethics of justifiable slaughter a little closer, maybe, than you have. Now, you can hand in your resignation the first of next week if you are so minded. But if you do,' says Sam, 'I'll order a corporal's guard to take you over by that limestone bluff on the creek and shoot enough lead into you to ballast a submarine airship. I'm captain of this company, and I've swore allegiance to the Amalgamated States regardless of sectional, secessional, and Congressional differences. Have you got any smoking-tobacco?' winds up Sam. 'Mine got wet when I swum the creek this morning.'

"The reason I drag all this *non ex parte* evidence in is because Willie Robbins was standing there listening to us. I was a second sergeant and he was a private then, but among us Texans and Westerners there never was as much tactics and subordination as there was in the regular army. We never called our captain anything but 'Sam' except when there was a lot of major-generals and admirals around, so as to preserve the discipline.

"And says Willie Robbins to me, in a sharp construction of voice much unbecoming to his light hair and previous record:

" 'You ought to be shot, Ben, for emitting any such sentiments. A man that won't fight for his country is worse than a horse-thief. If I was the cap, I'd put you in the guard-house for thirty days on round steak and tamales. War,' says Willie, 'is great and glorious. I didn't know you were a coward.'

" 'I'm not,' says I. 'If I was, I'd knock some of the pallidness off your marble brow. I'm lenient with you,' I says, 'just as I am with the Spaniards, because you have always reminded me of something with mushrooms on the side. Why, you little Lady of Shalott,' says I, 'you underdone leader of cotillions, you glassy fashion and moulded form, you white-pine soldier made in the Cisalpine Alps in Germany for the late New-Year trade, do you know of whom you are talking to? We've been in the same social circle,' says I, 'and I've put up with you because you seemed so meek and self-unsatisfying. I don't understand why you have so sudden taken a personal interest in chivalrousness and murder. Your nature's undergone a complete revelation. Now, how is it?'

" 'Well, you wouldn't understand, Ben,' says Willie, giving one of his refined smiles and turning away.

" 'Come back here!' says I, catching him by the tail of his khaki coat. 'You've made me kind of mad, in spite of the aloofness in which I have heretofore held you. You are out for making a success in this hero business, and I believe I know what for. You are doing it either because you are crazy or because you expect to catch some girl by it. Now, if it's a girl, I've got something here to show you.'

"I wouldn't have done it, but I was plumb mad. I pulled a San Augustine paper out of my hip-pocket, and showed him an item. It was a half column about the marriage of Myra Allison and Joe Granberry.

"Willie laughed, and I saw I hadn't touched him.

" 'Oh,' says he, 'everybody knew that was going to happen. I heard about that a week ago.' And then he gave me the laugh again.

" 'All right,' says I. 'Then why do you so recklessly chase the bright rainbow of fame? Do you expect to be elected President, or do you belong to a suicide club?'

"And then Captain Sam interferes.

" 'You gentlemen quit jawing and go back to your quarters,' says he, 'or I'll have you escorted to the guardhouse. Now, scat, both of you! Before you go, which one of you has got any chewing-tobacco?'

" 'We're off, Sam,' says I. 'It's supper-time, anyhow. But what do you think of what we was talking about? I've noticed you throwing out a good many grappling-hooks for this here balloon called fame—— What's ambition, anyhow? What does a man risk his life day after day for? Do you know of anything he gets in the end that can pay him for the trouble? I want to go back home,' says I. 'I don't care whether Cuba sinks or swims, and I don't give a pipeful of rabbit tobacco whether Queen Sophia Christina or Charlie Culberson rules these fairy isles; and I don't want my name on any list except the list of survivors. But I've noticed you, Sam,' says I, 'seeking the bubble of notoriety in the cannon's larynx a number of times. Now, what do you do it for? Is it ambition, business, or some freckle-faced Phœbe at home that you are heroing for?'

" 'Well, Ben,' says Sam, king of hefting his sword out from between his knees, 'as your superior officer I could court-martial you for attempted cowardice and desertion. But I won't. And I'll tell you why I'm trying for promotion and the usual honors of war and conquest. A major gets more pay than a captain, and I need the money.'

" 'Correct for you!' says I. 'I can understand that. Your system of fame-seeking is rooted in the deepest soil of patriotism. But I can't comprehend,' says I, 'why Willie Robbins, whose folks at home are well off, and who used to be as meek and undesirous of notice as a cat with cream on his whiskers, should all at once develop into a warrior bold with the most fire-eating kind of proclivities. And the girl in his case seems to have been eliminated by marriage to another fellow. I reckon,' says I, 'it's a plain case of just common ambition. He wants his name, maybe, to go thundering down the corners of time. It must be that.'

"Well, without itemizing his deeds, Willie sure made good as a hero. He simply spent most of his time on his knees begging our captain to send him on forlorn hopes and dangerous scouting expeditions. In every fight he was the first man to mix it at close quarters with the Don Alfonsos. He got three or four bullets planted in various parts of his autonomy. Once he went off with a detail of eight men and captured a whole company of Spanish. He kept Captain Floyd busy writing out recommendations of his bravery to send in to headquarters; and he began to accumulate medals for all kinds of things—heroism and target-shooting and valor and tactics and uninsubordination, and all the little accomplishments that look good to the third assistant secretaries of the War Department.

"Finally, Cap Floyd got promoted to be a major general, or a knight commander of the main herd, or something like that. He pounded around on a white horse, all desecrated up with gold-leaf and hen-feathers and a Good Templar's hat, and wasn't allowed by the regulations to speak to us. And Willie Robbins was made captain of our company.

"And maybe he didn't go after the wreath of fame then! As far as I could see it was him that ended the war. He got eighteen of us boys—friends of his, too—killed in battles that he stirred up himself and that didn't seem to me necessary at all. One night he took twelve of us and waded through a little rill about a hundred and ninety yards wide, and climbed a couple of mountains, and sneaked through a mile of neglected shrubbery and a couple of rock-quarries and into a rye-straw village, and captured a Spanish general named, as they said, Benny Veedus. Benny seemed to me hardly worth the trouble, being a blackish man without shoes or cuffs, and anxious to surrender and throw himself on the commissary of his foe.

"But that job gave Willie the big boost he wanted. The San Augustine *News* and the Galveston, St. Louis, New York, and Kansas City papers printed his picture and columns of stuff about him. Old San Augustine simply went crazy over its 'gallant son.' The *News* had an editorial tearfully begging the government to call off the regular army and the national guard, and let Willie carry on the rest of the war single-handed. It said that a refusal to do so would be regarded as a proof that the Northern jealousy of the South was still as rampant as ever.

"If the war hadn't ended pretty soon, I don't know to what heights of gold braid and encomiums Willie would have climbed; but it did. There was a secession of hostilities just three days after he was appointed a colonel, and got in three more medals by registered mail and shot two Spaniards while they were drinking lemonade in an ambuscade.

"Our company went back to San Augustine when the war was over. There wasn't anywhere else for it to go. And what do you think? The old town notified us in print, by wire cable, special delivery, and a nigger named Saul sent on a gray mule to San Antone, that they was going to give us the biggest blowout, complimentary, alimentary, and elementary, that ever disturbed the kildees on the sand-flats outside of the immediate contiguity of the city.

"I say 'we,' but it was all meant for ex-Private, Captain *de facto,* and Colonel-elect Willie Robbins. The town was crazy about him. They notified us that the reception they were going to put up would make the Mardi Gras in New Orleans look like an afternoon tea in Bury St. Edmonds with a curate's aunt.

"Well, the San Augustine Rifles got back home on schedule time. Everybody was at the depot giving forth Roosevelt-Democrat—they used to be called Rebel—yells. There was two brass-bands, and the mayor, and schoolgirls in white frightening the street-car horses by throwing Cherokee roses in the streets, and—well, maybe you've seen a celebration by a town that was inland and out of water.

"They wanted Brevet Colonel Willie to get into a carriage and be drawn by prominent citizens and some of the city aldermen to the armory, but he stuck to his company and marched at the head of it up Sam Houston Avenue. The buildings on both sides was covered with flags and audiences, and everybody hollered 'Robbins!' or 'Hello, Willie!' as we marched up in files of fours. I never saw a illustriouser-looking human in my life than Willie was. He had at least seven or eight medals and diplomas and decorations on the breast of his khaki coat; he was sunburnt the color of a saddle, and he certainly done himself proud.

"They told us at the depot that the court-house was to be illuminated at half-past seven, and there would be speeches and chili-concarne at the Palace Hotel. Miss Delphine Thompson was to read an original poem by James Whitcomb Ryan, and Constable Hooker had promised us a salute of nine guns from Chicago that he had arrested that day.

"After we had disbanded in the armory, Willie says to me:

" 'Want to walk out a piece with me?'

" 'Why, yes,' says I, 'if it ain't so far that we can't hear the tumult and the shouting die away. I'm hungry myself,' says I, 'and I'm pining for some home grub, but I'll go with you.'

"Willie steered me down some side streets till we came to a little white cottage in a new lot with a twenty-by-thirty-foot lawn decorated with brickbats and old barrel-staves.

" 'Halt and give the countersign,' says I to Willie. 'Don't you know this dugout? It's the bird's-nest that Joe Granberry built before he married Myra Allison. What you going there for?'

"But Willie already had the gate open. He walked up the brick walk to the steps, and I went with him. Myra was sitting in a rocking chair on the porch, sewing. Her hair was smoothed back kind of hasty and tied in a knot. I never noticed till then that she had freckles. Joe was at one side of the porch, in his shirt-sleeves, with no collar on, and no signs of a shave, trying to scrape out a hole among the brickbats and tin cans to plant a little fruit-tree in. He looked up but never said a word, and neither did Myra.

"Willie was sure dandy-looking in his uniform, with medals strung on his breast and his new gold-handled sword. You'd never have taken him for the little white-headed snipe that the girls used to order about and make fun of. He just stood there for a minute, looking at Myra with a peculiar little smile on his face; and then he says to her, slow, and kind of holding on to his words with his teeth:

" *'Oh, I don't know! Maybe I could if I tried!'*

"That was all that was said. Willie raised his hat, and we walked away.

"And, somehow, when he said that, I remembered, all of a

sudden, the night of that dance and Willie brushing his hair before the looking glass, and Myra sticking her head in the door to guy him.

"When we got back to Sam Houston Avenue, Willie says:

" 'Well, so long, Ben. I'm going down home and get off my shoes and take a rest.'

" 'You?' says I. 'What's the matter with you? Ain't the courthouse jammed with everybody in town waiting to honor the hero? And two brass-bands, and recitations and flags and jags, and grub to follow waiting for you?'

"Willie sighs.

" 'All right, Ben,' says he. 'Darned if I didn't forget all about that.'

"And that's why I say," concluded Ben Granger, "that you can't tell where ambition begins any more than you can where it is going to wind up."

Our Neighbors
to the South

Foreign

~

Two Renegades

In the Gate City of the South the Confederate Veterans were reuniting; and I stood to see them march, beneath the tangled flags of the great conflict, to the hall of their oratory and commemoration.

While the irregular and halting line was passing I made onslaught upon it and dragged forth from the ranks my friend Barnard O'Keefe, who had no right to be there. For he was a Northerner born and bred; and what should he be doing hallooing for the Stars and Bars among those gray and moribund veterans? And why should he be trudging, with his shining, martial, humorous, broad face, among those warriors of a previous and alien generation?

I say I dragged him forth, and held him till the last hickory leg and waving goatee had stumbled past. And then I hustled him out of the crowd into a cool interior; for the Gate City was stirred that day, and the hand-organs wisely eliminated "Marching Through Georgia" from their repertories.

"Now, what deviltry are you up to?" I asked of O'Keefe when there were a table and things in glasses between us.

O'Keefe wiped his heated face and instigated a commotion among the floating ice in his glass before he chose to answer.

"I am assisting at the wake," said he, "of the only nation on earth that ever did me a good turn. As one gentleman to another, I am ratifying and celebrating the foreign policy of the late Jefferson Davis, as fine a statesman as ever settled the financial question of a country. Equal ratio—that was his platform—a barrel of money for a barrel of flour—a pair of $20 bills for a pair of boots—a hatful of currency for a new

337

hat—say, ain't that simple compared with W.J.B.'s little old oxidized plank?''

"What talk is this?" I asked. "Your financial digression is merely a subterfuge. Why were you marching in the ranks of the Confederate Veterans?"

"Because, my lad," answered O'Keefe, "the Confederate Government in its might and power interposed to protect and defend Barnard O'Keefe against immediate and dangerous assassination at the hands of a blood-thirsty foreign country after the United States of America had overruled his appeal for protection, and had instructed Private Secretary Cortelyou to reduce his estimate of the Republican majority for 1905 by one vote."

"Come, Barney," said I, "the Confederate States of America has been out of existence nearly forty years. You do not look older yourself. When was it that the deceased government exerted its foreign policy in your behalf?"

"Four months ago," said O'Keefe, promptly. "The infamous foreign power I alluded to is still staggering from the official blow dealt it by Mr. Davis's contraband aggregation of states. That's why you see me cake-walking with the ex-rebs to the illegitimate tune about 'simmonseels and cotton. I vote for the Great Father in Washington, but I am not going back on Mars' Jeff. You say the Confederacy has been dead forty years? Well, if it hadn't been for it, I'd have been breathing today with soul so dead I couldn't have whispered a single cussword about my native land. The O'Keefes are not overburdened with ingratitude."

I must have looked bewildered. "The war was over," I said vacantly, "in——"

O'Keefe laughed loudly, scattering my thoughts.

"Ask old Doc Millikin if the war is over!" he shouted, hugely diverted. "Oh, no! Doc hasn't surrendered yet. And the Confederate States! Well, I just told you they bucked officially and solidly and nationally against a foreign government four months ago and kept me from being shot. Old Jeff's country stepped in and brought me off under its wing while Roosevelt was having a gunboat painted and waiting for the National Campaign Committee to look up whether I had ever scratched the ticket."

"Isn't there a story in this, Barney?" I asked.

"No," said O'Keefe; "but I'll give you the facts. You know I went down to Panama when this irritation about a canal began. I thought I'd get in on the ground floor. I did, and had to sleep on it, and drink water with little zoos in it; so, of course, I got the Chagres fever. That was in a little town called San Juan on the coast.

"After I got the fever hard enough to kill a Port-au-Prince nigger, I had a relapse in the shape of Doc Millikin.

"There was a doctor to attend a sick man! If Doc Millikin had your case, he made the terrors of death seem like an invitation to a donkey-party. He had the bedside manners of a Piute medicine-man and the soothing presence of a dray loaded with iron bridge-girders. When he laid his hand on your fevered brow you felt like Cap John Smith just before Pocahontas went his bail.

"Well, this old medical outrage floated down to my shack when I sent for him. He was built like a shad, and his eyebrows was black, and his white whiskers trickled down from his chin like milk coming out of a sprinkling-pot. He had a nigger boy along carrying an old tomato-can full of calomel, and a saw.

"Doc felt my pulse, and then he began to mess up some calomel with an agricultural implement that belonged to the trowel class.

" 'I don't want any death-mask made yet, Doc,' I says, 'nor my liver put in a plaster-of-paris cast. I'm sick; and it's medicine I need, not frescoing.'

" 'You're a blame Yankee, ain't you?' asked Doc, going on mixing up his Portland cement.

" 'I'm from the North,' says I, 'but I'm a plain man, and don't care for mural decorations. When you get the Isthmus all asphalted over with that boll-weevil prescription, would you mind giving me a dose of painkiller, or a little strychnine on toast to ease up this feeling of unhealthiness that I have got?'

" 'They was all sassy, just like you,' says old Doc, 'but we lowered their temperature considerable. Yes, sir, I reckon we sent a good many of ye over to old *mortuis nisi bonum*. Look at Antietam and Bull Run and Seven Pines and around Nashville! There never was a battle where we didn't lick ye unless you was ten to our one. I knew you were a blame Yankee the minute I laid eyes on you.'

" 'Don't reopen the chasm, Doc,' I begs him. 'Any Yankeeness I may have is geographical; and, as far as I am concerned a Southerner is as good as a Filipino any day. I'm feeling too bad to argue. Let's have secession without misrepresentation, if you say so; but what I need is more laudanum and less Lundy's Lane. If you're mixing that compound gefloxide of gefloxicum for me, please fill my ears with it before you get around to the battle of Gettysburg, for there is a subject full of talk.'

"By this time Doc Millikin had thrown up a line of fortifications on square pieces of paper; and he says to me: 'Yank, take one of these powders every two hours. They won't kill you. I'll be around again about sundown to see if you're alive.'

"Old Doc's powders knocked the chagres. I stayed in San Juan, and got to knowing him better. He was from Mississippi, and the red-hottest Southerner that ever smelled mint. He made Stonewall Jackson and R. E. Lee look like Abolitionists. He had a family somewhere down near Yazoo City; but he stayed away from the States on account of an uncontrollable liking he had for the absence of a Yankee government. Him and me got as thick personally as the Emperor of Russia and the dove of peace, but sectionally we didn't amalgamate.

" 'Twas a beautiful system of medical practice introduced by old Doc into that isthmus of land. He'd take that bracket-saw and the mild chloride and his hypodermic, and treat anything from yellow fever to a personal friend.

"Besides his other liabilities Doc could play a flute for a minute or two. He was guilty of two tunes—'Dixie' and another one that was mighty close to the 'Suwanee River' —you might say one of its tributaries. He used to come down and sit with me while I was getting well, and aggrieve his flute and say unreconstructed things about the North. You'd have thought the smoke from the first gun at Fort Sumter was still floating around in the air.

"You know that was about the time they staged them property revolutions down there, that wound up in the fifth act with the thrilling canal scene where Uncle Sam has nine curtain-calls holding Miss Panama by the hand, while the bloodhounds keep Senator Morgan treed up in a cocoanut-palm.

"That's the way it wound up; but at first it seemed as if Colombia was going to make Panama look like one of the $3.98 kind, with dents made in it in the factory, like they wear at North Beach fish fries. For mine, I played the straw-hat crowd to win; and they gave me a colonel's commission over a brigade of twenty-seven men in the left wing and second joint of the insurgent army.

"The Colombian troops were awfully rude to us. One day when I had my brigade in a sandy spot, with its shoes off doing a battalion drill by squads, the Government army rushed from behind a bush at us, acting as noisy and disagreeable as they could.

"My troops enfiladed, left-faced, and left the spot. After enticing the enemy for three miles or so we struck a brier-patch and had to sit down. When we were ordered to throw up our toes and surrender we obeyed. Five of my best staff-officers fell, suffering extremely with stone-bruised heels.

"Then and there those Colombians took your friend Barney, sir, stripped him of the insignia of his rank, consisting of a pair of brass knuckles and a canteen of rum, and dragged him before a military court. The presiding general went through the usual legal formalities that sometimes cause a case to hang on the calendar of a South American military court as long as ten minutes. He asked me my age, and then sentenced me to be shot.

"They woke up the court interpreter, an American named Jenks, who was in the rum business and vice versa, and told him to translate the verdict.

"Jenks stretched himself and took a morphine tablet.

" 'You've got to back up against th' 'dobe, old man,' says he to me. 'Three weeks, I believe, you get. Haven't got a chew of fine-cut on you, have you?'

" 'Translate that again, with footnotes and a glossary,' says I. 'I don't know whether I'm discharged, condemned, or handed over to the Gerry Society.'

" 'Oh,' says Jenks, 'don't you understand? You're to be stood up against a 'dobe wall and shot in two or three weeks—three, I think, they said.'

" 'Would you mind asking 'em which?' says I. 'A week

don't amount to much after you are dead, but it seems a real nice long spell while you are alive.'

" 'It's two weeks,' says the interpreter, after inquiring in Spanish of the court. 'Shall I ask 'em again?'

" 'Let be,' says I. 'Let's have a stationary verdict. If I keep on appealing this way they'll have me shot about ten days before I was captured. No, I haven't got any fine-cut.'

"They sends me over to the *calaboza* with a detachment of colored postal-telegraph boys carrying Enfield rifles, and I am locked up in a kind of brick bakery. The temperature in there was just about the kind mentioned in the cooking recipes that call for a quick oven.

"Then I gives a silver dollar to one of the guards to send for the United States consul. He comes around in pajamas with a pair of glasses on his nose and a dozen or two inside of him.

" 'I'm to be shot in two weeks,' says I. 'And although I've made a memorandum of it, I don't seem to get it off my mind. You want to call up Uncle Sam on the cable as quick as you can and get him all worked up about it. Have 'em send the *Kentucky* and the *Kearsarge* and the *Oregon* down right away. That'll be about enough battleships; but it wouldn't hurt to have a couple of cruisers and a torpedo-boat destroyer, too. And—say, if Dewey isn't busy, better have him come along on the fastest one of the fleet.'

" 'Now, see here, O'Keefe,' says the consul, getting the best of a hiccup, 'what do you want to bother the State Department about this matter for?'

" 'Didn't you hear me?' says I; 'I'm to be shot in two weeks. Did you think I said I was going to a lawn-party? And it wouldn't hurt if Roosevelt could get the Japs to send down the *Yellowyamstiskookum* or the *Ogotosingsing* or some other first-class cruiser to help. It would make me feel safer.'

" 'Now, what you want,' says the consul, 'is not to get excited. I'll send you over some chewing tobacco and some banana fritters when I go back. The United States can't interfere in this. You know you were caught insurging against the government, and you're subject to the laws of this country. Tell you the truth, I've had an intimation from the State Department—unofficially, of course—that whenever a soldier of fortune demands a fleet of gunboats in a case of revolutionary *katzenjammer*, I should cut the cable, give him all the tobacco he wants, and after he's shot take his clothes, if they fit me, for part payment of my salary.'

" 'Consul,' says I to him, 'this is a serious question. You are representing Uncle Sam. This ain't any little international tomfoolery, like a universal peace congress or the christening of the *Shamrock IV*. I'm an American citizen and I demand protection. I demand the Mosquito fleet, and Schley, and the Atlantic squadron, and Bob Evans, and General E. Byrd Grubb, and two or three protocols. What are you going to do about it?'

" 'Nothing doing,' says the consul.

" 'Be off with you, then,' says I, out of patience with him, 'and send me Doc Millikin. Ask Doc to come and see me.'

"Doc comes and looks through the bars at me, surrounded by dirty soldiers, with even my shoes and canteen confiscated, and he looks mightily pleased.

" 'Hello, Yank,' says he, 'getting a little taste of Johnson's Island, now, ain't ye?'

" 'Doc,' says I, 'I've just had an interview with the U.S. consul. I gather from his remarks that I might just as well have been caught selling suspenders in Kishineff under the name of Rosenstein as to be in my present condition. It seems that the only maritime aid I am to receive from the United States is some navy-plug to chew. Doc,' says I, 'can't you suspend hostilities on the slavery question long enough to do something for me?'

" 'It ain't been my habit,' Doc Millikin answers, 'to do any painless dentistry when I find a Yank cutting an eyetooth. So the Stars and Stripes ain't landing any marines to shell the huts of the Colombian cannibals, hey? Oh, say, can you see by the dawn's early light the star-spangled banner has fluked in the fight? What's the matter with the War Department, hey? It's a great thing to be a citizen of a gold-standard nation, ain't it?'

" 'Rub it in, Doc, all you want,' says I. 'I guess we're weak on foreign policy.'

" 'For a Yank,' says Doc, putting on his specs and talking more mild, 'you ain't so bad. If you had come from below the line I reckon I would have liked you right smart. Now since your country has gone back on you, you have to come to the old doctor whose cotton you burned and whose mules you stole and whose niggers you freed to help you. Ain't that so, Yank?'

" 'It is,' says I heartily, 'and let's have a diagnosis of the case right away, for in two weeks' time all you can do is to hold an autopsy and I don't want to be amputated if I can help it.'

" 'Now,' says Doc, business-like, 'it's easy enough for you to get out of this scrape. Money'll do it. You've got to pay a long string of 'em from General Pomposo down to this anthropoid ape guarding your door. About $10,000 will do the trick. Have you got the money?'

" 'Me?' says I. 'I've got one Chili dollar, two *real* pieces, and a *medio*.'

" 'Then if you've any last words, utter 'em,' says that old reb. 'The roster of your financial budget sounds quite much to me like the noise of a requiem.'

" 'Change the treatment,' says I. 'I admit that I'm short. Call a consultation or use radium or smuggle me in some saws or something.'

" 'Yank,' says Doc Millikin, 'I've a good notion to help you. There's only one government in the world that can get you out of this difficulty; and that's the Confederate States of America, the grandest nation that ever existed.'

"Just as you said to me I says to Doc: 'Why, the Confederacy ain't a nation. It's been absolved forty years ago.'

" 'That's a campaign lie,' says Doc. 'She's running along as solid as the Roman Empire. She's the only hope you've got. Now, you, being a Yank, have got to go through with some preliminary obsequies before you can get official aid. You've got to take the oath of allegiance to the Confederate Government. Then I'll guarantee she does all she can for you. What do you say, Yank?—it's your last chance.'

" 'If you're fooling with me, Doc,' I answered, 'you're no better than the United States. But as you say it's the last chance, hurry up and swear me. I always did like corn whisky and 'possum anyhow. I believe I'm half Southerner by nature. I'm willing to try the Ku Klux in place of the khaki. Get brisk.'

"Doc Millikin thinks awhile, and then he offers me this oath of allegiance to take without any kind of a chaser:

" 'I, Barnard O'Keefe, Yank, being of sound body but a Republican mind, hereby swear to transfer my fealty, respect, and allegiance to the Confederate States of America, and the Government thereof, in consideration of said government, through its official acts and powers, obtaining my freedom and release from confinement and sentence of death brought about by the exuberance of my Irish proclivities and my general pizenness as a Yank.'

"I repeated these words after Doc, but they seemed to me a kind of hocus-pocus; and I don't believe any life-insurance company in the country would have issued me a policy on the strength of 'em.

"Doc went away saying he would communicate with his government immediately.

"Say—you can imagine how I felt—me to be shot in two weeks and my only hope for help being a government that's been dead so long that it isn't even remembered except on Decoration Day and when Joe Wheeler signs the voucher for his pay-check. But it was all there was in sight; and somehow I thought Doc Millikin had something up his old alpaca sleeve that wasn't all foolishness.

"Around to the jail comes old Doc again in about a week. I was flea-bitten, a mite sarcastic, and fundamentally hungry.

" 'Any Confederate ironclads in the offing?' I asks. 'Do you notice any sounds resembling the approach of Jeb Stewart's cavalry overland or Stonewall Jackson sneaking up in the rear? If you do, I wish you'd say so.'

" 'It's too soon yet for help to come,' says Doc.

" 'The sooner the better,' says I. 'I don't care if it gets in fully fifteen minutes before I am shot; and if you happen to lay eyes on Beauregard or Albert Sidney Johnson or any of the relief corps, wig-wag 'em to hike along.'

" 'There's been no answer received yet,' says Doc.

" 'Don't forget,' says I, 'that there's only four days more. I don't know how you propose to work this thing, Doc,' I says to him; 'but it seems to me I'd sleep better if you had got a government that was alive and on the map—like Afghanistan or Great Britain, or old man Kruger's kingdom, to take this matter up. I don't mean any disrespect to your Confederate States, but I can't help feeling that my chances of being pulled out of this scrape was decidedly weakened when General Lee surrendered.'

" 'It's your only chance,' said Doc; 'don't quarrel with it. What did your own country do for you?'

"It was only two days before the morning I was to be shot when Doc Millikin came around again.

" 'All right, Yank,' says he. 'Help's come. The Confederate States of America is going to apply for your release. The representatives of the government arrived on a fruit-steamer last night.'

" 'Bully!' says I—'bully for you, Doc! I suppose it's marines with a Gatling. I'm going to love your country all I can for this.'

" 'Negotiations,' says old Doc, 'will be opened between the two governments at once. You will know later on to-day if they are successful.'

"About four in the afternoon a soldier in red trousers brings a paper round to the jail, and they unlocks the door and I walks out. The guard at the door bows and I bows, and I steps into the grass and wades around to Doc Millikin's shack.

"Doc was sitting in his hammock playing 'Dixie,' soft and low and out of tune, on his flute. I interrupted him at 'Look away! look away!' and shook his hand for five minutes.

" 'I never thought,' says Doc, taking a chew fretfully, 'that I'd ever try to save any blame Yank's life. But, Mr. O'Keefe, I don't see but what you are entitled to be considered part human, anyhow. I never thought Yanks had any of the rudiments of decorum and laudability about them. I reckon I might have been too aggregative in my tabulation. But it ain't me you want to thank—it's the Confederate States of America.'

" 'And I'm much obliged to 'em,' says I. 'It's a poor man that wouldn't be patriotic with a country that's saved his life. I'll drink to the Stars and Bars whenever there's a flag-staff and a glass convenient. But where,' says I, 'are the rescuing troops? If there was a gun fired or a shell burst, I didn't hear it.'

"Doc Millikin raises up and points out the window with his flute at the banana-steamer loading with fruit.

" 'Yank,' says he, 'there's a steamer that's going to sail in the morning. If I was you, I'd sail on it. The Confederate Government's done all it can for you. There wasn't a gun fired. The negotiations was carried on secretly between the two nations by the purser of that steamer. I got him to do it because I didn't want to appear in it. Twelve thousand dollars was paid to the officials in bribes to let you go.'

" 'Man!' says I, sitting down hard—'twelve thousand— how will I ever—who could have—where did the money come from?'

" 'Yazoo City,' says Doc Millikin; 'I've got a little bit saved up there. Two barrels full. It looks good to these Colombians. 'Twas Confederate money, every dollar of it. Now do you see why you'd better leave before they try to pass some of it on an expert?'

" 'I do,' says I.

" 'Now, let's hear you give the password,' says Doc Millikin.

" 'Hurrah for Jeff Davis!' says I.

" 'Correct,' says Doc. 'And let me tell you something. The next tune I learn on my flute is going to be "Yankee Doodle." I reckon there's some Yanks that are not so pizen. Or, if you was me, would you try "The Red, White, and Blue"?' "

He Also Serves

If I could have a thousand years—just one little thousand years—more of life, I might, in that time, draw near enough to true Romance to touch the hem of her robe.

Up from ships men come, and from waste places and forest and road and garret and cellar to maunder to me in strangely distributed words of the things they have seen and considered.

The recording of their tales is no more than a matter of ears and fingers. There are only two fates I dread—deafness and writer's cramp. The hand is yet steady; let the ear bear the blame if these printed words be not in the order they were delivered to me by Hunky Magee, true camp-follower of fortune.

Biography shall claim you but an instant—I first knew Hunky when he was head-waiter at Chubb's little beefsteak restaurant and café on Third Avenue. There was only one waiter besides.

Then, successively, I caromed against him in the little streets of the Big City after his trip to Alaska, his voyage as cook with a treasure-seeking expedition to the Caribbean, and his failure as a pearl-fisher in the Arkansas River. Between these dashes into the land of adventure he usually came back to Chubb's for a while. Chubb's was a port for him when gales blew too high; but when you dined there and Hunky went for your steak you never knew whether he would come to anchor in the kitchen or in the Malayan Archipelago. You wouldn't care for his description—he was soft of voice and hard to face, and rarely had to use more than one eye to quell any approach to a disturbance among Chubb's customers.

One night I found Hunky standing at a corner of Twenty-third Street and Third Avenue after an absence of several months. In ten minutes we had a little round table between us in a quiet corner, and my ears began to get busy. I leave out my sly ruses and feints to draw Hunky's word-of-mouth blows—it all came to something like this:

"Speaking of the next election," said Hunky, "did you ever know much about Indians? No; I don't mean the Cooper, Beadle, cigarstore, or Laughing Water kind—I mean the modern Indian—the kind that takes Greek prizes in colleges and scalps the half-back on the other side in football games. The kind that eats macaroons and tea in the afternoons with the daughter of the professor of biology, and fills up on grasshoppers and fried rattlesnake when they get back to the ancestral wickiup.

"Well, they ain't so bad. I like 'em better than most foreigners that have come over in the last few hundred years.

One thing about the Indian is this: when he mixes with the white race he swaps all his own vices for them of the pale-faces—and he retains all his own virtues. Well, his virtues are enough to call out the reserves whenever he lets 'em loose. But the imported foreigners adopt our virtues and keep their own vices—and it's going to take our whole standing army some day to police that gang.

"But let me tell you about the trip I took to Mexico with High Jack Snakefeeder, a Cherokee twice removed, a graduate of a Pennsylvania college and the latest thing in pointed-toed, rubber-heeled, patent kid moccasins and Madras hunting-shirt with turned-back cuffs. He was a friend of mine. I met him in Tahlequah when I was out there during the land boom, and we got thick. He had got all there was out of colleges and had come back to lead his people out of Egypt. He was a man of first-class style and wrote essays, and had been invited to visit rich guys' houses in Boston and such places.

"There was a Cherokee girl in Muscogee that High Jack was foolish about. He took me to see her a few times. Her name was Florence Blue Feather—but you want to clear your mind of all ideas of squaws with nose-rings and army blankets. This young lady was whiter than you are, and better educated than I ever was. You couldn't have told her from any of the girls shopping in the swell Third Avenue stores. I liked her so well that I got to calling on her now and then when High Jack wasn't along, which is the way of friends in such matters. She was educated at the Muscogee College, and was making a specialty of—let's see—eth—yes, ethnology. That's the art that goes back and traces the descent of different races of people, leading up from jelly-fish through monkeys and to the O'Briens. High Jack had took up that line too, and had read papers about it before all kinds of riotous assemblies—Chautauquas and Choctaws and chowder-parties and such. Having a mutual taste for musty information like that was what made 'em like each other, I suppose. But I don't know! What they call congeniality of tastes ain't always it. Now, when Miss Blue Feather and me was talking together, I listened to her affidavits about the first families of the Land of Nod being cousins german (well, if the Germans don't nod, who does?) to the mound-builders of Ohio with incomprehension and respect. And when I'd tell her about the Bowery and Coney Island, and sing her a few songs that I'd heard the Jamaica niggers sing at their church lawn-parties, she didn't look much less interested than she did when High Jack would tell her that he had a pipe that the first inhabitants of America originally arrived here on stilts after a freshet at Tenafly, New Jersey.

"But I was going to tell you more about High Jack.

"About six months ago I get a letter from him, saying he'd been commissioned by the Minority Report Bureau of Ethnology at Washington to go down to Mexico and translate some excavations or dig up the meaning of some shorthand notes on some ruins—or something of that sort. And if I'd go along he could squeeze the price into the expense account.

"Well, I'd been holding a napkin over my arm at Chubb's about long enough then, so I wired High Jack 'Yes'; and he sent me a ticket, and I met him in Washington, and he had a lot of news to tell me. First of all was that Florence Blue Feather had suddenly disappeared from her home and environments.

" 'Run away?' I asked.

" 'Vanished,' says High Jack. 'Disappeared like your shadow when the sun goes under a cloud. She was seen on the street, and then she turned a corner and nobody ever seen her afterward. The whole community turned out to look for her, but we never found a clue.'

" 'That's bad—that's bad,' says I. 'She was a mighty nice girl, and as smart as you find 'em.'

"High Jack seemed to take it hard. I guess he must have esteemed Miss Blue Feather quite highly. I could see that he'd referred the matter to the whiskey-jug. That was his weak point—and many another man's. I've noticed that when a man loses a girl he generally takes to drink either just before or just after it happens.

"From Washington we railroaded it to New Orleans, and there took a tramp steamer bound for Belize. And a gale pounded us all down the Caribbean, and nearly wrecked us on the Yucatan coast opposite a little town without a harbor called Boca de Coacoyula. Suppose the ship had run against that name in the dark!

" 'Better fifty years of Europe than a cyclone in the bay,' says High Jack Snakefeeder. So we get the captain to send us ashore in a dory when the squall seemed to cease from squalling.

" 'We will find ruins here or make 'em,' says High. 'The Government doesn't care which we do. An appropriation is an appropriation.'

"Boca de Coacoyula was a dead town. Them biblical towns we read about—Tired and Siphon—after they were destroyed, they must have looked like Forty-second Street and Broadway compared to this Boca place. It still claimed 1300 inhabitants as estimated and engraved on the stone courthouse by the census-taker in 1597. The citizens were a mixture of Indians and other Indians; but some of 'em was light-colored, which I was surprised to see. The town was huddled up on the shore, with woods so thick around it that a subpoena-server couldn't have reached a monkey ten years away with the papers. We wondered what kept it from being annexed to Kansas; but we soon found out that it was Major Bing.

"Major Bing was the ointment around the fly. He had the cochineal, sarsaparilla, logwood, annatto hemp, and all other dye-woods and pure food adulteration concessions cornered. He had five sixths of the Boca de Thingamajiggers working for him on shares. It was a beautiful graft. We used to brag about Morgan and E. H. and others of our wisest when I was in the provinces—but now no more. That peninsula has got our little country turned into a submarine without even the observation tower showing.

"Major Bing's idea was this: He had the population go forth into the forest and gather these products. When they brought 'em in he gave 'em one fifth for their trouble. Sometimes they'd strike and demand a sixth. The Major always gave in to 'em.

"The Major had a bungalow so close on the sea that the nine-inch tide seeped through the cracks in the kitchen floor. Me and him and High Jack Snakefeeder sat on the porch and drank rum from noon till midnight. He said he had piled up $300,000 in New Orleans banks, and High and me could stay with him forever if we would. But High Jack happened to think of the United States, and began to talk ethnology.

" 'Ruins!' says Major Bing. 'The woods are full of 'em. I don't know how far they date back, but they was here before I came.'

"High Jack asks what form of worship the citizens of that locality are addicted to.

" 'Why,' says the Major, rubbing his nose, 'I can't hardly say. I imagine it's infidel or Aztec or Nonconformist or something like that. There's a church here—a Methodist or some other kind—with a parson named Skidder. He claims to have converted the people to Christianity. He and me don't assimilate except on state occasions. I imagine they worship some kind of gods or idols yet. But Skidder says he has 'em in the fold.'

"A few days later High Jack and me, prowling around, strikes a plain path into the forest, and follows it a good four miles. Then a branch turns to the left. We go a mile, maybe, down that, and run up against the finest ruin you ever saw— solid stone with trees and vines and underbrush all growing up against it and in it and through it. All over it was chiselled carvings of funny beasts and people, that would have been arrested if they'd ever come out in vaudeville that way. We approached it from the rear.

"High Jack had been drinking too much rum ever since we landed in Boca. You know how an Indian is—the palefaces fixed his clock when they introduced him to firewater. He'd brought a quart along with him.

" 'Hunky,' says he, 'we'll explore the ancient temple. It may be that the storm that landed us here was propitious. The Minority Report Bureau of Ethnology,' says he, 'may yet profit by the vagaries of wind and tide.'

"We went in the rear door of the bum edifice. We struck a kind of alcove without bath. There was a granite davenport, and a stone washstand without any soap or exit for the water and some hardwood pegs drove into holes in the wall, and that was all. To go out of that furnished apartment into a Harlem hall bedroom would make you feel like getting back home from an amateur violoncello solo at an East Side Settlement house.

"While High was examining some hieroglyphics on the

wall that the stone-masons must have made when their tools slipped, I stepped into the front room. That was at least thirty by fifty feet, stone floor, six little windows like square-port-holes that didn't let much light in.

"I looked back over my shoulder, and sees High Jack's face three feet away.

" 'High,' says I, 'of all the——'

And then I noticed he looked funny, and I turned around.

"He'd taken off his clothes to the waist, and he didn't seem to hear me. I touched him, and came near beating it. High Jack had turned to stone. I had been drinking some rum myself.

" 'Ossified!' I says to him, loudly. 'I knew what would happen if you kept it up.'

"And then High Jack comes in from the alcove when he hears me conversing with nobody, and we have a look at Mr. Snakefeeder No. 2. It's a stone idol, or god, or revised statue or something, and it looks as much like High Jack as one green pea looks like itself. It's got exactly his face and size and color, but it's steadier on its pins. It stands on a kind of rostrum or pedestal, and you can see it's been there ten million years.

" 'He's a cousin of mine,' sings High, and then he turns solemn.

" 'Hunky,' he says, putting one hand on my shoulder and one on the statue's, 'I'm in the holy temple of my ancestors.'

" 'Well, if looks goes for anything,' says I, 'you've struck a twin. Stand side by side with buddy, and let's see if there's any difference.'

"There wasn't. You know an Indian can keep his face as still as an iron dog's when he wants to, so when High Jack froze his features you couldn't have told him from the other one.

" 'There's some letters,' says I, 'on his nob's pedestal, but I can't make 'em out. The alphabet of this country seems to be composed of sometimes a, e, i, o, and u, generally, z's, l's, and t's.

"High Jack's ethnology gets the upper hand of his rum for a minute, and he investigates the inscription.

" 'Hunky,' says he, 'this is a statue of Tlotopaxl, one of the most powerful gods of the ancient Aztecs.'

" 'Glad to know him,' says I, 'but in his present condition he reminds me of the joke Shakespeare got off on Julius Caesar. We might say about your friend:

"Imperious What's his-name, dead and turned to stone—
No use to write or call him on the phone."

" 'Hunky,' says High Jack Snakefeeder, looking at me funny, 'do you believe in reincarnation?'

" 'It sounds to me,' says I, 'like either a clean-up of the slaughter-houses or a new kind of Boston pink. I don't know.'

" 'I believe,' says he, 'that I am the reincarnation of Tlotopaxl. My researches have convinced me that the Cherokees, of all the North American tribes, can boast of the straightest descent from the proud Aztec race. That,' says he, 'was a favorite theory of mine and Florence Blue Feather's. And she—what if she——'

"High Jack grabs my arm and walls his eyes at me. Just then he looked more like his eminent co-Indian murderer, Crazy Horse.

" 'Well,' says I, 'what if she, what if she, what if she? You're drunk,' says I. 'Impersonating idols and believing in—what was it?—recarnalization? Let's have a drink,' says I. 'It's as spooky here as a Brooklyn artificial-limb factory at midnight with the gas turned down.'

"Just then I heard somebody coming, and I dragged High Jack into the bedless bedchamber. There was peepholes bored through the wall, so we could see the whole front part of the temple. Major Bing told me afterward that the ancient priests in charge used to rubber through them at the congregation.

"In a few minutes an old Indian woman came in with a big oval earthen dish full of grub. She set it on a square block of stone in front of the graven image, and laid down and walloped her face on the floor a few times, and then took a walk for herself.

"High Jack and me was hungry, so we came out and looked it over. There was goat steaks and fried rice-cakes, and plaintains and casava, and broiled land-crabs and mangoes—nothing like what you get at Chubb's.

"We ate hearty—and had another round of rum.

" 'It must be old Tecumseh's—or whatever you call him—

birthday,' says I. 'Or do they feed him every day? I thought gods only drank vanilla on Mount Catawampus.'

"Then some more native parties in short kimonos that showed their aboriginees puncture the near-horizon, and me and Hugh had to skip back into Father Axletree's private boudoir. They came by ones, twos, and threes, and left all sorts of offerings—there was enough grub for Bingham's nine gods of war, with plenty left over for the Peace Conference at The Hague. They brought jars of honey, and bunches of bananas, and bottles of wine, and stacks of tortillas, and beautiful shawls worth one hundred dollars apiece that the Indian women weave of a kind of vegetable fiber like silk. All of 'em got down and wriggled on the floor in front of that hard-finish god, and then sneaked off through the woods again.

" 'I wonder who gets this rake-off?' remarks High Jack.

" 'Oh,' says I, 'there's priests or deputy idols or a committee of disarrangements somewhere in the woods on the job. Wherever you find a god you'll find somebody waiting to take charge of the burnt offerings.'

"And then we took another swig of rum and walked out to the parlor front door to cool off, for it was as hot inside as a summer camp on the Palisades.

"And while we stood there in the breeze we looks down the path and sees a young lady approaching the blasted ruin. She was barefooted and had on a white robe, and carried a wreath of white flowers in her hand. When she got nearer we saw she had a long blue feather stuck through her black hair. And when she got nearer still me and High Jack Snakefeeder grabbed each other to keep from tumbling down on the floor; for the girl's face was as much like Florence Blue Feather's as his was like old King Toxicology's.

"And then was when High Jack's booze drowned his system of ethnology. He dragged me inside back of the statue, and says:

" 'Lay hold of it, Hunky. We'll pack it into the other room. I felt it all the time,' says he. 'I'm the reconsideration of the god Locomotorataxia, and Florence Blue Feather was my bride a thousand years ago. She has come to seek me in the temple where I used to reign.'

" 'All right,' says I. 'There's no use arguing against the rum question. You take his feet.'

"We lifted the three-hundred-pound stone god, and carried him into the back room of the café—the temple, I mean—and leaned him against the wall. It was more work than bouncing three live ones from an all night Broadway joint on New-Year's Eve.

"Then High Jack ran out and brought in a couple of them Indian silk shawls and began to undress himself.

" 'Oh, figs!' says I. 'Is it thus? Strong drink is an adder and subtractor, too. Is it the heat or the call of the wild that's got you?'

"But High Jack is too full of exaltation and cane-juice to reply. He stops the disrobing business just short of the Manhattan Beach rules, and then winds them red-and-white shawls around him, and goes out and stands on the pedestal as steady as any platinum deity you ever saw. And I looks through a peekhole to see what he is up to.

"In a few minutes in comes the girl with the flower wreath. Danged if I wasn't knocked a little silly when she got close, she looked so exactly much like Florence Blue Feather. 'I wonder,' says I to myself, 'if she has been reincarcerated, too? If I could see,' says I to myself, 'whether she has a mole on her left——' " But the next minute I thought she looked one eighth of a shade darker than Florence; but she looked good at that. And High Jack hadn't drunk all the rum that had been drank.

"The girl went up within ten feet of the bum idol, and got down and massaged her nose with the floor, like the rest did. Then she went nearer and laid the flower wreath on the block of stone at High Jack's feet. Rummy as I was, I thought it was kind of nice of her to think of offering flowers instead of household and kitchen provisions. Even a stone god ought to appreciate a little sentiment like that on top of the fancy groceries they had piled up in front of him.

"And then High Jack steps down from his pedestal, quiet, and mentions a few words that sounded just like the hieroglyphics carved on the walls of the ruin. The girl gives a little jump backward, and her eyes fly open as big as doughnuts; but she don't beat it.

"Why didn't she? I'll tell you why I think why. It don't

seem to a girl so supernatural, unlikely, strange, and startling that a stone god should come to life for *her*. If he was to do it for one of them snub-nosed brown girls on the other side of the woods, now, it would be different—but *her!* I'll bet she said to herself: 'Well, goodness me! you've been a long time getting on your job. I've half a mind not to speak to you.'

"But she and High Jack holds hands and walks away out of the temple together. By the time I'd had time to take another drink and enter upon the scene they was twenty yards away, going up the path in the woods that the girl had come down. With the natural scenery already in place, it was just like a play to watch 'em—she looking up at him, and him giving her back the best that an Indian can hand out in the way of a goo-goo eye. But there wasn't anything in the recarnification and revulsion to tintype for me.

" 'Hey! Injun!' I yells out to High Jack. 'We've got a board-bill due in town, and you're leaving me without a cent. Brace up and cut out the Neapolitan fisher-maiden, and let's go back home.'

"But on the two goes without looking once back until, as you might say, the forest swallowed 'em up. And I never saw or heard of High Jack Snakefeeder from that day to this. I don't know if the Cherokees came from the Aspics; but if they did, one of 'em went back.

"All I could do was to hustle back to that Boca place and panhandle Major Bing. He detached himself from enough of his winnings to buy me a ticket home. And I'm back again on the job at Chubb's, sir, and I'm going to hold it steady. Come round, and you'll find the steaks as good as ever."

I wondered what Hunky Magee thought about his own story; so I asked him if he had any theories about reincarnation and transmogrification and such mysteries as he had touched upon.

"Nothing like that," said Hunky, positively. "What ailed High Jack was too much booze and education. They'll do an Indian up every time."

"But what about Miss Blue Feather?" I persisted.

"Say," said Hunky, with a grin, "that little lady that stole High Jack certainly did give me a jar when I first took a look at her, but it was only for a minute. You remember I told you High Jack said that Miss Florence Blue Feather disappeared from home about a year ago? Well, where she landed four days later was in as neat a five-room flat on East Twenty-third Street as you ever walked sideways through—and she's been Mrs. Magee ever since.''

The Lotus and the Bottle

Willard Geddie, consul for the United States in Coralio, was working leisurely on his yearly report. Goodwin, who had strolled in as he did daily for a smoke on the much coveted porch, had found him so absorbed in his work that he departed after roundly abusing the consul for his lack of hospitality.

"I shall complain to the civil service department," said Goodwin;—"or is it a department?—perhaps it's only a theory. One gets neither civility nor service from you. You won't talk; and you won't set out anything to drink. What kind of a way is that of representing your government?''

Goodwin strolled out and across to the hotel to see if he could bully the quarantine doctor into a game on Coralio's solitary billiard table. His plans were completed for the interception of the fugitives from the capital; and now it was but a waiting game that he had to play.

The consul was interested in his report. He was only twenty-four; and he had not been in Coralio long enough for his enthusiasm to cool in the heat of the tropics—a paradox that may be allowed between Cancer and Capricorn.

So many thousand bunches of bananas, so many thousand oranges and cocoanuts, so many ounces of gold dust, pounds of rubber, coffee, indigo and sarsaparilla—actually, exports were twenty per cent. greater than for the previous year!

A little thrill of satisfaction ran through the consul. Perhaps, he thought, the State Department, upon reading his introduction, would notice—and then he leaned back in his chair and laughed. He was getting as bad as the others. For the moment he had forgotten that Coralio was an insignificant town in an insignificant republic lying along the by-ways of a second-rate sea. He thought of Gregg, the quarantine doctor, who subscribed for the London *Lancet,* expecting to find it quoting his reports to the home Board of Health concerning the yellow fever germ. The consul knew that not one in fifty of his acquaintances in the States had ever heard of Coralio. He knew that two men, at any rate, would have to read his report—some underling in the State Department and a compositor in the Public Printing Office. Perhaps the typesticker would note the increase of commerce in Coralio, and speak of it, over the cheese and beer, to a friend.

He had just written: "Most unaccountable is the supineness of the large exporters in the United States in permitting the French and German houses to practically control the trade interests of this rich and productive country"—when he heard the hoarse notes of a steamer's siren.

Geddie laid down his pen and gathered his Panama hat and umbrella. By the sound he knew it to be the *Valhalla,* one of the line of fruit vessels plying for the Vesuvius Company. Down to *niños* of five years, everyone in Coralio could name you each incoming steamer by the note of her siren.

The consul sauntered by a roundabout, shaded way to the beach. By reason of long practice he gauged his stroll so accurately that by the time he arrived on the sandy shore the boat of the customs officials was rowing back from the steamer, which had been boarded and inspected according to the laws of Anchuria.

There is no harbor at Coralio. Vessels of the draught of the *Valhalla* must ride at anchor a mile from shore. When they take on fruit it is conveyed on lighters and freighter sloops. At Solitas, where there was a fine harbor, ships of many kinds were to be seen, but in the roadstead off Coralio scarcely any save the fruiters paused. Now and then a tramp coaster, or a mysterious brig from Spain, or a saucy French barque would hang innocently for a few days in the offing. Then the custom-house crew would become doubly vigilant and wary. At night a sloop or two would be making strange trips in and out along the shore; and in the morning the stock of Three-Star Hennessey, wines and drygoods in Coralio would be found vastly increased. It has also been said that the customs officials jingled more silver in the pockets of their red-striped trousers, and that the record books showed no increase in import duties received.

The customs boat and the *Valhalla* gig reached the shore at the same time. When they grounded in the shallow water there was still five yards of rolling surf between them and dry sand. Then half-clothed Caribs dashed into the water, and brought in on their backs the *Valhalla's* purser and the native officials in their cotton undershirts, blue trousers with red stripes, and flapping straw hats.

At college Geddie had been a treasure as a first-baseman. He now closed his umbrella, stuck it upright in the sand, and stooped, with his hands resting upon his knees. The purser, burlesquing the pitcher's contortions, hurled at the consul the heavy roll of newspapers, tied with a string, that the steamer always brought for him. Geddie leaped high and caught the roll with a sounding "thwack." The loungers on the beach— about a third of the population of the town—laughed and applauded delightedly. Every week they expected to see that roll of papers delivered and received in that same manner, and they were never disappointed. Innovations did not flourish in Coralio.

The consul re-hoisted his umbrella and walked back to the consulate.

This home of a great nation's representative was a wooden structure of two rooms, with a native-built gallery of poles, bamboo and nipa palm running on three sides of it. One room was the official apartment, furnished chastely with a flat-top desk, a hammock, and three uncomfortable cane-seated chairs. Engravings of the first and latest president of the country represented hung against the wall. The other room was the consul's living apartment.

It was eleven o'clock when he returned from the beach, and therefore breakfast time. Chanca, the Carib woman who cooked for him, was just serving the meal on the side of the gallery facing the sea—a spot famous as the coolest in Coralio. The breakfast consisted of shark's fin soup, stew of land crabs, breadfruit, a boiled iguana steak, aguacates, a freshly cut pineapple, claret and coffee.

Geddie took his seat, and unrolled with luxurious laziness his bundle of newspapers. Here in Coralio for two days or longer he would read of goings-on in the world very much as we of the world read those whimsical contributions to inexact science that assume to portray the doings of the Martians. After he had finished with the papers they would be sent on the rounds of the other English-speaking residents of the town.

The paper that came first to his hand was one of those bulky mattresses of printed stuff upon which the readers of certain New York journals are supposed to take their Sabbath literary nap. Opening this the consul rested it upon the table, supporting its weight with the aid of the back of a chair. Then he partook of his meal deliberately, turning the leaves from time to time and glancing half idly at the contents.

Presently he was struck by something familiar to him in a picture—a half-page, badly printed reproduction of a photograph of a vessel. Languidly interested, he leaned for a nearer scrutiny and a view of the florid headlines of the column next to the picture.

Yes; he was not mistaken. The engraving was of the eight-hundred-ton yacht *Idalia,* belonging to "that prince of good fellows, Midas of the money market, and society's pink of perfection, J. Ward Tolliver."

Slowly sipping his black coffee, Geddie read the column of print. Following a listed statement of Mr. Tolliver's real estate and bonds, came a description of the yacht's furnishings, and then the grain of news no bigger than a mustard seed. Mr. Tolliver, with a party of favored guests, would sail the next day on a six weeks' cruise along the Central American and South American coasts and among the Bahama Islands. Among the guests were Mrs. Cumberland Payne and Miss Ida Payne, of Norfolk.

The writer, with the fatuous presumption that was demanded of him by his readers, had concocted a romance suited to their palates. He bracketed the names of Miss Payne and Mr. Tolliver until he had well-nigh read the marriage ceremony over them. He played coyly and insinuatingly upon the strings of *"on dit"* and "Madame Rumor" and "a little bird" and "no one would be surprised," and ended with congratulations.

Geddie, having finished his breakfast, took his papers to the edge of the gallery, and sat there in his favorite steamer chair with his feet on the bamboo railing. He lighted a cigar, and looked out upon the sea. He felt a glow of satisfaction at finding he was so little disturbed by what he had read. He told himself that he had conquered the distress that had sent him, a voluntary exile, to this far land of the lotus. He could never forget Ida, of course; but there was no longer any pain in thinking about her. When they had had that misunderstanding and quarrel he had impulsively sought his consulship with the desire to retaliate upon her by detaching himself from her world and presence. He had succeeded thoroughly in that. During the twelve months of his life in Coralio no word had passed between them, though he had sometimes heard of her through the dilatory correspondence with the few friends to whom he still wrote. Still he could not repress a little thrill of satisfaction at knowing that she had not yet married Tolliver or any one else. But evidently Tolliver had not yet abandoned hope.

Well, it made no difference to him now. He had eaten of the lotus. He was happy and content in this land of perpetual afternoon. Those old days of life in the States seemed like an irritating dream. He hoped Ida would be as happy as he was. The climate as balmy as that of distant Avalon; the fetterless, idyllic round of enchanted days; the life among this indolent, romantic people—a life full of music, flowers, and low laughter; the influence of the imminent sea and mountains, and the many shapes of love and magic and beauty that bloomed in the white tropic nights—with all he was more than content. Also, there was Paula Brannigan.

Geddie intended to marry Paula—if, of course, she would consent; but he felt rather sure that she would do that. Somehow, he kept postponing his proposal. Several times he had been quite near to it; but a mysterious something always held him back. Perhaps it was only the unconscious, instinctive conviction that the act would sever the last tie that bound him to his old world.

He could be very happy with Paula. Few of the native girls could be compared with her. She had attended a convent school in New Orleans for two years; and when she chose to display her accomplishments no one could detect any difference between her and the girls of Norfolk and Manhattan. But it was delicious to see her at home dressed, as she sometimes was, in the native costume, with bare shoulders and flowing sleeves.

Bernard Brannigan was the great merchant of Coralio. Besides his store, he maintained a train of pack mules, and carried on a lively trade with the interior towns and villages. He had married a native lady of high Castilian descent, but with a tinge of Indian brown showing through her olive cheek. The union of the Irish and the Spanish had produced, as it so often has, an offshoot of rare beauty and variety. They were very excellent people indeed, and the upper story of their house was ready to be placed at the service of Geddie and Paula as soon as he should make up his mind to speak about it.

By the time two hours were whiled away the consul tired of reading. The papers lay scattered about him on the gallery. Reclining there, he gazed dreamily out upon an Eden. A clump of banana plants interposed their broad shields between him and the sun. The gentle slope from the consulate to the sea was covered with the dark-green foliage of lemon-trees and orange-trees just bursting into bloom. A lagoon pierced the land like a dark, jagged crystal, and above it a pale ceiba-tree rose almost to the clouds. The waving cocoanut palms on the beach flared their decorative green leaves against the slate of an almost quiescent sea. His senses were cognizant of brilliant scarlet and ochres amid the vert of the coppice, of odors of fruit and bloom and the smoke from Chanca's clay oven under the calabash-tree; of the treble laughter of the native women in their huts, the song of the robin, the salt taste of the breeze, the diminuendo of the faint surf running along the shore—and, gradually, of a white speck, growing to a blur, that introduced itself upon the drab prospect of the sea.

Lazily interested, he watched this blur increase until it became the *Idalia* steaming at full speed, coming down the coast. Without changing his position he kept his eyes upon the beautiful white yacht as she drew swiftly near and came opposite to Coralio. Then, sitting upright, he saw her float steadily past and on. Scarcely a mile of sea had separated her from the shore. He had seen the frequent flash of her polished brass work and the stripes of her deck-awnings—so much, and no more. Like a ship on a magic lantern slide the *Idalia* had crossed the illuminated circle of the consul's little world, and was gone. Save for the tiny cloud of smoke that was left hanging over the brim of the sea, she might have been an immaterial thing, a chimera of his idle brain.

Geddie went into his office and sat down to dawdle over his report. If the reading of the article in the paper had left him unshaken, this silent passing of the *Idalia* had done for him still more. It had brought the calm and peace of a situation from which all uncertainty had been erased. He knew that men sometimes hope without being aware of it. Now, since she had come two thousand miles and had passed without a sign, not even his unconscious self need cling to the past any longer.

After dinner, when the sun was low behind the mountains, Geddie walked on the little strip of beach under the cocoanuts. The wind was blowing mildly landward, and the surface of the sea was rippled by tiny wavelets.

A miniature breaker, spreading with a soft "swish" upon the sand, brought with it something round and shiny that rolled back again as the wave receded. The next influx beached it clear, and Geddie picked it up. The thing was a long-necked wine bottle of colorless glass. The cork had been driven in tightly to the level of the mouth, and the end covered with dark-red sealing-wax. The bottle contained only what seemed to be a sheet of paper, much curled from the manipulation it had undergone while being inserted. In the sealing-wax was the impression of a seal—probably of a signet-ring, bearing the initials of a monogram; but the impression had been hastily made, and the letters were past anything more certain than a shrewd conjecture. Ida Payne had always worn a signet-ring in preference to any other finger decoration. Geddie thought he could make out the familiar "I P"; and a queer sensation of disquietude went over him. More personal and intimate was this reminder of her than had been the sight of the vessel she was doubtless on. He walked back to his house, and set the bottle on his desk.

Throwing off his hat and coat, and lighting a lamp—for the night had crowded precipitately upon the brief twilight—he began to examine his piece of sea salvage.

By holding the bottle near the light and turning it judiciously, he made out that it contained a double sheet of note-paper filled with close writing; further, that the paper was of the same size and shade as that always used by Ida; and that, to the best of his belief, the handwriting was hers. The imperfect glass of the bottle so distorted the rays of light that he could read no word of the writing; but certain capital letters, of which he caught comprehensive glimpses, were Ida's, he felt sure.

There was a little smile both of perplexity and amusement in Geddie's eyes as he set the bottle down, and laid three cigars side by side on his desk. He fetched his steamer chair from the gallery, and stretched himself comfortably. He would smoke those three cigars while considering the problem.

For it amounted to a problem. He almost wished that he had not found the bottle; but the bottle was there. Why should it have drifted in from the sea, whence come so many disquieting things, to disturb his peace?

In this dreamy land, where time seemed so redundant, he had fallen into the habit of bestowing much thought upon even trifling matters.

He began to speculate upon many fanciful theories concerning the story of the bottle, rejecting each in turn.

Ships in danger of wreck or disablement sometimes cast forth such precarious messengers calling for aid. But he had seen the *Idalia* not three hours before, safe and speeding. Suppose the crew had mutinied and imprisoned the passengers below, and the message was one begging for succor! But, premising such an improbable outrage, would the agitated captives have taken the pains to fill four pages of note-paper with carefully penned arguments to their rescue?

Thus by elimination he soon rid the matter of the more unlikely theories, and was reduced—though aversely—to the less assailable one that the bottle contained a message to himself. Ida knew he was in Coralio; she must have launched the bottle while the yacht was passing and the wind blowing fairly toward the shore.

As soon as Geddie reached this conclusion a wrinkle came

between his brows and a stubborn look settled around his mouth. He sat looking out through the doorway at the gigantic fire-flies traversing the quiet streets.

If this was a message to him from Ida, what could it mean save an overture toward a reconciliation? And if that, why had she not used the safe methods of the post instead of this uncertain and even flippant means of communication? A note in an empty bottle, cast into the sea! There was something light and frivolous about it, if not actually contemptuous.

The thought stirred his pride and subdued whatever emotions had been resurrected by the finding of the bottle.

Geddie put on his coat and hat and walked out. He followed a street that led him along the border of the little plaza where a band was playing and people were rambling, carefree and indolent. Some timorous *señoritas* scurrying past with fire-flies tangled in the jetty braids of their hair glanced at him with shy, flattering eyes. The air was languorous with the scent of jasmin and orange-blossoms.

The consul stayed his steps at the house of Bernard Brannigan. Paula was swinging in a hammock on the gallery. She rose from it like a bird from its nest. The color came to her cheek at the sound of Geddie's voice.

He was charmed at the sight of her costume—a flounced muslin dress, with a little jacket of white flannel, all made with neatness and style. He suggested a stroll, and they walked out to the old Indian well on the hill road. They sat on the curb, and there Geddie made the expected but long-deferred speech. Certain though he had been that she would not say him nay, he was thrilled with joy at the completeness and sweetness of her surrender. Here was surely a heart made for love and steadfastness. Here was no caprice or questionings or captious standards of convention.

When Geddie kissed Paula at her door that night he was happier than he had ever been before. "Here in this hollow lotus land, ever to live and lie reclined" seemed to him, as it has seemed to many mariners, the best as well as the easiest. His future would be an ideal one. He had attained a Paradise without a serpent. His Eve would be indeed a part of him, unbeguiled, and therefore more beguiling. He had made his decision to-night, and his heart was full of serene, assured content.

Geddie went back to his house whistling that finest and saddest love song, "La Golondrina." At the door his tame monkey leaped down from his shelf, chattering briskly. The consul turned to his desk to get him some nuts he usually kept there. Reaching in the half-darkness, his hand struck against the bottle. He started as if he had touched the cold rotundity of a serpent.

He had forgotten that the bottle was there.

He lighted the lamp and fed the monkey. Then, very deliberately, he lighted a cigar, and took the bottle in his hand, and walked down the path to the beach.

There was a moon, and the sea was glorious. The breeze had shifted, as it did each evening, and was now rushing steadily seaward.

Stepping to the water's edge, Geddie hurled the unopened bottle far out into the sea. It disappeared for a moment, and then shot upward twice its length. Geddie stood still, watching it. The moonlight was so bright that he could see it bobbing up and down with the little waves. Slowly it receded from the shore, flashing and turning as it went. The wind was carrying it out to sea. Soon it became a mere speck, doubtfully discerned at irregular intervals; and then the mystery of it was swallowed up by the greater mystery of the ocean. Geddie stood still upon the beach, smoking and looking out upon the water.

"Simon!—Oh, Simon!—wake up there, Simon!" bawled a sonorous voice at the edge of the water.

Old Simon Cruz was a half-breed fisherman and smuggler who lived in a hut on the beach. Out of his earliest nap Simon was thus awakened.

He slipped on his shoes and went outside. Just landing from one of the *Valhalla's* boats was the third mate of that vessel, who was an acquaintance of Simon's, and three sailors from the fruiter.

"Go up, Simon," called the mate, "and find Dr. Gregg or Mr. Goodwin or anybody that's a friend of Mr. Geddie, and bring 'em here at once."

"Saints of the skies!" said Simon, sleepily, "nothing has happened to Mr. Geddie?"

"He's under that tarpauling," said the mate, pointing to the boat, "and he's rather more than half drowned. We seen him from the steamer nearly a mile out from shore, swimmin' like mad after a bottle that was floatin' in the water, outward bound. We lowered the gig and started for him. He nearly had his hand on the bottle, when he gave out and went under. We pulled him out in time to save him, maybe; but the doctor is the one to decide that."

"A bottle?" said the old man, rubbing his eyes. He was not yet fully awake. "Where is the bottle?"

"Driftin' along out there some'eres," said the mate, jerking his thumb toward the sea. "Get on with you, Simon."

The Shamrock and the Palm

One night when there was no breeze, and Coralio seemed closer than ever to the gratings of Avernus, five men were grouped about the door of the photograph establishment of Keogh and Clancy. Thus, in all the scorched and exotic places of the earth, Caucasians meet when the day's work is done to preserve the fulness of the heritage by the aspersion of alien things.

Johnny Atwood lay stretched upon the grass in the undress uniform of a Carib, and prated feebly of the cool water to be had in the cucumberwood pumps of Dalesburg. Dr. Gregg, through the prestige of his whiskers and as a bribe against the relation of his imminent professional tales, was conceded the hammock that was swung between the door jamb and a calabash-tree. Keogh had moved out upon the grass a little table that held the instrument for burnishing completed photographs. He was the only busy one of the group. Industriously from between the cylinders of the burnisher rolled the finished depictments of Coralio's citizens. Blanchard, the French mining engineer, in his cool linen viewed the smoke of his cigarette through his calm glasses, impervious to the heat. Clancy sat on the steps, smoking his short pipe. His mood was the gossip's; the others were reduced, by the humidity, to the state of disability desirable in an audience.

Clancy was an American with an Irish diathesis and cosmopolitan proclivities. Many businesses had claimed him, but not for long. The roadster's blood was in his veins. The voice of the tintype was but one of the many callings that had wooed him upon so many roads. Sometimes he could be persuaded to oral construction of his voyages into the informal and egregious. To-night there were symptoms of divulgement in him.

" 'Tis elegant weather for filibusterin'," he volunteered. "It reminds me of the time I struggled to liberate a nation from the poisonous breath of a tyrant's clutch. 'Twas hard work. 'Tis strainin' to the back and makes corns on the hands."

"I didn't know you had ever lent your sword to an oppressed people," murmured Atwood, from the grass.

"I did," said Clancy; "and they turned it into a plowshare."

"What country was so fortunate as to secure your aid?" airily inquired Blanchard.

"Where's Kamchatka?" asked Clancy, with seeming irrelevance.

"Why, off Siberia somewhere in the Arctic regions," somebody answered, doubtfully.

"I thought that was the cold one," said Clancy, with a satisfied nod. "I'm always gettin' the two names mixed. 'Twas Guatemala, then—the hot one—I've been filibusterin' with. Ye'll find that country on the map. 'Tis in the district known as the tropics. By the foresight of Providence, it lies on the coast so the geography man could run the names of the towns off into the water. They're an inch long, small type, composed of Spanish dialects, and, 'tis my opinion, of the same system of syntax that blew up the *Maine*. Yes, 'twas that country I sailed against, single-handed, and endeavored to liberate it from a tyrannical government with a single-barreled pickaxe, unloaded at that. Ye don't understand, of course. 'Tis a statement demandin' elucidation and apologies.

" 'Twas in New Orleans one morning about the first of June; I was standin' down on the wharf, lookin' about at the ships in the river. There was a little steamer moored right opposite me that seemed about ready to sail. The funnels of it were throwin' out smoke, and a gang of roustabouts were carryin' aboard a pile of boxes that was stacked up on the wharf. The boxes were about two feet square, and somethin' like four feet long, and they seemed to be pretty heavy.

"I walked over, careless, to the stack of boxes. I saw one of them had been broken in handlin'. 'Twas curiosity made me pull up the loose top and look inside. The box was packed full of Winchester rifles. 'So, so,' says I to myself; 'somebody's gettin' a twist on the neutrality laws. Somebody's aidin' with munitions of war. I wonder where the popguns are goin'?'

"I heard somebody cough, and I turned around. There stood a little, round, fat man with a brown face and white clothes, a first-class-looking little man, with a four-karat diamond on his finger and his eye full of interrogations and respects. I judged he was a kind of foreigner—maybe from Russia or Japan or the archipelagoes.

" 'Hist!' says the round man, full of concealments and confidences. 'Will the señor respect the discoveryments he has made, that the mans on the ship shall not be acquaint? The señor will be a gentleman that shall not expose one thing that by accident occur.'

" 'Monseer,' says I—for I judged him to be a kind of Frenchman—'receive my most exasperated assurances that your secret is safe with James Clancy. Furthermore, I will go so far as to remark, Veev la Liberty—veev it good and strong. Whenever you hear of a Clancy obstructin' the abolishment of existin' governments you may notify me by return mail.'

" 'The señor is good,' says the dark, fat man, smilin' under his black mustache. 'Wish you to come aboard my ship and drink of wine a glass.'

"Bein' a Clancy, in two minutes me and the foreigner man were seated at a table in the cabin of the steamer, with a bottle between us. I could hear the heavy boxes bein' dumped into the hold. I judged that cargo must consist of at least 2,000 Winchesters. Me and the brown man drank the bottle of stuff, and he called the steward to bring another. When you amalgamate a Clancy with the contents of a bottle you practically instigate secession. I had heard a good deal about these revolutions in them tropical localities, and I began to want a hand in it.

" 'You goin' to stir things up in your country ain't you, monseer?' says I, with a wink to let him know I was on.

" 'Yes, yes,' said the little man, pounding his fist on the table. 'A change of the greatest will occur. Too long have the people been oppressed with the promises and the never-to-happen things to become. The great work it shall be carry on. Yes. Our forces shall in the capital city strike of the soonest. *Carrambos!'*

" '*Carrambos* is the word,' says I, beginning to invest myself with enthusiasm and more wine, 'likewise veeva, as I said before. May the shamrock of old—I mean the banana-vine or the pie-plant, or whatever the imperial emblem may be of your down-trodden country, wave forever.'

" 'A thousand thank-yous,' says the round man; 'for your emission of amicable utterances. What our cause needs of the very most is mans who will work do, to lift it along. Oh, for one thousands strong, good mans to aid the General De Vega that he shall to his country bring those success and glory! It is hard—oh, so hard to find good mans to help in the work.'

" 'Monseer,' says I, leanin' over the table and graspin' his hand, 'I don't know where your country is, but me heart bleeds for it. The heart of a Clancy was never deaf to the sight of an oppressed people. The family is filibusterers by birth, and foreigners by trade. If you can use James Clancy's arms and his blood in denudin' your shores of the tyrant's yoke they're yours to command.'

"General De Vega was overcome with joy to confiscate my condolence of his conspiracies and predicaments. He tried to embrace me across the table, but his fatness, and the wine that had been in the bottles, prevented. Thus was I welcomed into the ranks of filibustery. Then the general man told me his country had the name of Guatemala, and was the greatest nation laved by any ocean whatever anywhere. He looked at me with tears in his eyes, and from time to time he would emit the remark, 'Ah! big, strong, brave mans! That is what my country need.'

"General De Vega, as was the name by which he denounced himself, brought out a document for me to sign, which I did, makin' a fine flourish and curlycue with the tail of the 'y.'

"'Your passage-money,' says the general, business-like, 'shall from your pay be deduct.'

"'Twill not,' says I, haughty. 'I'll pay my own passage.' A hundred and eighty dollars I had in my inside pocket, and 'twas no common filibuster I was goin' to be, filibusterin' for me board and clothes.

"The steamer was to sail in two hours, and I went ashore to get some things together I'd need. When I came aboard I showed the general with pride the outfit. 'Twas a fine Chinchilla overcoat, Arctic over-shoes, fur cap and earmuffs, with elegant fleece-lined gloves and woolen muffler.

"'*Carrambos!*' says the little general. 'What clothes are these that shall go to the tropic?' And then the little spalpeen laughs, and he calls the captain, and the captain calls the purser, and they pipe up the chief engineer, and the whole gang leans against the cabin and laughs at Clancy's wardrobe for Guatemala.

"I reflects a bit, serious, and asks the general again to denominate the terms by which his country is called. He tells me, and I see then that 'twas the t'other one, Kamchatka, I had in mind. Since then I've had difficulty in separatin' the two nations in name, climate, and geographic disposition.

"I paid my passage—twenty-four dollars, first cabin—and ate at table with the officer crowd. Down on the lower deck was a gang of second-class passengers, about forty of them, seemin' to be Dagoes and the like. I wondered what so many of them were goin' along for.

"Well, then, in three days we sailed alongside that Guatemala. 'Twas a blue country, and not yellow as 'tis miscolored on the map. We landed at a town on the coast, where a train of cars was waitin' for us on a dinky little railroad. The boxes on the steamer were brought ashore and loaded on the cars. The gang of Dagoes got aboard, too, the general and me in the front car. Yes, me and General De Vega headed the revolution, as it pulled out of the seaport town. That train travelled about as fast as a policeman goin' to a riot. It penetrated the most conspicuous lot of fuzzy scenery ever seen outside a geography. We run some forty miles in seven hours, and the train stopped. There was no more railroad. 'Twas a sort of camp in a damp gorge full of wildness and melancholies. They was gradin' and choppin' out the forests ahead to continue the road. 'Here,' says I to myself, 'is the romantic haunt of the revolutionists. Here will Clancy, by the virtue that is in a superior race and the inculcation of Fenian tactics, strike a tremendous blow for liberty.'

"They unloaded the boxes from the train and begun to knock the tops off. From the first one that was open I saw General De Vega take the Winchester rifles and pass them around to a squad of morbid soldiery. The other boxes was opened next, and, believe me or not, divil another gun was to be seen. Every other box in the load was full of pickaxes and spades.

"And then—sorrow be upon them tropics—the proud Clancy and the dishonored Dagoes, each one of them, had to shoulder a pick or a spade, and march away to work on that dirty little railroad. Yes; 'twas that the Dagoes shipped for, and 'twas that the filibusterin' Clancy signed for, though unbeknownst to himself at the time. In after days I found out about it. It seems 'twas hard to get hands to work on that road. The intelligent natives of the country was too lazy to work. Indeed the saints know, 'twas unnecessary. By stretchin' out one hand, they could seize the most delicate and costly fruits of the earth, and, by stretchin' out the other, they could sleep for days at a time without hearin' a seven-o'clock whistle or the footsteps of the rent man upon the stairs. So, regular, the steamers travelled to the United States to seduce labor. Usually the imported spade-slingers died in two or three months from eatin' the over-ripe water and breathin' the violent tropical scenery. Wherefore they made them sign contracts for a year, when they hired them, and put an armed guard over the poor divils to keep them from runnin' away.

" 'Twas thus I was double-crossed by the tropics through a family failin' of goin' out of the way to hunt disturbances.

"They gave me a pick, and I took it, meditatin' an insurrection on the spot; but there was the guards handlin' the Winchesters careless, and I come to the conclusion that discretion was the best part of filibusterin'. There was about a hundred of us in the gang startin' out to work, and the word was given to move. I steps out of the ranks and goes up to that General

De Vega man, who was smokin' a cigar and gazin' upon the scene with satisfactions and glory. He smiles at me polite and devilish. 'Plenty work,' says he, 'for big, strong mans in Guatemala. Yes. T'irty dollars in the month. Good pay. Ah, yes. You strong, brave man. Bimeby we push those railroad in the capital very quick. They want you go work now. *Adios,* strong mans.'

" 'Monseer,' says I, lingerin', 'will you tell a poor little Irishman this: When I sét foot on your cockroachy steamer, and breathed liberal and revolutionary sentiments into your sour wine, did you think I was conspirin' to sling a pick on your contemptuous little railroad? And when you answered me with patriotic recitations, humping up the star-spangled cause of liberty, did you have meditations of reducin' me to the ranks of the stump-grubbin' Dagoes in the chain-gangs of your vile and grovelin' country?'

"The general man expanded his rotundity and laughed considerable. Yes, he laughed very long and loud, and I, Clancy, stood and waited.

" 'Comical mans!' he shouts, at last. 'So you will kill me from the laughing. Yes; it is hard to find the brave, strong mans to aid my country. Revolutions? Did I speak of r-r-revolutions? Not one word. I say, big, strong mans is need in Guatemala. So. The mistake is of you. You have looked in those one box containing those gun for the guard. You think all boxes is contain gun? No.

" 'There is not war in Guatemala. But work? Yes. Good. T'irty dollar in the month. You shall shoulder one pickaxe, señor, and dig for the liberty and prosperity of Guatemala. Off to your work. The guard waits for you.'

" 'Little, fat poodle dog of a brown man,' says I, quiet, but full of indignations and discomforts, 'things shall happen to you. Maybe not right away, but as soon as J. Clancy can formulate somethin' in the way of repartee.'

"The boss of the gang orders us to work. I tramps off with the Dagoes, and I hears the distinguished patriot and kidnapper laughin' hearty as we go.

" 'Tis a sorrowful fact, for eight weeks I built railroads for that misbehavin' country. I filibustered twelve hours a day with a heavy pick and a spade, choppin' away the luxurious landscape that grew upon the right of way. We worked in swamps that smelled like there was a leak in the gas mains, trampin' down a fine assortment of the most expensive hot-house plants and vegetables. The scene was tropical beyond the wildest imagination of the geography man. The trees was all sky-scrapers; the under-brush was full of needles and pins; there was monkeys jumpin' around and crocodiles and pink-tailed mockin'-birds, and ye stood knee-deep in the rotten water and grabbed roots for the liberation of Guatemala. Of nights we would build smudges in camp to discourage the mosquitoes, and sit in the smoke, with the guards pacin' all around us. There was two hundred men workin' on the road—mostly Dagoes, nigger-men, Spanish-men and Swedes. Three or four were Irish.

"One old man named Halloran—a man of Hibernian entitlements and discretions, explained it to me. He had been workin' on the road a year. Most of them died in less than six months. He was dried up to gristle and bone and shook with chills every third night.

" 'When you first come,' says he, 'ye think ye'll leave right away. But they hold out your first month's pay for your passage over, and by that time the tropics has its grip on ye. Ye're surrounded by a ragin' forest full of disreputable beasts— lions and baboons and anacondas—waitin' to devour ye. The sun strikes ye hard, and melts the marrow in your bones. Ye get similar to the lettuce-eaters the poetry-book speaks about. Ye forget the elevated sintiments of life, such as patriotism, revenge, disturbances of the peace and the dacint love of a clane shirt. Ye do your work, and ye swallow the kerosene ile and rubber pipestems dished up to ye by the Dago cook for food. Ye light your pipeful, and say to yoursilf, "Nixt week I'll break away," and ye go to sleep and call yersilf a liar, for ye know ye'll never do it.'

" 'Who is this general man,' asks I, 'that calls himself De Vega?'

" ' 'Tis the man,' says Halloran, 'who is tryin' to complete the finishin' of the railroad. 'Twas the project of a private corporation, but it was busted, and then the government took it up. De Vegy is a big politician, and wants to be president. The people want the railroad completed, as they're taxed mighty on account of it. The De Vegy man is pushin' it along as a campaign move.'

" ' 'Tis not my way,' says I, 'to make threats against any man, but there's an account to be settled between the railroad man and James O'Dowd Clancy.'

" ' 'Twas that way I thought, mesilf, at first,' Halloran says, with a big sigh, 'until I got to be a lettuce-eater. The fault's wid these tropics. They rejuices a man's system. 'Tis a land, as the poet says, "Where it always seems to be after dinner." I does me work and smokes me pipe and sleeps. There's little else in life, anyway. Ye'll get that way yersilf, mighty soon. Don't be harborin' any sintiments at all, Clancy.'

" 'I can't help it,' says I; 'I'm full of 'em. I enlisted in the revolutionary army of this dark country in good faith to fight for its liberty, honors and silver candlesticks; instead of which I am set to amputatin' its scenery and grubbin' its roots. 'Tis the general man will have to pay for it.'

"Two months I worked on that railroad before I found a chance to get away. One day a gang of us was sent back to the end of the completed line to fetch some picks that had been sent down to Port Barrios to be sharpened. They were brought on a hand-car, and I noticed, when I started away, that the car was left there on the track.

"That night, about twelve, I woke up Halloran and told him my scheme.

" 'Run away?' says Halloran. 'Good Lord, Clancy, do ye mean it? Why, I ain't got the nerve. It's too chilly, and I ain't slept enough. Run away? I told you, Clancy, I've eat the lettuce. I've lost my grip. 'Tis the tropics that's done it. 'Tis like the poet says: "Forgotten are our friends that we have left behind; in the hollow lettuce-land we will live and lay reclined." You better go on, Clancy, I'll stay, I guess. It's too early and cold, and I'm sleepy.'

"So I had to leave Halloran. I dressed quiet, and slipped out of the tent we were in. When the guard came along I knocked him over, like a ninepin, with a green cocoanut I had, and made for the railroad. I got on that hand-car and made it fly. 'Twas yet a while before daybreak when I saw the lights of Port Barrios about a mile away. I stopped the hand-car there and walked to the town. I stepped inside the corporations of that town with care and hesitations. I was not afraid of the army of Guatemala, but me soul quaked at the prospect of a hand-to-hand struggle with its employment bureau. 'Tis a country that hires its help easy and keeps 'em long. Sure I can fancy Missis America and Missis Guatemala passin' a bit of gossip some fine, still night across the mountains. 'Oh, dear,' says Missis America, 'and it's a lot of trouble I'm havin' ag'in with the help, señora, ma'am.' 'Laws, now!' says Missis Guatemala, 'you don't say so, ma'am! Now, mine never think of leavin' me—te-he! ma'am,' snickers Missis Guatemala.

"I was wonderin' how I was goin' to move away from them tropics without bein' hired again. Dark as it was, I could see a steamer ridin' in the harbor, with smoke emergin' from her stacks. I turned down a little grass street that run down to the water. On the beach I found a little brown nigger-man just about to shove off in a skiff.

" 'Hold on, Sambo,' says I, 'savve English?'

" 'Heap plenty, yes,' says he, with a pleasant grin.

" 'What steamer is that?' I asks him, 'and where is it going? And what's the news, and the good word and the time of day?'

" 'That steamer the *Conchita*,' said the brown man, affable and easy, rollin' a cigarette. 'Him come from New Orleans for load banana. Him got load last night. I think him sail in one, two hour. Verree nice day we shall be goin' to have. You hear some talkee 'bout big battle, maybe so? You think catchee General De Vega, señor? Yes? No?'

" 'How's that, Sambo?' says I. 'Big battle? What battle? Who wants catchee General De Vega? I've been up at my old gold mines in the interior for a couple of months, and haven't heard any news.'

" 'Oh,' says the nigger-man, proud to speak the English, 'verree great revolution in Guatemala one week ago. General De Vega, him try be president. Him raise armee—one—five—ten thousand mans for fight at the government. Those one government send five—forty—hundred thousand soldiers to suppress revolution. They fight big battle yesterday at Lomagrande—that about nineteen or fifty mile in the mountain. That government soldier wheep General De Vega—oh, most bad. Five hundred—nine hundred—two thousand of his mans is kill. That revolution is smash suppress—bust—very quick. General De Vega, him r-r-run away fast on one big mule. Yes, *carrambos!* The general, him r-r-run away, and his armee is kill. That government soldier, they try to find General De Vega verree much. They want catchee him for shoot. You think they catchee that general, señor?'

" 'Saints grant it!' says I. ' 'Twould be the judgment of Providence for settin' the warlike talent of a Clancy to gradin' the tropics with a pick and shovel. But 'tis not so much a question of insurrections now, me little man, as 'tis of the hired-man problem. 'Tis anxious I am to resign a situation of responsibility and trust with the white wings department of your great and degraded country. Row me in your little boat out to that steamer, and I'll give ye five dollars—sinker pacers—sinker pacers,' says I, reducin' the offer to the language and denomination of the tropic dialects.

" *'Cinco pesos,'* repeats the little man. 'Five dollee, you give?'

" 'Twas not such a bad little man. He had hesitations at first, sayin' that passengers leaving the country had to have papers and passports, but at last he took me out alongside the steamer.

"Day was just breakin' as we struck her, and there wasn't a soul to be seen on board. The water was very still, and the nigger-man gave me a lift from the boat, and I climbed onto the steamer where her side was sliced to the deck for loadin' fruit. The hatches was open, and I looked down and saw the cargo of bananas that filled the hold to within six feet of the top. I thinks to myself, 'Clancy, you better go as a stowaway. It's safer. The steamer men might hand you back to the employment bureau. The tropic'll get you, Clancy, if you don't watch out.'

"So I jumps down easy among the bananas and digs out a hole to hide in among the bunches. In an hour or so I could hear the engines goin', and feel the steamer rockin', and I knew we were off to sea. They left the hatches open for ventilation, and pretty soon it was light enough in the hold to see fairly well. I got to feelin' a bit hungry, and thought I'd have a light fruit lunch, by way of refreshment. I creeped out of the hole I'd made and stood up straight. Just then I saw another man crawl up about ten feet away and reach out and skin a banana and stuff it into his mouth. 'Twas a dirty man, black-faced and ragged and disgraceful of aspect. Yes, the man was a ringer for the pictures of the fat Weary Willie in the funny papers. I looked again, and saw it was my general man—De Vega, the great revolutionist, mule-rider and pick-axe importer. When he saw me the general hesitated with his mouth filled with banana and his eyes the size of cocoanuts.

" 'Hist!' I says. 'Not a word, or they'll put us off and make us walk. "Veev la Liberty!"' ' I adds, copperin' the sentiment by shovin' a banana into the source of it. I was certain the general wouldn't recognize me. The nefarious work of the tropics had left me lookin' different. There was half an inch of roan whiskers coverin' me face, and me costume was a pair of blue overalls and a red shirt.

" 'How you come in the ship, señor?' asked the general as soon as he could speak.

" 'By the back door—whist!' says I. ' 'Twas a glorious blow for liberty we struck,' I continues; 'but we was overpowered by numbers. Let us accept our defeat like brave men and eat another banana.'

" 'Were you in the cause of liberty fightin', señor?' says the general, sheddin' tears on the cargo.

" 'To the last,' says I. ' 'Twas I led the last desperate charge against the minions of the tyrant. But it made them mad, and we was forced to retreat. 'Twas I, general, procured the mule upon which you escaped. Could you give that ripe bunch a little boost this way, general? It's a bit out of my reach. Thanks.'

" 'Say you so, brave patriot?' said the general, again weepin'. 'Ah, *Dios!* And I have not the means to reward your devotion. Barely did I my life bring away. *Carrambos!* what a devil's animal was that mule, señor! Like ships in one storm was I dashed about. The skin on myself was ripped away with the thorns and vines. Upon the bark of a hundred trees did that beast of the infernal bump, and cause outrage to the legs of mine. In the night to Port Barrios I came. I dispossess myself of that mountain of mule and hasten along the water shore. I find a little boat to be tied. I launch myself and row to the steamer. I cannot see any mans on board, so I climbed one rope which hang at the side. I then myself hide in the bananas. Surely, I say, if the ship captains view me, they shall throw me again to those Guatemala. Those things are not good. Guatemala will shoot General De Vega.

Therefore, I am hide and remain silent. Life itself is glorious. Liberty, it is pretty good; but so good as life I do not think.'

"Three days, as I said, was the trip to New Orleans. The general man and me got to be cronies of the deepest dye. Bananas we ate until they were distasteful to the sight and an eyesore to the palate, but to bananas alone was the bill of fare reduced. At night I crawls out, careful, on the lower deck, and gets a bucket of fresh water.

"That General De Vega was a man inhabited by an engorgement of words and sentences. He added to the monotony of the voyage by divestin' himself of conversation. He believed I was a revolutionist of his own party, there bein', as he told me, a good many Americans and other foreigners in its ranks. 'Twas a braggart and a conceited little gabbler it was, though he considered himself a hero. 'Twas on himself he wasted all his regrets at the failin' of his plot. Not a word did the little balloon have to say about the other misbehavin' idiots that had been shot, or run themselves to death in his revolution.

"The second day out he was feelin' pretty braggy and uppish for a stowed-away conspirator that owed his existence to a mule and stolen bananas. He was tellin' me about the great railroad he had been buildin', and he relates what he calls a comic incident about a fool Irishman he inveigled from New Orleans to sling a pick on his little morgue of a narrow-gauge line. 'Twas sorrowful to hear the little, dirty general tell the opprobrious story of how he put salt upon the tail of that reckless and silly bird, Clancy. Laugh, he did, hearty and long. He shook with laughin', the black-faced rebel and outcast, standin' neck-deep in bananas, without friends or country.

" 'Ah, señor,' he snickers, 'to the death you would have laughed at that drollest Irish. I say to him: "Strong, big mans is need very much in Guatemala." "I will blows strike for your down-pressed country," he say. "That shall you do," I tell him. Ah! it was an Irish so comic. He sees one box break upon the wharf that contain for the guard a few gun. He think there is gun in all the box. But that is all pick-axe. Yes. Ah! señor, could you the face of that Irish have seen when they set him to the work!'

" 'Twas thus the ex-boss of the employment bureau contributed to the tedium of the trip with merry jests and anecdote. But now and then he would weep upon the bananas and make oration about the lost cause of liberty and the mule.

" 'Twas a pleasant sound when the steamer bumped against the pier in New Orleans. Pretty soon we heard the pat-a-pat of hundreds of bare feet, and the Dago gang that unloads the fruit jumped on the deck and down into the hold. Me and the general worked a while at passin' up the bunches, and they thought we were part of the gang. After about an hour we managed to slip off the steamer onto the wharf.

" 'Twas a great honor on the hands of an obscure Clancy, havin' the entertainment of the representative of a great foreign filibusterin' power. I first bought for the general and myself many long drinks and things to eat that were not bananas. The general man trotted along at my side, leavin' all the arrangements to me. I led him up to Lafayette Square and set him on a bench in the little park. Cigarettes I had bought for him, and he humped himself down on the seat like a little fat, contented hobo. I look him over as he sets there, and what I see pleases me. Brown by nature and instinct, he is now brindled with dirt and dust. Praise to the mule, his clothes is mostly strings and flaps. Yes, the looks of the general man is agreeable to Clancy.

"I ask him, delicate, if, by any chance, he brought away anybody's money with him from Guatemala. He sighs and bumps his shoulders against the bench. Not a cent. All right. Maybe, he tells me, some of his friends in the tropic outfit will send him funds later. The general was as clear a case of no visible means as I ever saw.

"I told him not to move from the bench, and then I went up to the corner of Poydras and Carondelet. Along there is O'Hara's beat. In five minutes along comes O'Hara, a big, fine man, red-faced, with shinin' buttons, swingin' his club. 'Twould be a fine thing for Guatemala to move into O'Hara's precinct. 'Twould be a fine bit of recreation for Danny to suppress revolutions and uprisin's once or twice a week with his club.

" 'Is 5046 workin' yet, Danny?' says I, walkin' up to him.

" 'Overtime,' says O'Hara, lookin' over me suspicious. 'Want some of it?'

"Fifty-forty-six is the celebrated city ordinance authorizin'" arrest, conviction, and imprisonment of persons that succeed in concealin' their crimes from the police.

" 'Don't ye know Jimmy Clancy?' says I. 'Ye pink-gilled monster.' So, when O'Hara recognized me beneath the scandalous exterior bestowed upon me by the tropics, I backed him into a doorway and told him what I wanted, and why I wanted it. 'All right, Jimmy,' says O'Hara. 'Go back and hold the bench. I'll be along in ten minutes.'

"In that time O'Hara strolled through Lafayette Square and spied two Weary Willies disgracin' one of the benches. In ten minutes more J. Clancy and General De Vega, late candidate for the presidency of Guatemala, was in the station house. The general is badly frightened, and calls upon me to proclaim his distinguishments and rank.

" 'The man,' says I to the police, 'used to be a railroad man. He's on the bum now. 'Tis a little bughouse he is, on account of losin' his job.'

" '*Carrambos!*' says the general, fizzin' like a little soda-water fountain, 'you fought, señor, with my forces in my native country. Why do you say the lies? You shall say I am the General De Vega, one soldier, one *caballero*——'

" 'Railroader,' says I again. 'On the hog. No good. Been livin' for three days on stolen bananas. Look at him. Ain't that enough?'

"Twenty-five dollars or sixty days, was what the recorder gave the general. He didn't have a cent, so he took the time. They let me go, as I knew they would, for I had money to show, and O'Hara spoke for me. Yes; sixty days he got. 'Twas just so long that I slung a pick for the great country of Kam—Guatemala."

Clancy paused. The bright starlight showed a reminiscent look of happy content on his seasoned features. Keogh leaned in his chair and gave his partner a slap on his thinly-clad back that sounded like the crack of the surf on the sands.

"Tell 'em, you divil," he chuckled, 'how you got even with the tropical general in the way of agricultural maneuvrings."

"Havin' no money," concluded Clancy, with unction, "they set him to work his fine out with a gang from the parish prison clearing Ursulines Street. Around the corner was a saloon decorated genially with electric fans and cool merchandise. I made that me headquarters, and every fifteen minutes I'd walk around and take a look at the little man filibusterin' with a rake and shovel. 'Twas just such a hot broth of a day as this has been. And I'd call at him 'Hey, monseer!' and he'd look at me black, with the damp showin' through his shirt in places.

" 'Fat, strong mans,' says I to General De Vega, 'is needed in New Orleans. Yes. To carry on the good work. Carrambos! Erin go bragh!' "

Shoes

John de Graffenreid Atwood ate of the lotus, root, stem, and flower. The tropics gobbled him up. He plunged enthusiastically into his work, which was to try to forget Rosine.

Now, they who dine on the lotus rarely consume it plain. There is a sauce *au diable* that goes with it; and the distillers are the chefs who prepare it. And on Johnny's menu card it read "brandy." With a bottle between them, he and Billy Keogh would sit on the porch of the little consulate at night and roar out great, indecorous songs, until the natives, slipping hastily past, would shrug a shoulder and mutter things to themselves about the *"Americanos diablos."*

One day Johnny's *mozo* brought the mail and dumped it on the table. Johnny leaned from his hammock, and fingered the four or five letters dejectedly. Keogh was sitting on the edge of the table chopping lazily with a paper knife at the legs of a centipede that was crawling among the stationery. Johnny was in that phase of lotus-eating when all the world tastes bitter in one's mouth.

"Same old thing!" he complained. "Fool people writing for information about the country. They want to know all about raising fruit, and how to make a fortune without work.

Half of 'em don't even send stamps for a reply. They think a consul hasn't anything to do but write letters. Slit those envelopes for me, old man, and see what they want. I'm feeling too rocky to move."

Keogh, acclimated beyond all possibility of ill-humor, drew his chair to the table with smiling compliance on his rose-pink countenance, and began to slit open the letters. Four of them were from citizens in various parts of the United States who seemed to regard the consul at Coralio as a cyclopædia of information. They asked long lists of questions, numerically arranged, about the climate, products, possibilities, laws, business chances, and statistics of the country in which the consul had the honor of representing his own government.

"Write 'em, please, Billy," said that inert official, "just a line, referring them to the latest consular report. Tell 'em the State Department will be delighted to furnish the literary gems. Sign my name. Don't let your pen scratch, Billy; it'll keep me awake."

"Don't snore," said Keogh, amiably, "and I'll do your work for you. You need a corps of assistants, anyhow. Don't see how you ever get out a report. Wake up a minute! —here's one more letter—it's from your own town, too— Dalesburg."

"That so?" murmured Johnny, showing a mild obligatory interest. "What's it about?"

"Postmaster writes," explained Keogh. "Says a citizen of the town wants some facts and advice from you. Says the citizen has an idea in his head of coming down where you are and opening a shoe store. Wants to know if you think the business would pay. Says he's heard of the boom along this coast, and wants to get in on the ground floor."

In spite of the heat and his bad temper, Johnny's hammock swayed with his laughter. Keogh laughed too; and the pet monkey on the top shelf of the bookcase chattered in shrill sympathy with the ironical reception of the letter from Dalesburg.

"Great bunions!" exclaimed the consul. "Shoe store! What'll they ask about next, I wonder? Overcoat factory, I reckon. Say, Billy—of our 3,000 citizens, how many do you suppose ever had on a pair of shoes?"

Keogh reflected judicially.

"Let's see—there's you and me and——"

"Not me," said Johnny, promptly and incorrectly, holding up a foot encased in a disreputable deerskin *zapato*. "I haven't been a victim to shoes in months."

"But you've got 'em, though," went on Keogh. "And there's Goodwin and Blanchard and Geddie and old Lutz and Doc Gregg and that Italian that's agent for the banana company, and there's old Delgado—no; he wears sandals. And, oh, yes; there's Madama Ortiz, 'what kapes the hotel'—she had on a pair of red slippers at the *baile* the other night. And Miss Pasa, her daughter, that went to school in the States—she brought back some civilized notions in the way of footgear. And there's the *comandante's* sister that dresses up her feet on feast-days—and Mrs. Geddie, who wears a two with a Castilian instep—and that's about all the ladies. Let's see— don't some of the soldiers at the *cuartel*—no that's so; they're allowed shoes only when on the march. In barracks they turn their little toeses out to grass."

" 'Bout right," agreed the consul. "Not over twenty out of the three thousand ever felt leather on their walking arrangements. Oh, yes; Coralio is just the town for an enter-prising shoe store—that doesn't want to part with its goods. Wonder if old Patterson is trying to jolly me! He always was full of things he called jokes. Write him a letter, Billy. I'll dictate it. We'll jolly him back a few."

Keogh dipped his pen, and wrote at Johnny's dictation. With many pauses, filled in with smoke and sundry travel-lings of the bottle and glasses, the following reply to the Dalesburg communication was perpetrated:

Mr. Obadiah Patterson,
    Dalesburg, Ala.

Dear Sir: In reply to your favor of July 2d, I have the honor to inform you that, according to my opinion, there is no place on the habitable globe that presents to the eye stronger evidence of the need of a first-class shoe store than does the town of Coralio. There are 3,000 inhabitants in the place, and not a single shoe store! The situation speaks for itself. This coast is rap-idly becoming the goal of enterprising business men, but the shoe business is one that has been sadly overlooked or neglected. In fact, there are a considerable number of our citizens actually without shoes at present.

Besides the want above mentioned, there is also a crying need for a brewery, a college of higher mathematics, a coal yard, and a clean and intellectual Punch and Judy show. I have the honor to be, sir,

Your Obt. Servant,
John de Graffenreid Atwood,
U. S. Consul at Coralio.

P.S.—Hello! Uncle Obadiah. How's the old burg racking along? What would the government do without you and me? Look out for a green-headed parrot and a bunch of bananas soon, from your old friend

Johnny

"I throw in that postscript," explained the consul, "so Uncle Obadiah won't take offence at the official tone of the letter! Now, Billy, you get that correspondence fixed up, and send Pancho to the post-office with it. The *Ariadne* takes the mail out to-morrow if they make up that load of fruit to-day."

The night programme in Coralio never varied. The recreations of the people were soporific and flat. They wandered about, barefoot and aimless, speaking lowly and smoking cigar or cigarette. Looking down on the dimly lighted ways one seemed to see a threading maze of brunette ghosts tangled with a procession of insane fire-flies. In some houses the thrumming of lugubrious guitars added to the depression of the *triste* night. Giant tree-frogs rattled in the foliage as loudly as the end man's "bones" in a minstrel troupe. By nine o'clock the streets were almost deserted.

Not at the consulate was there often a change of bill. Keogh would come there nightly, for Coralio's one cool place with the little seaward porch of that official residence.

The brandy would be kept moving; and before midnight sentiment would begin to stir in the heart of the self-exiled consul. Then he would relate to Keogh the story of his ended romance. Each night Keogh would listen patiently to the tale, and be ready with untiring sympathy.

"But don't you think for a minute"—thus Johnny would always conclude his woeful narrative—"that I'm grieving about that girl, Billy. I've forgotten her. She never enters my mind. If she were to enter that door right now, my pulse wouldn't gain a beat. That's all over long ago."

"Don't I know it?" Keogh would answer. "Of course you've forgotten her. Proper thing to do. Wasn't quite O.K. of her to listen to the knocks that—er—Dink Pawson kept giving you."

"Pink Dawson!"—a world of contempt would be in Johnny's tones—"Poor white trash! That's what he was. Had five hundred acres of farming land, though; and that counted. Maybe I'll have a chance to get back at him some day. The Dawsons weren't anybody. Everybody in Alabama knows the Atwoods. Say, Billy—did you know my mother was a De Graffenreid?"

"Why, no," Keogh would say; "is that so?" He had heard it some three hundred times.

"Fact. The De Graffenreids of Hancock County. But I never think of that girl any more, do I, Billy?"

"Not for a minute, my boy," would be the last sounds heard by the conqueror of Cupid.

At this point Johnny would fall into a gentle slumber, and Keogh would saunter out to his own shack under the calabash tree at the edge of the plaza.

In a day or two the letter from the Dalesburg postmaster and its answer had been forgotten by the Coralio exiles. But on the 26th day of July the fruit of the reply appeared upon the tree of events.

The *Andador*, a fruit steamer that visited Coralio regularly, drew into the offing and anchored. The beach was lined with spectators while the quarantine doctor and the custom-house crew rowed out to attend to their duties.

An hour later Bill Keogh lounged into the consulate, clean and cool in his linen clothes, and grinning like a pleased shark.

"Guess what?" he said to Johnny, lounging in his hammock.

"Too hot to guess," said Johnny, lazily.

"Your shoe-store man's come," said Keogh, rolling the sweet morsel on his tongue, "with a stock of goods big enough to supply the continent as far down as Terra del Fuego. They're carting his cases over to the custom-house now. Six barges full they brought ashore and have paddled back for the rest. Oh, ye saints in glory! won't there be regalements in the air when he gets onto the joke and has an interview with Mr. Consul? It'll be worth nine years in the tropics just to witness that one joyful moment.''

Keogh loved to take his mirth easily. He selected a clean place on the matting and lay upon the floor. The walls shook with his enjoyment. Johnny turned half over and blinked.

"Don't tell me," he said, "that anybody was fool enough to take that letter seriously."

"Four-thousand-dollar stock of goods!" gasped Keogh, in ecstasy. "Talk about coals to Newcastle! Why didn't he take a ship-load of palm-leaf fans to Spitzbergen while he was about it? Saw the old codger on the beach. You ought to have been there when he put on his specs and squinted at the five hundred or so barefooted citizens standing around."

"Are you telling the truth, Billy?" asked the consul, weakly.

"Am I? You ought to see the buncoed gentleman's daughter he brought along. Looks! She makes the brick-dust señoritas here look like tar-babies."

"Go on," said Johnny, "if you can stop that asinine giggling. I hate to see a grown man make a laughing hyena of himself."

"Name is Hemstetter," went on Keogh. "He's a—— Hello! what's the matter now?"

Johnny's moccasined feet struck the floor with a thud as he wriggled out of his hammock.

"Get up, you idiot," he said, sternly, "or I'll brain you with this inkstand. That's Rosine and her father. Gad! what a drivelling idiot old Patterson is! Get up, here, Billy Keogh, and help me. What the devil are we going to do? Has all the world gone crazy?"

Keogh rose and dusted himself. He managed to regain a decorous demeanor.

"Situation has got to be met, Johnny," he said, with some success at seriousness. "I didn't think about its being your girl until you spoke. First thing to do is to get them comfortable quarters. You go down and face the music, and I'll trot out to Goodwin's and see if Mrs. Goodwin won't take them in. They've got the decentest house in town."

"Bless you, Billy!" said the consul. "I knew you wouldn't desert me. The world's bound to come to an end, but maybe we can stave it off for a day or two."

Keogh hoisted his umbrella and set out for Goodwin's house. Johnny put on his coat and hat. He picked up the brandy bottle, but set it down again without drinking, and marched bravely down to the beach.

In the shade of the custom-house walls he found Mr. Hemstetter and Rosine surrounded by a mass of gaping citizens. The customs officers were ducking and scraping, while the captain of the *Andador* interpreted the business of the new arrivals. Rosine looked healthy and very much alive. She was gazing at the strange scenes around her with amused interest. There was a faint blush upon her round cheek as she greeted her old admirer. Mr. Hemstetter shook hands with Johnny in a very friendly way. He was an oldish, impractical man—one of that numerous class of erratic business men who are forever dissatisfied, and seeking a change.

"I am very glad to see you, John—may I call you John?" he said. "Let me thank you for your prompt answer to our postmaster's letter of inquiry. He volunteered to write to you on my behalf. I was looking about for something different in the way of a business in which the profits would be greater. I had noticed in the papers that this coast was receiving much attention from investors. I am extremely grateful for your advice to come. I sold out everything that I possess, and invested the proceeds in as fine a stock of shoes as could be bought in the North. You have a picturesque town here, John. I hope business will be as good as your letter justifies me in expecting."

Johnny's agony was abbreviated by the arrival of Keogh, who hurried up with the news that Mrs. Goodwin would be much pleased to place rooms at the disposal of Mr. Hemstetter and his daughter. So there Mr. Hemstetter and Rosine were at once conducted and left to recuperate from the fatigue of the voyage, while Johnny went down to see that the cases of shoes were safely stored in the customs warehouse pending their examination by the officials. Keogh, grinning like a shark, skirmished about to find Goodwin, to instruct him not to expose to Mr. Hemstetter the true state of Coralio as a shoe market until Johnny had been given a chance to redeem the situation, if such a thing were possible.

That night the consul and Keogh held a desperate consultation on the breezy porch of the consulate.

"Send 'em back home," began Keogh, reading Johnny's thoughts.

"I would," said Johnny, after a little silence; "but I've been lying to you, Billy."

"All right about that," said Keogh, affably.

"I've told you hundreds of times," said Johnny, slowly, "that I had forgotten that girl, haven't I?"

"About three hundred and seventy-five," admitted the monument of patience.

"I lied," repeated the consul, "every time. I never forget her for one minute. I was an obstinate ass for running away just because she said 'No' once. And I was too proud a fool to go back. I talked with Rosine a few minutes this evening up at Goodwin's. I found out one thing. You remember that farmer fellow who was always after her?"

"Dink Pawson?" asked Keogh.

"Pink Dawson. Well, he wasn't a hill of beans to her. She says she didn't believe a word of the things he told her about me. But I'm sewed up now, Billy. That tomfool letter we sent ruined whatever chance I had left. She'll despise me when she finds out that her old father has been made the victim of a joke that a decent school boy wouldn't have been guilty of. Shoes! Why he couldn't sell twenty pairs of shoes in Coralio if he kept store here for twenty years. You put a pair of shoes on one of these Caribs or Spanish brown boys and what'd he do? Stand on his head and squeal until he'd kicked 'em off. None of 'em ever wore shoes and they never will. If I send 'em back home I'll have to tell the whole story, and what'll she think of me? I want that girl worse than ever, Billy, and now when she's in reach I've lost her forever because I tried to be funny when the thermometer was at 102."

"Keep cheerful," said the optimistic Keogh. "And let 'em open the store. I've been busy myself this afternoon. We can stir up a temporary boom in foot-gear anyhow. I'll buy six pairs when the doors open. I've been around and seen all the fellows and explained the catastrophe. They'll all buy shoes like they was centipedes. Frank Goodwin will take cases of 'em. The Geddies want about eleven pairs between 'em. Clancy is going to invest the savings of weeks, and even old Doc Gregg wants three pairs of alligator-hide slippers if they've got any tens. Blanchard got a look at Miss Hemstetter; and as he's a Frenchman, no less than a dozen pairs will do for him.''

"A dozen customers," said Johnny, "for a $4,000 stock of shoes! It won't work. There's a big problem here to figure out. You go home, Billy, and leave me alone. I've got to work at it all by myself. Take that bottle of Three-star along with you—no, sir; not another ounce of booze for the United States consul. I'll sit here to-night and pull out the think stop. If there's a soft place on this proposition anywhere I'll land on it. If there isn't there'll be another wreck to the credit of the gorgeous tropics.''

Keogh left, feeling that he could be of no use. Johnny laid a handful of cigars on a table and stretched himself in a steamer chair. When the sudden daylight broke, silvering the harbor ripples, he was still sitting there. Then he got up, whistling a little tune, and took his bath.

At nine o'clock he walked down to the dingy little cable office and hung for half an hour over a blank. The result of his application was the following message, which he signed and had transmitted at a cost of $33:

To Pinkney Dawson,
    Dalesburg, Ala.
  Draft for $100 comes to you next mail. Ship me immediately 500 pounds stiff, dry cockleburrs. New use here in arts. Market price twenty cents pound. Further orders likely. Rush.

A Double-Dyed Deceiver

The trouble began in Laredo. It was the Llano Kid's fault, for he should have confined his habit of manslaughter to Mexicans. But the Kid was past twenty; and to have only Mexicans to one's credit at twenty is to blush unseen on the Rio Grande border.

It happened in old Justo Valdo's gambling house. There was a poker game at which sat players who were not all friends, as happens often where men ride in from afar to shoot Folly as she gallops. There was a row over so small a matter as a pair of queens; and when the smoke had cleared away it was found that the Kid had committed an indiscretion, and his adversary had been guilty of a blunder. For, the unfortunate combatant, instead of being a Greaser, was a high-blooded youth from the cow ranches, of about the Kid's own age and possessed of friends and champions. His blunder in missing the Kid's right ear only a sixteenth of an inch when he pulled his gun did not lessen the indiscretion of the better marksman.

The Kid, not being equipped with a retinue, not bountifully supplied with personal admirers and supporters—on account of a rather umbrageous reputation, even for the border—considered it not incompatible with his indisputable gameness to perform that judicious tractional act known as "pulling his freight."

Quickly the avengers gathered and sought him. Three of them overtook him within a rod of the station. The Kid turned and showed his teeth in that brilliant but mirthless smile that usually preceded his deeds of insolence and violence, and his

pursuers fell back without making it necessary for him even
to reach for his weapon.

But in this affair the Kid had not felt the grim thirst for
encounter that usually urged him on to battle. It had been a
purely chance row, born of the cards and certain epithets
impossible for a gentleman to brook that had passed between
the two. The Kid had rather liked the slim, haughty, brown-
faced young chap whom his bullet had cut off in the first
pride of manhood. And now he wanted no more blood. He
wanted to get away and have a good long sleep somewhere in
the sun on the mesquite grass with his handkerchief over his
face. Even a Mexican might have crossed his path in safety
while he was in this mood.

The Kid openly boarded the north-bound passenger train
that departed five minutes later. But at Webb, a few miles
out, where it was flagged to take on a traveller, he abandoned
that manner of escape. There were telegraph stations ahead;
and the Kid looked askance at electricity and steam. Saddle
and spur were his rocks of safety.

The man whom he had shot was a stranger to him. But the
Kid knew that he was of the Coralitos outfit from Hidalgo;
and that the punchers from that ranch were more relentless
and vengeful than Kentucky feudists when wrong or harm
was done to one of them. So, with the wisdom that has
characterized many great fighters, the Kid decided to pile up
as many leagues as possible of chaparral and pear between
himself and the retaliation of the Coralitos bunch.

Near the station was a store; and near the store, scattered
among the mesquite and elms, stood the saddled horses of the
customers. Most of them waited, half asleep, with sagging
limbs and drooping heads. But one, a long-legged roan with a
curved neck, snorted and pawed the turf. Him the Kid mounted,
gripped with his knees, and slapped gently with the owner's
own quirt.

If the slaying of the temerarious card-player had cast a
cloud over the Kid's standing as a good and true citizen, this
last act of his veiled his figure in the darkest shadows of
disrepute. On the Rio Grande border if you take a man's life
you sometimes take trash; but if you take his horse, you take
a thing the loss of which renders him poor, indeed, and which

enriches you not—if you are caught. For the Kid there was no turning back now.

With the springing roan under him he felt little care or uneasiness. After a five-mile gallop he drew into the plains-man's jogging trot, and rode north-eastward toward the Nue-ces River bottoms. He knew the country well—its most tortu-ous and obscure trails through the great wilderness of brush and pear, and its camps and lonesome ranches where one might find safe entertainment. Always he bore to the east; for the Kid had never seen the ocean, and he had a fancy to lay his hand upon the mane of the great Gulf, the gamesome colt of the greater waters.

So after three days he stood on the shore at Corpus Christi, and looked out across the gentle ripples of a quiet sea.

Captain Boone, of the schooner *Flyaway*, stood near his skiff, which one of his crew was guarding in the surf. When ready to sail he had discovered that one of the necessaries of life, in the parallelogrammatic shape of plug tobacco, had been forgotten. A sailor had been dispatched for the missing cargo. Meanwhile the captain paced the sands, chewing pro-fanely at his pocket store.

A slim, wiry youth in high-heeled boots came down to the water's edge. His face was boyish, but with a premature severity that hinted at a man's experience. His complexion was naturally dark; and the sun and wind of an outdoor life had burned it to a coffee-brown. His hair was as black and straight as an Indian's; his face had not yet been upturned to the humiliation of a razor; his eyes were a cold and steady blue. He carried his left arm somewhat away from his body, for pearl-handled .45s are frowned upon by town marshals, and are a little bulky when packed in the left armhole of one's vest. He looked beyond Captain Boone at the gulf with the impersonal and expressionless dignity of a Chinese emperor.

"Thinkin' of buyin' that 'ar gulf, buddy?" asked the captain, made sarcastic by his narrow escape from the tobaccoless voyage.

"Why, no," said the Kid gently, "I reckon not. I never saw it before. I was just looking at it. Not thinking of selling it, are you?"

"Not this trip," said the captain. "I'll send it to you C.O.D. when I get back to Buenas Tierras. Here comes that capstan-footed lubber with the chewin'. I ought to've weighed anchor an hour ago.''

"Is that your ship out there?" asked the Kid.

"Why, yes," answered the captain, "if you want to call a schooner a ship, and I don't mind lyin'. But you better say Miller and Gonzales, owners, and ordinary plain, Billy-be-damned old Samuel K. Boone, skipper.''

"Where are you going to?" asked the refugee.

"Buenas Tierras, coast of South America—I forget what they called the country the last time I was there. Cargo—lumber, corrugated iron, and machetes.''

"What kind of a country is it?" asked the Kid—"hot or cold?''

"Warmish, buddy," said the captain. "But a regular Paradise Lost for elegance of scenery and be-yooty of geography. Ye're wakened every morning by the sweet singin' of red birds with seven purple tails, and the sighin' of breezes in the posies and roses. And the inhabitants never work, for they can reach out and pick steamer baskets of the choicest hothouse fruit without gettin' out of bed. And there's no Sunday and no ice and no rent and no troubles and no use and no nothin'. It's a great country for a man to go to sleep with, and wait for somethin' to turn up. The bananys and oranges and hurricanes and pineapples that ye eat comes from there.''

"That sounds to me!" said the Kid, at last betraying interest. "What'll the expressage be to take me out there with you?''

"Twenty-four dollars," said Captain Boone; "grub and transportation. Second cabin. I haven't got a first cabin.''

"You've got my company," said the Kid, pulling out a buckskin bag.

With three hundred dollars he had gone to Laredo for his regular "blowout." The duel in Valdos's had cut short his season of hilarity, but it had left him with nearly $200 for aid in the flight that it had made necessary.

"All right, buddy," said the captain. "I hope your ma won't blame me for this little childish escapade of yours.'' He beckoned to one of the boat's crew. "Let Sanchez lift you out to the skiff so you won't get your feet wet.''

*   *   *

Thacker, the United States consul at Buenas Tierras, was not yet drunk. It was only eleven o'clock; and he never arrived at his desired state of beatitude—a state where he sang ancient maudlin vaudeville songs and pelted his screaming parrot with banana peels—until the middle of the afternoon. So, when he looked up from his hammock at the sound of a slight cough, and saw the Kid standing in the door of the consulate, he was still in a condition to extend the hospitality and courtesy due from the representative of a great nation.

"Don't disturb yourself," said the Kid easily. "I just dropped in. They told me it was customary to light at your camp before starting in to round up the town. I just came in on a ship from Texas."

"Glad to see you, Mr.——," said the consul.

The Kid laughed.

"Sprague Dalton," he said. "It sounds funny to me to hear it. I'm called the Llano Kid in the Rio Grande country."

"I'm Thacker," said the consul. "Take that cane-bottom chair. Now if you've come to invest, you want somebody to advise you. These dingies will cheat you out of the gold in your teeth if you don't understand their ways. Try a cigar?"

"Much obliged," said the Kid, "but if it wasn't for my corn shucks and the little bag in my back pocket I couldn't live a minute." He took out his "makings," and rolled a cigarette.

"They speak Spanish here," said the consul. "You'll need an interpreter. If there's anything I can do, why, I'd be delighted. If you're buying fruit lands or looking for a concession of any sort, you'll want somebody who knows the ropes to look out for you."

"I speak Spanish," said the Kid, "about nine times better than I do English. Everybody speaks it on the range where I come from. And I'm not in the market for anything."

"You speak Spanish?" said Thacker, thoughtfully. He regarded the Kid absorbedly.

"You look like a Spaniard, too," he continued. "And you're from Texas. And you can't be more than twenty or twenty-one. I wonder if you've got any nerve."

"You got a deal of some kind to put through?" asked the Texan, with unexpected shrewdness.

"Are you open to a proposition?" said Thacker.

"What's the use to deny it?" said the Kid. "I got into a little gun frolic down in Laredo, and plugged a white man. There wasn't any Mexican handy. And I come down to your parrot-and-monkey range just for to smell the morning-glories and marigolds. Now, do you *sabe?*"

Thacker got up and closed the door.

"Let me see your hand," he said.

He took the Kid's left hand, and examined the back of it closely.

"I can do it," he said, excitedly. "Your flesh is as hard as wood and as healthy as a baby's. It will heal in a week."

"If it's a fist fight you want to back me for," said the Kid, "don't put your money up yet. Make it gun work, and I'll keep you company. But no bare-handed scrapping, like ladies at a tea-party, for me."

"It's easier than that," said Thacker. "Just step here, will you?"

Through the window he pointed to a two-story white-stuccoed house with wide galleries rising amid the deep-green tropical foliage on a wooded hill that sloped gently from the sea.

"In that house," said Thacker, "a fine old Castilian gentleman and his wife are yearning to gather you into their arms and fill your pockets with money. Old Santos Urique lives there. He owns half the gold-mines in the country."

"You haven't been eating loco weed, have you?" asked the Kid.

"Sit down again," said Thacker, "and I'll tell you. Twelve years ago they lost a kid. No, he didn't die—although most of 'em here do from drinking the surface water. He was a wild little devil, even if he wasn't but eight years old. Everybody knows about it. Some Americans who were through here prospecting for gold had letters to Señor Urique, and the boy who was a favorite with them. They filled his head with big stories about the States; and about a month after they left, the kid disappeared, too. He was supposed to have stowed himself away among the banana bunches on a fruit steamer, and gone to New Orleans. He was seen once afterward in Texas, it was thought, but they never heard anything more of him. Old Urique has spent thousands of dollars having him looked for. The madam was broken up worst of all. The kid was her life. She wears mourning yet. But they say she believes he'll come back to her some day, and never gives up hope. On the back of the boy's left hand was tattooed a flying eagle carrying a spear in his claws. That's old Urique's coat of arms or something that he inherited in Spain.''

The Kid raised his left hand slowly and gazed at it curiously.

"That's it," said Thacker, reaching behind the official desk for his bottle of smuggled brandy. "You're not so slow. I can do it. What was I consul at Sandakan for? I never knew till now. In a week I'll have the eagle bird with the frog-sticker blended in so you'd think you were born with it. I brought a set of the needles and ink just because I was sure you'd drop in some day, Mr. Dalton.''

"Oh, hell," said the Kid. "I thought I told you my name!''

"All right, 'Kid,' then. It won't be that long. How does 'Señorito Urique' sound, for a change?''

"I never played son any that I remember of," said the Kid. "If I had any parents to mention they went over the divide about the time I gave my first bleat. What is the plan of your round-up?''

Thacker leaned back against the wall and held his glass up to the light.

"We've come now," said he, "to the question of how far you're willing to go in a little matter of the sort.''

"I told you why I came down here," said the Kid simply.

"A good answer," said the consul. "But you won't have to go that far. Here's the scheme. After I get the trade-mark tattooed on your hand I'll notify old Urique. In the meantime I'll furnish you with all of the family history I can find out, so you can be studying up points to talk about. You've got the looks, you speak the Spanish, you know the facts, you can tell about Texas, you've got the tattoo mark. When I notify them that the rightful heir has returned and is waiting to know whether he will be received and pardoned what will happen? They'll simply rush down here and fall on your neck, and the curtain goes down for refreshments and a stroll in the lobby.''

"I'm waiting," said the Kid. "I haven't had my saddle off in your camp long, pardner, and I never met you before; but if you intend to let it go at a parental blessing, why, I'm mistaken in my man, that's all.''

"Thanks," said the consul. "I haven't met anybody in a long time that keeps up with an argument as well as you do. The rest of it is simple. If they take you in only for a while it's long enough. Don't give 'em time to hunt up the strawberry mark on your left shoulder. Old Urique keeps anywhere from $50,000 to $100,000 in his house all the time in a little safe that you could open with a shoe buttoner. Get it. My skill as a tattooer is worth half the boodle. We go halves and catch a tramp steamer for Rio Janeiro. Let the United States go to pieces if it can't get along without my services. *Qué dice, señor?*''

"It sounds to me!" said the Kid, nodding his head. "I'm out for the dust.''

"All right, then," said Thacker. "You'll have to keep close until we get the bird on you. You can live in the back room here. I do my own cooking, and I'll make you as comfortable as a parsimonious government will allow me.''

Thacker had set the time at a week, but it was two weeks before the design that he patiently tattooed upon the Kid's hand was to his notion. And then Thacker called a *muchacho,* and dispatched this note to the intended victim:

El Señor Don Santos Urique,
    La Casa Blanca,
My Dear Sir:
    I beg permission to inform you that there is in my house as a temporary guest a young man who arrived in Buenas Tierras from the United States some days ago. Without wishing to excite any hopes that may not be realized, I think there is a possibility of his being your long-absent son. It might be well for you to call and see him. If he is, it is my opinion that his intention was to return to his home, but upon arriving here, his courage failed him from doubts as to how he would be received.
                    Your true servant,
                    Thompson Thacker

Half an hour afterward—quick time for Buenas Tierras—Señor Urique's ancient landau drove to the consul's door, with the bare-footed coachman beating and shouting at the team of fat, awkward horses.

A tall man with a white moustache alighted, and assisted to the ground a lady who was dressed and veiled in unrelieved black.

The two hastened inside, and were met by Thacker with his best diplomatic bow. By his desk stood a slender young man with clear-cut, sunbrowned features and smoothly brushed black hair.

Señora Urique threw back her heavy veil with a quick gesture. She was past middle age, and her hair was beginning to silver, but her full, proud figure and clear olive skin retained traces of the beauty peculiar to the Basque province. But, once you had seen her eyes, and comprehended the great sadness that was revealed in their deep shadows and hopeless expression, you saw that the woman lived only in some memory.

She bent upon the young man a long look of the most agonized questioning. Then her great black eyes turned, and her gaze rested upon his left hand. And then with a sob, not loud, but seeming to shake the room, she cried *"Hijo mío!"* and caught the Llano Kid to her heart.

A month afterward the Kid came to the consulate in response to a message sent by Thacker.

He looked the young Spanish caballero. His clothes were imported, and the wiles of the jewellers had not been spent upon him in vain. A more than respectable diamond shone on his finger as he rolled a shuck cigarette.

"What's doing?" asked Thacker.

"Nothing much," said the Kid calmly. "I eat my first iguana steak to-day. They're them big lizards, you *sabe?* I reckon, though, that frijoles and side bacon would do me about as well. Do you care for iguanas, Thacker?"

"No, nor for some other kinds of reptiles," said Thacker.

It was three in the afternoon, and in another hour he would be in his state of beatitude.

"It's time you were making good, sonny," he went on, with an ugly look on his reddened face. "You're not playing up to me square. You've been the prodigal son for four weeks now, and you could have had veal for every meal on a gold dish if you'd wanted it. Now, Mr. Kid, do you think it's right to leave me out so long on a husk diet? What's the trouble? Don't you get your filial eyes on anything that looks like cash in the Casa Blanca? Don't tell me you don't. Everybody knows where old Urique keeps his stuff. It's U. S. currency, too; he don't accept anything else. What's doing? Don't say 'nothing' this time.''

"Why, sure," said the Kid, admiring his diamond, "there's plenty of money up there. I'm no judge of collateral in bunches, but I will undertake for to say that I've seen the rise of $50,000 at a time in that tin grub box that my adopted father calls his safe. And he lets me carry the key sometimes just to show me that he knows I'm the real little Francisco that strayed from the herd a long time ago.''

"Well, what are you waiting for?" asked Thacker angrily. "Don't you forget that I can upset your apple-cart any day I want to. If old Urique knew you were an impostor, what sort of things would happen to you? Oh, you don't know this country, Mr. Texas Kid. The laws here have got mustard spread between 'em. These people here'd stretch you out like a frog that had been stepped on, and give you about fifty sticks at every corner of the plaza. And they'd wear every stick out, too. What was left of you they'd feed to alligators.''

"I might as well tell you now, pardner," said the Kid, sliding down low on his steamer chair, "that things are going to stay just as they are. They're about right now.''

"What do you mean?" asked Thacker, rattling the bottom of his glass on his desk.

"The scheme's off," said the Kid. "And whenever you have the pleasure of speaking to me address me as Don Francisco Urique. I'll guarantee I'll answer to it. We'll let Colonel Urique keep his money. His little tin safe is as good as the time-locker in the First National Bank of Laredo as far as you and me are concerned.''

"You're going to throw me down, then, are you?" said the consul.

"Sure," said the Kid, cheerfully. "Throw you down. That's it. And now I'll tell you why. The first night I was up at the colonel's house they introduced me to a bedroom. No blankets on the floor—a real room, with a bed and things in it. And before I was asleep, in comes this artificial mother of mine and tucks in the covers. 'Panchito,' she says, 'my little lost one, God has brought you back to me. I bless His name forever.' It was that, or some truck like that, she said. And down comes a drop or two of rain and hits me on the nose. And all that stuck by me, Mr. Thacker. And it's been that way ever since. And it's got to stay that way. Don't you think that it's for what's in it for me, either, that I say so. If you have any such ideas keep 'em to yourself. I haven't had much truck with women in my life, and no mothers to speak of, but here's a lady that we've got to keep fooled. Once she stood it; twice she won't. I'm a lowdown wolf, and the devil may have sent me on this trail instead of God, but I'll travel it to the end. And now, don't forget that I'm Don Francisco Urique whenever you happen to mention my name.''

''I'll expose you to-day, you—you double-dyed traitor,'' stammered Thacker.

The Kid arose and, without violence, took Thacker by the throat with a hand of steel, and shoved him slowly into a corner. Then he drew from under his left arm his pearl-handled .45 and poked the cold muzzle of it against the consul's mouth.

''I told you why I come here,'' he said, with his old freezing smile. ''If I leave here, you'll be the reason. Never forget it, pardner. Now, what is my name?''

''Er—Don Francisco Urique,'' gasped Thacker.

From outside came a sound of wheels, and the shouting of someone, and the sharp thwacks of a wooden whipstock upon the backs of fat horses.

The Kid put up his gun, and walked toward the door. But he turned again and came back to the trembling Thacker, and held up his left hand with its back toward the consul.

''There's one more reason,'' he said, slowly, ''why things have got to stand as they are. The fellow I killed in Laredo had one of them same pictures on his left hand.''

Outside, the ancient landau of Don Santos Urique rattled to the door. The coachman ceased his bellowing. Señora Urique, in a voluminous gay gown of white lace and flying ribbons, leaned forward with a happy look in her great soft eyes.

''Are you within, dear son?'' she called, in the rippling Castilian.

''*Madre mía, yo vengo* [mother, I come],'' answered the young Don Francisco Urique.

The Fourth in Salvador

On a summer's day, while the city was rocking with the din and red uproar of patriotism, Billy Casparis told me this story.

In his way, Billy is Ulysses, Jr. Like Satan, he comes from going to and fro upon the earth and walking up and down in it. To-morrow morning while you are cracking your breakfast egg he may be off with his little alligator grip to boom a town site in the middle of Lake Okeechobee or to trade horses with the Patagonians.

We sat at a little, round table, and between us were glasses holding big lumps of ice, and above us leaned an artificial palm. And because our scene was set with the properties of the one they recalled to his mind, Billy was stirred to narrative.

"It reminds me," said he, "of a Fourth I helped to celebrate down in Salvador. 'Twas while I was running an ice factory down there, after I unloaded that silver mine I had in Colorado. I had what they called a 'conditional concession.' They made me put up a thousand dollars cash forfeit that I would make ice continuously for six months. If I did that I could draw down my ante. If I failed to do so the government took the pot. So the inspectors kept dropping in, trying to catch me without the goods.

"One day when the thermometer was at 110, the clock at half-past one, and the calendar at July third, two of the little, brown, oily nosers in red trousers slid in to make an inspection. Now, the factory hadn't turned out a pound of ice in three weeks, for a couple of reasons. The Salvador heathen wouldn't buy it; they said it made things cold they put it in. And I couldn't make any more, because I was broke. All I was holding on for was to get down my thousand so I could leave the country. The six months would be up on the sixth of July.

"Well, I showed 'em all the ice I had. I raised the lid of a darkish vat, and there was an elegant 100-pound block of ice, beautiful and convincing to the eye. I was about to close down the lid again when one of those brunette sleuths flops down on his red knees and lays a slanderous and violent hand on my guarantee of good faith. And in two minutes more they had dragged out on the floor that fine chunk of molded glass that had cost me fifty dollars to have shipped down from Frisco.

" 'Ice-y?' says the fellow that played me the dishonorable trick; 'verree warm ice-y. Yes. The day is that hot, señor. Yes. Maybeso it is of desirableness to leave him out to get the cool. Yes.'

" 'Yes,' says I, 'yes,' for I knew they had me. 'Touching's believing, ain't it, boys? Yes. Now there's some might say the seats of your trousers are sky blue, but 'tis my opinion they are red. Let's apply the tests of the laying on of hands and feet.' And so I hoisted both those inspectors out of the door on the toe of my shoe, and sat down to cool off on my block of disreputable glass.

"And, as I live without oats, while I sat there, homesick for money and without a cent to my ambition, there came on the breeze the most beautiful smell my nose had entered for a year. God knows where it came from in that backyard of a country—it was a bouquet of soaked lemon peel, cigar stumps, and stale beer—exactly the smell of Goldbrick Charley's place on Fourteenth Street where I used to play pinochle of afternoons with the third-rate actors. And that smell drove my troubles through me and clinched 'em at the back. I began to long for my country and feel sentiments about it; and I said words about Salvador that you wouldn't think could come legitimate out of an ice factory.

"And while I was sitting there, down through the blazing sunshine in his clean, white clothes comes Maximilian Jones, an American interested in rubber and rosewood.

" 'Great carrambos!' says I, when he stepped in, for I was in a bad temper, 'didn't I have catastrophes enough? I know what you want. You want to tell me that story again about

Johnny Ammiger and the widow on the train. You've told it nine times already this month.'

" 'It must be the heat,' says Jones, stopping in the door, amazed. 'Poor Billy. He's got bugs. Sitting on ice, and calling his best friends pseudonyms. Hi!—*muchacho!*' Jones called my force of employees, who was sitting in the sun, playing with his toes, and told him to put on his trousers and run for the doctor.

" 'Come back,' says I. 'Sit down, Maxy, and forget it. 'Tis not ice you see, nor a lunatic upon it. 'Tis only an exile full of homesickness sitting on a lump of glass that's just cost him a thousand dollars. Now, what was it Johnny said to the widow first? I'd like to hear it again, Maxy—honest. Don't mind what I said.'

"Maximilian Jones and I sat down and talked. He was about as sick of the country as I was, for the grafters were squeezing him for half the profits of his rosewood and rubber. Down in the bottom of a tank of water I had a dozen bottles of sticky Frisco beer; and I fished these up, and we fell to talking about home and the flag and Hail Columbia and home-fried potatoes; and the drivel we contributed would have sickened any man enjoying those blessings. But at that time we were out of 'em. You can't appreciate home till you've left it, money till it's spent, your wife till she's joined a woman's club, nor Old Glory till you see it hanging on a broomstick on the shanty of a consul in a foreign town.

"And sitting there me and Maximilian Jones, scratching at our prickly heat and kicking at the lizards on the floor, became afflicted with a dose of patriotism and affection for our country. There was me, Billy Casparis, reduced from a capitalist to a pauper by over-addiction to my glass (in the lump), declares my trouble off for the present and myself to be an uncrowned sovereign of the greatest country on earth. And Maximilian Jones pours out whole drug stores of his wrath on oligarchies and potentates in red trousers and calico shoes. And we issues a declaration of interference in which we guarantee that the fourth day of July shall be celebrated in Salvador with all the kinds of salutes, explosions, honors of war, oratory, and liquids known to tradition. Yes, neither me nor Jones breathed with soul so dead. There shall be rucuses in Salvador, we say, and the monkeys had better climb the tallest cocoanut trees and the fire department get out its red sashes and two tin buckets.

"About this time into the factory steps a native man incriminated by the name of General Mary Esperanza Dingo. He was some pumpkin both in politics and color, and the friend of me and Jones. He was full of politeness and a kind of intelligence, having picked up the latter and managed to preserve the former during a two years' residence in Philadelphia studying medicine. For a Salvadorian he was not such a calamitous little man, though he always would play jack, queen, king, ace, deuce for a straight.

"General Mary sits with us and has a bottle. While he was in the States he had acquired a synopsis of the English language and the art of admiring our institutions. By and by the General gets up and tiptoes to the doors and windows and other stage entrances, remarking 'Hist!' at each one. They all do that in Salvador before they ask for a drink of water or the time of day, being conspirators from the cradle and matinée idols by proclamation.

"'Hist!' says General Dingo again, and then he lays his chest on the table quite like Gaspard the Miser. 'Good friends, señores, to-morrow will be the great day of Liberty and Independence. The hearts of Americans and Salvadorians should beat together. Of your history and your great Washington I know. Is it not so?'

"Now, me and Jones thought that nice of the General to remember when the Fourth came. It made us feel good. He must have heard the news going round in Philadelphia about that disturbance we had with England.

"'Yes,' says me and Maxy together, 'we knew it. We were talking about it when you came in. And you can bet your bottom concession that there'll be fuss and feathers in the air to-morrow. We are few in numbers, but the welkin may as well reach out to push the button, for it's got to ring.'

"'I, too, shall assist,' says the General, thumping his collar-bone. 'I, too, am on the side of Liberty. Noble Americans, we will make the day one to be never forgotten.'

"'For us American whisky,' says Jones—'none of your Scotch smoke or anisada or Three Star Hennessey to-morrow.

We'll borrow the consul's flag; old man Billfinger shall make orations, and we'll have a barbecue on the plaza.'

" 'Fireworks,' says I, 'will be scarce; but we'll have all the cartridges in the shops for our guns. I've got two navy sixes I brought from Denver.''

" 'There is one cannon,' said the General; 'one big cannon that will go "BOOM!" And three hundred men with rifles to shoot.'

" 'Oh, say!' says Jones, 'Generalissimo, you're the real silk elastic. We'll make it a joint international celebration. Please, General, get a white horse and a blue sash and be grand marshal.'

" 'With my sword,' says the General, rolling his eyes, 'I shall ride at the head of the brave men who gather in the name of Liberty.'

".'And you might,' we suggest, 'see the comandante and advise him that we are going to prize things up a bit. We Americans, you know, are accustomed to using municipal regulations for gun wadding when we line up to help the eagle scream. He might suspend the rules for one day. We don't want to get in the calaboose for spanking his soldiers if they get in our way, do you see?'

" 'Hist!' says General Mary. 'The comandante is with us, heart and soul. He will aid us. He is one of us.'

"We made all the arrangements that afternoon. There was a buck coon from Georgia in Salvador who had drifted down there from a busted-up colored colony that had been started on some possumless land in Mexico. As soon as he heard us say 'barbecue' he wept for joy and groveled on the ground. He dug his trench on the plaza, and got half a beef on the coals for an all-night roast. Me and Maxy went to see the rest of the Americans in the town and they all sizzled like a seidlitz with joy at the idea of solemnizing an old-time Fourth.

"There were six of us all together—Martin Dillard, a coffee planter; Henry Barnes, a railroad man; old man Billfinger, an educated tintype taker; me and Jonesy, and Jerry, the boss of the barbecue. There was also an Englishman in town named Sterrett, who was there to write a book on Domestic Architecture of the Insect World. We felt some bashfulness about inviting a Britisher to help crow over his own country, but we decided to risk it, out of our personal regard for him.

"We found Sterrett in pajamas working at his manuscript with a bottle of brandy for a paper weight.

" 'Englishman,' says Jones, 'let us interrupt your disquisition on bug houses for a moment. To-morrow is the Fourth of July. We don't want to hurt your feelings, but we're going to commemorate the day when we licked you by a little refined debauchery and nonsense—something that can be heard about five miles off. If you are broad-gauged enough to taste whisky at your own wake, we'd be pleased to have you join us.'

" 'Do you know,' says Sterrett, setting his glasses on his nose, 'I like your cheek in asking me if I'll join you; blast me if I don't. You might have known I would, without asking. Not as a traitor to my own country, but for the intrinsic joy of a blooming row.'

"On the morning of the Fourth I woke up in that old shanty of an ice factory feeling sore. I looked around at the wreck of all I possessed, and my heart was full of bile. From where I lay on my cot I could look through the window and see the consul's old ragged Stars and Stripes hanging over his shack. 'You're all kinds of a fool, Billy Casparis,' I says to myself; 'and of all your crimes against sense it does look like this idea of celebrating the Fourth should receive the award of demerit. Your business is busted up, your thousand dollars is gone into the kitty of this corrupt country on that last bluff you made, you've got just fifteen Chili dollars left, worth forty-six cents each at bedtime last night and steadily going down. To-day you'll blow in your last cent hurrahing for that flag, and to-morrow you'll be living on bananas from the stalk and screwing your drinks out of your friends. What's the flag done for you? While you were under it you worked for what you got. You wore your finger nails down skinning suckers, and salting mines, and driving bears and alligators off your town lot additions. How much does patriotism count for on deposit when the little man with the green eye-shade in the savings-bank adds up your book? Suppose you were to get pinched over here in this irreligious country for some little crime or other, and appealed to your country for protection— what would it do for you? Turn your appeal over to a committee of one railroad man, an army officer, a member of each labour union, and a colored man to investigate whether any of your ancestors were ever related to a cousin of Mark Hanna, and then file the papers in the Smithsonian Institution until after the next election. That's the kind of a sidetrack the Stars and Stripes would switch you on to.'

"You can see that I was feeling like an indigo plant; but after I washed my face in some cool water, and got out my navys and ammunition, and started up to the Saloon of the Immaculate Saints where we were to meet, I felt better. And when I saw those other American boys come swaggering into the trysting place—cool, easy, conspicuous fellows, ready to risk any kind of a one-card draw, or to fight grizzlies, fire, or extradition, I began to feel glad I was one of 'em. So, I says to myself again: 'Billy, you've got fifteen dollars and a country left this morning—blow in the dollars and blow up the town as an American gentleman should on Independence Day.'

"It is my recollection that we began the day along conventional lines. The six of us—for Sterrett was along—made progress among the cantinas divesting the bars as we went of all strong drink bearing American labels. We kept informing the atmosphere as to the glory and preëminence of the United States and its ability to subdue, out-jump, and eradicate the other nations of the earth. And, as the findings of American labels grew more plentiful, we became more contaminated with patriotism. Maximilian Jones hopes that our late foe, Mr. Sterrett, will not take offense at our enthusiasm. He sets down his bottle and shakes Sterrett's hand. 'As white man to white man,' says he, 'denude our uproar of the slightest taint of personality. Excuse us for Bunker Hill, Patrick Henry, and Waldorf Astor, and such grievances as might lie between us as nations.'

" 'Fellow hoodlums,' says Sterrett, 'on behalf of the Queen I ask you to cheese it. It is an honor to be a guest at disturbing the peace under the American flag. Let us chant the passionate strains of "Yankee Doodle" while the señor behind the bar mitigates the occasion with another round of cochineal and aqua fortis.'

"Old Man Billfinger, being charged with a kind of rhetoric, makes speeches every time we stop. We explained to such citizens as we happened to step on that we were celebrating the dawn of our private brand of liberty, and to please enter such inhumanities as we might commit on the list of unavoidable casualties.

"About eleven o'clock our bulletins read: 'A considerable rise in temperature, accompanied by thirst and other alarming symptoms.' We hooked arms and stretched our line across the narrow streets, all of us armed with Winchesters and navys for purposes of noise and without malice. We stopped on a street corner and fired a dozen or so rounds, and began a serial assortment of United States whoops and yells, probably the first ever heard in that town.

"When we made that noise things began to liven up. We heard a pattering up a side street, and here came General Mary Esperanza Dingo on a white horse with a couple of hundred brown boys following him in red undershirts and bare feet, dragging guns ten feet long. Jones and me had forgot all about General Mary and his promise to help us celebrate. We fired another salute and gave another yell, while the General shook hands with us and waved his sword.

" 'Oh, General,' shouts Jones, 'this is great. This will be a real pleasure to the eagle. Get down and have a drink.'

" 'Drink?' says the general. 'No. There is no time to drink. *Viva la Libertad!*'

" 'Don't forget *E Pluribus Unum!*' says Henry Barnes.

" '*Viva* it good and strong,' says I. 'Likewise *viva* George Washington. God save the Union, and,' I says, bowing to Sterrett, 'don't discard the Queen.'

" 'Thanks,' says Sterrett. 'The next round's mine. All in to the bar Army, too.'

"But we were deprived of Sterrett's treat by a lot of gunshot several squares away, which General Dingo seemed to think he ought to look after. He spurred his old white plug up that way, and the soldiers scuttled along after him.

" 'Mary is a real tropical bird,' says Jones. 'He's turned out the infantry to help us do honor to the Fourth. We'll get that cannon he spoke of after a while and fire some window-breakers with it. But just now I want some of that barbecued beef. Let us on to the plaza.'

"There we found the meat gloriously done, and Jerry waiting, anxious. We sat around on the grass, and got hunks of it on our tin plates. Maximilian Jones, always made tenderhearted by drink, cried some because George Washington couldn't be there to enjoy the day. 'There was a man I love, Billy,' he says, weeping on my shoulder. 'Poor George! To think he's gone, and missed the fireworks. A little more salt, please, Jerry.'

"From what we could hear, General Dingo seemed to be kindly contributing some noise while we feasted. There were guns going off around town, and pretty soon we heard that cannon go 'BOOM!' just as he said it would. And then men began to skim along the edge of the plaza, dodging in among the orange trees and houses. We certainly had things stirred up in Salvador. We felt proud of the occasion and grateful to General Dingo. Sterrett was about to take a bite off a juicy piece of rib when a bullet took it away from his mouth.

" 'Somebody's celebrating with ball cartridges,' says he, reaching for another piece. 'Little over-zealous for a non-resident patriot, isn't it?'

" 'Don't mind it,' I says to him. ' 'Twas an accident. They happen, you know, on the Fourth. After one reading of the Declaration of Independence in New York I've known the S.R.O. sign to be hung out at all the hospitals and police stations.'

"But then Jerry gives a howl and jumps up with one hand clapped to the back of his leg where another bullet has acted over-zealous. And then comes a quantity of yells, and round a corner and across the plaza gallops General Mary Esperanza Dingo embracing the neck of his horse, with his men running behind him, mostly dropping their guns by way of discharging ballast. And chasing 'em all is a company of feverish little warriors wearing blue trousers and caps.

" 'Assistance, *amigos*,' the General shouts, trying to stop his horse. 'Assistance, in the name of Liberty!'

" 'That's the Compañía Azul, the President's bodyguard,' says Jones. 'What a shame! They've jumped on poor old Mary just because he was helping us to celebrate. Come on, boys, it's our Fourth;—do we let that little squad of A. D. T.'s break it up?'

" 'I vote No,' says Martin Dillard, gathering his Winchester. 'It's the privilege of an American citizen to drink, drill, dress up, and be dreadful on the Fourth of July, no matter whose country he's in.'

" 'Fellow citizens!' says old man Billfinger. 'In the darkest hour of Freedom's birth, when our brave forefathers promulgated the principles of undying liberty, they never expected that a bunch of blue jays like that should be allowed to bust up an anniversary. Let us preserve and protect the Constitution.'

"We made it unanimous, and then we gathered our guns and assaulted the blue troops in force. We fired over their heads, and then charged 'em with a yell, and they broke and ran. We were irritated at having our barbecue disturbed, and we chased 'em a quarter of a mile. Some of 'em we caught and kicked hard. The General rallied his troops and joined in the chase. Finally they scattered in a thick banana grove, and we couldn't flush a single one. So we sat down and rested.

"If I were to be put, severe, through the third degree, I wouldn't be able to tell much about the rest of the day. I mind that we pervaded the town considerable, calling upon the people to bring out more armies for us to destroy. I remember seeing a crowd somewhere, and a tall man that wasn't Billfinger making a Fourth of July speech from a balcony. And that was about all.

"Somebody must have hauled the old ice factory up to where I was, and put it around me, for there's where I was when I woke up the next morning. As soon as I could recollect my name and address I got up and held an inquest. My last cent was gone. I was all in.

"And then a neat black carriage drives to the door, and out steps General Dingo and a bay man in a silk hat and tan shoes.

" 'Yes,' says I to myself, 'I see it now. You're the Chief de Policeos and High Lord Chamberlain of the Calaboosum; and you want Billy Casparis for excess of patriotism and assault with intent. All right. Might as well be in jail, anyhow.'

"But it seems that General Mary is smiling, and the bay man shakes my hand, and speaks in the American dialect.

" 'General Dingo has informed me, Señor Casparis, of your gallant service in our cause. I desire to thank you with my person. The bravery of you and the other *señores Americanos* turned the struggle for liberty in our favor. Our party triumphed. The terrible battle will live forever in history.'

" 'Battle?' says I; 'what battle?' and I ran my mind back along history, trying to think.

" 'Señor Casparis is modest,' says General Dingo. 'He led his brave *compadres* into the thickest of the fearful conflict. Yes. Without their aid the revolution would have failed.'

" 'Why, now,' says I, 'don't tell me there was a revolution yestereday. That was only a Fourth of——'

"But right there I abbreviated. It seemed to me it might be best.

" 'After the terrible struggle,' says the bay man, 'President Bolano was forced to fly. To-day Caballo is President by proclamation. Ah, yes. Beneath the new administration I am the head of the Department of Mercantile Concessions. On my file I find one report, Señor Casparis, that you have not made ice in accord with your contract.' And here the bay man smiles at me, 'cute.

" 'Oh, well,' says I, 'I guess the report's straight. I know they caught me. That's all there is to it.'

" 'Do not say so,' says the bay man. He pulls off a glove and goes over and lays his hand on that chunk of glass.

" 'Ice,' says he, nodding his head, solemn.

"General Dingo also steps over and feels of it.

" 'Ice,' says the General; 'I'll swear to it.'

" 'If Señor Casparis,' says the bay man, 'will present himself to the treasury on the sixth day of this month he will receive back the thousand dollars he did deposit as a forfeit. *Adiós, señor.*'

"The General and the bay man bowed themselves out, and I bowed as often as they did.

"And when the carriage rolls away through the sand I bows once more, deeper than ever, till my hat touches the ground. But this time 'twas not intended for them. For, over their heads, I saw the old flag fluttering in the breeze above the consul's roof; and 'twas to it I made my profoundest salute.''

Afterword

~

All of us want to know what will happen next. In fiction, plot pulls events through a story. Plot is the demonstration that an action takes place as a consequence of what has gone before and is linked to what will come after it, and thus the fulfillment of plot is reassuring to a reader. Today the hunger for plot is often satisfied by media other than literary fiction. Television provides one example in the ubiquitous *Law and Order*, where our desire for the satisfactions of a clear beginning, middle, and end is understood. William Sidney Porter, best known as O. Henry, lived a discouraging life, but his stories with their well worked-out plots help his readers believe that what is difficult now can unfold into happiness.

In his time, O. Henry was considered to be an artist, not merely a commercial or popular writer. He was called the American Maupassant as a way to define his standing as a writer, the way today's writers are compared to Chekhov. At the height of O. Henry's production, he published a story a week, in newspapers and magazines, single-handedly doing his best to fill the need of his readers for more—more story, more characters, more satisfying plots that worked out for the good, however implausibly. Almost one hundred years after his death, his stories are still read in English and in translation. The present Signet Classics collection has been reprinted numerous times; each year it outsells most new works of fiction, which is to say that the stories of O. Henry have loyal readers and that they gain new ones.*

---

*One example of O. Henry's continuing presence in American letters is *The O. Henry Prize Stories.* To ensure the permanent identification

*   *   *

O. Henry's fictional world could hardly be more different from that of great writers who were roughly his contemporaries: James Joyce (1882–1941), Virginia Woolf (1882–1941), and Marcel Proust (1871–1922); also Henry James (1843–1916), though it's especially hard to imagine either writer caring a fig about the other. As for writers of our own day, O. Henry is comparatively unconcerned with time, a subject that haunts Alice Munro, one of our best short story writers. O. Henry's tales are broad humor compared to today's postmodernist satires.

O. Henry's endings with a twist are a hallmark of his style. He had the ability to create a seemingly insoluble dilemma and then to untie the knot. Today O. Henry's chosen approach to endings seems contrived to many readers. Even a story written in 1899, during O. Henry's lifetime, "The Lady with the Dog" by Anton Chekhov, has a markedly different sort of ending, one that defines the insoluble problem of the story's characters rather than solving it. For Gurov, the main character in Chekhov's story, understanding the nature of love is a transformative experience. If his understanding doesn't result in a solution to the profound problems presented in the story, that's because Chekhov wasn't interested in problems that could be solved.

But O. Henry was. O. Henry designed his stories around the establishment and solution of the problems of his characters. In this way, he's continued to please readers who might detest the open-endedness of modern stories.

O. Henry made sure his characters could be understood by a broad range of readers, for he had his own

_____

of O. Henry with the short story, after his death, his friends established a collection to appear annually, gathered from stories published in the preceding year, to be called *The O. Henry Prize Stories*. From 1919 to our own day, *The O. Henry Prize Stories* has been published to honor him and "to strengthen the art of the short story and to stimulate younger authors." *The O. Henry Prize Stories* has always included a wide variety of writers and styles, and winning an O. Henry is one of the most coveted honors among writers of stories.

mission: to connect his readers with a particular type of character, the uneducated (or self-educated) but natural man who sees clearly while those richer and better educated, more fortunate in every way, are blind. He made devastating fun gently, so that even the pompous, the pretentious, and the selfish live to see another day.

In his fiction, O. Henry often used places he'd really lived—the Texas of ranches and its capital, Austin; the American South; Latin America; New Orleans—but O. Henry's own life, unlike his fiction, was full of insoluble problems: incurable disease, poverty, debt, imprisonment, the deaths of his wife and infant son. As a writer, he chose deliberately to idealize and recolor human suffering. In the world of his stories, a plot working out was a way of giving his readers relief from their own lives. If O. Henry made everything in a story work out, often at the cost of verisimilitude, it was a price his readers were more than happy to pay. Until the end of his life, O. Henry eschewed writing in a realistic vein, and he preferred to twist events to create a world that was recognizable and yet comforting for his readers.

Only when he was too ill and exhausted to write at all did O. Henry express regret for the waste of his talent and think about writing a different kind of fiction, closer to the life he'd actually led.

William Sidney Porter was born on September 11, 1862, in Greensboro, North Carolina. Before he was three, his mother was dead of tuberculosis. His father, a physician and heavy drinker, gave up the practice of medicine and earning an income to invent a perpetual-motion machine. The care of Dr. Porter's two children, Will and Shirley, was left to their grandmother and their aunt Lina, who ran a local school. In his youth, Porter was poor. If he wasn't precisely neglected, he wasn't wanted as he might have been by his mother, had she lived, or by his father, if he hadn't succumbed to obsession and alcoholism. In his childhood, Porter was dependent on the kindness of relatives and friendly families, and he lived a kind of orphanhood that made him dreamy and a little passive, or at least willing his whole life to accept the generosity of others—his father-in-law and his friends who extended themselves and their resources to support him.

This is not to say that Porter didn't try. By the time he was fifteen, he was working at his uncle Clark's store, W. C. Porter and Company Drug Store. At nineteen, he was a licensed pharmacist. He was rescued from being trapped in a small-town drugstore when, in March 1882, Dr. and Mrs. Hall took him along to South Texas, where they were visiting their four sons. The Hall family, plus the Harrell family, with whom Porter lived in Austin when he left the Hall ranch, provided him with homes and emotional support, and gave him a chance to read as many books as he could get his hands on, to learn about the Texas countryside and its people, and eventually, to secure jobs in the Texas Land Office and at the First National Bank of Austin. That they did so is testimony not only to their kindness and generosity but to what must have been Porter's considerable charm and promise. Those were days of landgrabs and the piling up of wealth in Texas, but Porter was unable to gain material security. His luck in life, if he had any, lay in human relations and his ability to communicate what was worthwhile in people.

In Austin, he fell in love with and married Athol Estes; worked in the Land Office; performed in Gilbert and Sullivan's *Mikado*; started his own paper, *The Rolling Stone*; and eventually worked at the First National Bank, which was the undoing of his Austin life. The disastrous combination of Porter's unsuitability as a bookkeeper and the looseness of Texas banking practices ended in 1896 in his indictment for embezzlement. He fled Texas, first for New Orleans and then for Honduras, finally returning to Austin because Athol was dying of tuberculosis. He was convicted and sent to the federal penitentiary in Columbus, Ohio, to serve a term of five years, of which he ended up serving three. In prison he worked in the pharmacy, and soon was trusted enough to be allowed to sleep at the pharmacy rather than in a cell. He and an old acquaintance, a bank robber, formed a group of friends—embezzlers, train robbers, and one forger—and they called themselves the Recluse Club. Porter was gathering material, as he always did, and he was also writing, more than ever. Humiliated by his imprisonment, a widower and absent father to his daughter, Margaret, he poured his failure and loss into the hard work of being a productive writer. He sent his stories out to magazines and newspapers, and left prison a published writer with a new name, that of O. Henry.

Released in 1901, he moved to New York City, and there he found the home of his heart. In the universe of New York, O. Henry could find all the stories he could write, more than enough editors who wanted his work and would pay in advance, and perhaps most important, a combination of friends and anonymity. He avoided confidences about his past, even with close friends.

O. Henry's second marriage, in late 1907, to Sara Coleman, an old sweetheart from Greensboro, was not happy. He'd lived too long on his own in hotels and boardinghouses, and his financial insecurity and unrelenting drinking habits would have been hard to take, along with his need to be by himself. O. Henry died in New York City on June 5, 1910, months before his forty-eighth birthday, of diabetes and cirrhosis of the liver, and perhaps also of exhaustion. He'd worked for years at a killing pace, always on deadline, always behind. However much he wrote, however much he was paid, O. Henry gave away and spent all that he had and more. Many of his characters seek money, but few find it, and even if they do, it's likely to evaporate sooner rather than later. Money, as much as or even more than love, is the Holy Grail of his stories—not surprising since O. Henry spent his life in pursuit of it. For him it always remained a will-o'-the-wisp.*

*I'm especially indebted in writing this afterword to two books: *Alias O. Henry* by Gerald Langford (New York: The Macmillan Company, 1957) and *Time to Write: How William Sidney Porter Became O. Henry*

*　　*　　*

As a master of plot, O. Henry deliberately twisted his endings to establish a symmetry rarely seen in life. One of the most appealing things about an O. Henry story is its demonstration of balance in an unjust world.

O. Henry starts "The Last Leaf," included in the present collection, with a lively description of Greenwich Village, a section of New York where the "art people" live on winding streets in a quaint place of "north windows and eighteenth-century gables and Dutch attics and low rents." The last phrase makes the quartet of descriptives vintage O. Henry; what he elevates in idealized terms, he brings back to earth with a reminder of the insoluble, ever-present problem of money.

"At the top of a squatty, three-story brick," two young artists live: Johnsy, or Joanna, and Sue. Sue came to Greenwich Village from Maine, Johnsy from California; they met and decided to share a studio.

It is a cold, unforgiving winter, and Johnsy has pneumonia. The doctor doesn't hold out much hope for her; Johnsy is waiting for death, and the doctor tells the faithful Sue, " 'Whenever my patient begins to count the carriages in her funeral procession I subtract 50 per cent from the curative power of medicines. If you will get her to ask one question about the new winter styles in cloak sleeves I will promise you a one-in-five chance for her, instead of one in ten.' "

Johnsy lies in bed, staring out the window, counting backward. "An old, old ivy vine, gnarled and decayed at the roots, climbed half way up the brick wall." There are only five leaves left on the vine and, Johnsy tells Sue, " 'When the last one falls I must go, too.' " She refuses fortifying wine and nourishing food. She desires nothing that will keep her in the world, and wants to see the last leaf fall. " 'I'm tired of waiting,' " she says. " 'I'm tired of thinking. I want to turn loose my hold on everything,

by Truemann E. O'Quinn and Jenny Lind Porter (Austin: Eakin Press, 1986).

and go sailing down, down, like one of those poor, tired leaves.' "

The cleverness in the story rests in the establishment of a seemingly insoluble problem. There's no way to control the falling of leaves, or the death of a friend, however much Sue—and the reader—wishes to. Johnsy is young and talented. It's unjust that she should give up and die. Most important, her death matters to Sue.

Enter salvation in the form of Behrman, an old German painter who speaks in a vaudeville dialect and lives in the same building as Johnsy and Sue. Behrman has been talking forever about painting his masterpiece but never touches the blank canvas that's rested on his easel for twenty-five years. Sue persuades him to pose for an illustration so she can earn money for Johnsy's care. She tells him of Johnsy's fancy that she'll die when the last leaf falls, and he declares, " 'Is dere people in de world mit der foolishness to die because the leafs dey drop off from a confounded vine?' "

That night there's a terrible storm, but in the morning, when Sue raises the blind, the last leaf is still on the vine. Another night, another storm, and still the leaf persists.

Johnsy rallies, deciding, " 'Something has made that last leaf stay to show me how wicked I was. It is a sin to want to die. You may bring me a little broth now, and some milk with port in it, and—no; bring me a hand-mirror first. . . .' " The reader cheers up, remembering the doctor's statement, and agreeing that nothing is more of this world than an interest in one's appearance.

When Johnsy is well enough to leave her bed, Sue tells her that Behrman has died of pneumonia. During the dreadful night of the first storm, he carried a lantern up a ladder to provide light while he painted the last leaf on the brick wall. He painted the last leaf so beautifully that Johnsy never noticed that the leaf didn't move in the wind and rain.

" 'Ah, darling,' " says Sue, " 'it's Behrman's masterpiece— he painted it there the night the last leaf fell.' "

The ending of "The Last Leaf" is sad and completely

satisfying. The seemingly impossible problem is solved; the real leaf fell but couldn't kill Johnsy. The gears of injustice are jammed, not for supernatural reasons but by the effort of an old man, whom everyone thought a failure. Best of all, Behrman has painted his masterpiece at last.

For a moment the world is balanced and fair, and so it will remain until the reader enters O. Henry's next tale.

—LAURA FURMAN